Cocoa Beach

Cocoa Beach

BEATRIZ WILLIAMS

wm

WILLIAM MORROW
An Imprint of HarperCollins*Publishers*

COCOA BEACH. Copyright © 2017 by Beatriz Williams. All rights reserved. Printed in the United States of America. No part of this book may be used or reproduced in any manner whatsoever without written permission except in the case of brief quotations embodied in critical articles and reviews. For information, address HarperCollins Publishers, 195 Broadway, New York, NY 10007.

HarperCollins books may be purchased for educational, business, or sales promotional use. For information, please email the Special Markets Department at SPsales@harpercollins.com.

FIRST EDITION

Designed by Bonni Leon-Berman

Library of Congress Cataloging-in-Publication Data has been applied for.

ISBN 978-0-06-240498-5

17 18 19 20 21   LSC   10 9 8 7 6 5 4 3 2 1

To the land of Florida—its dreamers, its builders, its mavericks, and its scoundrels. (Sometimes all four at once.)

May 16, 1919

My dear wife,

Let me tell you about this pen.

Handsome object, made of black enamel, repeating fleur-de-lis motif in gold leaf. Casing somewhat scratched owing to years of hard use (rather like its owner). Knows you well enough, I expect, to write this letter without instruction. Anyway, I <u>wish</u> it would. I have been holding the damned thing for an hour at least. Turning it about between my fingers. Getting up and walking around the room. Sitting and staring and resolving.

The truth is, I'm afraid I don't know what to say—I don't know what to <u>write</u> to make you believe in me again. I stand accused and convicted of a despicable crime, and you never allowed me a word in my own defense. If I could, I'd whisper in your ear the <u>entire truth</u>, but I suspect you wouldn't believe me, would you? God knows, as a practical matter, you <u>shouldn't</u> believe me. Anyway, I can't tell you the truth, at least not yet, so that's that.

Instead of relying on your faith, then, I shall have to attempt the next best thing, the hardest thing. I am going to <u>prove</u> my—I was going to say innocence, but that's not quite true enough, is it? I am not an innocent man, and I've never pretended to be, at least with you—the one person with whom I never pretended. But I <u>can</u> insist I'm innocent of this <u>one</u> crime at least—that I married you for <u>yourself alone</u>—and since I'm afraid, in the wake of my parents' deaths, the house must now be sold for taxes and the estate broken up, I shall take up *the last inheritance remaining to me and make something of myself at last: something, I hope, you will one day recognize as the man you thought you had married.*

I shall write my next letter from the mosquito-bitten town of Cocoa, Florida, at the head of a once-grand shipping empire, which I intend to resurrect for your sake. And then—well, what? You will decide, my own dear phantom, my irreplaceable and inalienable wife, my own Virginia. If you'll remember—if you're honest in remembering me—I have always allowed you to choose for yourself.

In the meantime, may God watch over you.

Yours always,

S.F.

CHAPTER 1

Cocoa Beach, Florida, June 1922

S OMEONE HAS CLEARED the ruins away, but you can still see that a house burned to the ground here, not long ago. The earth is black and charred, and the air smells faintly of soot.

In the center of what must once have been a courtyard, a modest stone fountain has toppled from its pedestal. Already the weeds have begun to sprout from the base, encouraged by the hot, damp sunshine and the fertile soil. Everything grows in Florida. Grows and grows, unchecked by any puny human efforts to control nature's destiny. I sink to the edge of the pedestal and call to my daughter, who's poking a stick through the long, sharp grasses that grow along the perimeter of the paving stones. She looks up in surprise, as if she's forgotten I exist, and runs to me on her stubby bare legs. On her mouth is the same startling smile that used to light her father's face, and there are moments—such as this one—when the resemblance strikes me so forcefully, I can't breathe.

"Mama! Mama! There *mouse*!"

"A mouse? In the grass? Are you sure?"

"Yes, Mama! *Mouse!* He run away."

"Of course he did, darling, if you poked him with your stick."

Without another word she burrows her hot, wriggling body into my chest, and I'm not one to waste such an opportunity. Not me. Not now. I clasp Evelyn between my arms and bury my face in her sweet-smelling hair, and I breathe her in, great lungfuls of Evelyn, as if I could actually do that, if I inhaled with enough strength and will. Breathe my daughter's spirit into mine.

I haven't told her that her father died here four months ago, on this very patch of ground, or even that he built this house and lived in it while we—Evelyn and I—inhabited our comfortable brownstone on East Thirty-Second Street in New York City, together with Grandpapa and Aunt Sophie. For one thing, I don't want to frighten her with the idea that a person could burn to death at two o'clock in the morning in his own house, just like that. For another, she's not that curious about him, not yet. She's not yet three years old, after all, and she doesn't know any other little girls. Doesn't know that most of them have both mothers *and* fathers, living at home together, sometimes with brothers and sisters, too. One day, of course, she'll want to know more. She'll ask me questions, and I'll have to think of plausible answers.

And there is another reason, a final reason. The reason I'm here in Florida to begin with, examining this blackened ground with my jaded eyes. I suppose I'll tell Evelyn about that, too, when the time comes, but for now I'm holding this reason inside my own head and nowhere else. I've learned, over the years, to keep my private thoughts strictly to myself.

Behind us, Mr. Burnside clears his throat in that slight, unnecessary way that lawyers have. I imagine they think it conveys discretion. "Mrs. Fitzwilliam," he says.

"Yes, Mr. Burnside?"

"Have you seen enough? I hate to hurry you, but we do have a whole mess of appointments this morning."

Mr. Burnside, you understand, likes to keep to a tight schedule, especially in the face of this shimmering June sun, which forces all business around here to conclude by lunchtime. After which Mr. Burnside will spend the rest of his day inside a high-ceilinged, north-facing room, sipping a cool, strong drink while an electric fan rotates above him. If he can spare the energy, he might turn over a paper or two on his desk.

On the other hand, he's an extremely competent man of affairs, as I've had plenty of occasion to discover in the past two months, and the sound of his voice—practical, confident, somewhat impatient—is enough to stiffen my resolve. To blow away the dust of regret, or nostalgia, or grief, or whatever it is that's stinging my eyes, that's clogging my chest as I hold Simon's daughter in my arms and try to imagine that Simon is dead. *Dead*. What a word. An impossible word, as unlike Simon as clay is to fire. I kiss the top of Evelyn's head, detach her from my arms, and rise to my feet. The early sun catches my back. Not far away, the ocean beats against the yellow sand, and the sound makes me want to take off my shoes and socks and wander, aimless, into the surf.

Instead, I say: "Are you certain the remains belonged to my husband?"

"Yes, ma'am. His brother identified the body."

"Samuel."

"That's the man. Big fella."

"And this *was* Simon's house, of course. There's no mistake about that?"

"Oh, no, ma'am. No mistake about that. Had the pleasure of visiting here many times myself. Lovely place. Like one of those Italian villas. There were lemon trees in this courtyard, real pretty. A real shame, Mrs. Fitzwilliam. Terrible, terrible shame that you never saw how lovely it was."

I gaze at him coldly, and he coughs and turns away, as if to survey the empty, overgrown plot around us. The breeze touches the ends of his pale jacket. His straw hat glows in the sun. He inserts his fingers into his sweating collar and says, "Have you thought about what you'll do with the place? You can get a good price for the land, if you don't mind my saying so. Folks are paying top dollar these days for a plot of good Florida land, let alone one as nice and big as this, looking out on the ocean."

Across the road, at the edge of the yellow beach, an especially large wave rises to the sky, gathering strength and power, until it can't bear the strain any longer and dives for shore in a long, elegant undulation, from north to south. An instant later, the boom reaches us, like the firing of a seventy-five-millimeter artillery shell—a sound I know all too well. My nerves flinch obediently.

But I'm an old hand at disguising the flinch of my nerves. Instead of jumping at the sound of a crashing wave, I brush an imaginary patch of dirt from my dress and reach for Evelyn's sticky hand.

"I think we should visit the docks next, don't you think? So we don't run late on our schedule."

Mr. Burnside frowns, causing his bottlebrush mustache to twitch under his nose.

"Of course," he says. "It's your property, after all."

IN ADDITION TO A THOUSAND or so acres of mature citrus, a shipping company, the ruined house on Cocoa Beach, and a hotel in town (in which he kept a private apartment for his own use), Simon has also left me a beautiful sky-blue Twin Six Packard roadster, which Mr. Burnside now drives at thirty exuberant miles an hour toward the long, narrow bridge across the Indian River, where the little boomtown of Cocoa perches on the shore and makes itself a living.

On another day, I would have liked to drive myself. This is, after all, my car. But the estate is still in probate, and anyway Mr. Burnside knows the way, while Florida's still a mystery to me. Why, I don't even know the name for this thick, rampant vegetation that spreads around us, creeping along the edges of the road, but as the Packard plows along the raised bed, top down and windows lowered, I think—for the first time in years—of the hedgerows of Cornwall. The way they block everything else from view, everything ahead of you and everything to the side, so that you never know what's coming around the next curve. Those shrubs might be hiding anything.

"How much farther?" I call out above the roar of the engine and the heavy, warm draft blowing past our ears.

"Bridge is up ahead!"

"What are these shrubs and trees growing alongside?"

"That? Mangrove."

"Pardon me?"

"MANGROVE, Mrs. Fitzwilliam! That's MANGROVE! Grows EV-ERYWHERE around here, where the ground's LOW and SWAMPY, and it's mostly LOW and SWAMPY in these PARTS!"

Mangrove. Of course. One of those things you hear about—a *mangrove swamp*, how exotic—but never actually see. And here it is, spreading everywhere, tangled and salty and very much at home.

"Darned STUFF!" Mr. Burnside continues. "Breeds MOSQUITOES! I'm sure you've noticed all the MOSQUITOES!"

"Yes!"

He turns his head closer. "They used to call this Mosquito County, until someone got smart and saw it was keeping the settlers away. Changed the name to Brevard. Now they've got big plans to drain these swamps, at least on the mainland side, some of the bigger islands."

"What a shame!"

"Shame? About TIME, I say! You haven't seen 'em SWARM yet! Here's the bridge, now."

The mangrove falls away, replaced by the tranquil navy blue of the Indian River and the bustling shore on the other side. Across the waterway stretches the wooden bridge, straight as an arrow, except for the drawbridge and its wheelhouse. We crossed it this morning, rattling the boards from their morning slumber, much to Evelyn's delight. I nudge her now. "Look, darling! It's the bridge!"

She scrambles up into my lap and puts her hands on the doorframe. "Bridge! Bridge!"

"She's a PRETTY THING!" shouts Mr. Burnside.

"Thank you."

"Looks like her FATHER, if you don't MIND my SAYING so!"

I stroke Evelyn's hair. "Tell me, Mr. Burnside. When was the bridge built? It looks rather new."

Mr. Burnside flexes his fingers around the steering wheel and leans forward, as if to concentrate his attention on the progress of the Packard down the narrow roadway. He's driving more slowly now, as we cross from solid ground to fragile human construction, and the noise of the engine subsides, replaced by the rattle of wood.

"Oh, not that new, I guess. They finished it just about the time we got into the war—1917, it was. Seems like ages, though I guess that's only five years, by the calendar."

"Yes."

He spares a sideways glance. "You must have gone over there, isn't that right? The war, I mean. Over to France."

Evelyn's trying to stand on my lap, to get a better view over the edge of the car. With difficulty, not wanting to spoil her fun entirely, I brace my hands around her flapping upper arms. "Why do you ask?"

"Oh, just curious, I guess. What it was like. Pretty awful, I bet. I figured you must have met Mr. Fitzwilliam there, you know. Since he was fighting."

"He wasn't fighting," I say. "He was in the medical corps."

"Oh, that's right. Used to be a doctor, I think he said."

"Yes. He was a surgeon in the British Army."

"Yep, that's right. That was good luck for him, I guess. Do your bit without getting killed."

"I suppose so."

The Packard rattles on, toward the middle of the bridge. The sun's higher now, and without the shade of the mangroves, the interior of the car has grown intolerably hot, even in the draft. The perspiration trickles down the hollow of my spine, dampening my dress against the back of the seat.

Mr. Burnside, however, is persistent. "You must've been a nurse, then. Red Cross?"

"Yes." And then, reluctantly: "I wasn't really a nurse. I drove ambulances."

"Did you! Well, I'll be. Can't say I would have guessed. You're such an elegant thing. And that's man's work. Real man's work, driving those tin cans through the guns and the slop."

"There were a great many women driving, actually. So the men could go fight."

"Were there, now? I guess that's war for you. Where'd you learn to drive? In the service?"

"No. My father taught me."

"Well, well. And so you met Mr. Fitzwilliam in France, somewhere?"

We're approaching the drawbridge, and the stop signal appears. The Packard slows and slows. I point through the windshield. "Look, Evelyn. The bridge is going to go up so the boats can sail through."

Evelyn, squealing, throws herself toward the glass, fingers outstretched for the topmost edge, and I catch her by the chest just in time.

"You've got your hands full with that one," observes Mr. Burnside.

"She's a good girl, really. Just impulsive when she's excited. As most children are, at this age."

My voice is crisp, but he doesn't seem to notice. His hand reaches for the gear lever. "She doesn't get *that* from her daddy, that's for sure. Never saw a man with a more even temper than Mr. Fitzwilliam. Nothing troubled him. Cool as January. I always figured it was the war, see. You survive something like that, and . . . Oh, look at that. It's one of his ships. *Your* ships, I mean."

I turn my head to the cluster of vessels awaiting the lifting of the drawbridge. "Which one?"

"The steamer, there at the end. Loaded up with fruit, I'll bet, and headed for Europe. Though I'd have to check the schedule in the office to be sure."

"Yes, I'd like that."

"Oh, I don't mean *you,* ma'am. There's no need for you to trouble yourself with the business side of things."

The wooden deck draws slowly upward before us, foot by foot, and Evelyn gasps for joy. Claps her palms together, leans trustfully into my hands. The creaking of the gear reaches a breaking point, above the rumble of the Packard's idling engine, and the ships begin to bob forward.

"But that's why I'm here, Mr. Burnside. To learn about Simon's business. Since it now belongs to me."

"Now, Mrs. Fitzwilliam. Why bother yourself like that? That's what we're here for, to keep your affairs running all nice and smooth, so you don't need to dirty yourself. The dirt of commerce, I mean. Just you live in comfort and raise your daughter and maybe find yourself another husband. A nice, ladylike thing like you. It's hard work, you know, running a business like this."

"I'm not afraid of hard work."

"Well, now. Have you ever run a business before, Mrs. Fitzwilliam?"

"No. But that doesn't mean—"

"Then I think you'd best just leave everything to us, ma'am. Those of us who know the business, inside out." He leans back contentedly against the seat and crosses his arms over his broad, damp chest. "Trust me."

Well! At the sound of those words—*Trust me*—I'm nearly overcome by an urge to laugh. High and hysterical, a little mad, the kind of laugh that will make this kind, round-bellied lawyer shake his head and think, *Women*.

Trust me. My goodness. Trust me, indeed. I've heard that one before.

But I don't laugh. Poor fellow. Why disturb his satisfaction? Instead, I watch the progress of the ships through the gap in the bridge, paying particular attention to the nimble white steamship at the end, which—I now see—bears the name of its company in black block letters near the stern.

PHANTOM SHIPPING LINES

AS IT HAPPENS, SIMON'S DOCK is empty of ships, except for a small boat that Mr. Burnside informs me is a tender. "The others are out to sea," he says, chewing on the end of a long and unlit cigar, "which is a good thing, mind you. Good for profits. Our aim is always to turn the ships around as smart as we can."

We're standing at the end of the Phantom Shipping dock, and the Indian River swirls around the pilings at our feet while a hazy white sun cooks us inside our clothes. Evelyn, restless, swings from my hand to look for fish in the oily water. Thirty yards away, a tugboat steams slowly upstream, trailing gray smoke from its single stack. The air is almost too hot to breathe.

"What about the warehouse?" I ask.

"Warehouse?"

I turn and nod to the rectangular wooden building at the base of the dock. Like the ship at the drawbridge, the building identifies its ownership in confident, no-nonsense black letters above the massive double door: PHANTOM SHIPPING LINES. The paint is fresh, on both the signboard and the white walls of the warehouse itself. There are no windows. I understand this keeps the fruit fresh and cool in its crates, waiting for a ship to transport it across the ocean. Citrus, mostly, but some avocado as well. There's a growing taste for more exotic fare in the London drawing rooms, apparently, after so many years of restriction and rationing and self-denial. A growing taste for adventure.

"Oh, there won't be anything to see in there," says Mr. Burnside. "The ship's already loaded and left, and we're not due to receive any goods this morning."

"I'd like to have a look, all the same."

He nudges aside his sleeve to check his watch. "Well, I can't object to that. But it *is* nearly lunchtime, and we've still got the offices to visit, haven't we? And your poor daughter looks like she might stand in need of a rest and a cool drink, if you don't mind my saying so."

"If you don't mind *my* saying so, you do seem pleased to offer up your opinion on a variety of matters, Mr. Burnside." I strike off down the dock, holding Evelyn's hand. "Even without being asked for it."

"That's what I'm paid to do, Mrs. Fitzwilliam. Give you my opinion. Your husband, in his will, made very clear that—"

I turn so quickly, Mr. Burnside nearly stumbles into my chest. He's an inch shorter than I am, and his eyes are forced to turn up to meet mine. I can tell he doesn't necessarily welcome the mismatch.

"Let *me* make very clear, Mr. Burnside, that my late husband's wishes are really no longer the point. *My* wishes are your business now, and if you find that task impossible, I'm afraid I'll simply have to find myself a new lawyer."

He steps backward. Snatches the cigar from the corner of his mouth. Widens his eyes to regard the cast of my expression, which—after two and a half years of motherhood—is formed of iron.

"Of course, ma'am." He inclines his head. "I didn't mean to overstep."

"I'm sure you didn't. I presume the warehouse is locked?"

"Yes, ma'am."

"And you have the key?"

"I do."

"Then let's proceed, shall we?"

I swing Evelyn onto my hip and cut through the sweating atmosphere in long, masculine strides to the white double doors at the base of the dock.

As it turns out, Mr. Burnside is correct. The warehouse doors swing open to reveal nothing at all: no cargo, at any rate. No waiting crates of citrus and avocado. Along the walls, ropes and tools hang at neat intervals, and the air—unexpectedly cool—smells of the usual dockside perfume, hemp and tar and salt and warm wood.

And something else.

I tilt my chin and sniff carefully. There it is again, sweet and spicy and tonic.

"Is something the matter, Mrs. Fitzwilliam?" asks Mr. Burnside, lighting his cigar.

"Nothing at all."

"What *smell*, Mama?"

Evelyn's wrinkling her tiny nose. Her face has grown pink from the heat, and I consider the possibility that Mr. Burnside's correct about this, as well: she needs a rest and a cool drink.

"Smell, darling? What do you smell?"

"It's my cigar, I expect," Mr. Burnside says quickly.

"No, it's not that. I smelled it, too."

"Just the fruit, then."

"Possibly." I try the air again, but the flavor has disappeared in the overpowering fog of the lawyer's cigar. "Though it didn't smell like fruit to me. If anything, it smelled like brandy."

Mr. Burnside turns for the door and laughs. "Ha-ha. *Brandy?* Your nose is playing tricks on you, Mrs. Fitzwilliam. Though I guess, if some of last night's shipment had gone off in the heat . . . happens sometimes . . . sitting in the sun like that . . ."

I wave away a delicate blue plume of smoke and cast a final gaze along the clean, well-organized walls of my late husband's warehouse, and as I do I'm reminded, against my will, of the neat canvas walls of a casualty clearing station in northern France, everything in its place, equipment and instruments and creature comforts, while the rain drummed outside. Of a pair of hazel eyes, turned toward me in supplication.

"Perhaps," I say.

Evelyn's squirming weight pulls at my arms. I allow my daughter to slide to the scrubbed wooden floor. I take her hand, and together we follow Mr. Burnside through the doorway, into the suffocating Florida noon.

WE'RE LATE FOR OUR VISIT to the offices of the Phantom Shipping Lines, on the second floor of a large, businesslike brick building set across from the Phantom Hotel, which now belongs to me, according to the terms of Simon's will. My husband, you see, articulated his last wishes in clear, simple terms: in the event of his death, everything—every single article he possessed—should pass to his wife, Virginia Fitzwilliam of New York City.

A dressmaker and a coffee shop occupy the storefronts on the ground floor, and the stairs for the upper floors lie behind a plain wooden door around the corner. Mr. Burnside reaches for the knob and unlocks it with a small Yale key from the chain in his jacket pocket.

The stairs are wide and bare, and Mr. Burnside tells me to watch my step as I climb, holding Evelyn by the hand. The wood creaks softly beneath our feet. Simon climbed these steps, I think. Simon's feet caused the same soft creak.

"If you'll allow me," Mr. Burnside says, stepping around my body as we reach the top of the staircase and a square, high-ceilinged foyer made white by the glare of the sun through the window at the opposite end. He strides for a door halfway down the wall on the right side, the one facing the river, and unlocks that, too. The top half is made of frosted glass and also bears the name PHANTOM SHIPPING LINES in the same uniform black letters.

"After you," says Mr. Burnside, stepping back, and Evelyn and I walk through the doorway into a beautiful, spacious room, lined on the east and south walls by large sash windows, shaded from the ferocity of the Florida sun by a series of green-and-white striped awnings. Above our heads, four electric fans rotate quickly. The walls are white, the furniture simple: a pair of desks, a sofa, armchairs, table, cabinets. Everything necessary, I suppose, to run a small, legitimate shipping company, sending fresh, nutritious Florida citrus and avocadoes to the kitchens and dining rooms of Great Britain.

The room is occupied, of course. After all, business goes on, though the owner of Phantom Shipping Lines has died shockingly in a house fire four months earlier, leaving his company and all the rest of his worldly goods to a wife who, I suspect, most people here in Cocoa never knew existed. A young woman in a navy suit sits erect before a curving black typing machine, the clattering of which has abruptly ceased, and a middle-aged man looks up from the desk on the other side of the room and gazes at us from beneath the green shade covering his brow.

More. There's another man, stepping just now from a doorway along the north wall, closing the portal behind him and turning to face me. But he's not the man that—at some hidden depth of consciousness, unknown to logic—I suppose I'm expecting to find before me. Whole and alive.

No. This man is burly and straight-shouldered, grim-faced and dark-haired, bearing a jaw and a pair of hazel eyes so resembling those of my husband, my heart jolts in my chest and my legs turn to sand, and I squeeze Evelyn's tiny hand in order to remain upright.

Samuel Fitzwilliam.

CHAPTER 2

France, February 1917

HUNKA TIN

. . . But when the night is black,
And there's *blessés* to take back,
And they hardly give you time to take a smoke;
It's mighty good to feel,
When you're sitting at the wheel,
She'll be running when the bigger cars are broke.

Yes, Tin, Tin, Tin!
You exasperating puzzle, Hunka Tin!
I've abused you and I've flayed you
But by Henry Ford who made you,
You are better than a Packard, Hunka Tin!

—FROM THE *AMERICAN FIELD SERVICE BULLETIN*, 1917

(IN THE SPIRIT OF KIPLING'S "GUNGA DIN")

I MET MY husband in the least romantic setting possible: a casualty clearing station in northern France in the middle of February. A cold drizzle fell and the air stank of human rot. I suppose this constituted a warning from Providence, though Providence needn't have bothered. I had always known better than to fall in love. I had always known love was something you would later regret.

The CCS occupied the barn of an ancient farm, and by the time I reached it, late in the afternoon, the sky was dark and the ambulance wheels had choked with thawed mud. For weeks the winter had frozen the saturated ground; today, on the first day of a new offensive, the roads had turned to sludge. That was the war for you.

I brought the motor to a grinding halt in what had once been a stable yard and yanked back the brake. No other vehicles inhabited the swamp around me, and for a moment I thought I'd got the directions wrong. It was all just a hunch, after all: Hazel bursting back from the village, rushing down the empty ward, calling out that there was a battle on! A new attack into some salient or another, and if we wanted patients we should take the ambulance down to the nearest CCS, they'd be lousy with casualties! We were all rolling bandages at the time, there was nothing else to do. No patients to care for. Everyone turned to me. And what could I say? *Take the ambulance,* Hazel had said: the ambulance just brought down from Paris, our precious Hunka Tin, a bastard born of much wheedling and carrying-on with the American Red Cross Ambulance Service. A tattered, battered Model T that, in our entire sisterhood of accomplished Manhattan ladies, only I could drive.

Take the ambulance, Virginia, do! It's not as if you have anything better to do.

She was right, of course. The rain was crackling on the great windows overlooking the courtyard. An infinite roll of lint lay in my lap like a death sentence. What else could I have said? *Yes.* I dumped that damned lint back into the basket and said *yes.*

A reckless act. *Impetuous,* my father would have said, shaking his head, and an hour later I'd regretted it passionately, but now that I'd arrived at my destination, the regret was gone. I rubbed my sleeve against the windshield fog—my breath kept clouding the glass—and spied the grim, erratic movements of a stretcher party lurching through the field beyond, half-obscured by mist. Above my head, a delicate whine pierced the air, high and gliding, ending in a percussive *crump* that rattled my bones. I reached for the door handle and forced myself out.

Four hours ago, as I left the hospital, Hazel suggested I borrow her rubber boots—*The mud's just awful, Virginia*—but I hadn't listened. I had my leather shoes, and from there I'd wrapped army-style puttees around my trousers, all the way to the knee, like a pair of gaiters, and I thought that was enough. Smart and efficient. That was all the soldiers wore, wasn't it? In those days, newly freed from my father's house, I thought I didn't have to follow anyone's advice if I didn't want to. I thought I was free. From the moment of departure, from the instant the gray-sided ocean liner cast off into the Hudson River, I had soaked up the knowledge of my independence. I had reveled in reliance on my own common sense.

And that was all very well, except that the mud of northern France didn't give a damn for my independence and my common sense. The mud didn't give a damn for anything. I stuck my left leg out of the cab of the ambulance and into the wet French earth, and the muck swallowed up my neat leather shoe right past the ankle. You can't imagine the greedy, sucking noises it made as I staggered across that stable yard, foot by foot, while the drizzle struck my helmet in metallic pings and the shells screamed and popped at some worryingly unknown distance. The front-line trenches were supposed to be miles away, but you couldn't tell that to your ears, or to your heart that crashed every time those screaming whistles pierced the air in twos and threes, inhuman and relentless, followed by those acoustic *crump*s that meant someone had just gotten hell. Shellfire had a way of sounding as if it was going to drop directly on the crown of your head, every time.

I was making for the stretcher party, not the barn. I don't know why. I think I just wanted to help, right that second, after so many weeks and months of preparation. Like the rest of us American volunteers, I was simply dying for a real live patient. Two men carried the wounded soldier, who was covered by a blanket and nothing else, and my God, how I wondered that he hadn't fallen off the canvas altogether as the stretcher-bearers staggered through the mud, drunken and exhausted. The rain dripped from their helmets. "Need a hand?" I called out, and their heads jerked hopefully upward at the sound of my voice.

"Jesus," the first one swore, "who the devil are you?"

"I'm from the American Red Cross," I said. "I was sent out to bring patients to a hospital nearby. They said you were overloaded."

"You're a *driver?*"

Of the two, the second man looked the worst, whey-faced and vertiginous, as if the next step might kill him. I leapt across a puddle and reached for the handles of the stretcher. "Yes," I said. "What have we got?"

The man was too tired—or else too astonished—to dispute the stretcher with me. He fell away, rubbing his blistered palms against his trousers, and I took the load in my own hands. It was lighter than I expected, a strange living weight, like a child instead of a man. The wounded soldier's face was pale and wet; I couldn't tell where he was hit, beneath the blanket.

"Right leg," said the second man. "Sent back straightaway for amputation."

"Can they amputate here?"

"Got no choice, have they?"

The soldier moved his head and groaned. Still wore his helmet, slipped to one side, covering his ear and part of his jaw while his face and young brow remained exposed to the drizzle. His pack lay next to him on the stretcher, shielded by the gray blanket.

"Almost there," I told him, and his startled eyelids swooped open and his eyes met mine, very briefly, before a patch of mud sent me wallowing for balance.

"Blimey," he said, blinking, "am I dead already?"

"You ain't dead, mate," the second man said. "It's the American Red Cross, innit."

"Blimey." The soldier closed his eyes. "God bless America."

Ahead of us a door swung open on the face of the barn, and a man's shoulders appeared in silhouette against the electric light within. "Goddamn it!" he shouted. "I told the last party we haven't got room!"

"Well, they ain't told us back up the line, sir," the first man said.

"We can't bloody well take him!"

"He needs the leg off, sir, on the double."

The other man pounded his fist against the side of the doorway. He took a step toward us, into the soggy remains of the daylight. Stopped, frowned. He wore a dilapidated khaki tunic, officer's stripes. The rain struck his bare head. "Who the devil's this?"

"The American Red Cross, sir," said the first man.

"How in the hell did she get here?"

I nodded toward the Model T. "I drove, sir."

"You drove *that*? From where?"

"From Marieux, sir. We've set up a private hospital there, only we weren't getting any patients, so I went back to Paris and found a Model T from the American Ambulance—" The stretcher handle slipped in my wet right hand.

"Never mind." The doctor stepped forward and yanked the stretcher handles from my fingers. "Carry on, for God's sake. Get the poor sod out of the rain. Now!"

He had the kind of manner you couldn't refuse, the kind of resolve you couldn't just turn. I think I admired him right then, whether or not I realized it. I couldn't help it. After all, I was used to a strong masculine will. His authority seemed natural and just, derived from the consent of those governed. I scampered like a damned puppy at his heels. Followed him into the barn, refusing to be shunted. "We've got plenty of beds at the hospital," I said. "I can take three stretchers or six sitting in the ambulance."

"I don't know this hospital of yours."

"We're fully staffed, sir. Eight nurses, two doctors. Both experienced surgeons. You said you're full."

"All Americans, I suppose."

"Yes."

We ducked through the doorway of the barn, into a shower of electric light that stung my eyes. Around us stretched a ward of perhaps fifty beds, all of them occupied; a number of cots seemed to have been put up along the walls, staffed by a thin swarm of orderlies and a few nursing sisters in gray dresses and white pinafores. The smell of disinfectant saturated the damp air, swirling with the primeval odors of blood and earth. And not just any earth: this was the mud of France, battlefield mud, in which living things had died and decayed, and even now—years later—the stench still rots in the cavities of my nose like the memory of death. There is not enough disinfectant in the world to cleanse that smell.

The doctor didn't pause. I don't think he even heard me, any more than he would have heard an actual puppy scampering at his heels. He called out commands to a series of orderlies—*Prepare the theater, Pass the word for Captain Winston*—and only when he handed off the stretcher to the men assisting in the operating theater did he turn and fix his full attention upon me, like the next item on a long list of daily tasks, to be checked off and disposed of.

But the funny thing was—the really *momentous* thing, when I look back on the entire episode, trying to pinpoint this or that instant that might have constituted a turning point, a point of flexion at which my life might have taken an entirely different course—the funny thing was that his expression then changed. Transformed, like a man engaged in an obsessive quest, who had just parted a final pair of jungle branches and made the discovery for which he'd longed all his life.

His face, as I later learned, had that natural capability for transformation.

Where I had expected sternness, and frowns, and orders crossly delivered, I received something else. A smile, quite gentle. A movement of eyebrows that suggested understanding, and a little wonder. A bit of crinkling around a pair of eyes that had to be called hazel, though they tended, in certain light, toward green; surely that signified admiration?

My face turned warm.

"Miss—?"

"Fortescue."

"Miss Fortescue. You're the only evacuation ambulance to get through the roads today, did you know that? Either from the dressing station or the railway depot. How the devil did you do it?"

"I—I just drove, sir. Pushed her out when she got stuck."

He drove a hand through his hair, which was sparkling with gray and cropped short, so that the bones of his face thrust out with additional clout. I thought he looked as if he came from the countryside, from some sort of vast outdoors; there was something a little rough-hewn about his cheeks and jaw, blunt, like a gamekeeper or else a poacher, although his creased skin was pale and sunless. His fingers, by contrast, contained all the delicate, tensile strength of a surgeon. I thought he must be exotically old, thirty-five at least. "Well, well. I'll be damned," he said. "You're a heroine."

"Not at all, sir. Just doing my best."

"As are we all, Miss Fortescue, but you're the only driver who actually made it through. *That's* heroism."

My cheeks burned. Of course. My chest, too, I think, while everything else went a little cold. At that point in my life—aged only twenty, sheltered for most of those years by a few square miles of tough Manhattan Island and a grim, reclusive father—I'd never received a compliment like that. Certainly not from a grown man, a man of mating age. I didn't even *know* that kind of man, other than that he existed, a separate and untamed species, kept in another cage from mine on the opposite end of the zoo. And that was well enough with me. I had no interest in mating. Having survived such a childhood, I thought myself practical and resourceful— and I was, by God!—but not tender. Not susceptible to blandishment, and not susceptible to that particular kind of charm, the kind of charm you're warned about in all the magazines: hazel eyes and a huntsman's bones and an angel's smile.

But now, at this instant, it turned out that I wasn't immune at all. I was only innocent. Like a child who had never been exposed to measles, I thought I couldn't catch them. That I was somehow stronger than all those weak, febrile children who had gotten sick.

I didn't know how to answer him. I mumbled something. I forget what.

His smile, if possible, grew warmer. *Incandescent,* if I had to choose a word for it, which I did only at a much later hour, when I had the time and the composure to think rationally about him. He said, looking fearlessly into my eyes, "All right, then, Miss Fortescue. Heroine of the hour. If you want patients so badly."

"Yes, we do," I said, but he had already turned and barked out something to someone, and down we went along the rows of cots, selecting patients for transport. He gave me six, along with their paperwork, and asked me again for the name of the hospital.

"It's a château, really," I said. "Near Marieux. It belongs to the de Créouville family. Mrs. DeForest arranged to lease it—"

"Who the devil's Mrs. DeForest?"

"Our chapter president."

"Your chapter president," he said, mock wearily, shaking his head. He was filling out the transfer papers with a beaten enamel fountain pen, using a medical dictionary as a desk. A small, sharp widow's peak marked the exact center of his forehead. "What would we do without ladies' committees?"

"A great deal less, I think."

He looked up and handed me the papers. "You're right, of course. God bless them all. I don't suppose you have an orderly with you?"

"No."

"Nurse?"

"There's just me."

"Just you. Of course." He turned and called out to the nearest man, who straightened away from a bandage and looked afraid. "Miss Fortescue . . . is that right?"

"Yes. Fortescue."

"Miss Fortescue from the American Red Cross has driven an ambulance all the way here from Marieux without an orderly, hell for leather, through mud and shellfire, in order to relieve us of some of our patients. Is Pritchard on duty?"

"No, sir. He's on rest."

"Fetch him up on the double and tell him we've got to escort six wounded men to the Château de Créouville, in Marieux." Then, to me: "You'll bring us back in the morning, won't you?"

"Of course."

Back to the orderly. "And find Miss Fortescue a cup of coffee and a sandwich, while you're passing the mess. She looks like death. Perfectly charming death, but death nonetheless. We shall have no further harm come to her, do you hear me? She is absolutely essential."

"Yes, sir."

I tucked the papers under my arm. "If I may say so, sir, *you* should get some rest. You look like death yourself."

"It's Captain Fitzwilliam, Miss Fortescue. As well I should. But I'm afraid I shall have to make do with a ride in an American ambulance instead. You'll be ready to shove off in twenty minutes?"

"Of course."

That was all. A final smile, and he turned away and headed off into the maze of rubber curtains that partitioned the far end of the barn, while I stood there, dripping and bewildered, scintillating, waiting for my coffee and sandwich, for Corporal Pritchard. For my six wounded British soldiers.

For Captain Fitzwilliam, in his greatcoat and gum boots, who wanted to inspect us personally.

CHAPTER 3

Cocoa, Florida, June 1922

ON SECOND THOUGHT, maybe I'm not exactly surprised to see Simon's brother emerging from an office in the headquarters of Simon's shipping company. It's been three years, after all, and even England and Germany are allies now. But certainly I'm shocked, with all the usual physical symptoms of shock, which I do my best to disguise. (You might say I've had a lot of practice at that.)

Does he notice? I can't really say. Like me, he's the kind of person who disguises his untoward emotions behind a set of frigid, automatic manners. He just holds out his hand and says, "Virginia. It's good to see you again."

"Yes." I recover my balance and release Evelyn's small fingers to take his palm. The contrast startles me. I had forgotten how large Samuel's hands are. How large, my God, is the rest of him. "How are you?"

"Well enough." His gaze falls upon Evelyn, who's crept behind my right leg and now looks out from the shelter of my skirt.

"I didn't know you and Simon were partners here."

"We weren't."

"Then, if you'll pardon my asking—"

He looks back up. "Your husband never actually allowed me a share in the business, Virginia. Despite the close nature of our relationship."

"To be perfectly honest, I'm surprised he took you on at all. Given the close nature of your relationship." I put the same ironic emphasis on those words as my brother-in-law did. Why not? We share a certain understanding, after all.

"Well, I guess he'd run out of other men to trust. Anyway, he got his money's worth out of me."

"Did he? I haven't had the chance to examine the books yet. I'm sure I'll find everything in order, won't I?"

Mr. Burnside steps up on my other side. "Mr. Fitzwilliam was kind enough to stay on with the company, after his brother's death."

"I'm grateful."

"The least I could do," says Samuel. "And I was happily able to set Mr. Burnside straight about your existence, and where you might be found, and in the meantime—well. Here we are."

"Here we are."

Mr. Burnside says, "In your absence, ma'am, and acting for the estate, I appointed Mr. Fitzwilliam temporary director of Phantom Shipping and its affiliate concerns. There was really nobody else. The citrus plantation, as you know, has been in the family for some time."

"Our grandfather's American wife," says Samuel.

"Yes. I remember Simon once told me something about it. A wedding present from her father to the happy couple, wasn't that right?"

"Something like that. Although really more in the nature of a bribe, the rich old devil. I believe he hoped the glorious sunshine of Maitland Plantation would tempt the two of them near, but they preferred the pile of soggy family stones in Cornwall, God knows why, and poor old Maitland's been mostly left to the incompetence of estate managers ever since. Well, until Simon came along, after the war."

"And now you. You're in charge of everything."

Samuel shrugs. "So it seems."

Mr. Burnside breaks in. "Of course, if you don't think Mr. Fitzwilliam's the right man for the job, I'm happy to look about for a replacement."

You know, there's something about Mr. Burnside's tone that brings out the streak of perversity in me. I don't know why. Maybe it's because I've been such a very *good* girl the past few years, a model of respectability, absorbed in my child and my home, never once mentioning the thing that plagues me. Smiling serenely, while the world buckles and shifts around us, while women bob their hair and run out to smoke cigarettes and to vote, while fortunes are made by the illegal importation of liquor, while broad new highways are laid in their hundreds and I am not.

Or perhaps I'm just wondering—and surely you noticed it, too—why Mr. Burnside so artfully changed the subject when I mentioned those company accounts.

"Well, then. Maybe you should look around for a replacement, Mr. Burnside, just to be prepared. I think Samuel understands that he's here on trial. I'll be in a better position to make these decisions once I'm fully intimate with the details of the business."

My exceptional height gives me a small advantage in making this pronouncement. Even as large as Samuel is—and I judge he's a good four inches over six feet—I don't have to turn up all that far to meet his gaze, and I can see that I've startled him. You know the look. His eyebrows shoot to the roof; his lips part.

But that's nothing compared with Mr. Burnside, who gasps and mutters by my side, flapping his mouth and his eyelids, while Samuel and I lock eyes like a pair of rival giants.

"Come now, Mrs. Fitzwilliam!"

"She's right, however," says Samuel, not looking away. "It's *her* business now, isn't it? Once the estate clears probate."

"But she's just—"

"A woman?" Samuel breaks our little encounter at last and turns to the lawyer. "Mr. Burnside, I'm surprised a man your age doesn't know better by now than to put those words together. *Just a woman.* Women rule the earth, don't you know? A man doesn't do a single thing that isn't somehow inspired by a woman's will. Sometimes all it takes is her mere existence. Anyway, you haven't seen this particular woman drive a rattletrap Model T through the mud of a French battlefield, swearing like a sailor."

"You're wrong about that," I say. "I never swore."

"Didn't you? Well, I suppose I never saw you in action, either. I only have it secondhand. Now, then. Would you like to see the rest of the offices, Virginia? All the accounts are in order and ready for your inspection."

I glance at the clock on the wall, and the two other occupants of the room—the typist and the accountant—turn sharply back to their work. The steady undertone clatter of typewriter keys picks up again. The sound of business. Good, solid, American business, rushing on to meet the brash new age before us.

"I'm afraid I'm going to have to defer that pleasure until later this afternoon, Mr. Fitzwilliam. My daughter needs her nap."

WHEN I FIRST MADE ACQUAINTANCE with the name of Mr. Cornelius Burnside, I was sitting at the desk of my suite in the Pickwick Arms Hotel on the Boston Post Road in Greenwich, Connecticut, sifting my way through a thick collection of mail that had been forwarded from the house in New York City. It was the middle of May and I was exhausted, having sat through yet another court hearing in the days before Father's trial, and at first I didn't quite understand the neat, typewritten words before me. (Typewritten, quite possibly, by that silent young lady in the navy blue suit in the office of the Phantom Shipping Company.)

I still have the letter, packed in a separate valise, the one that contains all my important papers, though I hardly need to see it. I must know every word by now. It's short, after all, and I have read it many times.

Dear Mrs. Fitzwilliam,

You will forgive my intrusion on your notice at such a busy time, but I have reason to believe that you may be the surviving relic of Mr. Simon Fitzwilliam, late of the city of Cocoa, Florida, who I regret to inform you passed away in a fire at his home in Cocoa Beach, in the early hours of February 19 of this year.

I must beg you to confirm your receipt of this letter, and your identity as the former Miss Virginia Fortescue of New York, married to Mr. Simon Fitzwilliam of Penderleath, England [Cornwall, I thought automatically] in the borough of

Kensington and Chelsea on the 31st of March, 1919, at your earliest convenience,
so that we may proceed with the proper settlement of Mr. Fitzwilliam's estate.
　　Yours respectfully,
　　Mr. Cornelius S. Burnside, Jr., Esq.

On the first reading, I didn't understand at all. Something about the
sight of my husband's name—Mr. Simon Fitzwilliam—all typewritten
and impersonal, as if I were reading about him in a newspaper, simply froze
my thoughts in place. My eyes skimmed over the rest of the words without
absorbing a single one.

Only upon a second reading did I realize that something had happened
to Simon, and only after the third did I perceive that Simon was dead. That
he had burned to death in a house in Florida, a terrible accident, and left to
me—Virginia Fitzwilliam, his legal wife—the entirety of his estate. His
estate, whatever that was.

Because while houses burned down regularly, and people died all the
time, I had never imagined that Simon could meet his end like that. You
could not extinguish my husband in mere flame. It simply wasn't possible.

And while I had never tried to forget Simon—how could I, when his
daughter gazed up at me every morning, an incarnate reminder of our brief
life together?—I had, over the course of the previous three years, seques-
tered his image into its own tidy corner of my head, rigid and unchanged, a
two-dimensional portrait covered by a sheet against the dust. I had refused
to allow any memories out of that corner, because those might bring him
back to life, and where would I be if Simon became human to me again?

But the shock of seeing his name, understanding the bare facts of his
death, had a catastrophic effect on that mental frame I had erected around
Simon, confining him in two dimensions. Simon: dead. I couldn't comprehend it. It simply didn't make sense. I stared and stared at that letter, and I
put it away in the desk, and then I woke up at midnight and pulled it out and
read it again while my sister, Sophie, slept in her nearby bed.

A week passed before I found the composure to answer that letter, and when I did, my reply was just as slim and factual as the original, though I wrote it in pen on Pickwick Arms notepaper. I simply confirmed my identity as Simon's widow, indicated that I would not be at liberty to attend Mr. Burnside in person for some weeks, but that I would be happy to answer any inquiries by letter in the meantime.

At the time, however, I made no mention of Evelyn. For one thing, I doubted Mr. Burnside—or Samuel Fitzwilliam, for that matter—would have any idea of her existence.

I'M CARRYING EVELYN IN MY arms this minute, as we cross the street to the Phantom Hotel and Simon's private apartment on the fifth floor, overlooking the docks. I haven't seen it yet. We spent a few brief moments in the hotel lobby this morning, Evelyn and I, depositing our luggage and waiting for Mr. Burnside to appear. I'm afraid I didn't notice any details, other than a clean-lined, simple décor and the impression of light and mirrors.

Samuel offers to carry Evelyn, but I decline politely, even though my arms ache under her weight. Instead, he puts his hand on my elbow and makes sure there's no traffic as we start across the pitted street. It's the first time he's touched me since we shook hands in the office, and his fingers are unexpectedly light against the sharp point of my humerus. As we reach the safety of the paved sidewalk, the hand drops away.

This time the hotel staff recognizes me, and the manager hurries over the instant I pass through the doorway and hoist Evelyn—already half-asleep—further up my hip. "Mrs. Fitzwilliam!" he cries in dismay. He turns and snaps his fingers to the lobby boy, who hurries to press the call button on the elevator at the other end of the room. By the time we reach the apartment and I've tucked Evelyn into her bed, a tray's arrived, bearing sandwiches and a pitcher of lemonade. Samuel, who stands by the window looking at the river, offers to pour me a glass.

The humble question brings me up short in the middle of an enormous silk rug.

"Yes, thank you."

He strikes out across the floor while I settle myself on the edge of a sleek leather armchair. The drawing room yawns around us, vast and spare, containing only a few necessary pieces of clean-edged furniture and no sentiment whatsoever. Even the curtains are pale and plain, a uniform gray-green that merges immaculately with the paint on the high, long walls. I can just glimpse the river over the edge of the nearest windowsill, and the dark mass of the mangrove on the opposite shore—the barrier that separates us from the Atlantic. A convenient, protected harbor. No wonder Cocoa's a boomtown.

Samuel hands me a damp glass of lemonade. Our fingertips brush, and he doesn't move away.

"I didn't realize Simon's taste was so modern," I say.

"I didn't either, when I first arrived. I suppose neither of us had the opportunity to know him particularly well."

"I knew him well enough."

"In hospitals and hotels. But you never set up a home together, did you?"

The question is rhetorical. Samuel knows the solution to this hypothesis as well as I do. Wasn't he the very man who drove me away from Cornwall, in an ancient Daimler whose cracked leather seats released a particular smell that still hangs in my nostrils? Still: "That's true," I say, and I settle in my chair, back still rigid, away from his looming figure.

Samuel tilts his head and returns to his station by the window. "I *am* sorry about all this. It must have been the devil of a shock."

"Yes, it was. I still can't imagine him dead."

"Neither can I. Of all of us, he was the one most alive."

"But you saw him dead. You identified the body."

"Only by the ring." Samuel taps his finger on the window frame, and the action reminds me so much of Simon, I turn away to drink my lemonade. "The body itself was burned beyond recognition. Poor chap."

"*Poor chap?* You can still say that, after everything?"

"Yes, I can. He *was* my brother, after all."

I think of Sophie, and the invisible thread that connects my heart to hers, even when an ocean opens between us. How my sister could commit no possible evil—even if she were capable of evil, and Sophie is as pure as a child—that would snap that thread.

"I suppose so."

"And we had a row, you know, not too long before he died. The last time we met, a god-awful almighty row. I think you should know that, before you hear it from someone else. It's been a weight on my mind ever since. And he stormed back to Maitland, to the plantation, and that was the last I saw of him. Until I went to identify his body. What there was of it."

My lips are numb from the ice. I set the glass on the round marble table next to the armchair, and as the two connect in a soft clink, something else occurs to me. "What ring?"

"Ring?"

"How you identified him. He had a ring, you said."

Samuel turns. "Yes. It was your wedding ring. The one you gave back. He kept it on him. I'm not sure how, in a pocket or something. The fire got to it. But I could still make out the inscription. Your initials, and his." He reaches into his pocket. "Here it is, if you want a look."

I stare at his grim expression. At his outstretched hand. The sunlight catches a glint from somewhere within that dense landscape of palm and mangrove, and I think, *It can't be my ring; it's too small.* But of course it is. Dull and bent, no longer a ring but a piece of burnt scrap. It might be anyone's old ring, but Samuel says it's mine, Samuel says it's the ring that Simon placed on my finger three years ago amid a litany of Christian vows, and unlike my late husband, and for all his faults, Samuel is a straightforward man who speaks only truth.

I realize I have stopped moving, stopped breathing, and before this paralysis becomes permanent I spring from the armchair and make for the opposite end of the room, where a broad, high window looks not eastward toward Europe but north, in the direction of New York City. I place my hands on the windowsill and breathe in large, shallow gasps, staring up-river at the ships coursing the tranquil blue water.

Behind me, Samuel swears and apologizes. I hear footsteps, and the click of wood, and the clink of glass, and a moment later, just as I've recovered the ordinary rhythms of respiration, my lemonade glass reappears at my elbow. I snatch it away and Samuel says, *Careful!*

But it's too late. I've already gulped down the first few ounces, and my throat bursts into flame. The cavities of my head fill with smoke.

"My God! What did you put in it?"

"Gin."

Another spasm. I set down the glass on the ledge. "Isn't that against the law?"

"Not to drink. Only to buy."

"You had to have bought it somewhere."

Samuel shrugged. "The liquor cabinet was already full when I arrived. What's a fellow to do but drink?"

I lift the glass again, and this time I sip more carefully, and the gin has its proper effect. Tamed by lemonade, in fact, it's what you might call tran-quilizing. My pulse settles, my nerves simmer down. The chasm between my ribs fills with something or other. The warmth on my shoulder, I real-ize, belongs to Samuel's hand. I shrug it off and turn to face him, and that's my second mistake, greater even than the reckless gulping of Samuel's par-ticular recipe for refreshment.

Maybe it's his grim, unhappy expression. Maybe it's the color of his eyes. His smell, or the gin, or the memory of my wedding night, or God knows. Maybe it's the effect of a sleepless Pullman sleeper, *clackety-clack* all the way from New York. My eyes, which have remained dry for the past three years, dry and dignified throughout every last thing, start to liquefy at last. I bend my face to the side, but not soon enough.

"Stupid girl," he says, "crying for him."

But his voice isn't without sympathy, and his chest—broad, covered with characteristic plainness in a white shirt and a light gray jacket, unbuttoned—possesses a strange power of gravity, like the earth itself. I find myself leaning toward him, or rather toppling, like a stone tower whose foundation has just turned to sand. An inch or two away from his collar, I catch myself, startling, but not before his right hand discovers the blade of my shoulder, and this gentle, masculine pressure finishes me. My forehead connects with the side of his neck, at the slope where it meets his clavicle, and my fingers rise to hang from the ridge of his shoulders. He goes on cradling my back with his one palm—the other hand, I believe, remains at his side—and says nothing, not even the traditional *Hush, now* or *There, there*. Thank God. I don't think I could have survived any words. His skin and his collar turn wet, though I'm not really sobbing. Not crying as you ordinarily imagine the act of sorrow. Just a small heave every so often, and the streaming from my eyes, which continues for some time. I don't know how long. I've lost the sense of passing minutes, here in the damp, warm hollow of my brother-in-law's neck.

I WAKE UNSTEADILY, DISCOMBOBULATED BY the heat and the sunlight slanting through the window glass between a pair of pale, billowy curtains. By the unfamiliarity of the bed in which I lie. A white sheet covers me, and beneath that I'm wearing only a petticoat. A clock chimes from somewhere in the room, but by the time I remember to count the strokes, it's too late. Several, at any rate. A soft knock sounds on the door, and I realize that's the sound that roused me in the first place.

I straighten myself. Lift the sheet to my neck, and that's when I remember Samuel, and our embrace, and going to bed for a nap. The rest is blurry. I glance fearfully to the side, and I'm relieved to discover I'm alone.

"Who is it?" I call.

"It's me. It's Clara." A tiny pause. "Simon's sister."

THERE'S SOMETHING ABOUT SISTERS, ISN'T there? At the sound of
Clara's voice, I find myself struck by a gust of yearning for my Sophie, as
fierce and destructive as one of those tropical hurricanes that are said to
strike these shores from time to time. Sophie, all grown up now, whom I
have left once more to bear the burden of our past on her own slim shoulders while I pursue some chimera of my own making, some delusion of
salvation in a foreign land.

Clara. Another surprise. But why not? Of course she would accompany
her brother Samuel to Florida, since she didn't have any other family of her
own. Parents dead, and all the marriageable men killed in France. That's
what you did, if you were a good maiden sister: help your brother carry his
burden. I should have been expecting her, really.

"Come in," I say.

The door cracks open. "Someone wants to see you," says a woman's
sweet voice, and Evelyn races through the crack and bounds onto the bed.

"Mama! Mama! Aunt Clarrie *cake*!"

"Oh, my! Did Aunt Clara give you *cake*, sweetheart?"

"I hope you don't mind. Samuel said you needed rest, and that's what
aunties are for, isn't it? Giving sweets without permission!"

From the last time—the only time—I saw Clara Fitzwilliam, I retain
only a vague recollection that her face was drawn and pale, and her voice
was somber. But that was years ago, when her parents lay dying. Now she's
transformed. It must be the absence of grief, or maybe the Florida sun has
touched some seam of gold inside her; who knows? Her skin is luminous,
her dark hair bobbed and cheerful. She's wearing a sundress of polka-
dotted periwinkle blue, the hem of which flutters around the middle of her
dainty calves. Beneath it, her stockings are white and extremely fine. She
gazes on my bare shoulders without the slightest shred of embarrassment.

"Of course I don't mind. How are you, Clara?"

A banal, inadequate question at such a moment, as if we're the ordinary
kind of sisters-in-law, meeting again after a month or two abroad. But if
she finds me awkward, she doesn't take any notice.

"Hot and sunburnt! I've spent the day at the beach. I can't seem to soak it in enough, after all those years in the English rain."

"But you've lived here for years, haven't you? You and Samuel."

"Years? Dear me, no. Samuel came over all by himself, the rotter, the year after Simon left England. Leaving me all alone and friendless in soggy old Blighty. I only arrived last winter, after Simon died. Samuel cabled me. Simply ghastly. Have you slept enough? Your daughter's charming. What a delicious surprise. We had no idea. A real live niece! Like finding a shilling in the pocket of one's winter coat." She goes to the window, throws open the curtains to their farthest possible extent, and closes her eyes like a goddess summoning the sun. (Or maybe sending it over the horizon—the quality of the light suggests sunset.) She adds, without opening her eyes, "You look well, by the way. Quite stunning. Far better than I imagined you would, after all you've been through."

Evelyn wriggles out of my arms and slides from the bed to join her aunt.

"Thank you. What time is it? I suppose I should be dressing for dinner."

"Only seven o'clock. But—"

"Seven o'clock! But Evelyn goes to bed in half an hour!"

Clara turns and smiles. "I've already given her tea. That should suffice, shouldn't it? But you needn't wear anything particular. I'll ring down and order us a supper. They do a frightfully nice supper, you know. And the best thing is, you don't have to pay. Because it's already yours!"

"I suppose that's true."

"Of course, I expect you're used to being rich. But it's all been rather novel for Samuel and yours truly. I say, I do hope you don't mind that we've been living here like parasites, waiting for you to arrive? Or rather, *I'm* the parasite. Samuel works like a bee. No, not like a bee. Like a beast! A beast in harness, poor dear. But *I'm* simply useless. Just lying about in the sun, trying to warm my poor English blood, and then coming home to *all this*"—she waves her hand—"and drinking all your champagne."

I can't help smiling. "You do know you're not supposed to be drinking champagne in America?"

"It's awfully bad of me. But I promise, not a penny's changed hands. So we're quite in the clear, legally speaking, at least according to Samuel."

"Yes. Samuel."

She steps forward to sit on the edge of the bed, and Evelyn, who has been peering out the window behind her, sidles up to grab her knees. Without looking down, Clara covers Evelyn's tiny fingers with her own, a gesture of unconscious affection that ought to disturb me, I suppose, since I hardly know Clara at all. She's Simon's sister, she's almost a stranger. Instead the touch of hands warms me. I don't know why. A craving for Sophie, maybe, who is so different and yet so strangely like this newfound Clara—full of energy and enthusiasm and a boundless capacity for love. A never-ending faith in tomorrow's joys.

"Samuel is such a rock," she says. "I never knew what a rock he could be, until all this."

"Do you mean what happened to Simon?"

She caresses Evelyn's fingers, and her voice turns kind. "You say it so calmly. You're not grieved at all?"

"I've already grieved."

"Oh, you're *that* sort, then."

"What sort?"

"The practical sort, the kind who puts things behind them and moves on. How I envy you. I think about Simon every day. It consumes me. Wondering what I might have done differently, if I might have changed him somehow. How I might have saved things. If only I'd—" She glances at Evelyn. "Well, never mind. I suppose we'll speak about it eventually. In the meantime, you must dress, and I'll put our wee darling here in her bath."

"Oh, but I should do that."

"Dearest, it's no bother. I adore children. And you *must* rest, you really must."

"But she's only two—"

"I promise, I shall keep my most beady of beadiest eyes on her well-being. You're not to worry about a thing, do you understand? She's my only niece, after all. I shall worship her idolatrously. My darling only niece."

I lean back against the pillows. "Yes. Of course. She's your niece."

"There we are. Is there anything I can get for you?"

"No, thank you. I believe my trunks are already unpacked."

"Yes, they are. I saw to it personally. Such fun, to be ordering maids about in your service. I do hope everything's comfortable. I *do* so want you to be comfortable, after everything you've endured. Now that we've found you at last. Our *sister*." She reaches forward and squeezes my hand.

I thank her, and she hoists Evelyn onto her hip and carries her out of the room, like any adoring auntie, leaving the smell of roses behind her—a scent I hadn't noticed until now, in the draft of her leaving.

As she passes through the doorway, she pauses and says over her shoulder, "Oh! I've forgot. I'm meant to tell you that Samuel has gone to the docks to supervise some shipment or another. He won't be back until late, so we're not to wait up."

AT THE SOUND OF THE clicking latch, I gather up my knees in my arms. The sheets are soft and fine, and I realize this must have been Simon's bedroom. Simon's bed. Something about the size of the room, and the windows overlooking the river, and the white-painted door in the corner that leads, I suspect, to a private bathroom. Simon's bathroom. Simon slept on these soft sheets and gazed at this ceiling and bathed behind that door. As I concentrate my mind, as I tread my gaze carefully along the pale walls and the draperies, the few pieces of dark, elegant furniture, this intuition grows into a certainty. This is Simon's room. Simon was here.

Simon is still here.

I suppose you think I'm crazy. Simon's death is a legal fact, after all. No one disputes the evidence. His own brother identified Simon's burned body, and I have reason to trust the integrity of Samuel Fitzwilliam.

And there is the ring. Who can argue with the presence of a ring, recovered from a body in a fire? I look down at my right hand, and there sits the battered gold band, fit with some effort around my fourth finger, just above the knuckle. It's my wedding ring, my genuine twenty-four-karat wedding ring, the worse for wear; I don't question that fact for an instant.

But the sight of this poor, tormented bauble, curled in the center of Samuel's palm, struck me not with grief—as Samuel supposed—but with something else. Some kind of psychological crisis, some kind of dissonance of the mind, in which the solid, indisputable object before your eyes clamors against the understanding in your brain, and that understanding is defeated, pulverized, crushed under the physical evidence of your husband's demise. And how are you supposed to contemplate what remains? You can't. You fall asleep instead.

But now I've awakened. I have awakened in Simon's bed and spoken to Simon's sister, and the cool suggestion of Simon's presence returns to me, as naturally as the sun climbs above the ocean in the morning, as unsettling as the fingers of a wraith pressed against your neck.

The faint sound of running water drifts through the plaster walls—a sound that should probably fill me with anxiety but instead leaves me weightless with gratitude. Aunt Clara, giving my daughter her evening bath, so I can rest at last. *Our sister,* Clara said. And it was true. All along, as I plodded through my days in New York, waiting for some kind of inevitable denouement, I had this family. I had a brother-in-law, and a sister-in-law, and a husband whose existence I tried to ignore. And I know nearly nothing about them. The history of the past three years is as mysterious to me as the mangroves growing on the opposite shore of the river, the mangroves surrounding Simon's burned house on Cocoa Beach.

I turn my head to the window, and the hot blue sky of this foreign land. This Florida, where Simon went to seek his fortune after I left him in Cornwall three years ago, and where he has met some kind of end, and now the remains of him drift about me, his presence slips in and out of my vision, and I have got to find a way to grasp him.

Because that's the real reason I've come, isn't it? Not because of duty, and certainly not because of love. Not even in order give my daughter a sense of her father, or any of those fine, sentimental things.

No. I'm here because I've done enough running away, haven't I? Enough hiding from what terrifies me. I'm twenty-five years old, a wife and a mother and a sister, and I've just watched a jury of twelve sensible men convict my father of murdering my mother. I've survived the worst possible ordeal, the question that's haunted me since I was eight years old, the source of all my waking dread. I have courage now. I have resolve. I have discovered the truth about one man.

Now the time has come to discover the truth about the other.

OVER BREAKFAST THE NEXT MORNING, I inform Clara that I'm taking Evelyn to Miami for a few days. We'll drive off in the Packard as soon as the dishes are cleared and the suitcases packed.

"Miami?" she says. Toast suspended in midair.

"Yes. Miami."

"Whatever for?"

For fun, I tell her.

Clara finishes her toast and her tea, dabs her mouth with a delicate napkin, and informs me that she's not going to let us run off without her, oh no.

And by the way, if it's fun I'm after, the place to go is Miami Beach.

CHAPTER 4

France, February 1917

A PERSONAL INSPECTION. That's what Captain Fitzwilliam told me, anyway, once we had started on our way, out of the stable yard and down the turgid road, twenty military minutes later. The drizzle had let up; the chill descended. Corporal Pritchard rode in the back with the wounded men, while Fitzwilliam sat next to me on the Ford's narrow seat, bracing one hand on the corner of the windshield while the damp crept in through the cracks in the rubber curtains.

"To inspect your hospital personally, of course," he said, in answer to my question. "I can't send patients to an auxiliary hospital without a thorough inspection of the premises."

Was he smiling? I couldn't take my eyes from the road in order to see his face, even if I'd had the courage to do it. In any case, the winter daylight was already retiring behind the thickening fog. But I thought I heard warmth in his voice. An impish emphasis on the word *thorough,* which I was then too unworldly to understand.

"I suppose not," I said.

"You're a Red Cross outfit, you said?"

"Yes. The Eighth New York chapter, the Overseas Unit."

"Which the redoubtable Mrs. DeForest organized."

"Yes. Mrs. DeForest was very eager to assist in the war effort. Directly, I mean."

"Of course she was. I can just picture her now. I do wonder if she'll match the image in my head. But what about *you*, Miss Fortescue? The *astonishing* Miss Fortescue."

I switched on the headlamps, not that it made much difference. The road went around a slight downhill curve, ending in a muddy hollow that required my concentration. When we had plunged through and emerged on the other side, a flatter stretch, straight and bordered by lindens at even intervals, he relaxed his grip on the windshield and repeated the question.

"I'm afraid I don't know what you mean."

"I mean what you're doing here, plowing your ambulance through shellfire and whatnot, along roads deemed impassable by my doughty British drivers. Are you a nurse?"

"Not a qualified one, no. That is, I've had first aid training and the Red Cross coursework, of course, but I'm mostly here as an auxiliary."

"A dogsbody, you mean."

"Not at all."

"But Mrs. DeForest has you doing all this wretched driving."

"I happen to like driving." The road was drier here, slightly elevated. I moved the throttle, and Hunka Tin reached forward. Engine screaming, mud flying from the tires. "My father taught me."

"What's that?" he said over the noise of the engine.

"My father! He's—well, he likes to work with machines."

"What, a mechanic?"

"Not exactly. An inventor, I guess."

"More and more extraordinary. What has your father invented?"

"Nothing, really. Industrial gadgets."

"Aha. Lucrative stuff, I suppose? Greasing the wheels of American commerce?"

We jumped hard over a rut. Fitzwilliam crashed into me. Straightened, apologized. I said don't be silly. He smelled of disinfectant and human skin and exhaustion. His beard stood in need of shaving; I had felt it briefly on my cheek, warm and raspy, and I thought, *That's what it feels like, a man's unshaven jaw, like the rasp of sandpaper.*

You know, it's a cozy roost, the cab of a Model T. And the ambulance cab was cozier than, say, a Ford roadster or a coupe, because you had that wooden box stuffed up behind you, and you were perched on the narrow seat, while your legs crowded into the narrower dash. Put a fully grown male in the passenger seat—a man like Captain Fitzwilliam, long-legged and loose-shouldered, oh yes, *fully grown indeed*—and there was just enough room for breath and awkwardness, for human sweat and anxiety.

"I don't know about lucrative," I said. "We don't much speak about money at home."

Fitzwilliam rubbed his jaw. I imagined the soft scratch of bristles, somewhere beneath the engine's rattle. A pair of headlamps surfaced in the gloaming, and a moment later a supply truck labored heavily past, plastered with mud, the driver's shattered face visible for an instant in the glow of Hunka Tin's blinders. Then another one, following close. Headed for the front.

"I suppose that was an impertinent question," he said.

"Impertinent?"

"About your father's inventions. Quite out of order. It's been rather a frightful two days, I'm afraid. Stretchers arriving every few minutes. Scrambles the gray matter."

"Of course."

"And then I've almost forgotten what it's like, speaking to a lady."

"What about your nurses?"

"Oh, the nurses. Have you met any of them? They're all ancient and exactly like schoolmarms. The RANS does it on purpose, to prevent fraternizing. Amazingly successful. One forgets they're women at all. Liberates conversation to a shocking degree. Mind you, they're terribly good at what they—oh, look out!"

Hunka Tin blew her left front tire.

IF YOU'VE NEVER HAD THE pleasure of inhabiting an old French château, let me assure you: the reality's less charming than you'd think.

Oh, they have a way of bewitching you from the outside. A black night had fallen utterly by the time we reached the Château de Créouville—not so much as a breath of moonlight behind all that cloud—but the lamps blazed from the windows of the great hall and the bedrooms above, so that you emerged from the surrounding forest to encounter seven cone-topped stone turrets rising dreamlike against the sky, and a lake shimmering with gold. Captain Fitzwilliam straightened in his seat. "By God, is that it? Isn't there supposed to be a blackout?"

"Mrs. DeForest isn't one for hiding."

"Must be damned expensive, however, burning up all those lights."

"She doesn't care about expense."

"Yes, that's the lovely thing about having blunt, isn't it? Well, she's failed one test already. She's got to observe the blackout. I suppose the Boche reconnaissance haven't found you yet, but they will. They'll think you're the new staff headquarters, and bomb the blazes out of you." He sat back and folded his arms against the solid khaki bulk of his greatcoat. Our elbows met, and I was surprised by the size and strength of his, by how much more assertive the male elbow could be. How confidential, there inside a humid little enclave, where you couldn't help tasting his vaporous breath and the flavor of his soap, detecting each movement of his fingers and jaw, while a castle glimmered nearby against a sooty night. He went on, more whispery: "It's beautiful, however. Good God. Like a fairy story. Is it built on that lake?"

"Yes. The lake forms a kind of moat around it, only much prettier than a real moat."

"Oh, agreed. Nasty, swampish things, moats. Imagine this in summer, set against a blue sky."

Well, I already had. I'd imagined the château in full, vigorous, fertile summer, five centuries ago: teeming with knights and stags, each stone pink in a rising dawn. I had imagined people inside. I had imagined love affairs and troubadours. Long ago, I had learned that you could imagine anything you wanted, that the space inside your head belonged only to you. Furnished and decorated and inhabited only by you, so that your insides teemed and seethed while your outward aspect remained serene.

"You've got some imagination," I said. "If you look closely enough, it's falling apart."

"Of course it is. Everyone's skint these days, including and perhaps especially the upper classes. Except your Mrs. DeForest, it seems. Or is it just Americans in general?"

"Not all Americans are rich."

"No, but the ones who *are* . . ."

We were climbing the drive now, a slight incline, and the tires slipped in the mud. I reached down with my left hand and shifted the Ford into low gear. The windows grew before us; the exuberant decoration took shape. The ripples on the lake made you think of enchantments.

Because everything looks better in lamplight, doesn't it? Tomorrow, in the harshness of the winter morning, Captain Fitzwilliam would see the crumbling of the old stones, the chunks of fallen fretwork, the brown weeds thrusting from the seams. The sordid state of the gravel, the broken paving stones in the courtyard. How Mrs. DeForest had grumbled! But now, at dusk, in the glow of a hundred lamps, everything was new and luminous. You couldn't speak for the beauty of it.

And we didn't. We didn't say another word, either of us, all the way up the drive and over the stone bridge, beneath the rusting portcullis and into the courtyard. Captain Fitzwilliam leaned forward, and the movement brought his leg into contact with mine. He didn't seem to notice; the spectacle of the château immersed him. One gloved hand reached out to grasp the top edge of the dashboard, and I thought how gamely he had helped me change the flat tire, how he'd knelt in the mud and turned the bolts while I held the rectangular pocket flashlight, turning it off and on at intervals so the battery wouldn't quit. The cheerful way he'd risen from the half-frozen slop and said, *I could just about do with a bottle of brandy, couldn't you?* As if I were a partner of some kind, a person of equal footing, deserving of brandy and respect.

I hadn't replied. How could I reply to a thing like that?

I brought Hunka Tin to a careful, battered stop just before the main steps and switched off the engine. There was an instant of rare silence, like a prayer. Captain Fitzwilliam turned to me and said, "Miss Fortescue, I—"

The door flew open, and Hazel popped outside in her woolen dressing gown.

"Good grief! We thought you'd been killed!" she said, and then Captain Fitzwilliam unfolded himself onto the gravel, muddy and unshaven, wet and weathered, and she paused. One foot hovering on the next step, one hand covering her mouth. Behind her, the hinges squeaked rustily, and somebody shrilled about the draft.

"Home sweet home," I muttered, and went around back to release the doors.

MY FATHER BOUGHT OUR FIRST Ford secondhand when I was eleven years old. We had just moved into a narrow, respectable brownstone house on East Thirty-Second Street, after two years of renting a basement apartment somewhere on the West Side—I don't recall the exact neighborhood, just that it was quiet and slightly downtrodden, the kind of place where you minded your own business and didn't get to know your neighbors—and Father came home one day and said he had a surprise for us. I still don't know why he bought it. We hardly ever drove anywhere; we never left Manhattan. I think he just wanted something to tinker with, or maybe to keep my sister busy. She shared his joy in mechanical things. I didn't; I learned how to drive and how to keep the flivver in working order, but only because I had to. Because Father said so. When Sophie was old enough, I washed my hands and turned the Ford over to her.

But even if you didn't take joy in engines, you couldn't help admiring that car. It was blue—before the war, you could buy a Model T in red

or green or blue, just about any color *except* black—and really a marvel
of simple utility, easily understood, made of durable modern vanadium
steel, lightweight and versatile, so that you could jam the family inside for
a Sunday drive or build a wooden truck atop the chassis and call it a delivery van.

Or an ambulance.

And when I went to Paris and knocked on the door (metaphorically
speaking) of the American Ambulance Field Service in Neuilly and begged
for a vehicle, I didn't tell them I hadn't bent over the hood of a Model T in
five years. I just bent like I knew what I was doing, and it all made sense
again. The neat, economic logic of engine and gearbox. The floor pedals
and the gear lever, the spark retard on the left of the steering wheel and the
throttle on the right. And I thanked my father for making me learn, even
though I hadn't wanted to, and I thought—as I drove out of Neuilly, truck
packed tight with hospital supplies and spare parts—about that first driving
lesson. How frustrated I had been, how angry at Father's unsympathetic
sternness. *But* why *do I have to learn? I don't care a jot for automobiles*, I said
recklessly, and he said implacably, *Because a car can make you free, Virginia,
a car can take you anywhere you want to go.*

But maybe *need* was a better word. A car could take you anywhere
you *needed* to go. Like the garage of a medieval château in north-central
France—a garage that wasn't really a garage, just an old stable, lacking
electricity, lit by a pair of kerosene lanterns, smelling of grease and wet
stone and melancholy. I didn't *want* to be here, cleaning the mud from
Hunka Tin's brave, scarred sides, changing her oil and examining her tires,
but I *needed* to be here. And needing was of a higher order than wanting,
wasn't it? A nobler calling.

BY THE TIME I FINISHED, it was nearly midnight, and the lamps in the
great hall had darkened at last. The atmosphere lay black and dank on the
stones of the courtyard. I strode from the garage to the main house, car-

rying one of the kerosene lanterns, so absorbed by the question of Hunka Tin's suspect fuel line—to replace or not to replace?—that I didn't notice the fiery orange dot zigzagging at the corner of the western wing until the smell of burning tobacco startled my nose.

I lifted the lantern. "Who's there?"

The orange dot flared and disappeared. "Your humble servant."

"Captain Fitzwilliam?"

"I didn't mean to disturb you. Have you been taking care of your ambulance all this time?"

"Yes." I raised the lantern higher, and at last I found him, resting against the damp stone wall, arms folded, cigarette extinguished. The peak of his cap shadowed his eyes. "How are the patients?"

"Tip-top. Showered in grateful attention from the ladies of the Overseas Delegation of the—which chapter is it?"

"The Eighth New York Chapter."

"Of the American Red Cross. Yes. They were *delighted* to see us. I was reminded of Jason and the women of Lemnos. Except that ended rather badly, didn't it? In any case, commendable zeal. Commendable."

"Does that mean we've passed your inspection?"

"With flying colors."

I wondered if he had been drinking. I thought I smelled some sort of spirits on his breath, though I wasn't close enough to be sure, and the pungency of the recent cigarette still disguised any other smell that might have inhabited the air. His voice was steady, his words beautifully precise. I couldn't fault his diction. Still. There was something, wasn't there? Some ironic note at play. I stepped once in his direction, so that the light caught the bristling edge of his jaw. "You're making fun of us, aren't you?"

"I? No, indeed. Perish the thought. I admire you extremely, the entire enthusiastic lot of you. So fresh and dear and unspoiled. The fires of heroism burning in your eyes."

I lowered the lantern and turned away. "Good night, Captain."

"No, don't go. I apologize."

"You've been drinking."

"I have not been drinking." Injured air. "I've had a glass or two of wine, served over dinner by your redoubtable directrix, but I haven't been drinking. Not as the term is commonly known."

"You had dinner with Mrs. DeForest?"

"She insisted."

Yes, I had lowered the lantern and turned away, but I hadn't taken a step. The soles of my shoes had stuck to the pavement by some invisible cement. I don't know why. Yes, I do. Captain Fitzwilliam had that quality; he could hold you fast with a single word, a single instant of sincerity. *Don't go. I apologize.* And there you stood, rapt, wanting to know what he really meant. Wanting to know the truth. All that charm, all that marvelously arid English wit—there had to be something *behind* it, didn't there? It couldn't just dangle out there on its own, a signboard without a shop.

A light flickered to life in one of the bedrooms above us. Fitzwilliam went on. "I made my escape, however. As you see."

"You might have chosen a warmer place for it."

"Ah, but I wanted a cigarette, you see, after all that. Rather badly. And my mother, who detests cigarettes, always made us smoke outdoors."

"I see. An old habit."

"That, and I was hoping to encounter a certain intrepid young ambulance driver, to thank her for her fortitude. And for enduring the cynicism of a jaded old soldier along the way."

"That wasn't necessary."

"Not to you, perhaps. But essential to me."

The handle of the lantern had become slippery in my bare palm. I had left my gloves in the garage. *Essential.* That word again. "Well, I'm sorry to have put you to the trouble. I hope you weren't waiting long."

"Not too long." He levered himself from the wall. "I just want to be clear. I wasn't mocking *you*, Miss Fortescue. I was mocking myself."

I started walking toward the door, or rather the rectangle-shaped hole in the darkness where the door should have been. The air was opaque and full of weight. I heard the crunch of his footsteps behind me. "It doesn't matter," I said.

"Yes, it does. It matters terribly. All this, it's no excuse to lose one's humanity."

"You haven't lost your humanity. I saw you working, back there. You cared for those men; you were—you were *passionate*."

"The way a butcher cares for his pieces of meat."

"That's not true."

"It shouldn't be, but it is. It's the only way to get along, you see."

"I don't think that's true."

"Because you haven't been here long enough. Believe me, once you've seen enough chaps minus their limbs or their faces or *guts,* that's the worst, entrails hanging from a gaping hole in what once was a nobly intact human abdomen . . ."

He stopped talking. Stopped walking. I stopped, too, and turned my head, pulse racketing. His eyes were stark and gray, his skin was gray. But that was just the light, the feeble light from the lantern I held at my knee.

"Forgive me," he said.

"There's no need."

"It's the wine, I suppose. One should never obey one's impulses after drinking a bottle of wine."

"You said it was a glass or two."

"I might have been modest."

How strange. He wouldn't look away. I wanted to look away, but it seemed rude, didn't it, turning my eyes somewhere else when he held my gaze so zealously. As if he had something important to say. In fact, I couldn't move at all, even if I wanted to. Like a nocturnal animal caught in the light from the kitchen door. My knuckles locked around the lantern, my cheeks frozen in shock.

"You should rest," I said softly. "You shouldn't be out like this."

"I might say the same of you. Shall we go in together?"

"Of course."

He reached forward and took the lantern from my hand. My fingers gave way without a fight. Shameful, I thought. He lifted his elbow as well, but I ignored that. I ignored all of him, in fact, as we walked silently toward the entrance of the château, through which the great had once streamed, the ancient de Créouvilles in all their glory, shimmering and laughing, and now it was just wounded soldiers, common men, nurses and doctors in bleak clothing. I ignored him because I didn't know what to say, I didn't know what to do. When he opened the door for me, I stepped through and sped for the staircase.

"Miss Fortescue?"

"Yes?" Breathlessly, without looking down. Hand on the bannister. Under my foot, the stair creaked noisily.

"My room is in the west wing."

"Yes."

"So I suppose it's good night."

The word *night* tended upward, like a question to which I was supposed to know the answer.

I said, "Yes. Good night."

THE KINGSTON ACADEMY GIRLS KNEW I was different from them. Girls always do. I was too afraid to speak to anyone—too afraid I would say something I shouldn't—so I sat by myself on that first day and didn't say a word.

There was one girl. Amelia. She was the ringleader, the girl everybody listened to. "Let's play the husband game," she said when we were outside in the small courtyard after lunch, and everybody wrote something on a piece of paper and put it inside the crown of Amelia's hat, and when they drew out the pieces of paper and read the words aloud, they were the names of boys, and the name you drew was the name of the man you were going to marry. Henry, John, Theodore, George. The girls all giggled when they read the names, as if they actually believed in it, and I sat there on a wooden bench next to the brick wall of the courtyard—there was a cherry tree growing feebly nearby, I remember that—and I hoped no one would notice me.

But Amelia did. That was why she was the ringleader; she never missed a thing. She came up to me, and her brown eyes were like keyholes, small and well guarded. "Pick a name, Fortescue," she said, shaking the hat. "That *is* your name, isn't it, Fortescue?"

I now know she only meant the question rhetorically, but at the time I quaked in panic. Because my surname wasn't Fortescue, was it? I was really Faninal, unique and infamous. I shook my head at Amelia and said No, thank you.

Well, Amelia wouldn't stand for that, not right there in front of the other girls. You couldn't allow any petty rebellions. The new girl always had to be put in her place.

"I said, pick a *name*, Fortescue!" She rattled the hat again, right in my face, and again I refused, and her eyes, which had been keyholes, became tiny slits. "All right. If you're too scared," she said, and she picked a piece of paper from the hat and read out the name, and everybody—all the girls—burst into hysterical giggles.

I sometimes wonder if I should have obeyed Amelia. Would everything have taken a different path? Would I have become like the other girls, and my old Faninal life dissolve harmlessly into my past? Would I have entered into the Kingston universe, the ordinary female universe, in which pretty dresses hung like stars and marriage was the gravity that held everything together?

Or would I have remained stranded on my bench, while the other girls went to parties, met boys, discovered dark corners, were kissed and fell, unafraid, into love?

EXCEPT FOR MRS. DEFOREST, WHO HAD a grand suite in the west wing, the nurses slept in a row of narrow bedrooms, like nuns in a convent. Mary's door was closed and dark, and Hazel's. We were all so exhausted after so much excitement.

And me. Virginia Fortescue. I climbed into bed at last, trembling and aching, incurably awake, my nerves shot through with some kind of foreign stimulant I could not identify.

She is absolutely essential.

I stared at the gilded ceiling and thought, over and over, I have certainly not fallen in love; that is impossible.

CHAPTER 5

Dixie Highway, Florida, June 1922

WE'RE RUSHING DOWN the highway in the blue Packard, Evelyn wedged happily between us, suitcases lashed precariously into the rumble seat, and I'm laughing at some joke of Clara's, laughing and trying to keep the Packard straight on the road, which is soaked and slick from a morning downpour.

"Miami Beach is just heavenly," Clara's saying, "just endless fun. I know all the right people, too. They think I'm a proper aristocrat, and they've fallen all over themselves to make my acquaintance. There's nothing an English accent won't get you, in American society. I suppose there's some tremendous meditation there on republicanism and human nature, but I haven't got the brains for it this morning."

"Have you been there often? Miami Beach?"

"Oh, back and forth, really. Samuel goes to Miami on business, and I won't be left by myself in dull old Cocoa, not if you paid me. I've done enough of *that* all my life! Being left behind."

"What kind of business?"

"Heaven knows. Banks, I suppose. Or estate agents. Everybody's buying land in Florida these days, you know. Oh, look! There's the ocean. Isn't it dazzling? You couldn't pay me to return to England, either. For one thing, there aren't any men left, and you've got heaps of strapping young fellows here. To be perfectly honest—you don't mind if I'm perfectly honest, do you?"

"I don't think I could stop you."

"Well, as I said, to be perfectly honest, I was rather shocked to discover that you were still married at all. To Simon, I mean. That you hadn't divorced him and married someone else. Some devastatingly attractive Yankee chap. You can't have lacked for admirers."

The Packard's wheels slip in the mud, and I use this momentary distraction—righting a motorcar on a treacherous road, a nimble skill I still possess, thank God—to think of a suitable reply. When the Packard's running straight and smooth once more, I squint briefly at the sun and say, "Not really. I didn't go out. I was too busy with Evelyn."

"But your sister! Surely your sister must have wanted to go out. Didn't you chaperone her, or something like that? I think I read she had a suitor."

"Read where?"

"Why, in the papers, of course! How do you think we discovered where to find you? Your father's trial occupied all the headlines. I'm afraid I devoured them shamelessly. You were such a mystery to us, after all." She pauses and turns to me. "I hope you don't mind? I couldn't very well not look. I'm not *that* noble."

Unlike the sloppy road, the sky is blue and clear, the sun white against the windshield. Not so hot as yesterday, either, though it's only nine o'clock in the morning. Plenty of time for the heat to build, plenty of time for the tropical air to move in like a well-cooked sponge. For now, though, I'm enjoying the coolness of the breeze on my neck, the tiny goose bumps that raise the hair on my arms. I glance in the rear mirror, almost as if I'm expecting another car behind us, and say, "Then I guess you probably know more than I do. I haven't looked at a newspaper in five months."

"Really? Don't you want to know what people are saying?"

"Not at all."

"But your father! My goodness! Aren't you curious to know what becomes of him now?"

I glance down at my daughter, nestled between my right leg and Clara's left. Her soft head is already drooping against my ribs, her eyelids heavy and inattentive. The honeysuckle smell of her hair drifts upward into my throat. I turn a few inches to make absolutely sure my sister-in-law can hear my words over the engine.

"A court of law has just convicted my father of the crime of capital murder, Clara. So you'll forgive me if I really don't give a damn what becomes of him now."

TWO HUNDRED MILES AND SEVEN hours later, I point the Packard eastward along a narrow causeway, according to Clara's confident directions. The afternoon sun glitters joyfully on the water around us. To the left, a pair of oval islands slumber in the sunshine, too perfect for nature.

"Isn't it clever?" Clara says, standing up on the floorboards, clutching the top of the windshield. The draft whips her bobbed hair about her cheekbones. "Carl's dredging the bay to make beaches and islands. Just wait until you see the hotel."

"Who's Carl?"

"Carl Fisher, of course. He's an absolute genius. He's the one developing all this." She makes a sweeping arc of her right hand, taking in everything spreading out before us: the oval islands made of dredged sand, the long strip of palms and mangrove and building plots on the barrier island beyond. "Miami Beach," Clara says dreamily, and closes her eyes.

"I don't see any beaches."

"Those are on the other side, facing the ocean. The hotel's right over there, along the bay, so you can watch the speedboat regattas right from your window. Or moor your yacht out front!" She laughs.

"If you've got a yacht, of course."

"Even better if it's someone else's yacht, though. That way you haven't got to take care of it, or remember to pay your staff."

"Crew."

"Yes, of course. Crew!" She laughs again and sits down, pulling Evelyn onto her lap. "You're going to love Miami Beach, darling girl. We'll take you to the casino first thing tomorrow."

"The *casino?*"

"Oh, it's not that kind of casino. At least, not by daylight. It's a bathing casino. Lovely beach right on the ocean. Swimming pools. It's heavenly. If I were going to build a mansion, I'd build it right here in Miami Beach. On the ocean side, I think, so I can watch the waves arrive from across the world."

I don't know if I agree with her. In the first place, I wouldn't want to live in a mansion—too much grandeur, too much trouble—and in the second place, the ocean's such an unreliable neighbor, isn't it? Noisy, wet, tempestuous. Apt to spit up storms and unwanted visitors on your doorstep, without warning.

But my eyes and my shoulders are drained by the long drive in the sun, and I don't possess the strength to argue, or really to speak at all. I grip the Packard's large steering wheel between my hands—the white cotton gloves gone gray with dust—and concentrate what force remains on the slim, straight causeway before me, until our wheels roll onto dry land once more, and Clara points me left, up a wide and unhurried avenue, toward the Flamingo Hotel.

AN ELEPHANT BROWSES THE LAWN outside the hotel entrance.

"Look, there's Rosie!" Clara exclaims. She hoists Evelyn onto her lap— much hoisting has been done this day—and points one graceful finger toward the beast, while I attempt, between astonished gapes, to keep the Packard in a straight line for the hotel entrance. If I'm not mistaken, a pair of golf bags hangs on a yoke from Rosie's shoulders. Evelyn squeals and throws herself against Clara's restraining hands.

"Why on earth do they keep an elephant?" I ask.

"For *fun*, darling! My goodness. Haven't you ever heard of fun? There are two of them, actually. Elephants, I mean. Carl and Rosie. They do children's birthday parties and caddy for the golfers and that sort of thing. Better than being cooped up in a zoo or a circus, I should think."

Evelyn wants to stop the car and say hello to Rosie. I tell her we'll meet the elephant later. My daughter's face is brown from the sun, and she's full of spirit after being cooped—in the manner of an elephant in a zoo, I suppose—inside the narrow front seat of a Packard roadster all day. Our several stops at fruit stands and service stations seem only to have fueled her excitement. She exclaims at the palms lining the drive, the red-suited bellboys scrambling to meet us, and as I steer the car to the curb at the grand portico entrance, I think, *Maybe this trip has been good for her.* Maybe Florida is good for her.

Maybe little girls should have a chance to see the world a bit, while they're still young enough to see it in wonder.

"NOW THEN," CLARA SAYS, WHEN the last of the room service dinner is cleared away and Evelyn's bathed and put to bed. "Where shall we go tonight?"

"Go?"

"Yes. Go. Go *out*, Mrs. Fitzwilliam, because you can't tell me you're actually in mourning for my brother, God rest his villainous soul."

"No, of course not. But—"

She wags a finger. "But nothing! Of course, the winter season's long over, so there's not nearly so much going on. But the casino will be open, and I know a dashing little place up the coast—"

"You must be joking. Who's going to look after Evelyn?"

"Evelyn?" She looks to the connecting door.

"Yes. My daughter. We can't just go running off like that and leave her alone."

"But why not? She's sleeping, isn't she?" Clara's delicate face is a picture of puzzlement. Brows all bent, lips all parted.

"She might wake up, and then what?"

"Can't we just—well, lock the door?"

"If there's a fire?"

"Oh, for God's sake. There won't be a fire. Even if there is, look at all this marvelous water! They'll have it out in a flash."

I laugh, a little weary, and sink onto the settee. "Clara. I don't mean to be rude, but I can see you're not a mother."

"Well, if I were, I shouldn't be so frightfully dull about it as you are. Children need to learn a little independence, don't they?"

"She's not yet three years old."

"Well!" Clara sits, too, in a ripple of accordion-like pleats, atop the arm-chair before the desk. Or rather she perches, right on the edge, like a bird about to take flight, and I think again how unexpectedly young she looks, though she must be in her late thirties. I can't remember exactly how old. Her skin is so fresh and unlined, her hair so dark, her brows so crisp. She doesn't wear any cosmetics, except for a bit of lipstick, now smudged, as if she doesn't know how to blot. Maybe it's a cream she uses, or maybe it's a trait she's inherited from some fortunate ancestor. Maybe it's her good spirits. I've heard good spirits make all the difference.

"Yes. Well."

"What a nuisance. I suppose we'll have to stay in, then. I don't suppose your scruples will allow us to roam so far as the hotel restaurant?"

"No."

"The tea garden?"

"Even worse. It's outside."

"The *lobby*?"

"Maybe for a minute or two, to collect messages or leave instructions."

"My goodness. How reckless. Well, then." She springs back to her feet and dusts off her hands. Her dress floats around her narrow little figure. "You leave me no choice."

"You're not going out *alone*, are you?"

"I might, if I were here by myself. In fact, I rather believe I would." She pauses. Bites her lower lip. Gazes upon me with remorseful huge eyes. "Oh, rats! Look at you. I can't lie. Very well. To be perfectly honest, I've already done so, on frequent occasion."

"*Here?* In Miami Beach?" I glance out the nearby window at the yacht basin below, where perhaps a dozen golden-lit pleasure craft bob like apples in a barrel. Our suite occupies the seventh floor, at least a hundred and fifty feet from the nearest boat, and still I can hear the trails of mad, giddy laughter, the drunken song rising upward to drift through the crack in the window. "Do you think that's wise?"

"Of course it's not *wise*. Goodness me, no. But you never have any fun if you're wise. You never get the chance to live, and why did we go through all the trouble of surviving that awful war and everything else, if we don't mean to *live?*"

How my throat fills with bitter words. I can taste them at the back of my mouth, flavored with experience. Because the opposite of wisdom is folly. Because when you're foolish, you get hurt. When you abandon your good common sense for the sake of your impulses, you find yourself in trouble.

But Clara doesn't wait for me to answer her question. Her face has gone aglow, like the lights strung along the decks of those yachts in the harbor below. As she turns for the door, she continues in her confident, modern voice. "But this time I'm here with *you*, dearest, and I'd never abandon a sister to an evening of stultifying boredom, just for the sake of my own amusement. No, no. As the saying goes, If Mohammed won't go to the mountain . . ."

"*What* are you doing?"

Clara pauses before the door, tilting her chin in a martyred pose. "I'm off to collect a mountain for you, my darling. Or at least a bottle of champagne, which is just as difficult in this strange Puritanical teetotal nation of yours."

BEING CLARA, SHE RETURNS BEARING not just champagne but dessert, pushed through the doorway on a mirrored serving trolley by a waiter who's paid to ignore the distinctive round-bellied bottles dangling from each of Clara's slender hands. "I couldn't decide," she says, setting down each one, "so I had him bring them all."

I can't tell her that I hate champagne, the taste and the smell and the zing of bubbles against my nose, which brings such painful memories rushing against my skull, I sometimes hold my breath on those rare occasions when champagne must be endured. Clara's so triumphant, so full of joy at her successful mission—God only knows where she found these bottles, and what she had to do to obtain them for us—I just keep quiet. Wince at the *shhh-pop* of the first cork. Take my glass and sip as small as I can: a toothful of bubbling wine.

Clara drains half a pint or so and reaches for the strawberries. "That's better. Now where were we?"

"We weren't anywhere."

"Do have one of these chocolates. The pastry chef makes them himself. One by one. I watched him once. Mesmerizing."

I took a chocolate.

"And for heaven's sake, drink your fizz. You've no idea what promises I made to obtain it. No, no. Not another miserable little sip. Properly. Like *this*." She tipped back her head and finished off the glass and poured herself another.

"I can see you're an expert."

"You don't need to be an *expert* to enjoy champagne." She made a little leap and plopped herself on one of the beds. "How I do adore this hotel! We stayed here when we first came to Miami Beach, Samuel and I. That was March, after we'd been to identify poor Simon's body. I couldn't stand to stay in that dreary little town, so we came here to recover. Just like you! That's why I thought of this place, when you said *Miami*."

I lower myself to the edge of the other bed. "That wasn't necessary."

"Yes, it was. I could see it in your face, when we saw the elephant. You were enchanted—as enchanted as darling Evelyn—only you wouldn't admit it. You daren't admit your enchantment anymore. Because of Simon, I suppose." She drinks her champagne and stares at the ceiling. "I say, I rather fancy a fag. You don't mind, do you?"

I tell her I don't mind at all, and she leaps up again and rummages through her handbag until her hand emerges in possession of a slim gold case. She knocks out a cigarette and lights it in a series of quick, graceful movements that mesmerize me. When she's finished, and the cigarette burns from her fingers, she lifts the champagne bottle and wanders dreamily across the room to where I sit on the edge of my bed. "Refill, darling. Now be a good girl and drink it."

For some impossible reason, I obey her and drink deep, and this time it isn't so bad. As if those first few sips have numbed the nerves that connect sensation to memory. Anyway, everything's different now, isn't it? This is Florida, sun-warmed and hibiscus-scented. The icy champagne just fits, somehow.

Clara watches my face. "That's better, isn't it? There's nothing a bottle of vintage fizz can't cure, I always say. And you need it more than anyone. You're in desperate need of a good roaring drunk, Virginia Fitzwilliam."

"Am I?"

"Oh, yes. Poor thing. I'll bet you've been blaming yourself for the past three years, telling yourself you can't have any fun, that you don't *deserve* any fun because you made such a dreadful, dreadful mistake trusting Simon."

"It wasn't a mistake. I thought so in the beginning, after I realized what he really was. But then Evelyn came."

"Oh, Evelyn. Of course. No, I don't suppose you can regret *her*."

"Never."

"And you can't really hate Simon, can you, when he gave you *such* a daughter. Oh, my darling! What a terrible burden you've been carrying, between Simon and your father. All these dreadful men pressing around you." She wandered back to her own bed and made that same little skipping motion, landing on her back, one white-stockinged leg dangling from the side. "You mustn't blame yourself, you know. It's not your fault that men are such beastly bounders."

"I don't blame myself."

"Oh, lies! Yes, you do. And you're punishing yourself for it. You're doing penance for allowing yourself to be taken in. Not once, but twice! First your father, and then Simon. Or is it the other way around?"

In a single awkward, unpracticed movement, I lift the glass to my lips and drink all the champagne, all of it, jiggling the stem so that the last drop tracks along the bowl and into my mouth.

Clara turns on her side and examines me. "Ah! I've got it right, haven't I?"

"Not at all."

"Yes, I have. I'm a terribly keen observer of other people, you understand. We younger siblings always are. I knew right away, as soon as I saw you. My poor Virginia. My poor brave darling."

I rise from the bed, and this time I'm the one who takes the bottle in my hand. I'm the one who pours the champagne into my glass, almost to the rim. "I'm not brave at all, though. If anything, I've been weak. Weak and blind."

"Because you wanted to be *loved*. You had no mother, no other family. My God! That man was your *father*. And Simon was your lover. Of course you wanted to believe in them. I remember the first time I saw you, clinging to Simon like a lovely pale little vine—you're so tall, and yet you didn't look tall at all then—and I thought, oh, the poor dear sweet thing. What am I going to tell her? How am I going to *warn* her?" She reaches forward—I'm standing next to her, because she left the champagne bottle on the small table between our two single beds—and she seizes my empty left hand. "And your father, too. It's the same thing. You wanted so desperately to believe that he was good, that he wasn't a murderer. You had no *choice* but to believe in him. He had all the money, and you had a sister, and then the baby. Where else could you go? You simply *had* to believe he was innocent. To go on believing. Oh, come here, darling." She pulls me onto the bed with her and puts her arms around me, and while I'm absolutely not crying a bit—my eyes are dry, my chest still—I find myself helpless to resist her. She has paralyzed me. "You're safe now, anyway. They can't lie to you anymore."

"What a shame. They were both excellent liars."

"Oh, you don't need to tell *me* that! Simon was just—what's the word? He was congenital. I don't know about your father, but Simon was simply born that way. A liar. He was an expert, a natural. He knew exactly what to say to you, to make you believe him. He knew exactly what you wanted to hear."

"Yes," I whisper.

"Of course, it made him terribly charming. All the local girls used to go mad for him, whenever he came down from school at the end of term. You can only imagine what a clever seducer he was. He was no more than fifteen, I think, when he got started. Yes, fifteen at the oldest. I remember because I happened upon him with a girl one afternoon, the summer I turned ten. There was a pretty little secret garden on the grounds, you see, just perfect for that sort of thing, all walled and sunken and loads of benches and sweet-smelling roses. I used to play there all the time. I thought it was a fairy garden. Don't laugh! Oh, the stories I used to make up, the darling little fairies of my youth. Anyway, that's where I saw them together, although I was so young at the time, I had only the vaguest idea what was going on. Just that it seemed rather beastly, like a pair of naked white rabbits."

We're lying on our sides, spoon-fashion, because the bed is so narrow. Clara's arms are secure around my chest, her breath sweet in my hair. I've drunk the champagne too quickly. The opposite wall floats before me. A pair of watercolor landscapes, framed in white, bob and merge along the sea-green wallpaper. I picture a ten-year-old Clara wandering across a wet Cornwall lawn. Turning the corner of a brick wall and finding Simon stretched on a bench or a blanket, atop some faceless, budding, writhing girl. In my imagination, she has blond hair and smells of peaches.

"How awful for you," I whisper. "And for her. Poor girl."

"She was lovely. An utter innocent, of course, just like you. I think he preferred them that way: virgins, or else someone's naïve young wife. The purer the better. And she wasn't a village girl, either, this one. She was a proper middle-class sort of girl, an attorney's daughter, the kind of girl who's supposed to preserve her virginity at all costs until marriage. Partic-

ularly in those days, you know, before the war. The poor darling! I don't
know how he convinced her. The usual way, I suppose. He didn't give a
damn for your feelings; that was his strength. You can do anything if you
don't care how other people feel."

"I don't understand that. How he could seem so sympathetic, if he didn't
really care."

"Because he *knew* what *you* were feeling. Don't you see? He knew, but
he didn't care. He was a tremendous actor. He acted his way through life,
manipulating us all like puppets. Everyone else was taken in by him, but *I*
knew. I knew how rotten he was inside. I could just *smell* it, the rottenness.
I've always sensed things like that, as if I could just sort of *see* someone's
spirit, like the color in a rainbow."

"A *color?*"

"Yes! Everybody has a color. Oh, not *visible*, I mean, not exactly. I can't
explain it. Like a sort of halo, I suppose, or rather the impression of a halo.
The color I think of, the color that *floods* me when I see you. I feel myself
rather purple, for example, veering between a kind of lurid violet and a
lavender, depending on my surroundings."

I make an awkward laugh. "Really? And what color am I?"

"Oh, darling! You're blue. Dear, true, pure, melancholy blue! And I
adore you for it. My sweet new sister."

I want to know what kind of color she saw in Simon, but for some reason
I can't bring myself to ask. I gaze at the wall instead, breathing quietly,
thinking *Blue*. A dark blue or a light blue? Or, as with Clara, does my particular shade depend on my surroundings?

She speaks up suddenly. "That's why he made such a good surgeon, you
know. Simon. He wasn't troubled by what he saw. He could operate on you
as if you were an automobile engine. Quite without mercy, but of course it
worked. I suppose you might say that human civilization *needs* people like
that—people to do our dirty work, to do all the horrible necessary things
we can't bring ourselves to do. It's just you don't want to fall in love with
them."

I sit up. The pins in my hair have loosened, and a few locks drop free. I brace my hands on the edge of the mattress, concentrating my attention on the wall, until the merged watercolors separate once more into two distinct forms. Then I reach for the champagne glass on the nightstand.

Behind me, Clara lifts herself to a sitting position and slips her arms around my waist. Her head rests gently on my back. She's forgotten about her cigarette. I watch the dying wisps of smoke drift from the white ceramic ashtray next to the champagne bottle. It's shaped like a shell—the ashtray, of course, not the champagne bottle—and the delicate flutes make a perfect hollow for the cigarette's round shape. How clever.

I lift the cigarette, rimmed in smudges of Clara's lipstick, and stub it out. "Still. I can't regret it."

"Of course not. You have Evelyn."

"She is worth everything to me. She's worth anything."

Clara reaches past me for the cigarette case. "And your sister? What was her name?"

"Sophie. Her name is Sophie."

"She's all right, too?"

"Yes. She's engaged to be married. A nice, well-bred fellow. Harmless and simple, from a stately old family. He hasn't got much money, but then he doesn't need to, does he? I think they'll be happy together."

Clara lights the cigarette and leans back against the pillow, watching my profile. "And you? What about *you*, dearest?"

"What about me?"

"Have *you* thought of marrying again?"

"Me?"

"Yes, you. You might as well make a fresh start, mightn't you? Simon's dead. The trial's over, and your father's got what he deserved. Your sister's got someone to watch over her. You have your daughter and all your lovely, lovely money. Why not find yourself a handsome, trustworthy lad to share it all with?"

"Because I can't!"

She leans forward. "What's the matter? Are you afraid of *all* men now? I assure you, you've only been frightfully unlucky. Most of them are quite decent. Anyway, you'd better marry quickly, or you'll attract all the rotten ones. The ones after your dosh."

"I'm not afraid of that. I don't have any intention of forming any—any—"

"Attachments?"

"Is that what you call them?"

"My poor love. Look at you, all frightened and trembling. And you are so *blue,* you know. You're not the sort that can take up with one chap and another, flitting about like a bee sipping nectar, and yet you need love. You need love desperately." She snatches a quick bite from her cigarette. "No. We've got to find you a husband. What about Samuel?"

I spring to my feet. *"Samuel?"*

"He's handsome enough, isn't he? And he's a dear, loyal boy who won't run about on you. You're already terribly fond of him."

"I hardly know him."

She shakes the cigarette at me. "Now, don't be coy. I know all about your embrace yesterday."

"It wasn't an embrace. Not *that* kind of embrace."

"Perhaps on your side it wasn't. But Samuel! He told me, you know. In his gruff little way. In fact, I suspect you quite overcame him. I shouldn't wonder if he's been in love with you all this time. Just like him, to form a passion for an impossible object. It's illegal, you know, back home. To marry your brother's widow."

"Is it?"

"Yes. The Church thinks it's a kind of incest, apparently. Ghastly archaic old men. Anyway, it all makes tremendous sense. He's just enough like Simon to attract you, but not enough to put you in danger for your life. In fact, the opposite. Samuel will protect you from anything. Protect you with his own heart's blood, I daresay, or whatever manner of nonsense you like. He's a warrior, you know. That's what they do."

I walk to the mirror that hangs above the desk. The image appalls me. I suppose I'm not the sort of woman who looks enchanting in dishabille. My hair straggles gracelessly from its pins; my face is wan, protected from sunburn today by the brim of a sensible hat. My bones stick out everywhere. Over my shoulder, Clara's dark head bobs and wavers. "I am *not* going to marry Samuel," I tell the reflection in the mirror, in slow, forceful words. "I'm not going to marry anyone again."

"Really?"

I turn to face her. "Really."

She reaches out to crush the cigarette into the crustacean ashtray. "I have agitated you terribly."

"I'm not agitated. I'm simply not going to marry again. I can't. I will take a thousand lovers before I marry again. But not that. Not marriage."

"Why? Because you're afraid they all *are* only in it for the dosh? Because Samuel—"

"Actually, there isn't any dosh. Not much, anyway."

"I mean when your father's dead, of course—"

"No. After he was arrested, he transferred everything, all he had, the patents and the money and the house, to Sophie and me, first thing. But I couldn't keep my share."

Clara's still rolling the end of the cigarette in the ashtray. She stops now, holding the stub against the porcelain, eyebrows high and sweetly arched. "You gave it all away?"

"Not quite all. But I couldn't take Father's money, any more than I needed. I've put almost all of it, including the patent rights, into trust for Evelyn."

Clara drops the cigarette at last. Rubs her thumb and forefinger together, as if to brush away the ash. "That's awfully noble."

I turn back to the mirror. "Not really. It isn't as if money has ever given me what I really wanted. You might say it's the opposite."

"Oh, my darling."

The bedsprings squeak, the rug rustles. Clara lays her small head against my back and wraps her arms around my waist.

"You poor thing," she whispers against the thin fabric of my dress.

"I'm not poor. I'm rich. I have Evelyn, I have my sister."

"What about Simon's estate? Are you going to give that away, too?"

"I haven't decided yet. Yes, probably. I guess I'll likely sell it all and put the money in Evelyn's trust. Once I've found out . . ."

"Found out what?"

"I don't know. Once I've seen everything. Everything Simon left behind."

"That may take a little time. He left behind a great many things."

My hollow eyes regard me. A bit accusingly, maybe, as if I'm blaming myself for my current state. My current gloom. I should eat more, I think. I should eat more and drink more and go outside without my hat and generally enjoy myself. Why not? I should learn something about this world that Simon inhabited, until I discover what I'm looking for. Whatever that is. A sign or a clue or an elegant solution to the puzzle of Simon's death. Until I discover whether or not I'm really free.

A foot or so to the left of the mirror, a window frames the western landscape, catching the glare of the dying sun. If I shade my eyes, I can see the smudge of buildings on the opposite shore of the bay. The striving blocks of Miami, where Simon occasionally made visits, to transact business with his bankers.

I say softly, "I've got nothing but time."

CHAPTER 6

DURING THE NIGHT before I left for France, I slept in Sophie's room, in her bed, the way we used to do when she was small. After Mama died.

Slept. I don't think we actually slept. We talked until our throats hurt, we laughed into our pillows, and Sophie cried a little. Sophie's the sentimental one; she tears up at everything, Fourth of July parades and baskets of puppies. Maybe I've spoiled her; maybe I've been too protective. I held her while she wept, and the old flannel of her nightgown scratched my neck, and the honeysuckle smell of her hair filled my head, raising all kinds of memories. My chest ached. She asked me why I had to go, and I didn't tell her the truth. I didn't tell her that I was going to explode, I was going to go mad, I was a pot of salted water coming on to boil under the pressure of an eternal cast-iron lid, and someone was going to get scalded.

Instead, I stroked her honeysuckle hair and said, *Because there's a war on, Baby. There's a terrible war going on overseas, and I have to help.*

She said, *I'm going to miss you so much, what am I going to do without you here,* and I kept on stroking that hair, blinking my bee-stung eyes, and when I could speak I said, *You'll be fine, you'll be safe, Father will take good care of you.*

I said it over and over, until I believed it myself. Until it almost felt true.

But I couldn't numb the anguish beneath my sternum. I couldn't cure the absence of my sister, or the fear that sometimes roused me in those sooty moments before dawn, when the terrible new day smoldered at the horizon, streaked with unknown danger.

AS IT DID NOW, THE morning after I first met Captain Fitzwilliam. I lay on my back and stared at the crumbling ceiling, while my nerves stung and my temples burst. While the tension hurt the muscles of my jaw. Like I hadn't slept at all, and maybe I hadn't.

I rolled over and opened the drawer in the bedside table, where I kept a clumsily embroidered sachet that Sophie had given me for my birthday when she was ten. Before I left New York, I had removed the exhausted lavender and slipped inside a small cake of soap, the honeysuckle soap with which I always bathed her, until she was old enough to bathe herself. I held the sachet to my nose and thought, *If I can still smell her, she must be all right, she must be safe. Father must be taking good care of her.*

The light grew. Time to rise. Time for breakfast, time to wash and to dress and to drive out into the bitter February morning. The bitter February mud. I absorbed a last breath of honeysuckle and threw off the covers.

Mrs. DeForest was one of those women who believed in a sturdy, early breakfast, stocked with protein and vitamins. She worshipped vitamins, the entire alphabet of them. She'd brought her own hens from Long Island, and not one bird had dared to expire along the way. When I stepped downstairs into the refectory at six o'clock, she sat already at the head of the long wooden table, looking clean and practical. At her left sat Corporal Pritchard, shoveling food silently into his mouth, and at her right sat Captain Fitzwilliam, wearing his tunic (but not his belt) and drinking coffee. I saw that his hair was lighter than I had supposed. It was almost golden—or maybe that was only the effect of the vast electric chandelier overhead—and spiked all over in stiff, reflective gray. I was shocked at the familiarity of his face, how I already recognized each angle of bone and each line embedded around his eyes and mouth. How I could say to myself, *His skin looks better this morning, less wan, full of color, plumper. He must have slept well, after all.*

Mrs. DeForest was speaking. She nodded to me but she didn't pause. She never paused. "It's the result of so much planning, you know. No detail too small when it comes to people's health. I'm a firm believer in clean sheets and fresh, abundant food. We've brought our own supplies, and there's more on the way from our chapter back home. We have an awfully enthusiastic chapter. Nothing is too good for our patients, Captain Fitzwilliam."

"Indeed." The captain looked at me. His eyes crinkled some sort of message. I went to the sideboard and lifted a plate. A mirror hung before me, at such an angle that I could watch the two of them, at right angles, his left knuckles nearly brushing her right knuckles.

"Our main ward is the old great hall. That was my idea. You can't understate the healthful benefits of the circulation of air, and the ceilings in that hall are no less than twenty-five feet high, served by no fewer than twenty fully operational windows. I saw to the refurbishment myself."

"But doesn't it get cold? So many windows? The men do hate a draft, Mrs. DeForest."

Mrs. DeForest set down her fork and steepled her fingers over her plate. She ate eggs and fruit for breakfast—always fresh, no toast—after an hour of morning calisthenics. She had gone to college, you know, and was all up-to-date. She was the first woman I knew who cut her hair short, though pretty soon we were all doing it, bobbing our hair. But she was the first. She said that short hair saved her an hour a day, at least. Her husband was older, and they had never had children. Maybe that accounted for her skin, which was so untroubled and resilient, as she leaned forward over the de Créouville porcelain, that you could have bounced a tennis ball from her cheek, if you wanted to. (Not that I wanted to! It's only an illustration.) Her fingers were equally young and strong, linked together now at the middle joints, though she must have been forty-one, by my own calculation. "As for warmth," she said, "you'll notice two rather *spacious* hearths, one on each end of the hall, which provide a *great deal* of heat. Nice, *dry* heat, Captain, in this awful damp."

"An inestimable virtue at this time of year."

My dish was full. I went to my usual chair, to the left of Corporal Pritchard, two seats down. Four nurses sat at the other end of the table, hunched over their plates, eating swiftly, each movement straining with suppressed excitement. The other nurses, I supposed, were on duty in the ward. Mrs. DeForest had worked out a careful system of shifts, based on scientific principles of human efficiency.

"I understand your patients are housed in a *barn*, Captain?" she said.

Corporal Pritchard set down his fork, lifted his head, and answered for his captain. "Indeed they are, ma'am. A regular French barnyard. Smells like the devil."

Mrs. DeForest turned to me. "Is this true, Miss Fortescue?"

"I think the corporal—that is, the building *was* a barn. Before the war. But it's perfectly clean now, just like a regular kind of hospital. Everything sanitary, as far as I could see."

Corporal Pritchard shook his head, very mournful. He was a thin, hollow-cheeked man with an oversized nose and a gaze of perpetual hunger, and mournfulness just about hung on his face as if he'd given birth to it, millimeter by millimeter, through his nostrils. I thought he was around thirty years old, but maybe I was wrong. Maybe the war made boys look older, and he was really eighteen. "It's the summer that's the trouble, miss. Them pigs running about. But we don't like to complain."

At the word *pigs,* I pressed my coffee cup to my lips and glanced at Captain Fitzwilliam, who concentrated on his toast. The clock ticked, the air yawned. The soft thump of busy feet approached and receded. Mrs. DeForest looked at me, at Captain Fitzwilliam. At Corporal Pritchard.

"*Pigs,* Corporal?"

"Just in summer."

"Hmm." The fingertips tapped. The brow furrowed. The gaze returned to Captain Fitzwilliam, but not the head itself. She had a way of doing that, looking at you sideways. "A *barn*," she said.

The captain spoke cheerfully. "You see, Mrs. DeForest, the Royal Army Medical Corps established this particular clearing station in the early days, when we were dashing about digging trenches, and nobody had the least idea we'd still be churning over the same ground two years later. There wasn't time to build any of your fine modern compounds of huts and wards, according to all those marvelous diagrams prepared beforehand by our diligent staff. Luckily—well, for the men, at least—it's only temporary accommodation. Until they're well enough to go back up the line, you know, or else bad enough to continue on to the base hospitals, or even Blighty itself. Well, the really fortunate blokes, anyway, too ripped up to be any use to Haig."

Mrs. DeForest smacked the table with the flat of her palm. "There. Do you see, Miss Fortescue? *This* is why we came to France. *This* makes it all worthwhile. Barns! *Barns,* if you will!"

I wanted to tell her that this wasn't why I came to France, not really. That the barn wasn't all that bad, and the British Army seemed, after two and a half years of war, to be taking care of its wounded in a pretty resourceful manner, given the circumstances. I thought of Captain Fitzwilliam's keen face, and the competent way he shot an order in its proper direction, hitting the mark bang on the nose, before turning to me and smiling, smiling, as if he'd been playing at darts. But how could you say that to Mrs. DeForest, the president of the Eighth New York Chapter of the American Red Cross, who never got out of bed except to rescue some lesser creature from an awful fate? How could you admit to a variety of motives, not all of them noble?

Captain Fitzwilliam saved me. "You're an angel of mercy, Mrs. DeForest, and on behalf of the entire British nation, I thank you for your service. That's a splendid cut of ham, by the way. *Splendid.*"

She snatched his plate, darted to the sideboard, and heaped on the slices of pink French ham, one after another. How she came by the ham in the middle of the beleaguered Western Front, I never understood. She was just that kind of person. She could pluck priceless haunches of *jambon* from thin air. She set the plate back before the captain and resumed her seat.

"So you'll be sending more? Patients?"

"As many as we possibly can."

"And you'll tell your colonel how well we've cared for your men, isn't that right? The many advantages of the château?" She lifted the coffeepot and dangled the spout above his cup. "More coffee?"

He nudged the saucer forward.

"My dear Mrs. DeForest. Advantages it is."

IN FACT, AS I WALKED down the ward on my way to the entrance, I thought the men were maybe a little *too* well cared for. The zeal of eight Red Cross nurses had left them cocooned in immaculate white sheets, immobile, a little stunned, like flies in the web of an especially greedy spider. The sisters were serving hot breakfast by the spoonful—whether or not the patient was capable of lifting a spoon—and as each man opened his mouth he seemed to be uttering a silent cry for escape.

"It's a bleeding palace," muttered Corporal Pritchard, who walked at my side. If you looked carefully, you could actually see the bulge in his stomach where the breakfast lay. Like a massive, self-satisfied tumor hanging from his ribs.

"A château."

"Like that what them staff officers got." At either end of the hall, just as Mrs. DeForest promised, two fires burned up the DeForest fortune at a magisterial rate of combustion. A wind-up gramophone played tinny Mozart between the two central windows.

"Your headquarters, you mean? In a château?"

"Yes, miss. A great big one, they say, but that's just to be expected, innit? The staff sacrificing their youth and health, day and night, for our sake. It's only right they should have a nice posh castle to lay their weary heads in." He stood back politely to allow me through the doorway. I liked the way he spoke, the peculiar accent (*youf an' elf*) and the natural sarcasm. Outside, on the gravel drive, Hunka Tin stood waiting. I had spent the hour before breakfast in the makeshift garage—the former stables, actually, except all the horses were long gone—while Mrs. DeForest did her calisthenics, and now the Ford looked as bright as new, almost. Mud washed away and engine tuned. Tires all repaired and axles checked. I hadn't replaced that fuel line, however. Hoped I wouldn't regret the omission.

"Blimey," said the corporal, "you've ain't half got a good mechanic."

"Actually, I'm the mechanic."

"*You*, miss?"

The air was bitter, and the engine would be cold. I went around front, released the choke, and turned the engine. "My father had a Model T for years, and my sister and I kept it running for him. He thought we should be self-reliant. Could you switch the ignition for me?"

When the engine was puttering at an easy, patient pace, the corporal slid from the seat and made room for me. "Your chariot, m'lady," he said. Courtly bow.

"Where's your captain?"

"Making his regards, I think."

"His regards?"

He nodded at the steps. "To herself."

"Oh. Of course."

"Now, don't you think anything of that, miss. It's only what he does."

"Think anything of what?"

The corporal nudged the brim of his hat and reached into his pocket. He lit a cheap, brown-wrapped cigarette and walked away, a few polite steps, smoking and staring into the dry fountain in the center of the driveway, where a suite of lichen-crusted cherubs stood frozen in frolic. A dark fog wrapped the trees beyond. I realized he wasn't going to reply and climbed into my seat. The smell of exhaust. The steady vibration of the engine under my hands and my bottom. The things I knew.

After a minute or two, Captain Fitzwilliam emerged from the château, hat and belt in place, and swung into the seat beside me. He smelled of coffee and soap and just the faintest hint of cigarettes, and his cheeks were pink against the ecru of his shirt collar. "Off we go, then," he said, striking the dash with his palm, like a signal, and he propped one boot against the frame, leaned back his head, and fell asleep.

SO I DROVE, BECAUSE I could do that well, and it steadied my nerves to do something well. Something practical. The fog persisted, and the damp, bitter wind blew on my temples. Behind me, the wooden truck rattled and groaned on its metal chassis. The engine ground faithfully, smelling of burnt oil and gasoline. The road was even more churned and muddy than yesterday, but this time I knew the way, and the morning light was still young and hopeful. I kept to the middle of the road, where the mud wasn't so bad, though I had to give way to other vehicles: supply trucks and artillery wagons and even, as we drew closer, other ambulances. All crusted with mire. They were headed to the railway station at Albert, for the sanitary trains to the coast, where the base hospitals lay in a chain along the sea, from Étaples to Boulogne.

Beyond them, England. The source of all these vehicles. The quarry from which all this manhood was mined, was cut and honed and shipped here in its millions. To do what? To live and fight and die. To construct and occupy this vast, temporary civilization that existed for a single object.

I caught myself wondering, at that moment, where Captain Fitzwilliam lived, when he wasn't patching up bodies in a casualty clearing station in northern France. When he wasn't asleep beside me, heavy and silent, pressing his big left knee across my right. Where he was raised, who were his parents. The ambulance pitched and wallowed. The wet air had soaked through my woolen gloves, and my fingers, clenching the wheel, should have felt the cold. Instead they glowed. *She is absolutely essential.* I was not falling in love; I was certainly not falling in love. Love was a fiction, written by Nature to disguise her real purpose. This sick, breathless sensation in my belly was only biology. This heat on my nerves. Only the instinct to procreate.

Or something else, maybe. The recognition of imminent danger.

"YOU'RE DAMNED QUIET," CAPTAIN FITZWILLIAM said an hour later, making me jump. "Are you always so quiet?"

"I thought you were asleep."

"Only resting my eyes. I rarely sleep."

"Why not?"

"I don't know. Troubled conscience, perhaps."

The ambulance lurched through a hollow. Fitzwilliam gripped the doorframe, while a series of thuds vibrated the wood behind us, and Pritchard swore.

"Aren't you going to ask?" he said.

"Ask what?"

"Why my conscience is troubled."

"Isn't that your own business? I don't even know you."

"Miss Fortescue," he said gravely, "this is a time of war, not a drawing room in peacetime."

"I don't understand. What difference does that make? People are people."

"I mean that we've shared a most intimate space for several hours now. Can't we dispense with the niceties and be friends?"

I said nothing.

"Look. I'll start. My conscience, since you're curious—"

"I'm not curious."

"Yes, you are. You're desperately curious. You *like* me, Miss Fortescue; admit it."

"I do *not*—"

"My conscience, Miss Fortescue, coincidentally enough, is troubled because of you."

"Me?"

"Yes, you. Because a young lady of tremendous youth and merit, to say nothing of beauty, has traveled such a great distance to cover herself in mud and motor oil and to make conversation with an old bounder like me, and most especially to put herself under the command of a Mrs. DeForest—"

"Mrs. DeForest is an *admirable* woman."

"Oh, most admirable. No doubt at all. But she's rather a tyrant, isn't she?"

I was still too rattled by the word *beauty*. "Of course not," I lied.

"And I ask myself why. Why you should do such a thing, and why I should be so fortunate as to deserve you."

"*Deserve* me!"

"Deserve, I should say, your entrance into my particular butcher shop at a quarter past five on an otherwise ordinary February afternoon. Ordinary in the sense of this mad, atrocious war, I mean."

Another vehicle approached us along the narrow road, a large truck painted in dull olive green, covered in canvas. I pointed Hunka Tin carefully to the right-hand side, and the truck thundered past, engine screaming, mire flying from the wheels.

"I don't understand why you say these things. How you can be so flippant."

He placed one hand on his woolen heart. "You wound me."

"Nonsense."

"I protest. In the first place, I'm not being flippant. I'm quite sincere. In the second place, you'll find there are two ways to cope with the madness in this godforsaken Hades. The first is to pretend that it's all a great—if rather unsporting—outdoor game. A match of cricket prolonged by inclement weather and unlucky batsmen."

"And the second?"

"I'd rather not say."

Another truck came by, identical to the first. A supply convoy, probably, returning from the lines. I rubbed my thumbs against the wheel. My back ached, my jaw ached. Every muscle strung tight.

"In any case," Captain Fitzwilliam went on, when the clamor died away, "we have roamed far from the question at hand. What exactly are you running away from, Miss Fortescue? I find I should very much like to know."

"Nothing at all."

"Tyrant parents? Failed love affair? Creditors at your heels?"

"None of those things."

"Nothing left behind? No heartache, no loved ones pining?"

I gripped the wheel and leaned forward. Stared through the windshield. The bleak, brown, lurching winter landscape. I remember I was considering how long to remain silent before starting another topic, and what kind of topic I could safely introduce. Weather or war news or staff incompetence. Something even more impersonal, like the quality of wartime coffee, and whether you could call it coffee at all. Then—

"I have a sister."

"What's that?"

"A sister!"

"Older or younger?"

"Younger."

"Are you close?"

"Very much."

"Well, then. Why the devil should you leave her behind, if you love her?"

"Because I—"

Well. I stopped right there, right there on the edge, right in the split second before I tumbled off. Shocked that I had crept so close without realizing. Or shocked, really, that I had allowed this man to lead me there. Why? Because he was handsome and weary and crammed with easy manners, because he was solid and smoke-scented by my side, because I was breathing the fog of his breath and he was breathing mine, and his big left knee connected with my slender right one. Because he was a doctor, after all, and how could you not trust a doctor with your miseries? That was why doctors existed.

"Because I wanted to help," I said instead.

He shifted in his seat, and his knee left mine.

"Well," he said, tilting his head back again, crossing his arms across his ribs, "if you change your mind, I should be glad to serve as your confidant."

I didn't reply. I didn't think I could. I felt sick, perspiring, the way you do when you stand by yourself on the brink of some vertiginous cliff, and

the whole world undulates around you, and you're overcome by the tantalizing power of suicide. The death that lies within your immediate grasp.
A single, easy step.

When the silence ripened, and the road flattened, and I felt I could risk
a sidelong glance, I saw that Captain Fitzwilliam's eyes were closed once
more.

But I knew he was not asleep.

WHEN WE WALLOWED INTO THE stable-yard entrance at half past ten,
the scene had changed from the day before. Two ambulances occupied the
corner nearest the barn, and for a moment I couldn't tell if they were loading patients or unloading them. I pulled the brake and the car lurched and
stopped. "We're here!" I shouted, banging a fist on the wood behind me,
and I didn't wait for Captain Fitzwilliam to stir, I didn't wait for Corporal
Pritchard to wake up and crawl from his stretcher. I jumped out of my seat
and into the soft earth, and I floundered around back to toss open the door.

Pritchard was sitting on the floor, dazed and sleepy. He lifted his head
and swore. "That was quick."

I stuck out my hand and lifted him free. The other ambulances, I now
saw, were loading men. They were headed for the railway station, for the
sanitary trains to the base hospitals. From the east came the sound of artillery, a steady barrage, round after round firing into the German defenses.
This time there was no returning fire, no long whistle and low, shattering
explosion, but I stuck my head to the crown of my helmet anyway, as if
that would protect me, and staggered through the sucking mud back to the
front of the ambulance.

Just as I ducked around the corner, a stretcher party charged from the
doorway, awash in wet khaki and as urgent and muscular as a set of race-
horses. I stopped just in time and flattened myself against the wall. "Watch
it, mate!" the orderly said, the one in front, and for some reason this rebuke
brought me back from the nauseous precipice. Reminded me, I suppose,

of my own unimportance in this place. My insignificance. I was not *absolutely essential;* I was intruding. I was in the way. There was no impending collision. No Virginia at the center of some fearful, imagined impact. Just wounded men, who were fighting a war.

The stretcher passed. "Go on, then," said Fitzwilliam's voice behind me, and I obeyed him. Crossed the threshold into the barn.

Less crowded now. A few of the cots lay stripped and empty, and the orderlies and nursing sisters moved around like people instead of rabbits. But the architecture was the same, the brown walls, the rows of lumpy beds to the right, the curiously identical white faces stuck above each blanket, the curtains to the left that partitioned the operating theater, the recovery room, the mess and the barracks. The smell of disinfectant, of earth and wet wool and old wood, enclosed me in its familiar cloud. If I cared to listen, I could discern the restless moans, the low chatter of a hundred injured men. Like any hospital, I thought. Captain Fitzwilliam pushed past me and caught the elbow of one of the nurses, speaking earnestly, head a little bowed, so that the electric light caught the tender skin of the back of his neck, and I found that I was wrong. That the threat of annihilation didn't matter.

But that's how it happens, when you have no defense, no immunity whatsoever. When you thought you were strong, and you were only untested. I made a movement, preparing to turn away, and at that instant Fitzwilliam lifted his gray-speckled head and looked at me, and his lips parted.

"Miss Fortescue—"

A clatter of boots overtook him, a choir of exhausted male shouts, and our heads snapped to the doorway of the barn, where a new stretcher party had arrived, flinging mud and chill onto the floorboards.

"Damn," said Captain Fitzwilliam. "You'll excuse me."

He strode to the door, and I turned to look for Corporal Pritchard. But Pritchard had gone as well, and I was left standing alone near the entrance to the operating theater, a useless obstruction, a thick American branch tossed into the orderly flow of treatment and evacuation, treatment and evacuation. We were two years late, weren't we? In the early months of invasion and repulsion, the race to the sea—before so many clearing stations were established, before the base hospitals were built on the northern coast, before all the manuals were written and the procedures put in place—when the trains were stuffed with casualties and the depots lined with stretchers and panic, a hospital like ours might have made a difference.

In this brutal, methodical February of 1917, our zeal was nothing but vanity.

I stood there, feet planted on the old wooden boards of that French barn, and watched Captain Fitzwilliam approach the stretcher and trade a few words with the man in front. Step forward and bend his head to address the wounded soldier inside. Behind them, the door was still open, and the corner of an ambulance flashed in and out of view as the driver and the orderly secured the doors. A nurse hurried past, carrying a tub of soiled and stinking bandages. Fitzwilliam stepped away from the stretcher and issued some direction to the stretcher-bearers, pointing his finger to one of the empty cots, bleached new sheets yellow-white under the electric bulbs, and I thought, *It is time to go, Virginia.*

Time to go.

I stepped aside for the stretcher party, and the soldier's pale face jogged by. Every roof beam, the arrangement of every cot was familiar to me, as if I'd known them for years. As if I'd been born and raised here, and maybe I had. Maybe I had lived an entire new life inside the space of the last twenty-four hours, been reborn and struggled and hoped and strived, and now . . . and now . . .

What now?

Did I die and return to the old life?

"Miss Fortescue," said a voice next to my shoulder, "will you come to my office? I'm afraid some paperwork remains to be sorted out."

AND SO I CAME, WITHOUT even striving for it, to stand inside that canvas-partitioned square that constituted Captain Fitzwilliam's office, while he made his final notes on the papers that would accompany my new patients to the Château de Créouville. He had offered me coffee, and I had refused it. I didn't want him to see how my hands shook. I gazed at the pink lobe of his right ear and said, *Of course*.

"I don't know how to say this—I'm sure you'll think me a little mad . . ."

I leaned forward and gathered up the papers from the desk. He was standing on the other side; he reached out and stopped my hands.

"You don't need to speak. I'll speak. I'll tell you something I'm not supposed to tell you, which is that we're moving. The unit, I mean. Next week. Long overdue. We've got a proper site, modern regulation huts, that sort of thing, just yards away from the railway, about two miles from here. Your Mrs. DeForest ought to be perfectly mollified about *that*, at any rate."

"No more barns," I said throatily.

"Of course we shall continue to send patients your way for rehabilitation; we stand very much in need, as I said before, of a hospital to manage all the ambulatory cases, trench foot and frostbite and that kind of thing, and while it's not as glamorous as—"

"Oh, for God's sake, I don't care about *that*."

"No, of course not. You wouldn't. But I'm afraid Mrs. DeForest has loftier dreams."

"Well, she doesn't have a choice, does she?"

"No."

I stared at the desk before us. My hands still rested on either side of the sheaf of documents, held at the wrist by Captain Fitzwilliam's agile, gentle fingers. A surgeon's fingers, trained at great expense. His thumbs lay upon the backs of my bare hands, like a pair of anchors. The intimate contact seemed at odds with our businesslike communication, but what did I know? No man had ever held my wrists like this before.

And then his hands sprang back, as if only just realizing what they were doing, and settled behind his back. I gathered up the papers to my chest. From beyond the canvas partition came a metallic crash, an angry shout. I thought, *Someone's going to walk in, right this second. Someone's going to see us like this, standing here without speaking.* The desk between us was one of those collapsible designs, made of thin, light wood: a camp desk, bearing only a kerosene lantern, a couple of medical volumes topped by a messy leather notebook, a tin of pens, and a silver-framed photograph of a woman in a white dress.

I said, without moving, "If that's all, then——"

"Wait! Damn." He turned, stepped a few paces to the right, and stopped square. Behind his back, his thumbs dug into his palms.

"Yes, sir?"

"Don't call me that. Don't call me *sir,* in that voice."

The lantern was lit, and the glow fell on the silver frame of the photograph. The metal was tarnished from the damp. From this angle, I couldn't see the subject very well, but she seemed to be smiling. I leaned forward an inch or two and tilted my head for a better look. The photograph, it seemed, was not taken in a studio. The girl sat on a large boulder, both shoes visible beneath the hem of her frothy white dress, and she carried her hat in her hand. Her hair seemed to be escaping its pins. There was an inscription at the bottom. I couldn't read it.

"That's a lovely photograph," I said.

"Photograph?"

"On your desk."

He turned back. His face was pale, except for a pair of reddish patches on the outer edges of his cheekbones. You might have thought he would look at the photograph, but he didn't. He looked at me instead, fixing his gaze so intently on my face, I almost turned away. Instead, I said, in a high voice, "She's lovely. Is she your sister?"

"Yes. Do you mind if I smoke?"

"Of course not."

He reached inside the breast pocket of his tunic and pulled out a gold cigarette case. There were initials engraved on the outside, in plain Roman lettering. My heart beat in such enormous, galloping strokes, I couldn't breathe. "It must be difficult, being apart from your family like this," I said.

"Yes. Well. We do what we must." He lit the cigarette quickly and shook out the match. "I seem to have lost my train of thought. What were we saying?"

"I don't recall. Something about the unit moving elsewhere."

"You seem upset."

"I'm not upset."

"I hope I haven't made you ill at ease. I never meant—you see, it's the strangest thing. Since yesterday, I have been struck—I have wanted—I *want* most intently—most unaccountably—to see you again, to see how you're getting on—to be a friend, I suppose." The cigarette twitched between his fingers. "Do you see what I mean?"

"I—not really, no. I'm afraid I don't. I think it would be better if—"

"Stop!" He held up his hand. "Don't say it, please. Don't say some damned prim little thing about prudence and discretion."

I pressed my lips together.

He turned away and stared at the canvas wall.

"I have been wrestling with this all day, Miss—what *is* your first name?"

"Virginia."

He closed his eyes and said *Virginia*. Like a prayer, like the answer to an ancient mystery. The sound of voices intensified on the other side of the canvas. Someone was getting dressed down, a few yards away. Captain Fitzwilliam sucked on the cigarette and blew the smoke out slowly, in a wide, thin stream. "I suppose you think I'm a bounder."

"No."

"Ah, but you hesitated."

"I—I don't know. I don't know you at all."

"May I write to you, at least? Convince you of my innocent intentions."

"What *are* your intentions?"

"To be friends, Virginia. There's nothing wrong with friendship, is there?"

"I've often heard it's impossible for men and women to be friends."

"Then let's prove them wrong, shall we?" He stubbed out the cigarette and turned to me, and he was smiling. A little wildly, I thought, like somebody drunk. "You see, I find I can't quite bear to cut you off so soon, like the limb of a precious new seedling. If friendship is all we're given on this earth, why, I'll be the most steadfast, honorable friend you ever knew. We can discuss poetry and history and botany. Whatever you damned well like. The latest sensational novel. Anything but the state of the war. God knows we've got enough of that without talking about it."

"I'm sure you have enough friends already."

"Yes. Well. I *have* had friends. The trouble is, they keep dying. It's a damned nuisance, but there it is. One's obliged to hunt further afield these days, when one's old school chums no longer exist. And now you've dropped like a ripe pear before me. A friend. A fascinating, unexpected friend, rich with all kinds of interesting mysteries I look forward to discovering."

He held out his hand. I took it. What else could I do? We shook briskly. His other hand came up to seal our palms together.

"Very good, Virginia. You can call me Simon, at least when nobody's looking."

"I'm not sure——"

He leaned forward. "Be sure. *Trust* me. And if you need anything, anything at all, you've only to ask. Your welfare shall remain uppermost in my heart."

His face was so close, his smile so certain and mesmerizing, I couldn't move. I thought, *I must look away, I must get away,* but instead I just stood there, trapped, while his hand actually lifted mine and turned it over, palm up, and I gazed stupidly at his face. His head bent briefly as he kissed my palm, and I stared at the part of his hair, the speckled gold and silver, and thought how dry his lips felt, yet his breath was damp.

"You see? Harmless and devoted. Your loyal English hound. I shall write when we settle in our new quarters——"

"Captain Fitzwilliam——"

"Simon. And you'll write back, won't you? And if you should happen

by the CCS to pick up patients, or if I should happen by your château, on
my way to the village—"

"Captain—"

"Simon. You'll find a few moments to chat, won't you? A little human
contact in this damned squalid show—"

"Simon."

Those bright, drunk eyes blinked once, the way you wake from a dream.
His gaze fell to the photograph on his desk. He squeezed my hand a final
time and released me.

"Yes," I said. "I will."

Captain Fitzwilliam reached into his breast pocket, removed another
cigarette from the case—the last one—and smiled softly as he struck the
match. His hand seemed to be shaking, or maybe it was only the building
around us, rattling in fear. I remember wondering why on earth he should
be so nervous as I was.

"Thank God," he said.

WHEN I RETURNED TO THE château that evening, cold and thrilled, nerves
vibrating to a strange new pitch, Hazel came to find me in my room. To
warn me, she said. She had noticed the way I looked at the British doctor,
and the way he looked at me.

Warn me about what? I asked.

She leaned forward and took my hands. She spoke in a whisper, the way
you tell someone a terrible secret. I can still picture the sympathetic slant
to her eyebrows.

Because he was married, she said. Corporal Pritchard told her last night.
He had a wife and a baby son, back home in England.

July 28, 1919

Dearest V,

    You will pardon my crude language, but there's really no other way to express oneself in these conditions: Florida is <u>bloody</u> hot. (There, I've said it.) Indeed, if God should be so good as to send you back to me one day, and we should be so fortunate as to make a little family of our own, I should carry us all back to cooler climes for the course of the summer months, on my own back if necessary. The Adirondack Mountains, I hear, are suitable as a seasonal retreat; or else the primeval woodlands of Maine or of Washington State. Anywhere but England.

    I am in Miami at the moment, meeting with my bankers, who are not particularly pleased to see me. The company overdraft, it seems, has formed a most hideous scar on their balance sheets for some time. All my powers of persuasion are now put to the task of extracting a few coins of additional capital from their sticky paws, for the purpose of getting our business back into productive order. I am nothing if not persuasive, however—even you must allow me that virtue, having happily succumbed to my charm more than once, to my great and (I hope) <u>everlasting</u> fortune.

    I wonder if you will like Miami at all, my dear. It is frightfully busy, chockfull of speculators and hedonists. A chap called Fisher is dredging up the bay nearby, at his own unimaginable expense, in order to create a beachside paradise out of the mangrove peninsula protecting us from the open ocean. Of course we could live wherever you like. But I rather prefer the territory further north at Cocoa, which is less frenetic. Last week, I engaged in a spot of tramping about the beaches there, and I wonder if a pretty villa by the sea might not be just the thing for us both. We could listen to the waves roll in beneath the moonlight and be perfectly content.

    Yours faithfully,

    S.F.

CHAPTER 7

Miami, Florida, June 1922

THE PRESIDENT OF the First National Bank of Miami apologizes for our modest surroundings. They're constructing a brand-new building on the corner of Forsyth, he tells me, and these quarters are only temporary. Slapdash.

A pair of electric fans whir furiously overhead. I lift my voice to reply that I don't mind a bit.

He pulls back one of the armchairs before his massive desk. "The wait'll be worth it, though. Steel frame, ten stories high. The finest building in downtown Miami, if not the entire Southeast. Drink? Iced tea?"

"No, thank you."

"Indiana limestone façade, marble floors. Hired a New York outfit to design it. Mowbray and Uffinger?" He settles himself in the chair behind the desk and lifts his eyebrows, as if he expects me to know the architects personally. I don't reply—what is there to say, really?—and he raises one hand to cough gently into his fist. His gaze darts to Evelyn, who's arranging herself on my lap, and back to me. "I'm terribly sorry for your loss, of course. Mr. Fitzwilliam was one of my favorite customers."

"Oh, I'm sure he was."

"A real shock. Terrible accident. Young fellow like that, in the prime of life." Shakes his head. Steeples his fingers. "I hope you've found the papers are all in order? Accounts all shipshape? Anything more I can do for you?"

You know, for all his banker-statesman airs, Mr. Edward Romfh doesn't look as if he's much older than Simon himself. Forty, forty-five at the most.

His brown hair parts straight down the middle, lustrous with some sort of invincible pomade, and his healthy Florida sportsman's tan sets off a pair of clear, bright eyes. He smells of laundry starch and leather: the kind of man who regards you from behind round, wire-rimmed spectacles as if he's calculating your precise value in dollars and cents, down to the last copper penny. As if he knows what you're going to say, even before you do.

Evelyn wriggles in my arms. I allow her to slide free and dart for the window, where you can see all ten stories of the new First National Bank of Miami Building, a few blocks away and nearly complete, as it scrapes the hazy sky. The fans stir the hair at my nape and temples. I'm wearing one of Clara's hats, which are much smarter than mine, close and brimless like a cap. Isn't it funny, how a smart new hat gives you moral strength? I cross my legs and say crisply—surprising even myself with the backbone in my voice—"I just want to learn more about my husband's time here in Florida, Mr. Romfh. His—the fire was so sudden, you know. I never had the chance to come down and see the business firsthand. His life here."

"Yes. Well. You'll forgive me, Mrs. Fitzwilliam, but down here in Miami, we frankly didn't know he had a wife to begin with. Not until I heard from that fellow up in Cocoa. His lawyer."

"Mr. Burnside."

"That's the one."

Again, the expression of male expectation. I suppose he wants to know more—why I didn't live here in Florida with my lawful husband, why I've only journeyed south now that he's dead. Whether I loved my husband. Whether my husband loved me. I suppose you'd have to be made of stone not to wonder these things, and bankers make it their business to know as much as possible about their clients, don't they? To learn every detail—however everyday and inconsequential—that might affect a man's willingness and ability to repay his creditors.

Well, let him wonder.

"Mr. Burnside's been very kind, of course," I say, "but he's the kind of man who thinks that women aren't capable of understanding business matters."

"Well!"

"Yes. Would you believe it? But he's older, you know. You have to make allowances for the prejudices of an earlier generation. I'm sure he means well."

"I'm sure he does, though in all truth—"

I wrap my hands around the ends of the chair arms and lean forward over my crossed knees. "But *you*, Mr. Romfh. You strike me as a much keener sort of man. A *modern* man. The kind of man who really *comprehends* women. Who respects our native intelligence, to say nothing of our peculiar intuition."

"Well. Yes, of course."

"I'm sure I can rely on you to treat me as a human being of reasonable acumen. Capable of understanding a figure or two." Here I smile, nice and warm. Conspiratorial. To my right, Evelyn's lost interest in the view of the new bank building and skips across a dark Oriental rug to the windows on the other side. "Do you know how we met, Mr. Romfh? Mr. Fitzwilliam and me? I was driving ambulances for the American Red Cross in France. Why, if you've got a Model T Ford outside, Mr. Romfh, I'll bet I can take the engine apart and put it back together again, all without dirtying my gloves." I hold up my hands, clad in white cotton.

And my stars, if that doesn't do the trick. Mr. Romfh unsteeples his thick hands and draws his chair closer to the desk. He reaches for a drawer and asks if I mind if he smokes. I say of course not. And he takes out a cigar—a cigar, mind you!—and lights it up slowly, *puff puff puff,* until they're both content, man and cigar, smoking quietly in that hot Miami room, while the electric fans suck the fog upward in mighty drafts.

"What do you want to know, Mrs. Fitzwilliam?" he asks.

BY THE TIME I RETURN to the Flamingo Hotel and arrange the Packard in the lot outside, under the shade of a cocoanut palm, it's eleven o'clock in the morning and the golfers are trudging indoors, sweating and flushed.

"There you are!" says Clara, rising from the bed, fully dressed and holding a crisp new novel, which she tosses on the pillow behind her. The room is already made up, though a breakfast tray lingers untidily on the desk, covered by a careless napkin. "Where on earth have you been?"

"Just to meet with Simon's bankers."

"You might have woken me first."

"You looked so peaceful. What have you been reading?"

"A detective story. Too clever. What did the bankers say?"

I remove the hat and set it on the desk, next to the tray, while Evelyn dashes into her room. The scent of coffee and toast lingers in the air, and I find I'm rather hungry. "What I expected, more or less. Despite the bank's known reluctance to invest in anything but the soundest of ventures, Simon managed to persuade Mr. Romfh to extend him over a hundred thousand dollars in credit, in the form of a mortgage on Maitland Plantation."

"My goodness! A hundred thousand dollars! It sounds like a very great deal of money. What's that in pounds sterling?"

"About twenty or thirty thousand, more or less."

Clara whistles low and moves across the room to examine her reflection in the mirror. Nudging this, tidying that. "I suppose I'm not surprised. He had a knack for that sort of thing. Convincing people to do impossible things for him. I doubt the plantation is worth a tenth of that. What do you think he did with all the money?"

I angle my neck to peer through the connecting door, where I can just glimpse Evelyn on the rug in the middle of the room, scribbling on a piece of paper.

"I'll have to look at the accounts, to be sure. But I presume he used it to rebuild the hotel and shipping business. The house on the beach."

"His little empire."

"Yes. But that's not the strange part, you see. It seems the whole thing's been paid off in full."

"Paid off! By who?"

"Mr. Romfh wouldn't tell me that. Just the name of the bank that issued payment, and that it came in February, soon after Simon's death."

"*After* his death. How strange. Samuel said nothing about it."

"Samuel might not have known. It was a mortgage, after all. Not part of the shipping business."

"Still."

I shrug my shoulders and follow Evelyn into her bedroom, which is much smaller than ours. Just a single bed, a wardrobe, a chair, a white enamel sink in the corner. Designed for maids and children. Evelyn looks up and shows me the paper, on which she's drawn a picture of some kind of person. A woman in a sharp triangle dress with long arms and stubby legs.

"Oh, that's lovely, darling. Who is it?"

Evelyn totters to her feet and points to the doorway. "Auntie Clara!"

"Do you know," says Clara, standing in the doorway, "when I'm feeling rather low, I find an outing to the beach cheers me up straightaway. What do you say to that?"

FOR MANY YEARS AFTER WE first moved to New York, an uncanny sensation dogged the pattern of my daily life: the certainty that someone was watching me.

I felt it continuously, in those early months. That first brutal winter in our grubby, alien basement apartment that reeked of beer and wet earth and vomit, when Father slept on the creaking Victorian sofa in the front room and Sophie and I huddled together in a tiny cot in what I guess was the back room, though it was really more like a cupboard. A cold, damp cupboard. And yet it was a relief to descend those dark steps and duck into our cave—a small relief, anyway—because at least here, unlike the streets and buildings of Manhattan, a billion eyes didn't follow your every movement. At least here you didn't have to resist the physical urge to look over your shoulder every two seconds, to scour the surface of every reflective shop window; at least here, in our tiny apartment, you knew that the crawling sensation of somebody's eyes on your skin, penetrating your secrets, was only an illusion.

As the weeks trudged on, however, the feeling began to fade. In the anonymity of city life, the months upon years in which our obscurity remained undisturbed, I came to escape—first for an hour or two, then for an entire day—the immediate, visceral awareness of being observed, of being stalked and hunted, a consciousness in which every window was a menace and every patch of open space a danger.

But I have never lost it entirely. The sensation still returns from time to time, like an unwelcome relative: sometimes in faint, gradual steps and sometimes suddenly, with such debilitating force that my reason scatters, my logic crumbles, leaving me alive on instinct alone.

And I am nothing more than a rabbit, caught in the open.

I MENTION THIS NOT BECAUSE the hunted feeling strikes me anew, as Clara directs the casino attendant in the proper fixing of a pair of striped beach umbrellas, but because a man really *is* watching us. From a round table at the edge of the boardwalk, all by himself, nursing a tall glass of something-or-other and a grim, clean-shaved expression. Rather handsome, in a thick-boned way, if you imagined away the scar on his chin and the ruggedness of his nose. He's wearing a worn straw boater, adorned above the brim with a thin strip of grosgrain, a plain navy blue.

I don't think Clara notices, and I'm certainly not going to mention him. For once, I'm not troubled. Isn't that funny? All those years of false alarm, and now a real live man observes my every gesture from a corner table, and I don't give a flying damn. The sun is fierce, the ocean beats on the nearby sand. The salt breeze rushes against my face, electric with life. I hold Evelyn's hand and wade into the foam, and a wave hurtles through the skirt of my old serge bathing costume, washes between my legs, cool and tempestuous, swirling and sucking as I hoist Evelyn free of the undertow. If a man wants to watch us play in the sea, then let him. The murder trial's over. All our secrets are out. Nothing left to fear, is there?

Clara wades by, wearing a different bathing costume altogether, modern and daring. No thick black stockings for her; oh no. She looks like a child, lean and narrow-hipped, navy suit clinging to her skin. At least six inches of fair, bare English thigh separate the edge of the skirt from the top of her knee, and yet she thrashes her arms and legs, she laughs and skips as if she doesn't think anyone's watching. As if she's not trying to excite any male attention whatsoever by this lascivious display, as if she just wants to be free. She takes Evelyn's other hand, and together we swing my daughter up into another wave, giggling and gasping, while the sun burns our skin and the ocean washes us clean, and the sand scrubs our feet all smooth. As smooth and pure as a newborn's tummy.

But you can't endure such pleasure for long, and the sun really does burn your skin. A quarter of an hour later we take shelter under the umbrellas, and Evelyn starts to work with a bucket and spade while Clara fetches drinks to cool us down. "Lemon ice!" she announces, handing me a paper cup. "Isn't it divine? You Americans are so terribly clever. Where *do* you get all this lovely ice?"

"The iceman, of course."

"Cheeky." She plops into the canvas chair beside me and stretches her legs into the sand. "I say. What heaven. Imagine Simon having his own house, right on the beach like that. I wonder what he used it for. I don't believe he had any particular passion for the sea, when we were young. Do you?"

"I don't know. I wasn't there."

She kicks me with her toe. "Aren't you the smart one! You know what I mean."

"No. He never spoke about the sea."

"You see? And you can't get much better beach than this. But why?"

"I suppose he had his reasons."

Clara sucks on her ice. "What are you going to do with it, then? The house on the beach, I mean. Or what's left of it."

"I haven't decided."

"But what do you *want* to do?"

"I don't know. We'll see."

Clara leans forward to the edge of the shade, where Evelyn is dumping her pail of sand over her toes. "Evelyn, my darling. Do you absolutely *love* the beach?"

"Yes!"

"Would you like to *live* on the beach?"

Evelyn turns to me. "Can we, Mama? Can we?"

"Oh, darling—"

"Please, Mama!" She flings herself on my knees. "*Please* beach!"

I stroke her head and stare down at her limpet eyes, and I say to Clara, "Thanks very much."

"Anytime."

She closes her eyes and leans back in her chair, absorbing what dilute sunshine penetrates the thick striped canvas of the umbrella, and I direct Evelyn's attention back to the sand. I don't tell Clara that I've already given those ruins many hours of thought, and that any day—even now, perhaps—a steam shovel will cross the bridge from the mainland and start to work on that rectangle of charred land on Cocoa Beach, rebuilding Simon's house according to the original plans. If work progresses on schedule, the new villa will be ready for occupation by the end of winter. Perhaps even sooner.

No, I don't share this piece of information with Clara, because—for one thing—I expect she'll find out, soon enough. From Samuel, at least, who will surely learn that a new villa is rising atop the old, even though I've instructed Mr. Burnside to keep the matter secret for the time being.

For another thing, I haven't really decided who's going to live there.

Evelyn turns over her bucket onto the beach and lifts it carefully. The loose sand falls away in a flattened cone, and she begins to cry.

"What's the matter, darling?" I ask.

"Castle! I want castle!"

"A castle, is it? In that case, we're going to need water. Water makes the sand all sticky, so it doesn't fall apart like that."

But Evelyn's only two and a half, and the chemical properties of water and sand are unknown to her. So I take her hand and lead her down to the water, and together we fill the bucket with water and return to our umbrellas. I love the sun on my shoulders and chest, the sand clinging to my stockings. I stare down at the thick, loathsome scar on my left arm and wonder what it's like, having the sand and the water on your bare legs. Whether the salt stings your skin, or whether it just makes you more alive. Whether maybe I should go shopping while I'm here in Miami Beach, and buy myself a new swimming costume, one more like Clara's. Clara, whose legs splay comfortably into the sand, and whose dozing face now tilts into her shoulder, lips parted. I bend over the bucket with Evelyn, showing her how to send the water in a stream over the sand, and a finger touches the small of my back.

"Mrs. Fitzwilliam?"

I whirl about. A little scream rises in my throat. Dies away at the sight of the man before me: the grim, clean-shaven, thick-boned man watching us earlier from the table at the corner of the boardwalk. His eyes, staring hard, are the same opaque shade of navy blue as the ocean lying beyond the surf. His massive jaw might have been dug out of an ancient German valley. He lays his right forefinger vertically across his lips, hands me a piece of paper, and walks away through the sand, barefoot, shoes and stockings hanging from one hand. Back to the boardwalk.

At my feet, Evelyn squeals at the results of our little experiment. I stand there watching the man's broad back, his thick shoulders and swift stride, the swinging ends of his blue jacket, the scrap of short brown hair under the rim of his straw boater, until he turns the corner of the casino building and disappears from sight.

The paper in my hand is thick and white, folded once across the middle. The edges waver, but that's just my nerves. My shock. Clara's still lying there, not a single muscle awake, and Evelyn scoops the sand with her small hands. I close my eyes briefly, and when I open them the paper's still there, though the man who delivered it has gone, as if he never existed. A burst of screams carries across the surf, followed by the thundering crash of an especially large wave. I think, *It's just paper, fraidycat.* A note of some kind. Just read the damned thing.

I lift my left hand—and I'm surprised by the effort this takes, as if someone's attached a ten-pound weight to my wrist—and open the folded paper.

But it's not a note, after all. Would you believe it? There are no words. No message of any kind, unless you consider that a stranger's perfect sketch of your daughter, playing in the sand, her snub-nosed profile almost photographic in its uncanny resemblance to Evelyn, constitutes a message. The bile rises in my throat. I close the paper and start to crumple it in my fist, hoping that the dozing Clara hasn't noticed this little exchange, and that's when I see the small block letters running across the bottom edge of the back of the page, so even and regular as to appear almost typewritten.

Evelyn looks up at me, squinting her hazel eyes against the sun, and her expression, for an instant, recalls her father to my heart.

"Mama?" She tugs the end of my skirt.

"Just a moment, darling."

I crouch on the sand and tuck the sketch into my pocketbook, and as I do this, swift and discreet, I smooth away the wrinkles at the bottom of the page and read: REGARDING YOUR HUSBAND. FLAMINGO TEA GARDEN. 11 P.M.

"Something the matter?" asks Clara. Her eyes are open now; she's watching me fiddle with the pocketbook. On her face rests an expression of such sleepy, blinking, content curiosity, I'm reminded of a kitten.

"Nothing at all," I say. "But I think it's time to go back to the hotel for a rest, don't you?"

I HAVE A PHOTOGRAPH OF the house on Cocoa Beach, taken just before the fire. I'm staring at it now, as I lie alone on my narrow single bed in the Flamingo Hotel, while Evelyn sleeps in her little room next door and Clara attends a little party downstairs. We were both invited by no less a figure than Mrs. Fisher herself, the wife of Mr. Carl Fisher, who—as you know—owns this hotel and the beach casino and most of Miami Beach, really. But I pleaded a headache, so Clara went to the party on her own.

And now here I am. Staring at a photograph while the clock just ticks and ticks, ten o'clock drawing inevitably toward eleven.

This house, you see, is important. And yet it's not the importance of the house that matters to me, at this precise moment, but its beauty. When I first pulled the photograph free from its envelope, I couldn't quite believe that a house like that could possibly belong to Simon, that he could have approved its design and made himself at home there, right on the edge of the great, tempestuous Atlantic, in a villa plucked from some lazy Mediterranean shore. The roof of red tile, the inner courtyard anchored in place by a central fountain, the trees of lemon and eucalyptus, the wide windows and the simple lines: they aren't anything like—for example—Simon's ancient family seat in Cornwall, which he loved so much that he was willing to do anything to keep it. Anything at all.

But then I thought—as I gazed and closed my eyes and opened them to gaze again—I thought that maybe the simple, sunbaked beauty of this house made sense after all. Maybe the new architecture of this house represented a change in the architecture of Simon himself, or rather a reflection of Simon's true architecture, instead of the one I had imagined these past three years. Maybe I had been wrong after all. Maybe I had been unjust and fearful. Maybe some other explanation existed for the dark events in Cornwall that spring.

Or maybe not. But the sight of that photograph gave me reason to wonder. Gives me reason to wonder now, in my room at the Flamingo Hotel, as I examine its monochrome details once more. To remember the way I once felt about Simon, the way I once loved and trusted him, because while a man can lie in his words and his kisses, his letters and his embraces, he can't lie about the house that he lives in.

Or can he?

The clock ticks. 10:51.

CHAPTER 8

Paris, August 1917

I REMEMBER ANOTHER occasion I encountered that sensation of being watched. I was in Paris with Hazel, some months after I met Simon, and we had just entered a café in the avenue de l'Opéra with a pair of English officers, when I thought somebody's gaze found me, like a hand on my neck.

At the time, I dismissed the idea as ridiculous. I was in Paris, for heaven's sake! An ocean away from my previous life, a lifetime away from the secrets of my childhood. And the place was as jam-packed as any midday New York sidewalk, a favorite spot for soldiers on leave. You could hear the din halfway down the street, and inside, the atmosphere crackled with khaki and laughter and clinking glass, the smell of wine and cigarettes, the unnatural high-pitched gaiety of wartime. Nobody cared who you were inside that café, in the middle of Armageddon. Nobody paid us any attention. Not the slightest glance.

But I couldn't shrug it off: a pair of eyes on the back of my head, on my throat and arms and legs simultaneously. Not suspicious or even curious. Only watchful.

We found a table, I don't know how. Bribery, maybe. Our escorts— two sub-lieutenants, pathetically young, Johnson and someone else whose name I couldn't remember—greeted the maître d' like old friends, the kind whose generous palms make up for their excruciating schoolboy French. The tablecloth was yellowed and dirty, the glasses filmy. The café had no fresh meat, only sausages. The waiter was old and philosophical, and spread his hands before us: *C'est la guerre.*

"Of course," said Lieutenant Johnson. "Long live sausages. As long as the wine's still running, I'll eat whatever you've got."

Hazel laughed—not the kind of laugh she used to make at the hospital, but a new one, higher-pitched and sort of fragile, as if the sound of it might shatter when you flicked it invisibly with your finger. Because Hazel had already drunk a lot of wine, you see, and so had Lieutenant Johnson and his nameless friend. I didn't dare. At the time, I had hardly ever sipped any wine at all. Mother drank it often, after Sophie was born, glass after glass in the armchair in the parlor while I played with the baby in the nursery, and the sight and smell of wine always left me feeling ill and nervous. Brought on the familiar shroud of black dread. Something terrible was going to happen.

Hazel went on laughing. She wasn't troubled by dread. She had grown up in a nice middle-class brownstone in the East Eighties with a German cook and an Irish maid and five or six siblings, all watched over tenderly by a father in the insurance business and a mother who belonged to several charity committees. She reached confidently for the bottle of wine in the center of the table—it was that kind of establishment, you poured your own wine—and topped up Johnson's glass and then her own. Then the other lieutenant, who sat next to me—Green! That was his name!—and when she turned at last to my glass, she said, "Why, Virginia, you're not drinking your wine! For shame!"

"Drink your wine, like a good girl," said Lieutenant Green.

"Yes, do," said Hazel. "We're celebrating, after all. Free of old DeForest at last! Long live the American service. Jolly times ahead!"

Well, I nearly laughed at *that* one, anyway. Virginia Fortescue, jolly. The idea! Besides, who was to say that the American service wouldn't be just as oppressive as Mrs. DeForest's volunteer hospital, and probably less well run? But the United States had entered the war in the spring, and here we were in Paris, Hazel and me, transferring into the newborn U.S. Army Ambulance Service now headquartered in the hospital in Neuilly. No more châteaux, no more British patients and British doctors, no more searching of faces at every stop, hoping and dreading what you might find. Which was all for the best, of course. Wasn't this the reason I'd accepted Hazel's offer to begin with? Tendered my resignation to Mrs. DeForest? To remove myself from any possibility of contact. To slice myself off from the source of this strange, stubborn infatuation that refused, like some kind of suppurating wound, to close itself and heal.

Instead of laughing, I lifted my shoulders and told her I didn't like wine.

"Oh, that's all right," said Green. "You don't have to like it, after all. You only have to drink it."

Everyone laughed at that, even me. Nothing more awkward than not laughing along. I picked up my glass and pretended to sip, and when nobody was looking I switched my glass with Lieutenant Green's, and at that instant I felt him again: my unknown watchman, as if his palm lay flat between the blades of my shoulders.

But I don't think Green noticed the maneuver at all, and even if he did, he wasn't going to complain. Unlike me, Green and Johnson were out for a determined jolly time tonight, five days of coveted Paris leave—*ooh la la*—and Hazel and I were only the start of it.

"YOU REMEMBER LIEUTENANT JOHNSON, DON'T you? He spent a week with us last March, convalescing from trench foot," Hazel had said that afternoon as we changed into our evening clothes, such as they were. (She said the word *Lieutenant* in the English way, gluing an invisible and inexplicable *f* to the end of the first syllable.) The hotel, tucked in a respectable corner of Neuilly—was there any other kind?—smelled of cigarettes and camphor. I guess this kept the insects away. Hazel and I shared a miniature double room on the attic floor, looking down gloriously on the Bois de Boulogne from a dirty mansard window, which we kept open because of the heat.

"Not really. I only see the patients for a moment or two."

"Oh, right. Of course you do. Well, I'm sure you'll love him. Dashing fellow. He's bringing a friend."

"What kind of friend?"

"I don't know. A friend! A nice English gentleman, I'm sure. You can trust these English boys; they're not like the ones back home, all hands and promises and more hands. You know what I mean."

"Naturally."

She turned her back to me, so I could do up her buttons, and lifted her hair from her shoulders. "Please be nice to him, Virginia. The friend, I mean."

"Of course I will."

"I need him to like you, Virginia. Do you know what I *mean?* Please."

I concentrated on my fingers, maneuvering buttons into small, delicate holes, enclosing the soft, young skin of Hazel's back, and I found myself wondering whose fingers would slide those buttons out again. What fate lay waiting for Hazel's soft skin, in the hours ahead, if I did as she asked. If I was nice to Lieutenant Green.

I fastened the last button and patted the edge of her dress. "I'll do my best," I said.

AS IT TURNED OUT, IT didn't matter whether I was nice to Lieutenant Green or not. He was determined to like me, in the same way Johnson was determined to like Hazel, and she was determined to like him. Because if you couldn't actually fall in love in the space of a Paris evening in wartime, you could at least do yourself the favor of *pretending* to fall in love, to experience all the bedazzlement of love without the usual entanglement. Because your nerves and your chemistry didn't know the difference, did they?

And the restaurant was dark and hazy, and the air was warm and pungent with tobacco, and Johnson had a sharp, neat profile and Green wore a smile on his pink young face: a smile that grew broader as the evening wore on. I shrugged away the imaginary palm between my shoulder blades and thought—defiantly—*I will enjoy myself.* After the sausages, the waiter brought out four small, pale custards and a bottle of old Muscat—for the English soldiers and the pretty American girls, he said—and Johnson poured the wine and said, *Ah, that's the stuff* and closed his eyes in rapture, or else in agony. Hazel looped her arm around his elbow and leaned a dreamy head against his shoulder. Underneath the rim of the table, Lieutenant Green's hand touched mine, where I was certain nobody could possibly see him.

Nobody at all.

AT SOME POINT THE CAFÉ closed abruptly. Curfew. Everybody spilled out the doors into the twilight while the lamps shut off, one by one. There were no taxis. The Métro, out of respect for the rules, was also shut down. *C'est la guerre.*

So we walked along the nearby Seine. The boats were dark, the cobblestones oily after an evening cloudburst. The air hung around us in an unfathomable black cloud, and you could hear the laughter of couples taking advantage of this strange privacy in the middle of war-darkened Paris. You could smell the wet reek of the river, the ozone, the perfume of someone's soap. A motor ambulance roared by, streaking the riverbank with unexpected light, and somebody shrieked and giggled. Ahead of me, Hazel's face shone for an instant, turned not toward her lieutenant but toward the nearby street and the disappearing ambulance.

Then the light was gone.

"Where are we going?" she asked, in a very loud whisper.

"Wherever you like," said Lieutenant Johnson.

Suggested Green: "To the hotel?"

"Which hotel?"

"Ours, I think."

"Oooh, that sounds lovely," sang Hazel.

"I'd rather not," I said.

"What's that?"

"I'd rather not. I'm tired, and we're not supposed to be out at all, after curfew, are we? The Germans still fire off shells into Paris, during the night."

We had come to a stop. Still too dark to see one another's faces, but you could pick out the shapes, if you tried. The nearly indiscernible shadows, the snatches of electric, drunken breath, the wisps of heat drifting from beneath our clothes. Lieutenant Green's hand brushed mine. More confident, now. Single-minded. A hand bent on a certain goal.

"Shall we sit, then?" said Johnson.

"Oh, yes! Let's sit." Hazel moved away, toward the river, and we mingled after her until we reached the stone edge of the quayside and lowered ourselves to the ground, one by one, legs dangling above the restless water. Hazel sat on my left, but Johnson was closer on my right, so close that our legs lay side by side, pressed into one. Our clasped hands rested at the seam. His palm stuck to mine in a thin film of perspiration—his or mine, I wasn't sure—and as we sat there, the four of us, separated into pairs by those few extra inches of space between me and Hazel, trying to think of something to say, I felt it again: the warmth on my neck, the weight against my spine.

A pair of eyes, somewhere nearby, in the Paris night.

"So then," said Green. "Let's see. What do you think of Paris?"

I couldn't see his face, but I knew how he must look. Fresh and round-faced and fair, his skin spotted red from the wine. Rather nice-looking. Hopeful eyes of English china blue, pale eyelashes that were nevertheless thick. A sloping forehead, mopped with disobedient young hair, and a pair of damp palms.

"I love Paris," I said.

"Good, good."

His fingers crawled against mine. On my other side, Hazel and her lieutenant murmured and giggled. The river went *rush, rush* below my feet, and somewhere in the center of the current a barge slid by, dark and lugubrious, its few lights shaded. Green's face turned in to my cheek.

"So then. Do you think—"

I tore my hand away and jumped to my feet. "I'm sorry, I must be going!"

"Virginia!" exclaimed Hazel.

Lieutenant Green, thrown off-balance by my movements, tried to stagger to his feet, but something went wrong—maybe it was the wine—and he staggered the wrong way, hovered like a dancer for a second or two, and toppled into the Seine.

Like a coward, I bolted away.

I FLED WITHOUT THOUGHT, AND when I stopped, panting, a few minutes later, I had no idea where I stood. Paris was so curiously black, its monumental buildings reflecting only the faintest amount of moon, the thinnest streaks of golden lamplight from behind a million curtains. Who knew a city could become so dark and so still? Not a soul on the sidewalks, except me.

I had no map, only the plan of Paris in my head, like the web of a spider. I had inherited that much from my father—his orderly mind, his ability to conceive how something went together, like a three-dimensional model suspended within his brain. Strut A connected into plate B. I balanced on a corner, gazing at the massive shadow of the building across the street, the silver points where the moon touched its skin, the glimmer against a wrought iron balcony, and tried to summon my logic.

I could wait for a gendarme to pass by, and beg for directions.

I could knock upon a nearby door.

I could return to the river, and the scene of my shame, and make sure that Lieutenant Green was all right.

My veins throbbed. My feet ached in their new shoes. The air was humid and August-warm, and a trickle of perspiration began at the edge of my scalp and fell slowly down my temple. *You must do something, Virginia, you must* act, I thought, and as I repeated the word *act* in my head, I thought I heard a footstep on the pavement behind me.

And another.

Another.

Too slow for a gendarme, I thought—not in words, the idea was too swift and instinctual—*too slow for good works.*

I stepped off the curb and darted across the street, up the long avenue—I now saw it in my head, yes, superimposed against the map of Paris, an important spoke in the wheel that sprang from the Arc de Triomphe, the Porte Maillot near which our hotel stood—up the long avenue at a flat run. The heel of my right shoe caught against my foot. The five toes screamed into their narrow triangle. Just another corner, I thought, just another street and I'll stop.

But when I reached the next corner, I couldn't stop. I didn't hear the footsteps pounding behind me, but I felt them in my ribs. I felt the stare of someone's omnivorous eyes on my spine and my skull, scouring out the secrets inside, and I thought my lungs would burst from my chest. The thick Paris air choked my throat. On I ran, aiming only at the next street, at the next corner, at the curbs that caught my ankle as I crossed them, and my mind turned white, my scalp burned, my limbs went numb.

A shadow appeared ahead, detaching itself from the long, irregular row of buildings and café awnings. Shaped like a man, broad and slope-shouldered, wearing a peaked cap.

I staggered to a walk, preparing to dart from his path, but he stuck out his arms. "Arretez-vous, mademoiselle! Qu'est-ce que vous faites?"

A gendarme.

I fell forward, nearly striking him. Recovered myself at the last instant and pressed a hand to my chest, as if this action might somehow restore my breath.

The man was old, far past the age of soldiering, incapable of violence. Only his voice was forceful.

I gasped. "Please help! There's someone following me!"

An electric torch sprang to life in his right hand. He held it high, aiming the beam first—briefly—at my face, and then at the pavement behind me. He interposed himself manfully between me and my pursuer, and his left hand went to his belt.

As he searched the sidewalk with his torch, lighting the doorways and the stacked café chairs and tables and the silent lampposts, I panted and rasped, following the slice of his torch through the darkness. Someone shouted faintly, from several streets away. Above us, inside one of the windows, a party of some kind seemed to be taking place; I could just hear the shower of glassware, the pitch of hysterical laughter. I could just see the glimmer of light on the sidewalk from behind the drawn curtains.

The gendarme turned. I could breathe now; my head was strangely light. My feet throbbed, hot and swollen.

"My dear mademoiselle," he said kindly, lisping his way through a number of missing teeth. "There is nobody there."

HE WALKED ME ALL THE way back to the hotel, telling me of his two grandsons at the front, the four grandsons who had already died, one at the Marne and three at Verdun. *C'est la guerre.* Of his many granddaughters, some nursing the wounded and some running canteens in the railway stations. One had married in April. She was already expecting a baby at Christmas, the gendarme's first great-grandchild, and her husband was dead, too. A shell had fallen precisely inside the reserve trench where he was trying to sleep, and had scattered him to pieces, mademoiselle, small and terrible pieces. Just a week ago.

But why did she get married, I asked, if she knew her husband was likely to die?

The gendarme shrugged his shoulders. Because they were in love, wasn't it so? And it was war. And now the poor dead soldier would have a baby to live on after him, so it wasn't for nothing. The two of them, his

precious Berthe and her young man, they had experienced a small moment
of happiness, and wasn't that enough, when you thought of all the misery
in this world? Better you had known that small joy than have gone to your
grave without it.

By the time he told me about his days during the siege of Paris, and the
rats he had shared with his children while the Prussians fired their daily
rounds into the city, we had reached my hotel. The windows were dark.
The gendarme made me a smart salute and opened the door for me to pass.
I thanked him and hurried inside.

The old foyer was lit by a single lamp, but even so small a light, after so
much darkness, was enough to blind me for an instant. I blinked. Rubbed
my eyes. When I lifted my head to discover the stairs at the back of the hallway, I realized that someone was already there, rising from the straight-
backed settee against the wall, stubbing out a cigarette in a small porcelain
ashtray. Removing his officer's cap to reveal a head of thick golden hair,
tarnished with gray.

Captain Fitzwilliam.

CHAPTER 9

Miami Beach, Florida, June 1922

A T NIGHT, THE Japanese tea garden at the Flamingo Hotel undergoes a remarkable metamorphosis. Gone are the ladies in white dresses, the gentlemen in linen suits, the perspiring waiters and the lilting atmosphere of the orchestra in the corner. The clink of porcelain and glass, the routine murmurs of civilization. The strings of lanterns, so festive in the twilight, have gone dark. The speedboats have returned to port. The air is damp and salty and still, and Biscayne Bay slaps quietly against the stone. You might call it peaceful. I find it menacing.

But I don't have much choice about being here, do I? This strange, hard-faced man didn't exactly ask me where I should prefer to meet him, or when. Didn't consider whether a simple telephone call or even a letter might serve as well. Anyway, he was probably right. Any operator can listen to your telephone call. The restaurant's still busy, the lobby crawling with bellboys and clerks. No, it had to be the garden: convenient, private, devoid of prying eyes. Within screaming distance, if screaming's required.

Still, as I navigate the warm, moist darkness, listening for some small disturbance in the air that might signal the presence of a waiting man, I begin to think this wasn't such a terrific idea after all. That the joyous merrymakers in the hotel ballroom behind me won't be listening for any trouble in the garden outside, and the night-blackened waters of Biscayne Bay make a discreet point of disposal for anything—or anyone—a fellow might wish to dispose of.

That, if this stranger really does have information about my husband, he's not likely to be the kind of man you could trust with your life.

A scrape of metal interrupts the stillness to my left. "Mrs. Fitzwilliam?" asks a familiar voice, like the passing of velvet over stone.

And I guess it's a good thing I'm standing near a garden chair of solid wrought iron, because even though I'm expecting this man, even though the weight of my small pistol hangs comfortably near my ribs, the sound causes my legs to buckle beneath me.

WHEN THE POLICE ARRESTED MY father last February, right there in the middle of my sister's engagement party, it was almost a relief. We'd been hiding for so long.

Sophie, of course, had no idea. My God, how shocked she was. All those years I had fought for her innocence, and now here I stood, holding her white and shaking body, explaining her true history to her as best I could. And it was terrible, just terrible, to see her world crumble around her, brick by brick, this careful storybook we had created for her, and yet it was still a relief. No more pretending. No more denying that a thing was so, when it wasn't. Or maybe it was the other way around?

Anyway, the next weeks blurred by, lawyers and papers and police interrogations. I was living on my nerves, living in fear that I would say the wrong thing, reveal things I couldn't reveal, and by March, Sophie and Evelyn and I had taken up residence at a suite in the Pickwick Arms Hotel in Greenwich, Connecticut, in order to be close to all these legal proceedings. So it was not until I received that brief, shattering notification from Mr. Burnside that I realized I hadn't received any more. Letters from Simon.

Yes, Simon's letters. I believe I mentioned them earlier. They arrived at regular intervals, at the beginning of each month, as reliable as if a machine had printed them out for the three years since I left him. Except it was not a machine who wrote them. It was Simon.

I hadn't read any of them. In the beginning, when the pain of losing Simon was so fresh, I couldn't bear the thought of reading his words again. Later, I suppose I was simply afraid: afraid of his powers of persuasion, afraid that he would convince me to set aside my convictions and return to him. Yes, I might have been living in a prison on Thirty-Second Street, but at least it was a prison I knew, a prison of my own making. A prison under my own command.

But the trouble was Sophie. In order to preserve Sophie's innocence—to preserve this delicate fiction that Evelyn's father and I were happily married, that Simon was only seeing to his complicated business affairs and would send for us in due time—my father and I had reached an unspoken agreement, by which I took each monthly letter from the hall table upstairs to my room and pretended to read it, and Father took the unopened letter from my dresser and—well, I didn't know exactly what he did with those letters. But I knew he wouldn't throw them away. Father was too meticulous for that. Everything in its place.

But Father had been held without bail in the Fairfield County Jail since the beginning of February, and as I lay in my sleepless Pickwick Arms bed that May night, tormented by the letter from Mr. Burnside, wrestling with the impossible notion that Simon had died, I realized that no new letters had arrived from my husband. That inside the packets of mail dutifully forwarded each day from our housekeeper on Thirty-Second Street, Simon's letters did not appear.

The next morning, cold with horror beneath a balmy spring sun, I left Evelyn in Sophie's care and drove down to New York City. I thundered up the stairs to Father's room and the locked secretary where he kept his papers, and I retrieved the key from the place I knew he kept it: inside the false bottom of a jar of threepenny nails resting atop the bookshelf.

The lock was stiff, because Father had been away so long, and even after I lowered the secretary's polished front I had to hunt among the pigeonholes and the drawers, sifting through bills and patent applications, bank statements and legal agreements, until I found a small leather portfolio tied with a faded scarlet ribbon, labeled in the corner with a single word: FITZWILLIAM.

And there they were: thirty-odd letters, crisp and still white, my name written so familiarly and invitingly in Simon's black spider scrawl that I could almost hear his voice caressing the words on our wedding day: *Mrs. Virginia Fitzwilliam.* I stood there next to the secretary, holding those envelopes, my blood beating through my veins and my breath jumping in my chest, caught between two opposing impulses: to hold these letters next to my skin and breathe in the scent of their ink, and to toss them out the window in a shower of poisonous white. But I didn't make either one of those ridiculous gestures. I gained some measure of control over my jumping nerves and sat down on the corner of Father's bed, and I stared at the first envelope, May of 1919, when Evelyn was only a tiny, fearful bud in the center of my womb, and the tulips were just beginning to wilt.

And it seemed to me, as I sat there, that someone whispered against my ear in a warm, English cadence.

Go on. Go on.

Everything you seek is here.

I reached for the stained silver letter opener in the jar on Father's desk and ripped open that first letter like a glutton, prepared to read all the letters at once, one after another, month after month, gorging myself on the thin black lines of Simon's handwriting. Ready to fill my lonely gut with the sound of his voice: reading them to me in my head, laying himself bare, dissecting each valve and channel of his heart for my amusement, while I pretended to believe him, to read those sentences as if they were true.

But the envelope was empty.

I picked up the next one. Empty. And the next, and the next. I didn't need to open them; I felt their thinness, their lack of weight. Not one single envelope held anything inside. Just a thin slice of open air, addressed to me in my husband's familiar handwriting.

And though I examined each envelope carefully, I could not determine whether my letters had been carefully opened and resealed or never opened to begin with. Whether this strange pantomime began with Simon or with my father, or whether some deeper mystery lay unfathomed beneath me.

As I replaced the last envelope in the portfolio, however, I noticed a curious detail. Curious, I say, because who really notices a postmark? I don't, unless I have some particular, practical reason, and yet as the paper slid past my gaze, I caught sight of the figures FEB 28 1922.

My hand went still, holding the envelope half in and half out of the portfolio. I stared for some time, but the letters didn't change. MIAMI FLA curving around the top part of the circle, and FEB 28 in the middle, and 1922 curving at the bottom.

I pushed the envelope the rest of the way inside the portfolio and fastened the latch, feeling in that moment as empty and dissatisfied as the letters themselves. Puzzled and unsteady. And I remember how, as I sat there in Father's chair and stared at the multitude of cracks spreading across the dry leather skin of his portfolio, like the turning up of new earth in a dead soil, a thought came to me. Or maybe more in the nature of a revelation.

I knew there was no possibility that my husband was dead.

ALL OF WHICH HAS BROUGHT me to this point, agreeing so foolishly to meet this strange man, just because he's drawn a picture of my daughter and claims to know something about Simon. I realize, as his voice reaches me through the darkness, just how very foolish I've been, how terribly reckless, all for the sake of a man who might or might not be worth the trouble.

"Please sit," the man says, stepping forward from the shadows—or rather the depth of the shadows, because we're still shrouded (as they say) in darkness. The glow from the hotel windows reaches only so far, and there isn't much moon to speak of. A perfect night to run in a boatload or two of rum from Cuba. I point this out to my companion, by way of idle conversation, as I obey his instructions and settle myself on the edge of a wrought iron chair, trying to steady my vision without looking as if I needed to.

"That's true," he replies, taking possession of the neighboring chair, "but a mere shipment or two of contraband isn't my chief concern, Mrs. Fitzwilliam, much as I deplore the activity."

"I'm afraid I don't understand."

"Don't you? I guess I should introduce myself, in that case. My name is Marshall, and I'm an agent for the Bureau of Internal Revenue."

"You're a Prohibition man?"

"Yes." He reaches into the inner breast pocket of his jacket. "If you'd care to see my badge."

"That's not necessary."

"Forgive me, Mrs. Fitzwilliam, but I believe it is. In fact, you ought to *insist* on official identification. The nature of this business is such that any number of unscrupulous men will try to convince you they're one thing, when they're really another."

"But badges can be faked, can't they?"

He lays an object on the table between us. "That's true. Still, I'm a fellow who likes to preserve the formalities. I imagine you've found it difficult to find men you can trust, Mrs. Fitzwilliam, and for what it's worth, you can trust me."

"Anyone can say that."

"Yes. I guess I might be any kind of villain, as far as you're concerned. God knows the bureau's got enough villains of its own, badge or no badge. Still." He lifts the object from the table and replaces it inside his jacket. He sits facing me, at a perpendicular angle to the hotel itself, so that one side of his face is faintly lit from the golden Flamingo windows and the other side is as dark as Biscayne Bay itself. His bones are just as solid as they appeared today on the beach, and across all the acreage of smooth, young skin covering that wide jaw, not a single particle of stubble dares to glitter above the surface. Mr. Marshall is the kind of man who shaves twice a day, come war or come hurricane, probably with an old-fashioned cutthroat blade instead of a modern double-edged safety razor.

"Assuming, then, you really are a Prohibition agent," I say, "what exactly was your business with my husband?"

He straightens his jacket and rests one elbow on the table. "Before I answer that, Mrs. Fitzwilliam, I feel myself obliged to inquire after your own health. As I understand it, you've been through something of an ordeal, these past several months."

"Oh? And what do you know about my ordeal?"

"It's my business to know things. And even if it weren't my business, I couldn't help but read the story. You've been featured in every newspaper in the country, Mrs. Fitzwilliam, or didn't you know?"

"I've been too busy to read the newspapers."

He nods. "Well, in any case, I apologize for disturbing you during your . . . well—"

"Bereavement? Time of distress?"

"If you want to call it that. Although I don't imagine you came down here to Florida for the purpose of relaxation."

"My purpose in Florida is none of your business, Mr. Marshall. All I really need from you is your information about my husband, if you really have it. And you might tell me why you felt yourself entitled to draw a portrait of my daughter, without my knowledge or permission."

"I apologize for the liberty. I only wanted to gain your attention."

"You have it. For the moment. Now bring yourself to the point, please, before they miss me inside."

Mr. Marshall tilts his head an inch or two, and I can't help thinking what a torpid man he is, compared with Simon, who always seemed to be in motion—always in the middle of some emotion or action or complex puzzle of logic. Or maybe that was only for my benefit. *Cool as January,* Mr. Burnside called him. Maybe this expressiveness was only another one of Simon's disguises, another of the masks he wore, each one custom-built for its intended audience.

"All right," Mr. Marshall says, moving his lips only the essential minimum required for speech. "I guess I might as well start by observing that you didn't seem a bit surprised, a moment ago, when I told you the nature of my work. Pursuing the illegal importation of intoxicating liquors into this country, I mean."

"Maybe not."

"Then it won't surprise you, either, to hear that we—the bureau, that is, and I personally—believe your husband's death, like the deaths of most men mixed up in the bootlegging business around here, was not a simple act of God."

A good thing it's so damned dark out here in the Japanese garden, because while I'm able to check the gasp in my throat as Mr. Marshall pronounces the words *your husband's death,* I feel pretty certain my face betrays a flinch. You know the kind: that involuntary spasm that follows an unexpected slap.

You see, I was expecting something else. I guess I was expecting that Mr. Marshall was about to reveal to me some kind of startling secret. That Mr. Marshall was going to lean forward and take my hand and tell me, in a voice of terrible quiet, to prepare myself for a great shock, because by some miracle or some improbable contortion of known fact, Simon is still alive. *Alive!* Alive, Mrs. Fitzwilliam. It's true. Because there's been a mistake, an extraordinary mistake, or maybe even a strange and complicated business afoot. That another, anonymous man died in the fire on Cocoa Beach that night, and Mr. Marshall is about to tell me why.

Not this. *Your husband's death.*

"Mrs. Fitzwilliam?" he says gently.

"No. I suppose I'm not surprised at all. I always thought there was something strange about the whole affair. Something more." I swallow back a sensation of nausea. Gather some kind of composure. "Do you have any idea who might be responsible?"

"We have a couple of ideas, yes. You see, that's my job at the moment. We're trying to take apart a ring of bootleggers, Mrs. Fitzwilliam, an illegal operation so large and complex, it's controlling pretty much all the traffic along the coast of Florida. I won't bore you with all the details—"

"Oh, I wouldn't be bored at all, Mr. Marshall. I like details. I'm not the kind of woman who sits back with her knitting, you know, and leaves the dirty tasks to the men."

He nods, and the tip of his nose catches a bit of light. "I hear you drove an ambulance in the war."

"Where did you hear that? Was that in the newspapers, too?"

"No. I just asked a few questions. Anyway, I thought that might be the case, when you turned up here in Florida like that, sticking yourself right in the middle of all these affairs as soon as your old man's trial was over. I figured you wouldn't have traveled down here so quickly, if you didn't want to know all about it."

"Well, yes. Of course I did."

"But why, exactly? If you don't mind my asking."

"Why?"

"Why come down to Florida. Stick your nose into all this ugly business."

"Isn't it obvious? Because I want to know more. I want to help, if I can."

"Help? Help with what?"

"With whatever it is you're doing. The truth about my husband."

"I see. And that's all?"

My God, what an inanimate man, this revenue agent. He doesn't fidget a bit. Maybe it comes with the job, this steadfast habit, scrubbed of all human influence. As I said, I can only see one side of his face—a rather unsettling effect, if you ask me—and there isn't much expression there to begin with. His hair is too short to shine in the light; it sort of bristles softly there, at his temples and around the curve of his skull. His one visible eye is black, too shadowed for color, and it hardly ever blinks. I believe I once heard that means he's telling the truth, or else he's an especially good liar.

Either way, I think, I might as well test him. What have I got to lose, really? He surely knows more than he's letting on. He's surely got all sorts of details tucked far up his sleeve. That's plain. I can see it in his unblinking eye, I can hear it in his voice. And I've already done the reckless thing. I've already met him here, in the garden of the Flamingo Hotel as the clock ticks toward midnight.

I lean forward and speak in the kind of firm, clear voice I use to reprimand my daughter, when she needs it.

"No. That isn't all."

"What, then?"

"Because I sometimes wonder if I'm being lied to, Mr. Marshall. I sometimes wonder if that body in the fire was really his."

If I'm expecting some sort of reaction—shock or dismay or anything at all—I suppose you could say I'm disappointed. That damned dark eye doesn't even blink. I think the crease around the corner of his mouth tightens a bit, like somebody wound the string another notch, but that's all.

"Well, that's strange," he says. "What makes you think that?"

"Because the man I married wouldn't have burned to death in his own house, that's why."

"You hesitated."

"What's that?"

"Before you spoke, you hesitated."

"I was just thinking of a way to explain it. You see, I've found that so many men have little regard for a woman's intuition."

A smile at last! At least on that one side of his mouth, nudging up the corner, pushing back the stiff muscle of his cheek. His voice, however, contains not a trace of amusement. "I have plenty of regard for female intuition, Mrs. Fitzwilliam, believe me. But in this case I'm afraid you're wrong."

"Am I?"

"I'm very sorry. But you see, if there's one thing I'm certain about in this entire wretched affair, it's that Simon Fitzwilliam died in a fire at his villa on Cocoa Beach, about two hours after midnight in the morning of February nineteenth of this year." He pauses. "Again. Very sorry."

I whisper, "And how can you be so certain of that, Mr. Marshall? The body was burned beyond recognition. His own brother had to identify him by the coincidental presence of a piece of metal."

Mr. Marshall flattens his hand on the table between us, and while I'm staring at his face and not his fingers, I have the impression that they're as wide and thick and rough as the branches of an oak tree. A peasant's hand.

"Because I was right there, that night on Cocoa Beach," he tells me. "And I guess, in some measure, I'm responsible for what happened."

WHATEVER MY OWN PRIVATE CONVICTIONS on the subject of my father's guilt, I was shocked when the jury returned its verdict. The jury, you see, did not possess all the relevant information. The jury didn't know what I knew: that my father was in love with another woman at the time of my mother's murder.

Well, I can't blame them. Nobody else knew, either. When I took the stand and described the contents of my memory, nobody asked me that particular thing—not the prosecution's lawyer, who treated me with great delicacy, and certainly not our own expensive table of defense attorneys, in their neat suits of charcoal and navy blue, sweating out the June heat. Who would expect such knowledge inside the dusty old memories of an eight-year-old girl? But of *course* I knew. Wasn't I the cool, steady center of the family maelstrom? Yes, I was. By the time of my mother's murder, I was a very old, perceptive, experienced eight-year-old, and I knew plenty of things I shouldn't, and I had seen plenty of things I shouldn't have. I had, for instance, many times spied the two of them together—my father and our kitchen maid, who happened to be cleaning an upstairs bedroom at the moment my mother was brutally stabbed—and even an eight-year-old girl knows what a kiss means, on the lips, lingering, between grownups. Even an eight-year-old girl understands that her father, having spent nearly three years a witness of his wife's extraordinary moods and her penchant for the intimate company of gardeners, might desire the lips of a more uncomplicated woman. And our kitchen maid was a young, pretty girl of about twenty who liked him back.

I never saw them do anything more than kiss. I would have sworn that on a Bible, if anyone had asked. But as I said, no one did, and by the end of my father's trial, everyone in the courtroom thought he should be acquitted. There was no real proof, just the possibilities suggested by circumstance, and my father, when you regard him in a sober suit, and consider his occupation, looks like nothing more than an absent-minded professor who wouldn't hurt a fly. Then again, the facts of my mother's promiscuous behavior and unsteady character had been firmly established by the defense. Even if you imagined that her husband might, under extraordinary provocation, have committed a single act of terrible and thoughtless passion, you might have thought the dame had it coming, mightn't you?

But it doesn't matter what the rest of the courtroom thinks. Only the jury matters, and the jury—for whatever reason—thought my father should be held to account for this unspeakable crime. This murder of his own wife. And as that word *guilty* echoed around the courtroom, I knew what I had always known, what I had spent a lifetime pretending I didn't know.

That they were right.

That I had been making believe all along, because the alternative was too dreadful to contemplate. Because who could still love a man who could commit a crime like that? A crime like murder.

AND IT'S THE SAME KIND of shock, delivered by Mr. Marshall here in the fragrant Japanese tea garden of the Flamingo Hotel. Only a mere few days since that Connecticut jury returned its verdict, in fact, though it seems like several lifetimes. Shock will do that.

I turn the words over in my head, examining them at various angles. Unlike in that Connecticut courtroom, there's no echo, no simultaneous gasp of surprise from a hundred or so lungs to tell me I've heard him properly. *Because I was right there, that night at Cocoa Beach.* My thumb touches the bent circle of metal clinching the fourth finger of my right hand. Spins it around a time or two.

At last: "I see."

"Yes. It's an awful thing. You see, he'd agreed to work with me, a while back. He'd agreed it might be in his best interest to help us gather up a bit of information. I think he'd realized, by then, he was in over his head, he and that brother of his. He's not a bad man, your husband. Why, the whole thing was Mr. Samuel Fitzwilliam's idea to begin with, when he took over managing the shipping company. They started out just wanting to make a few bucks, to tide the business over when the harvest had all been shipped out—he had a lot of debt, you know, a lot of money to pay back to the banks—and the bootleg money, why, it's a whole lot of dough, real hard for some men to resist. And I guess neither of them thought much of the Eighteenth Amendment to begin with. I understand that. I understand why some might object. I have my own opinions. But it's the law of the land, Mrs. Fitzwilliam, and I'm sworn to uphold the law of the land, and what happens when you start to break that law—my God, are you all right?"

"Yes. I'm fine. Please go on."

"Let me get you a glass of water."

"No! I want you to tell me the whole story."

But he doesn't listen. He reaches forward and grasps me by the shoulders and lifts me right out of my chair—he's much burlier than I thought—and into his arms. I guess this might count as a romantic gesture to some, but his arms are hard and businesslike, and he doesn't linger or comfort or anything like that, though he's careful not to hurt me, either. He carries me briskly across the garden toward the French doors of the hotel, and the truth is, I *am* a bit light-headed. A little dizzy, a little sick, such that even if I wanted to protest, I really couldn't. I *do* need a glass of water. I *do* need to lie down. There's only so much a body can endure in a single week.

At the last moment Mr. Marshall veers from the wall of French doors and carries me to a discreet entrance at the side of the building. He seems to know exactly where he's going. We proceed up the service elevator in absolute silence—thank God there's no one about—and I manage not to lean my head on his shoulder, not once, even as we turn sideways through the door and he places me gently on the bed. I glance at the other bed— Clara hasn't retired yet, it seems—and tell Mr. Marshall that this really wasn't necessary, and he should leave at once before my companion arrives.

He's pouring a glass of water from the pitcher and turns his head briefly to reply. "Miss Clara Fitzwilliam. Is that right?"

"Yes. My sister-in-law."

He hands me the water. "I know. Now listen to me. I sought you out, I arranged this little meeting only because I wanted to inform you in person of the substance of our investigation, and to deliver a warning."

"A warning?"

"Yes. Stay out of the way, do you hear me? These men are dangerous, extremely dangerous. So you're not going to *help,* as you put it. You're going to leave this entire matter to the bureau."

"But—"

"I promise you we'll catch the men who killed your husband, and we'll let you know when we do. God knows you've suffered enough already. You should go back to New York, Mrs. Fitzwilliam. You should go back to New York, where I'm sure your sister needs you more than we do."

I want to ask how he knows about my sister, but I suppose, once more— like Clara, like everyone else except me—he's read about her in the papers. I set down the water glass on the nightstand. "I'm in no condition to travel all the way back to New York at the moment, Mr. Marshall. I'll stay right here in Florida, if you don't mind."

"What about your daughter? You want to put her in danger? I'll tell you this: these men, these Florida gangs, they won't hesitate to hurt a baby girl. Or worse. I've seen what they can do, things no lady should have to imagine. That gun you're hiding in your pocket isn't going to do a damned bit of good. Thugs and murderers, every last one."

"I'm not afraid."

"You *ought* to be afraid. For your daughter, if not for yourself."

He speaks with terrible sternness. As I suppose he should; after all, he's got a point, hasn't he? He's just confirmed what I suppose I already knew; he's just slid a few pieces of this vast and complicated puzzle into place. The bootleggers, the Florida gangs, the acts of dangerous treachery. So I realize I should be afraid. I *am* afraid. I'm afraid for Evelyn, and I'm afraid for myself for Evelyn's sake. I know what it's like to grow up without a mother.

On the other hand—and this is important, mind you—just as in that courtroom in Connecticut, I happen to be in possession of a piece of information that nobody else knows, except Simon himself—a piece of information, a postmark, that constitutes my last particle of hope. If *hope*, indeed, is the word to describe this pitch of desperation that's overcome my every nerve.

"I appreciate your concern," I say, "but the fact is, I find I'm enjoying myself here in Florida. The sunshine, the sand, the ocean. It's the best kind of tonic."

"Then you're a fool."

"Maybe I am. But I'm not going to be chased out of anywhere, Mr. Marshall. Not by some Florida bootlegger, nor by a stranger with a square jaw and a short haircut who *claims* he's a revenue agent."

Up until this moment, Mr. Marshall's been looming over me as I lie on the bed, in the manner of a father trying to remonstrate with a recalcitrant child, while I have looked up at him in juvenile defiance. He straightens now, and his hard blue eyes—more lapis than sapphire, as the lamplight reveals—sort of widen. "*Claims* he's a revenue agent?"

"You're the one who told me not to trust anybody."

He blinks at last, a bit slowly, as if he's turning over rocks inside that prehistoric skull of his. "You know, Mrs. Fitzwilliam, for a woman who's lost a father and a husband inside of a few months, you've got a quick mouth. Tell me something. Do you know how to fire that gun?"

"Of course."

"Good. You might want to find a holster for it, though. You're liable to have an accident in that pocket of yours."

I nod to the door. "My friend will be back soon."

"Not for an hour at least, I'll bet," he says, reaching inside his jacket, "but I think you need your rest. Here's my card. If you need anything, or hear anything important, anything you think I might need to know, I want you to call that number right away. Do you understand? *Collect.*"

I accept the card between the tips of my fingers. "I will."

He puts his hat back on his head—all this time it's been dangling from the fingers of his left hand, a government-man fedora of dark gray felt, the sinister opposite of the tourist boater this afternoon—and turns to leave. "Oh, and Mrs. Fitzwilliam?"

"Yes?"

"I meant to ask. Have you happened to receive any relevant letters from your husband, over the years? Letters that mentioned business, I mean. Names, places, that kind of thing."

"Business? Why, no. Nothing as particular as that. Just love notes, really."

"I see. But if you remember anything, you'll let me know?"

I flutter the card in the air. "Of course. Good night, Mr. Marshall."

He stares at me a moment longer, narrowing those eyes in a most unsettling way, as if he's actually prying inside the contents of my mind. I suppose they train them that way, these revenue men, picking apart truth from prevarication. He's rather tall, for such a burly fellow, and I can't help feeling as if he's about to step forward and snap me in two.

Instead, he says, "I *am* very sorry about all this, Mrs. Fitzwilliam," and steps through the doorway as soundlessly as a six-foot cat, nearly brushing the lintel with his fedora.

CHAPTER 10

Paris, August 1917

A T FIRST I thought the man was a ghost. A figment of my imagination, or at least of my unconscious mind. He had flown up from the hole in the center of my soul—the one that hurt so much I had to ignore it—because you couldn't just go on ignoring the thing that hurt you. You couldn't go on fleeing the agony in your middle, the discord that plucked through your guts, just because you were afraid to acknowledge the truth.

So now he had come to haunt me.

"Captain Fitzwilliam?" I whispered.

He stepped forward into the light, and I saw that he was solid, not transparent. Whole and real: not a ghost. "I beg your pardon," he said. "I didn't mean to shock you."

"What are you doing here?"

"Can't you guess?"

I shook my head, and he smiled confidently.

"Because Mrs. DeForest told me you were in Paris, by yourself—"

"Not by myself."

"With only that silly nurse for company. Where is she now?"

My mouth was dry, my tongue almost too thick to speak. "She's with a friend."

"A friend. Hmm. As I thought. And you, Miss Fortescue? Why aren't *you* with a friend?"

"Because I—because—I was unwell."

He stepped forward. *"Unwell!"*

"Just for a moment."

He stopped, and I was already frozen, and so we stood for a moment. Still as forest animals. The wallpaper peeled behind him. The lamp cast a sinister shadow on his face. Above us, the floorboards creaked, while several thousand words floated like dust in the stuffy, sordid air between his lips and mine.

He moved first, shifting his hat from right hand to left. His voice was soft. "Did you receive my letters at all?"

"Yes."

"What did you think of them?"

"I thought—I thought—"

"Yes?"

"I didn't read them. I've been so busy, you know, with the hospital."

"I didn't think you would. But I had to write something, or I would have run mad. You see . . ."

"Yes?"

His pulse beat against the skin of his neck. "There's something I must tell you. Something I think—I hope—will change your mind about me."

"Oh."

"So I thought . . . well, I wanted to see you. To tell you the truth. To see if perhaps we might begin again."

I stood there, unmoving, thinking a hundred thoughts at once, not one of them expressible in words. His competent hands, operating on maimed and frightful bodies. The lines of his skin. The wool of his tunic. My painful feet. Lieutenant Green, pale under the ruddiness of wine. Footsteps on the pavement, and the uncanny instinct of being watched, and the even uncannier instinct that the danger had now passed, that I was safe. In good hands. I looked up from his collar and saw how earnestly his eyes were fixed on my face.

"Please. Virginia. If I could just *explain*. If I could just make you understand. Do you know what I mean?"

At the time, I didn't know what he meant. I could not comprehend why this man's gaze should be fixed on me, of all women. Now, of course, I understand wholly. I know the nature of his attraction to me. I know the exact length and breadth of his ardor, and why he felt it, and whether or not it could be trusted.

But in that suffocating August foyer in the middle of Paris, sexual love remained a mystery to me, and I sometimes wish I could go back to that moment: when the mystery was still pure, when the possibility of discovery still hovered before me. When I didn't know everything. When I was still innocent, and understanding lay in the future.

When I could say, in a surge of unfathomable trust that only a virgin could muster: *I suppose we could find somewhere to talk.*

SOMEWHERE, BY NECESSITY, MEANT *MY room upstairs*. For some reason, this suggestion didn't seem daring at all; maybe it was his uniform, or my independence. Acts we would have deemed impermissible before the war had now become ordinary. Who needed a chaperone to navigate your private behavior, when you spent your days navigating the churned earth of northern France in an ambulance packed with barbarian soldiers, all on your own? We were sensible adults, he and I. There was no need to fear each other.

Upstairs, I opened the window and asked Captain Fitzwilliam if he wanted a glass of water.

He placed his hat on the table beneath the lamp. "Thank you, yes."

I poured out two glasses from the pitcher, and as I handed him his drink I wondered if our fingers would touch. They did not. There was just the warmth of his hand, brief and ghostly.

"I'm afraid you can't stay long," I said. "Hazel will return any moment."

"Ah, yes. The irrepressible Hazel."

I sat in the armchair—a relic of the past century, wobbly at the legs, upholstered in threadbare velvet that might once have been burgundy but had since faded to a warm pink. Simon went to the window and parted the curtain an inch or so. "Is that the Bois de Boulogne?"

"Yes."

"Charming." He let the curtain fall and turned to lean against the window frame, crossing one leg over the other. His large hand swallowed the water glass. He looked so old and unnatural, standing before me in his dull uniform and polished shoes, his wide leather belt nicked and worn, the pips at his shoulder catching the light. I thought, *It can't be him, he can't really exist in my hotel room, propped against the window like a living statue.* When he was so far away, a moment ago. I was too unnerved to look at his face. Too stunned, and yet consumed by a paradoxical relief. He was safe. He was alive.

"Mrs. DeForest told me your CCS was bombed," I said.

"Yes, we were. A week ago. Lost three patients and a nurse. Terrible scene. Pritchard had a lucky escape, however." His mouth twitched.

"Lucky?"

"There are worse places to be hit, believe me."

A hysterical laugh rose in my throat. I said quickly, "And you? Were you injured?"

"No. Cuts and bruises. Superficial stuff. My pretty face emerged unscathed, as you see."

This time I did laugh.

"You see? That's better. I'm not such a monster, am I?"

"I never thought you were a monster."

"You looked at me as if I was, a moment ago."

"No. I thought you were a ghost at first, not a monster."

"My sincerest apologies. I didn't mean to startle you." He looked down at the glass. Behind him, the old green damask curtains made a somber frame. "But I'm none of those things, you know. Just a man. Nothing to be afraid of."

"I'm not afraid of you."

"Aren't you? Then why won't you look at me?"

Well, how was I supposed to answer that? *Because I'm afraid of myself when I look at you.* I'm afraid I'll lose my head. I'm afraid I already have.

The water trembled in my glass. I could hear another couple talking in a room nearby—he loud and bombastic, she sharp and quiet, the exact words muffled by plaster. The room was stuffy because of the curtains. I thought we should open a window, but of course we couldn't, not unless we turned off the lamp.

"Just tell me one thing," he said. "One thing, and I'll go."

"What's that?"

"Do you *like* me at all, Virginia?"

"Yes! Of course I do."

"I'm not repulsive to you? My letters. What have you done with them?"

"I destroyed them. I had to."

He drew in a gigantic sigh. I was staring at the water in my glass, but I felt his shoulders slump. The weight of his disappointment.

"Of course," he said. "Honorable soul that you are. But weren't you curious? Didn't you want to know what was inside them?"

"No. I couldn't. I couldn't allow myself."

"You might have found that I'm not so fearsome as you think. Not such a terrible villain. It's just that you've forced me out of my skin, to commit acts of unparalleled effrontery."

"Do you mean *this*? Seeking out one woman when you're already married to another?"

The words sounded so dreadful out loud. So harsh and vulgar and modern.

"Yes. That. I presume she's the reason you wouldn't read my letters? My wife?"

"How can you ask a thing like that?"

"But that's it, isn't it? You're an honorable woman. An innocent woman. Incorruptible. You won't let me plunge you into some kind of sordid, adulterous affair. Blackguard that I am."

I shook my head.

"Ah, Virginia."

He levered himself away from the window and walked toward me at a slow, heavy tread, until he was standing before the armchair and then kneeling, so I couldn't help accepting his gaze. It would have been rude otherwise. His eyes, as I said, were the kind of hazel that takes different forms as the light changes. Now they looked rather green and terribly focused. I almost didn't notice when his hand pried mine away from the glass. He set the tumbler on the table, under the lamp, and encircled my fingers with his. "Listen to me, Virginia. My marriage—my wife—it's not what you think."

"How can you possibly know what I think?"

"True. I don't have the faintest idea what you're thinking. Your telegram last winter was a masterpiece of brevity. You never replied to my letters. My entire hope existed in the knowledge that you hadn't exactly told me to go to the devil, at least."

"You're married. You have a child with her."

He hesitated. "Yes."

"You can't renounce that. I would never—"

"Of course not. My God. I don't intend to renounce them. I shall always be Sam's father. But you see, I can't go on with the lie of it. I can't pretend something is one thing, when it's another."

"I thought you said you cared for her."

"Of course I care for her. She's an old friend. But our marriage—you must understand—we weren't in love. We never were, not the least bit. We only married because of my family."

"Your family?"

"Yes. And little Sam."

"Your son."

"Don't say it like that. If only you knew. You *have* to know, Virginia. I have to tell you. I can't have you looking at me like that any longer. Thinking of me like that. It's like death. It's been killing me slowly for months.

You've got no idea. I've hardly slept. I can't think of anything else. Even there in the damned surgical hut in the middle of the night, the thought of you pounds in the back of my head. Your reproachful face. And I have *tried* to forget, believe me. I have *tried* to let you go. Not for my own sake, but for yours."

I pulled my hands away, but he snatched them back.

"We're broke, you know. My family. I expect I should tell you that, up front. We're absolutely dead broke. Utterly skint. Not a spare shilling in the till. Mortgaged to the hilt, estate falling to pieces. The old story. My parents are mostly to blame, I suppose, though old Granddad was no slouch when it came to ruination. I'd always known the bill would come due, sooner or later, and I'd have to pay it, having had the abominable bad luck to be born a few minutes earlier than my brother—"

"You have a brother?"

"I *had* a brother. Twin brother. Didn't I mention that? Samuel. He was in the regulars, one of the first regiments sent out. He lasted about three months. Went missing on patrol, presumed killed. Awful show."

"I'm so sorry."

"Yes. It was rather a shock, for all of us. But the point is, I'm the eldest, the one who inherits the old pile, and I've known since I was a child that I must marry money."

"And I suppose your wife . . . ?"

"Bags of it. Her father's in shipping. My parents own a few citrus groves in Florida—an old inheritance—and that's how they met, you know, ages and ages ago. My father-in-law's company exports the oranges, to put it simply. What there are of them, anymore, after two generations of utter neglect. So it seemed natural, to my parents, that—"

"That you would make her fall in love with you."

He rose without warning, dropping my hands, and patted his tunic for his cigarettes. "It wasn't like that. She was never in love with me."

"Then why did she marry you?"

He took out the case and lit a cigarette slowly, examining first the paper and then the match, striking twice against the side of the case. Drawing in the first gasp, so that the end flared orange. "Because she was carrying my brother's child."

My lips parted. "Oh."

"Yes. She was deeply in love with him, and he with her. I knew it, and they knew I knew it. A bit of a secret, because of course her parents wouldn't allow it, and neither would mine. She was supposed to marry me instead. So we were all three biding our time, I suppose, waiting for her father to die and leave her his fortune free and clear—he wasn't in the best of health, you see, and a disagreeable bloke to boot, drunkard and philanderer—and then the war started. Samuel was killed. She came to me in November and said that she was going to have a baby." He parted the curtains, cracked open the window, knocked out a bit of ash. Braced his hands on the sill and bent his head in my direction, over his shoulder. "You're not to say a word of this, of course. Nobody else knows, not even our parents. Everybody thinks Sam's mine, and for Lydia's sake—and his—I'd like to keep it that way."

"But—but—well, how did you do it?"

"Why, we got married at Christmas. Then I shipped out. We're friends, as I said, and Lydia was terribly grateful. She made it quite clear that I could do as I liked, as far as lovers are concerned, so long as I kept it quiet. Everyone was made happy, after all. My parents got her money, Lydia got a name for her child. The only trouble's that she's still in love with my brother."

My head was dizzy. Tongue all dry. I whispered, "How terrible for her. For both of you."

"Oh, she's got the worst of it. Mourning Samuel while pretending to be in love with me. Surrounded by my family. I daresay she's fairly miserable, except for little Sam." He paused to smoke. "We didn't have a wedding night, in case you're wondering. Did not consummate the marriage. My God, how could we? I suppose we reckoned we might try for a proper union, once the war was over and everything back to normal, but now . . ."

"Now?"

He straightened himself from the window and turned to me. The cigarette dangled above the floor, between his fingers. "Now I've met you."

I stared at him wordlessly.

"Well?" he said. "What do you think?"

"I don't know what to think. It's all so—I can't quite understand it all yet."

"She won't object, after everything. I'll take the blame, of course. Adultery. Shall have to get properly caught by a detective, as a formality, but that's easily done."

"*What?*"

He smiled. "I don't mean *actually* committing adultery, of course. Just for show. It's done all the time. The war's breaking up all the old rules."

His face was open and sincere; his hand, holding the cigarette, didn't quiver a fraction. Was it my imagination, or had his hair, in the past few months, gone a little more silver? But his skin seemed untroubled. The lines about his mouth had softened. He was almost smiling.

"I'm afraid I don't understand," I said.

"I mean I'm getting a divorce, Virginia. I'm going to ask my wife to divorce me."

I sprang to my feet, wobbled, and sat down again. "My God."

"Yes."

"A divorce?"

"Yes. Good Lord, what did you think? That I would ask you to become my mistress? Carry on with you behind Lydia's back?"

"I—I didn't know what to think. I didn't—I hardly know you at all, do I?"

He gazed at me quietly, letting the cigarette burn from his fingers. "No, I suppose not. Not in actual fact. And yet I feel as if I've known you all my life. I felt that from the first moment."

I pressed my lips together.

"And you? Have you felt that at all?"

"I can't say."

"Yes, you can. You must have felt it. I could tell that you did. I could see how you were struggling, just as I was. I tried to explain, in my letters—"

"Which I didn't read."

"No. But if you had, you might know me a little better. You might know that I would never ask you to commit any act repugnant to you. I would never ask you to be anything other than your own brave, honorable self."

His voice spun around my ears: too many words, too much to take in. I needed to think. I needed to piece through everything he had told me. And there was a light inside all this—I could just feel its warmth on my skin—a tiny, hopeful light glimmering somewhere at the end, but it disappeared every time I looked for it. I curled my fingers around the edge of the sofa and stared at his battered leather belt. "I don't what to say. I don't know what you're asking. I can't—I can't just—"

He stubbed out the cigarette. "I'm not asking you for a thing. I just wanted you to know."

"Is that all?"

"And to ask you, I suppose, if you care at all. If I have the slightest hope, when the divorce is final—"

I put my face into my palms.

"Dearest, it's not like that. You haven't done anything wrong."

"Then why do I feel as if I have?"

"If there's any sin, it's mine. But there isn't. I promise you that. Just tell me—"

"What? Tell you what?"

"Tell me you care, just a little."

I lifted my face away and stared at him bleakly. "But you don't really mean that. If I say *yes*—"

He took two giant strides to stand before me. His hands touched my elbows. "*Do* you? Say yes?"

"*If* I say yes, it means more than just that, doesn't it? Because if I only cared a little—"

"Then you wouldn't raise my hopes. You're too good for that."

My head was spinning a little. I could taste his breath on my tongue, at the back of my throat. I wanted to push him away; I wanted to draw him close. I wanted to hide; I wanted to be reckless. So close, so promisingly near. I wanted to touch his stubble and his eyebrows and the line of cheekbones. I craved the warmth of his skin. I desired the thoughts inside his brain, the electricity animating his nerves. I pressed my thumb against his, and his thick eyebrows rose. His lips parted.

"Don't be afraid," he said.

"I'm not afraid."

"Yes, you are. But you shouldn't be. I'm absolutely harmless. I'm here to cure whatever troubles you."

"But you can't. You can't cure this."

"Not true, Virginia. Not true at all. Whatever happens between us, between you and me, the divorce *will* go forward. For Lydia's sake, as much as mine. She deserves another chance to fall in love."

"I can't do this."

"Only if you don't care. If you don't care, I'll walk away this second. But you *do* care, don't you?"

I shook my head.

"You're holding back from me. Don't you trust me?"

"Of course I do."

"Again with the falsehoods. You won't let me in. All I want on this earth is to know everything about you, and you won't give me a single tiny clue."

"I've already told you more than I've ever told anybody."

"Really? My God, what a dry, *lonely* existence you're leading, my dear." His thumb was now stroking mine, the way you might stroke a nervous animal. And it struck me in that moment—an instinct, maybe—that he knew exactly what he was doing. That he was an expert in this kind of thing, making people feel at ease, and somehow the knowledge that I was being soothed—consciously, purposefully—was itself soothing. *No need to worry, Virginia. He's a doctor.* He knows what he's doing. He's dealt with your kind before.

You can trust him.

"Look," he said, "I know what you're afraid of. Do you think you're the only one? I *know.* The horrors I've seen. The damned sights that have kept me awake, the men I couldn't save. Hemorrhages that wouldn't stop. The infections that spread and spread. Going to bed streaked with blood, soaked with it, and you're too tired to give a damn. Then the voices. I still hear them, whenever I'm alone, like a Greek chorus. And every day, every morning you wake up thinking, *My God, what horrible thing awaits me today?* What fresh grief."

I bent my head over our clasped palms and gasped for breath. His other hand found the back of my head, my hair. His thumb comforted my ear.

"Shh. You see? I *know,* Virginia. But I think—for the past few months, I've had a bit of hope now, because of you. A little pinprick of light, and it's just out of reach, and do you *perhaps* understand, now, why I've written all those letters? Why I've kept writing, even when you didn't reply? Because I can't give it up. I can't give *you* up, the possibility of you. Not this single darling person whose vital spark I've craved, the way one craves water in a desert. Not unless I was wrong, and there isn't even that. Not even a spark left."

It was as if he knew exactly the words to win me over. Exactly what to say to overcome me. I knew I was sobbing, but I couldn't hear my own sobs, or feel my own wet tears. I only felt his hand in my hair, supporting my head.

"I *know,* Virginia. I know how you feel. I know your loneliness and your misery. I feel the same. We're all alone, the two of us. All alone in this frightful black world. Can we not at least *try* to give each other comfort? Light some small lamp together, against the darkness?"

And then, a quiet moment later: *Please, Virginia.*

And I believe, looking back, that this was the moment of my capitulation. *Please, Virginia.* This was the moment I chose my course, the moment I threw my heart over the cliff and leapt after it. I felt the tumbling of my resistance like a physical event, starting in my head and clattering down my spine and the bones of my skeleton, until I had nothing left to support myself. Only him.

And instead of feeling dread at this act of defeat, I felt freedom. I felt, in the instant of my leaping, as if I would never touch the ground again.

I lifted my head, or maybe he moved it for me, with that hand that now caressed the side of my face, the curve of my jaw. I met his eyes without fear. My fingers wrapped around his and squeezed for all life.

"Thank God," he said, closing his eyes, but the bang of the door smothered the words.

"Well!" said Hazel. "And to think we were worried to death."

CHAPTER 11

Cocoa Beach, Florida, June 1922

I SPOT MR. MARSHALL right away, the first thing I notice when I follow Clara inside the wood-framed house at the southern end of Cocoa Beach. He's sitting by himself, wearing a hat, hunched over a drink of some kind, but I'd know that prehistoric profile anywhere.

The building, as you might guess, is the kind of place I believe they call a speakeasy. It's just a shack, really—a plain wooden shack, big enough for tables and chairs and something that serves as a bar, not more than a couple of hundred yards down the beach from the old House of Refuge built by the Coast Guard in the previous century—so Clara tells me, anyway—in order to mop up survivors from all the shipwrecks. (The Florida coast, it seems, is a dangerous place to ply your sail, or whatever craft you happen to captain.) Whether the Coast Guard knows or cares what's going on under its lee, I can't say, but I certainly don't see any signs of knowing or caring here tonight. Just Mr. Marshall of the Bureau of Internal Revenue, all by himself, miraculously arrived on Cocoa Beach on this moonless evening, taking note of our entrance with a small salute of his glass.

In case you're wondering, I'm much recovered from the ordeal of two weeks ago. I woke up the day after that meeting in the Japanese garden filled with all kinds of resolve, and the first thing I did—well, the first thing once Clara was awake, which came long after the breakfast I shared downstairs with Evelyn—was to tell my sister-in-law to pack her bags, because we were heading straight back up to Cocoa. Back to the town of Cocoa,

Florida, where Simon Fitzwilliam, English doctor, captain in the British
Army Medical Corps, citrus grower and bootlegger, met his fate.

Cocoa, Florida. It sounds so lovely, doesn't it? Just saying the name
gives you a marvelous, exotic charge, however great your troubles. We've
passed our time at the beach, played all day in the heat and the blue ocean,
and the surf and sun have so exhausted my daughter that she falls asleep
almost before I tuck the blankets tenderly around her. Safe and sound.
And I've settled in for the evening like any old grieving widow, in the
lively company of my sister-in-law and the generally silent company of my
brother-in-law, and I've waited.

Waited for the turn of the moon.

Now the moon has turned—has disappeared into the great Florida
sky—and so this particular evening, instead of sitting down to a respectable supper, delivered on domed trays by hotel waiters dressed in crisp black
and white, eager to please, I came forth from Evelyn's room, smoothed my
dress, and asked Clara if she knew about a place on the beach where a girl
might have some fun this evening. (On the beach, mind you.) And her
eyes went all bright and she said, *Why, yes, I happen to know just the joint,*
and I said, *Excellent, let's go,* and she said, *But we're going to have to find you
something to wear, you know,* and all that took a certain amount of time, and
by good fortune Samuel happens to be working late tonight, because I dare
say he wouldn't have recognized us as we tripped out the lobby, having
arranged for a chambermaid to keep watch over Evelyn, and climbed into
the Packard baking quietly on the street outside.

And now the sun's gone down, and still the heat rises from the pavement
and the sand dunes, saturates the atmosphere like you could part it with
your two hands, except you can't. You can't just push it away. It's simply
there, eternal, whether you like it or not, sticking your flirty purple dress
to your back, coating your face in a tanned-pink sheen, wilting the ostrich
feathers that shimmer on your sequined headpiece, melting your crimson
lipstick. On Clara the effect is sultry and rather spectacular; I haven't dared

to look in a mirror and see what it's done for me. (The man in the corner isn't exactly smiling, after all.)

We sit at a small square table next to the musicians. It's some sort of jazz, I guess, a strange and hypnotic noise. A few feet away a pair of girls dance together in abandon, feet flying and hands jiggling, cosmetics tracking down their faces in lurid, colored lines. Two more conventional couples give them a wide berth. A man in perfect formal dress dances alone, eyes closed, swaying rather dangerously close to the trombone. And that's it. The other tables are empty. A barmaid makes a line for us; she must work on tips. I sit back in my chair and fan myself with my pocketbook while Clara orders for us. For such a tiny woman, she's got a remarkably long neck, especially when it's angled upward, as it is now, delivering our preferences to the waitress. She says something funny; they both laugh and glance at the man in the corner. Seems she's noticed him, too.

When the waitress moves away, Clara leans forward over the table. "Don't look now, but there's a chap sitting there in the corner, watching our every move. Just imagine!"

"I noticed."

"Did you? Clever thing. Mamie says he's some kind of bootlegger!" She says the word *bootlegger* with a particular breathless excitement, like *highwayman!*

"Mamie?"

"The waitress."

"Oh! Have you been here before?" (Innocently.)

"Of *course* I've been here before! My goodness. How do you think we got in?" She laughs.

"Well, it's awfully nice of you, keeping me company this week when you might have been kicking up your heels in this place."

"Oh? And how do you know I haven't? I do fancy a drink and a laugh, from time to time."

The door opens and a party spills inside, dressed in rakish elegance:

three women and four men. The smell of sweat and drunkenness invades the hot room. Mamie perks up from behind the bar, like a dog scenting a covey.

"Speaking of which," says Clara, "where the devil are our drinks? I want champagne tonight. I have the feeling we're celebrating."

"Celebrating what?"

"Why, your liberation! You're free at last, or hadn't you noticed?"

FOUR CHAMPAGNE COCKTAILS LATER, THE place is packed. I don't know where everybody comes from. It's rather wild and marvelously amoral, as if by defying the Eighteenth Amendment we are defying all the laws of ordinary society. The cocktails—even on my inexperienced palate—aren't very good, the cheapest of the cheap, but the satisfaction of your palate isn't the point. It's the satisfaction of your cravings, the satisfaction of the base animal inside you. Someone asks Clara to dance, and she takes his hand and dances, sweating and jiggling in the fug of jazz and cigarettes, a sick-sweet fume of rum and gin, and when he wraps his hand around her waist and bends to kiss her neck, I turn away, so swiftly that my shoulder hits a thick, dark-clad chest.

"Mrs. Fitzwilliam. Do you have a moment?"

"Mr. Marshall!"

He takes my astonishment for assent, I guess. Wraps one hand around my waist and the other around my fingers and starts to dance, far more competently than I imagined a Prohibition man was capable of.

"I don't want to dance," I say.

"Neither do I."

"Then what are we doing?"

He whirls me near a corner, where the music is muffled, and leans near my ear. "You need to go home, Mrs. Fitzwilliam. This isn't the place for you."

"I'll be the judge of that."

"Trust me."

"I don't trust you in the least. I don't know why you're here. Shouldn't a revenue agent be arresting everybody?"

"Look," he says, in a voice of pained exasperation, "just take your friend and get out of here. As far as you can. Back to town, safe and sound."

"What if I'd rather be here?"

He draws back and frowns at me. Only an inch or two taller, but terribly fierce. "Why? Why would you rather be *here,* of all places?"

"Because I want to have a little fun tonight, that's all."

And his fingers clench on mine, and his brow—if possible—takes on an even more terrible grimace. "This isn't *fun,* Mrs. Fitzwilliam. This is business, deadly business, and you're a fool to mix yourself up in it. You're a damned fool—pardon me—to think you can beat these fellows at their own game."

"I don't know what you're talking about."

"I think you do."

I open my mouth to make some indignant reply, and he just seizes me by the shoulders and stares at me, breath tasting of spearmint and virtue, nose parked a mere half inch away from mine, and after the shock wears off—a few seconds, that's all—I pull back and yank my hand free to smack him. He takes the blow with admirable calm, so I raise my hand for another try and someone grabs my wrist. Clara. She's smiling; her lips are smeared. "Is this poor fellow troubling you, my dear?"

"He was just leaving."

"Pity!" she says, giggling, and she tugs me away, into another room, more richly furnished than the last, where we collapse on a pair of red velvet chairs to be served a greasy, satisfying supper.

"TELL THE TRUTH. YOU'RE A regular here, aren't you?" I say.

"I cannot lie. But what about that chap of yours?"

"He's not my chap. He was making a nuisance of himself."

"That bad, was it? I'm surprised. He strikes me as the kind of fellow who knows how to kiss a girl properly." She extracts an olive pit from between her lips and reaches for the champagne. Not just the supper but the drinks are better in this room. The champagne—a vintage Pol Roger— rests in a bucket of ice next to our table, just as if we're not in America at all. Perhaps four or five tables occupy the space around us, filled mostly by men in dinner jackets who have presumably driven up here from various points of law-abiding civilization, just like us, along the road that keeps pace with the ocean.

"He didn't kiss me."

"He was about to."

"Far from it. He's not the kissing type."

"I don't know how you could judge a thing like that, on so little acquaintance. Unless you've met before?"

"No," I say swiftly.

Her eyes grow a little sharper, and she nods to her right. "There he is again, if you haven't noticed. He must be absolutely goofy for you. Are you quite certain you're not tempted?"

I follow her glance, and for an instant our eyes meet—his keen, mine resolute. In that second of contact, I have the familiar impression of a thick, unscalable jaw and hair so short as to bristle from his head.

"Quite certain."

"Because I expect he's a tremendous lover, once you work past his inhibitions. Think of all that feral energy he's got."

"My God. How do you imagine all these things?"

"Darling, I just know. Let's just say I haven't spent the last few years like you have, busy with hearth and home. For one thing, I haven't got either one. Hearth or home."

"No, you haven't."

Clara takes the bottle by the neck and refills my glass. "Well, then. A girl's got to keep busy somehow, if you take my meaning."

I don't quite take her meaning. I don't really want more champagne, either—my brain is already swimming—but I drink anyway, and then I venture, "The last time I saw you, you looked miserable."

"Well, I *was* miserable. I was frightfully miserable. It was awful at first, to be perfectly honest. I couldn't stay in dreary old Cornwall after all that, catching drizzle while the house fell to ruin, so after a bit, when the dust had properly settled, I moved to London and started living again."

"But what did you do? You must have taken work of some kind."

"Work? Oh, *darling*. Don't use such words." She waves her hand. "I had a bit of money from my parents. And the chaps paid for everything. If a girl learns how to play her cards properly, she shouldn't have to buy a thing."

I fall silent at that, because what can I say? I prod the remains of my supper. The giddy recklessness that carried me into this place tonight has died away, like the fizz in my champagne, leaving me flat and merely drunk. If this is what drunk is: muddy and blurred and pieced together, the Expressionist vision of yourself.

"I've shocked you," Clara says.

"No. Not really."

"Yes, I have. You think I'm some kind of prostitute."

"No! Of course not."

"I suppose it's a species of prostitution. But so is marriage, when you think about it. It's all just trade. His money and your—whatever it is you're inclined to give him. A meal, a well-ordered house, a bit of affection, a child or two. Sex, naturally, or else he's going to get that elsewhere, with women like me."

I touch the back of her hand with my fingers. "Don't say that."

"It's true, and I'm not ashamed. Why should I be? We're all ever so much more modern now. And I don't see why I should have become a dried-up little maiden aunt, just because some silly archduke got himself assassinated by a petty half-mad nationalist one June day and ended up taking most of Europe's eligible young men with him. The fellow I should have virtuously married lies under a cross in France somewhere, and I never even knew him."

"Not *all* the eligible men."

"No, that's true. But the ones who survived are practically useless, or else terribly maimed, and I've had enough of nursing. That sounds awful, doesn't it? It's true, though. That's one of the reasons I love America. You have so many strapping, healthy young men running about. Playing at their golf and tennis. Racing speedboats in Biscayne Bay. They're so tall and tanned and vigorous, I want to weep for the excess of it. If only I came here sooner, when I was young enough to get married."

"You're not that old."

"Oh, I am. I *am* old. I shall never marry now. I should never burden some poor chap with all my eccentric tendencies. It's too late for me. You see? You're the lucky one, really. You had a *moment* of marriage at least, even if you hadn't married the man you thought. A moment of content-ment, and a daughter to show for it. I've only got *this*." She waves her hand again, and when it returns she lets it fall on the neck of the bottle, at rest in its bucket. She pours the last dregs in democratic shares: a drizzle for her, a drizzle for me. "And if you're not going to encourage that fellow to drag his primeval jaw over here to seduce you with, I jolly well will."

"Oh, Clara, don't!"

But she's already tossed down that last drizzle of champagne, already risen from the table in a swish of fringed black gossamer. The look of flushed determination on her face terrifies me. I reach for her hand.

"Now, darling. You let me manage this," she says, and she bends her finger in the direction of Mr. Marshall.

I don't imagine he can resist her, even a man like him, a man doing his job, whatever it is. Clara is absolutely irresistible in her current moment, all lustrous and mettlesome, stylishly daring, a glossy trick pony you can't help watching. Waiting to see what she does next. But Marshall doesn't wait. He fixes on the doorway instead, as if something's going on in the main room, something of terrible interest, and only when Clara arrives at his table does he look at her, a second late, and then around her shoulder at me, and then back at her.

She places her two hands on the edge of the table and leans toward him. She's asking him something, and her endless necklace of imitation pearls, knotted in the middle—they *must* be imitation, right?—dangles exactly between them.

He replies. She replies back, pulls out a chair from a nearby table, and slides it into intimate proximity with his. Sits, graceful as a dancer, one leg extended to the side and the other folded atop, and rests her chin upon her laced fingers. Like a dreaming child, only dangerously grown up.

For some time I watch them converse. I can't see Clara's face, but I don't need to. Her pose says it all—angular, languid. I think of Clara in London, cadging a living at this, and compare her to the Clara I knew briefly in Cornwall, even the Clara who bounced into my bedroom in the Cocoa apartment, and I think, *This is Simon's fault; Simon created this creature.*

And then I think, *But is that so very bad?* The Cornwall Clara was a martyr in a gray dress. This Clara is happy, healthy, confident. Maybe this is Clara as she's meant to be, liberated from the shadow of her parents and of the war itself, and maybe Simon's done her a service, even if serving his sister was never Simon's object.

And then I think, out of the dark blue, as Clara lays her fingertips on the back of Mr. Marshall's considerable left hand: *What am I doing here?*

A small pool of flat champagne remains in my glass, the drizzle that Clara left for me. I drink it down, because I hate to waste anything, and I walk out of the inner chamber to the boisterous, middle-class main room, and straight on out the door into the black Florida midnight, and the reason I have come out to play this evening, under the new and invisible moon.

WE'RE ONLY A MILE OR two from the ruins of Simon's house, and a few miles more from the center of Cocoa, which still simmers with boomtown energy even in the sweltering start of summer, Florida's off-season, when most sensible midwesterners and New Englanders have retreated to their native lands. If I look behind me, I can see the creamy glow of lights on the night sky, but building lots and civilization haven't reached this far along the stretch of barrier sand, and the windows behind me are all shuttered, the doors bound tight. Not the slightest crack of light escapes. If you were plying your boat along the Atlantic shore this evening, you wouldn't know the place existed. The beach is as deserted and wild and midnight dark as an island in the Pacific.

Only the hum of gaiety betrays us.

In a few steps, my shoes have filled with grit. I take them off, balancing drunkenly on each foot. After a moment's consideration, I remove my stockings, too. The sand feels pleasant, still warm on the surface from the infinite sun, and then cool underneath, soothing my aching soles, which have been confined too long in sharp new leather. In pointy-toed glamour. As my eyes adjust to the darkness, the palms form shadows against the sky, and the sand takes on a slight luminescence from the stars, and I fall once more into enjoyment of my drunken state: the hazy peace, the physical comfort, the way you abandon thought and simply observe the altered world around you.

After a hundred yards or so, the gay noise recedes, and I settle myself in the sand, all blissfully alone for the first time since—well, I can't remember the last time I was alone. Not in New York. Certainly not since Evelyn was born. It's rather lovely, this solitary communion with the ocean. As I said, there isn't any moon, and the surf is gentle, building and cresting and surging and receding in succession. The bubbling phosphorescence fascinates me. Overhead, the palm fronds whisper to one another. The minutes leak away. I collect a few shells and stack them into a shaky tower, and when I lift my head again to stare across the vast dark water, I catch a flash of light.

Or maybe it's my imagination. The flash was so brief, a tiny explosion on the surface of the sea, and I can't be certain. Sometimes your eyes play tricks; sometimes your head plays tricks. Sometimes champagne plays tricks, God knows. I shouldn't have drunk so many glasses, with so much at stake. Shouldn't have let Clara pour so democratically. I draw my knees to my chest and wrap my arms around them and peer into a bar of surf, more curious than alarmed, my heart quickening pleasurably. But the flash doesn't repeat itself. The sea remains quiet, just the subdued crash of the miniature waves, and I am struck without warning by a sense of vital longing for my daughter.

Since her birth, I have felt this thing, this *need* to touch her skin, to hold her safe in my arms, to experience the movement of her breath and heartbeat: a need that supersedes all other physical requirements, for sleep or food or water or friendship. Almost all mothers experience this impulse, I'm told, and yet it remains so constant and so important, inhabiting my viscera, I wonder sometimes if I haven't poured all that repressed love for her father—that adoration cut off at the flood—into Evelyn's small body, swelling ordinary maternal instinct into something gargantuan, supernatural. That's what the psychologists might say, I suppose. Or maybe it's just that I have so little innocence left to me. Well, whatever. The flood swells anew, interrupting my peace, and I know I've made some kind of mistake; Marshall's right, I have no business here, no business staking myself in the middle of a game I don't understand.

I must return to Evelyn. I must protect her. I must make her safe.

And for God's sake, why did I ever leave her in the first place?

I rise to my feet and snatch up my shoes and stockings, and that's when the flash returns, a little longer this time, and then two quick additional flashes. I stand transfixed, articles hanging from my hand, waiting for the next tiny burst of light from the ocean, and concurrent with all this—the longing for Evelyn, the strange terror of the flashing lights—comes another awareness, most urgent and visceral of all.

Someone is watching me.

But there's no time to reflect on this sensation, to examine its authenticity or even to prepare myself to act on it. A pair of immense hands closes around my upper arms and yanks backward, throwing me to my knees, while a first connects against my left cheekbone.

I spin rightward. Crash into the sand. Dazed, without breath, brain white with pain. My mouth fills with grit; the sand coats my lips and tongue. I lift my face and spit and stagger back to my knees. Rise and turn. Someone seizes my shoulders, and I lift my head, and for an instant a spasm of yellow light illuminates his face, before another blow connects somewhere—my temple, possibly, though the impact strikes my entire head at once—and that's it.

Except for a pair of hazel eyes, barbarically fierce in a familiar face: an image so vivid that even as I drop into blackness and plop motionless at the bottom of the pit, the face remains, observing me in my unconscious state as if from a photograph stuck to the inside of my skull.

Simon's face.

CHAPTER 12

Versailles, France, August 1917

I N THE GARDENS of Versailles there are fifty fountains, but they don't all run at once, except on special occasions. I don't think there's enough water in France for that, and anyway, in the hot August afternoons of 1917, France had other things on her mind.

"They're a glorious sight, *les Grandes Eaux*," Simon told me, as we sat by the edge of the Grand Canal, cooling our feet. "I once saw the whole show when I was a young man."

"My goodness. You can't be that old?"

"Surely you've noticed my gray hair."

"How old are you, then?"

"Thirty-six." He paused. "I suppose that seems frightfully ancient to you."

"Not at all. I guessed thirty-five. And thirty-six is young enough. If you were over *forty*, now . . ."

"Ha. That's generous, coming from an absolute ingenue like you."

"I'm twenty-one. Not so *very* young."

"My God. You're a child." He sighed and swung his legs in the water, causing currents to ripple into my skin. "I was about your age when I first came here. Just after university. Eons ago."

"Only fifteen years."

"Oh? And where were *you*, fifteen years ago?"

I didn't answer.

"Exactly. Still in pinafores, no doubt. Six years old. It doesn't bear thinking about. What a wretch I am. Were you a pretty child?"

"No. My type never is. Too pale and dark-haired and bony."

"Well, you've aged beautifully. At this rate, you'll be another Helen in a year or two. Of course, I rather think you already are." He lifted my hand unexpectedly from the edge of the canal and kissed the knuckles.

"I'm not a Helen. I'm anything but."

"No, you're right. An empty compliment, that. I apologize. You're real and living and interesting. Not a mannequin. A painter's image. Anyway, Helen was a bit of a bitch, wasn't she? I always thought so. Poor thing, it's so hard for a truly beautiful woman to be otherwise, in this shallow human existence. When she's petted and praised for her beauty since birth, so she naturally goes about thinking beauty's the only thing that matters. The only thing people admire her for. So she imagines she's terribly smart, a cut above the ordinary sort of humanity, just because she happened to have the good luck to be born symmetrical, with the right sort of hair and the right sort of eyes, whatever those may be at any particular point in history. And yet, at the same time, her self-regard is of that wobbly sort that requires constant propping up from the world around her. Because it does things to your head, you know, when your face's the only thing people seem to care about. I suppose the psychologists have a word for it. In any case, in the end they're a great deal of trouble, these professional beauties." He kept my hand in his, and for an instant I thought of Lieutenant Green, clasping me clammily by the darkened Seine, except that Simon's palm was dry and warm, and the sun shone, and the canal flowed glassily before us.

"It sounds as if you know a great many beautiful women."

"I've known a few. Enough to know better."

"But when you were twenty-one?"

He laughed and stroked the back of my hand with his thumb. "Yes. Hmm. I see what you're getting at. But you shan't have it, you know. You shan't have the satisfaction of knowing all the details of my misspent youth. For one thing, I don't regret a bit of it."

I tried to pull my hand away, but he wouldn't let me.

"Don't be angry. I'm only being honest. I had the best of times. I'm not the sort of chap who's going to grovel on about what a stupid, callow fool he was in his salad days, how it was all a great waste of time, nothing but ruination. It wasn't. We had splendid times, those pretty girls and I. And it's all done, and I'm a different fellow now, older and wiser, and I want different things. Finer things. Things I shouldn't have properly appreciated, in those days. But I don't regret a minute of it. From experience comes knowledge." He kissed my hand again, the palm this time, and his lips lingered there for a moment.

"At least you're honest about it," I said.

"Have I shocked you terribly?"

"No, not really. I never expected you to be an innocent."

"But *you* are. Innocent. Aren't you?"

I hesitated. "Yes."

"I suppose that's unfair, really. These being modern times. An old sinner like me thinking he's got a right to pluck the untouched flower. Mind you, it wouldn't matter to me if you weren't. I may be a sinner, but I won't be some sort of damned middle-class hypocrite. Fair's fair. Logically speaking, you've got the same right to an improper past as I have." He kicked his legs out vigorously, splashing us both.

"That's not true. My innocence is what attracted you in the first place."

"No, it wasn't. It was the opposite. The way you seemed to know everything, in those mysterious eyes of yours. The way the grief of the world had somehow gone in and made house inside you. And then, at the very same time, your utter resolution. Your astonishing capability. I thought, *Here is a woman I can trust with my life*. Here is a woman who won't flinch at the dark corners of my soul."

"Do you have that many? Dark corners?"

"Everywhere, my dear. Everywhere. Don't we all?"

My God, how unspeakably luxurious it was, sitting there in the sultry French afternoon, talking like this while the sun beat on our necks and the water cooled our feet. I loved the shape of his legs, neither too beefy nor too slender, just exactly right, the trousers rolled to the knees and the shoes and stockings and puttees stacked military neat beside him. Luxurious to hear, from his own lips, how he had taken pleasure from many beautiful women, a man of tremendous carnal experience, and here he sat beside me, content with my company, wanting me above all.

"Tell me something," he said, after a long and deeply comfortable silence, in which the sun lowered an inch or two and the breeze began to rustle the hair at the nape of my neck. "Was I right?"

"Right about what?"

"About your eyes. All the world's sorrow?"

Across the canal, a pair of women walked briskly, as if taking exercise. They wore dark mourning dresses that whipped around their legs, and identical small hats that cast shadows across their cheekbones. One of them was much taller than the other, and I observed—as one tall woman to another—how she adjusted her stride to accommodate her shorter companion. A sort of vertical lurch at every step, wasting her forward momentum for the sake of unity.

I watched them cross before us and continue in the direction of the palace. Almost as a witness, I heard myself say, in a dead voice: "Yes. I lost my mother when I was eight."

"My God. I'm sorry. What a grotesque blow. Was she ill?"

"No. She was murdered."

The words came out, just like that. Shivered frightfully in the air before us, shocked by sudden exposure.

"My God," he said again, in a whisper. "No wonder."

"No wonder?"

"Why you wouldn't tell me."

"I've never told anyone else. We went into New York and started a whole new life because of it. The case was notorious. My father didn't want us to be exposed to public notice. So we left."

"I see."

I thought, *Nonsense, he doesn't see, he can't see.* Nobody who didn't live this thing could possibly imagine what it meant to a pair of girls, alone and motherless in the middle of Manhattan, like seedlings uprooted and transplanted into foreign soil and left to flourish or die by their own strength.

"My darling girl," he said. "How brave you've had to be. How utterly lonely you must have been, the two of you. You and your sister. Tell me her name."

"Sophie. Her name is Sophie," I said, and I turned my head into his shoulder.

HE HELD ME FOR MANY minutes, and when I raised my head at last he kissed me for the first time. To the west, the sun grew old and golden, and I imagined the taste of his mouth was golden, too, because the sunshine seemed to absorb us as we sat there in our virginal caress. His lips were warm and sweetly gentle, and his tongue stroked mine, the way you might lick the juice running down the side of a ripe peach. I didn't want him to stop. When he took my face between his palms and started to pull away, I yearned forward.

"Shh," he said. "Darling girl. Ghost girl. My own dear phantom."

"Not anymore."

"Yes. You're real now." He drew his thumbs over my cheeks and mouth and chin, kissed me again, and swore. "What are we going to do? I've got to be back on duty by noon tomorrow."

"Maybe that's best. It's best if we don't see each other right away."

"I'm due for a week next month. But I've got to run up to Cornwall to see my family. To speak to Lydia. To London, to speak to the solicitor. Go through this ridiculous pantomime for the lawyers."

I turned my head away. "Are you certain she wants this?"

"I think she will. I'm sure she will. She knows what it's like, after all. Being in love, I mean, and unable to do anything about it."

"And you. You did a noble thing for her sake."

He sighed and turned to the horizon, shading his face with one hand. We sat there for long moments, watching the sun descend. The taste of his kiss still lay on my tongue, rich and faintly exotic. His shoulder rested near my chin, close enough to touch, and the water dripped down my calves and around the knobs of my ankles, and the sun was so hot and abundant on my face that, for a single minute, I thought we would never have to move again, that the sun alone would nourish us, and we would graft onto each other like a pair of hardy plants, Simon and I, growing and blooming and dying together.

"There was this gardener we had, when I was a boy," Simon said suddenly. "Trevellyn. My parents—well, they were like most parents I knew, not altogether interested in children, leaving us mostly with nannies and governesses until we went off to school. We weren't awfully close. So I used to wander about the gardens—we had tremendous gardens, back home, though I expect they're suffering badly at the moment—and I struck up a friendship with old Trevellyn. He used to show me what he was doing. Teach me the names of the plants, that sort of thing. And one day he was grafting a new seedling, and he made me plant it for him. Stick my hands in all that rich, loamy earth. Place the new tree inside, carefully cut from the old. And I thought, my God, I can make things grow. I can make things live and thrive. And for a time I wanted to be a gardener, just like Trevellyn, and when I was old enough to realize that was impossible—impossible, I mean, in a professional capacity, for a chap from a family like mine—I decided I was going to be a doctor."

I didn't answer. I couldn't speak. How could he have known what I was thinking? It was impossible, and yet still more impossible that two such singular thoughts could have arisen at the same time, independent of each other. A few more people walked by. A woman, dressed in black—all the women of France were dressed in black, it was the national color—glanced at us and looked quickly away, as if she couldn't bear the sight. The sun touched the sharp tips of the trees before us and glinted. Simon, squeezing my hand, said that we'd better head into town for dinner, before the last train left for Paris.

IN THOSE DAYS BEFORE I became a mother myself, I often wondered what it was like to have one. A mother. And what kind of mother mine would have been, if someone hadn't murdered her.

I never discussed sex with my father. Well, my goodness, that hardly needs to be said, does it? I knew the bare mechanics of the act of procreation—the fact that sex existed, somewhere in the world, given the rampant evidence of humanity around me—but I didn't know what sex *meant*. Why you did it, and when, and what it was like. The string of smaller acts that led to this culmination. I thought I would never know. If you engaged in sexual inter-course, you must of course be married, and the subject of marriage never arose in my father's house. You might have thought we were a convent, governed by a grave and distant monk instead of an abbess. No young men, and certainly no marriage, and so—until the second evening of my visit to Paris in the summer of 1917—I had never given thought to what might happen if I fell in love.

In the end, it came down to the trains.

"Damn," said Simon, staring at the empty platform. He nudged his cuff aside to examine his wristwatch. "Five minutes past. How the devil? I thought we had bags of time."

"Are you sure that was the last train?"

"Yes. The damned curfew. What a nuisance. And no taxis to be had for love or money, of course. There's war for you."

I stared in shock at the deserted station, outlined in the vibrant indigo of deepest twilight. At the empty trough where the train should exist, if it hadn't already left. The last train to Paris until morning.

"Damn it all. It's my fault."

"No, it wasn't. I was the one who wanted to see Versailles."

"No, it was my idea to begin with. You only agreed out of kindness."

"It wasn't kindness. I did want to see Versailles."

"Well, at least it meant we shrugged off your Hazel and her damned pipsqueak—"

"Oh, he's a very nice fellow—"

"But all I really wanted to see was *you*. And now look what I've done."
He checked his wristwatch again. Gave his forearm a little shake, as if that
might change the result. "Well, there's nothing else for it. I shall have to
find us a hotel of some kind."

"A hotel!"

"I'm sure there's one about. Come along." He took my hand and turned
us both down the steps and into the motionless street, taking the pavement
in quick, long strides that I struggled to match. I think I was too shocked
to object. My God, a hotel! What did it mean? I might have known nothing about sex, but I knew you didn't just walk into a hotel with a man who
wasn't your husband.

Particularly when that man was married to someone else.

My legs were long, and I kept up well enough as we hurried along
the sidewalk, borne by some sort of urgency I didn't understand. Simon
didn't say anything. He seemed to know exactly where he was going,
as if Versailles were his second home. When we came to the next street,
he made a sharp left: so hard, in fact, that I stumbled on a crack in the
paving stones.

"Careful!" He reached out and caught me at the last instant. The action
brought us both to a stop. "My God! Are you all right?"

"Yes. I'm sorry. These shoes . . ."

"Good Lord. I'm so sorry. Charging along without thinking. I just
wanted to make sure we found a room before the doors start shutting. You
know these suburban towns."

I nodded. He took my other arm and held me at the elbows. The night
air swarmed around us, thick and August hot.

"Virginia. What's wrong?"

"Nothing! It's just a rather—a turn of events—"

"Are you angry with me?"

"Angry! No, of course not! It's just that I've never—of course, there's
nothing else to be done, but—well, what will Hazel think?"

"What will *Hazel* think? About what?"

"About—this. That we've—missed the train."

There was just enough light that I could detect a smile. "I see. You mean that we're going to spend the night together in a shameful hotel? Is *that* what you're worried about?"

"*I'm* not worried. But Hazel will wonder what's happened to us."

"Who gives a damn about that?"

"I do," I said pugnaciously.

"Well, you shouldn't. Hazel can think whatever the ruddy hell she wants. The only conscience I happen to care about is yours. What do *you* think about sharing a hotel with me?"

"I—well, it isn't as if we have a choice. Because of the train."

"You *do* trust me, don't you?"

"Of course I trust you."

Some wary expression must have taken shape on my face, because Simon's mouth split into another, greater smile. "Why, Miss Fortescue! Surely you don't think I mean to book us a *single* room, do you?"

I didn't answer. I didn't know how! I never had a mother to tell me how to conduct myself at a moment like this. I had some vague idea that I was supposed to draw a very firm line. That my mother, if she had lived, would have told me that under no circumstances were lovers to be trusted, that I should never enter a hotel with a man who was not my husband. That a lady's reputation might be destroyed in an instant, and virtue, once lost, could not be recovered. That kind of thing.

But my mother no longer existed, and Captain Fitzwilliam did. And Captain Fitzwilliam was now Simon, with whom I had just spent the most beautiful hours of my life. We had picnicked in the Versailles gardens; we had wandered among the fountains; we had examined our infinite reflections in the Hall of Mirrors. We had shared dinner in a small café, while pinpricks of light burst around us in the darkness, and now, in that naïve moment, standing there on the darkening Versailles pavement, I thought I knew Simon Fitzwilliam in the same way that I knew my own soul.

And if I couldn't trust my own soul, well, what was the point of anything?

I laid my hand on top of his, where it rested against my cheek.

"One room or two," I said. "It really doesn't matter."

IN THE END, THE HOTEL had plenty of rooms, and Simon booked two of them. The receptionist—a woman of about thirty, wearing a wedding ring like a clamp on her plump fourth finger—didn't seem to care. She had the glassy look of someone who has more fearful things to worry about than the precise moral rectitude of a paying customer. She handed us a pair of old brass keys and directed us upstairs. If she noticed our lack of baggage, she wasn't going to mention it.

Our rooms lay across a narrow, dark hall. Even in Versailles, the blackout had to be observed. Simon unlocked my door and ushered me inside. He checked the curtains and turned on the lamp, and the light revealed an unexpectedly pretty room, dressed in pale, flocked wallpaper and upholstered recently in shades of rose and cream. The two brass beds sat against the middle of the wall, side by side, as prim and white as virgins.

"I believe the bathroom's down the hall," said Simon, turning to face me.

"Naturally."

"I *am* sorry about this, Virginia. Don't be cross. I'll telephone Hazel. If there's any trouble—"

"Don't be ridiculous. I'm not cross at all."

"You *look* cross. All stiff and pale."

"Well, I'm not. It's an adventure, that's all. It isn't as if—"

"What's that?"

"Isn't as if we *meant* this to happen."

"My God, no." He smiled. "And even if we did . . ."

"Did you?"

"Of course not. But there are worse things than sharing a hotel with the woman you adore."

I tried to laugh. "Yes, I suppose so."

"And you? Do you mind so very much? Sharing a hotel with me?"

"I don't mind at all. After all—"

"Yes?"

"After all, your leave ends tomorrow."

"Yes." He had taken off his hat, and he fingered it now as he glanced toward the window. "That's true. And you're joining the American service, so God only knows when we'll have the chance again."

"Don't say that."

"It's the damned truth, that's all." He flung his hat against the wall. "The bloody war. The damned, bloody war. And we're just two people in it. Multiply this by a million, by ten million."

"Don't. There's no point."

"You're right. There's no point. There's no point in anything. We'll walk out of here tomorrow, we'll board our trains and say good-bye, and my heart's going to be ripped from my ribs, and what the devil use was all this? I shouldn't have come to Paris."

"That's not true."

"No, I've made things worse. It was just bearable before, knowing you were out there, beautiful and untouchable, like a dream. And now you're real, and this thing between us is real, and I've got to leave, I've got to go back to my wretched hut and patch bodies together again, I've got to see lawyers and go through hell in court—"

"Simon—"

"—and it's like having a glimpse of heaven, and then the gate slams shut, and you're not allowed to go inside, maybe not for a year or more. So maybe it would have been better not to have glimpsed it at all."

"Well, I think it was worth it."

He made a noise of exasperation. Ravaged his hair with one hand. Turned and paced to the window, thought better of it, turned back.

I said, "When we were sitting by the canal, cooling our feet, and you were telling me about the gardener—"

"Trevellyn."

"Trevellyn. And how he told you the names of the plants, and how to graft a seedling, and that was like a revelation, knowing you had the power to make things grow. To make things *live*. And you don't know what that meant to me. My father, he was always thinking about how things *worked*, inanimate things, machines and pieces of metal, but not about how living beings grew and thrived, and *you*—you're like . . . you're like—"

Simon came to a stop in the center of the room and went utterly still. His hand fell away from his hair. His eyes, wide and quite bright, fixed on my face.

I made myself wait, until the seams in my voice had knit back together. "That was worth everything. Just that moment. Even if I never feel that way again, I'll always be grateful we had so much as that."

My voice fell apart again, and this time I didn't try to retrieve it. I didn't think I could. I never thought I was capable of such a speech, in front of such a man, and that was all. Those were all the words I had.

Not that it mattered. He didn't seem to have heard me; he just went on staring, not even blinking, as if he'd slipped into a mesmeric trance. Taken gas of some kind, or been bitten by a paralytic spider. He wore his uniform, despite the heat—a man of fighting age couldn't go anywhere without his uniform, as a matter of general safety—and the collar of his shirt seemed to strangle his tanned neck. So maybe that was it. He wasn't getting enough air.

"What's the matter?" I asked.

"Nothing."

"What are you thinking?"

He shook his head. Movement at last! And a smile, small and bashful. "I can't say."

"Tell me."

"It's not the sort of thought one says aloud."

I flung out my hand. "You said you could trust me with all your thoughts. The dark corners of your soul."

"Did I say that?"

"Don't you remember? By the canal."

He folded his hands behind his back and examined the ceiling. I loved the cords of his neck, the curious tenderness of his skin. His square elbows, braced against his tunic. The lamplight surrounded him and made him glow; or maybe it was only my imagination. My imagination, *making* him glow.

"As the lady demands," he told the ceiling. "Very well. You're certain you wish to hear this?"

"Yes."

"*Quite* certain?"

I had to laugh. "Yes, of *course.*"

"Right, then. I was thinking how very much I want to go to bed with you."

My mouth formed a circle and said . . . nothing. Dark, soundless mouth.

"You see what I mean? Never press a man on his innermost thoughts." He dropped his gaze to consider my petrified face, my stricken throat, and I could have sworn his eyes actually sparkled, before he settled his cap back on his head. "Good night, Virginia."

I put out my hand to touch his arm. "Wait."

At the time, I didn't know what impelled me to act so boldly. Instinct, maybe, curious and terribly primal. And the fact that I desired him, too. Yes, that's what it was—*desire*—that heat in my veins, my mouth filling with water, though the Virginia of those days couldn't put a name on all those newfound sensations: the strange physical symptoms that had plagued me since he had turned the corner of the ticket windows at the Gare de l'Est at half past eleven, our appointed meeting, like a breath of gold air. I didn't really understand why the backs of his hands should fascinate me, or how the curve of his mouth could make me blush. Why the remembered sensation of his kiss should scintillate every pore of my skin. Why my every nerve had vibrated at a strange new pitch throughout the long afternoon and the evening, in tune with some harmonic I had never before detected.

Of course, I *know* now. I know everything about carnal lust. I know about kisses and gazes and heartbeats, that slow and primal dance that finds its finish in bed. I know the natural conclusion to such a day, with such a man. Gazing back upon that moment, I know perfectly well what I felt, and what I wanted.

I know perfectly well why—seething virgin as I was—I put my hand out to stop him as he prepared to leave me alone in that hotel room.

And I suppose Simon must have known, too, because he paused, as if that single act—my gentle hand on his arm—actually prevented him from continuing to the door. Maybe he had always known. Maybe he was only guiding me along, all day, to this point of decision. That's what his sister would say, wouldn't she? That he was an expert, that the seduction of innocents was Simon's particular specialty.

I can't say how long we stood there, silent and still, my right hand just above his right elbow, his shoulder a few inches from my chin, the back of his collar in view and the damp, burnished hairs above it. I thought he must have had a haircut recently, because the edge made such a flawless linear arc around the curve of his ear. I felt his heartbeat in the vein of his arm, throbbing in the same rhythm as mine. A floorboard creaked carefully above us.

After some unknown period of time—half a minute, half an hour—Simon lifted his left hand and covered my fingers.

"I should leave," he whispered.

But he didn't.

August 28, 1919

My dear phantom,

For so you are again, aren't you? We have come full circle. I have just been thinking of those early days, when I found and lost you, and how I wrote and wrote and eventually—great miracle—you came back to me. Well, if I'm honest, I did come to you first. But I only held out my hand, I believe, and you were the one who took it.

I have finished inspecting our crumbling warehouses and our rusting steamships—I say <u>our</u> because they belong to us both, you know—and am now writing to you from the commodious if rotting porch of our citrus plantation, about fifty miles to the west of Cocoa. You do remember my mentioning Maitland, don't you? My grandmother's dowry, badly neglected by my careless ancestors. The scale of the task before me is so enormous, I am sometimes tempted to take the next tramp steamer back to London and set up a modest surgery among my own kind, removing appendixes and treating venereal disease to the end of my days. But that would accomplish nothing, would it, and in order to win back your trust I must Accomplish Things. I must prove my devotion by acts of reparation. So this porch, which now slants rather dangerously to the south, will shortly be reconstructed by my own hand, and a new overseer found, and saplings planted to replace the dead trees. (You know I take comfort in such things.) You will, I trust, one day find yourself mistress of a gracious plantation house, overlooking a glorious vista of blossoming orange, the scent of which cannot properly be described by a mere English physician, who pines for his missing Virginia more each day, until sometimes, in the lonesome dark of night, he is so choked with desperation he considers he might be better off—and she might be better off—if he ended things altogether.

But then his courage returns with the dawn, and he sets aside his misery and begins again, each day another step, each hour closer to the dream. And each spring, when the oranges blossom again, their scent will carry you back into his heart.

Yours <u>always</u>,

S.F.

CHAPTER 13

Maitland Plantation, Florida, June 1922

THE STRANGEST THING happens as Simon's blue Packard draws around the last curve in the lane and Maitland Plantation appears before me, snow white and girdled in porches. I feel as if the roadway has split into a fathomless canyon and we are tumbling down its middle.

"Mama, Mama," says Evelyn, bouncing on my lap, "there house!"

"Yes, darling, a beautiful house."

Beside me, Clara lets out a low whistle and slows the Packard to a respectful crawl. "Well, gracious me. Look at that. Do you think it's got electricity?"

"I don't know. Until Mr. Burnside found me, I'd almost forgotten it existed."

"Well, I don't see any wires." She presses the accelerator, and the engine whines obediently higher, thrusting us forward down the muddy lane. It's nearly six o'clock, and an afternoon cloudburst has already stormed through; Clara stopped the car and raised the roof just in time to avoid the beautiful cloth interior getting drenched. Now the road is slick with thin, brown mud, and the Packard's rear axle slides back and forth as we accelerate up a gentle rise toward the house. My heart rushes, too, but not because of Clara's careless way with automobiles; it's the house, Simon's plantation house, square and tall-windowed, nestled among large, dense trees, while the wide green lawn spreads out like a skirt from her porticoes. The legacy of an American grandmother, according to Mr. Burnside, and if I shut my eyes, I can just recall Simon's voice as he told me about it, back in those early days, and how strange it seemed to me that a Cornish landowner might also produce oranges in Florida.

"To think it was practically a ruin four years ago," Clara says, grinding around in search of another gear, nearly sending us into a spin. "I saw the photographs from the overseer. He wrote us in desperation, begging for money for the repairs. And of course there wasn't any money."

"But Simon found the money, anyway."

"Yes. That's Simon for you. He always finds a way."

The gear slips into place at last, and the Packard surges forward. We've been driving all day, and I can't count the number of times I considered wrestling the wheel from her grasp and driving the car myself, down the long, overgrown roads while the hot sun engulfed us. Probably I should have done it. I doubt the additional strain on my injured head could be any worse than the fright and the nausea induced by Clara's driving.

But every time, the urge died away. I'm really not up to driving. Only three days have passed since the attack on Cocoa Beach, and I can't yet walk across a room without feeling sick. I can't lift my eyes to the sunlit sky. The doctor gave me a bottle of pills, which have relieved the ringing in my head, though I think they've sapped me somewhat—as pills sometimes do—of a bit of my will as well.

The lane flattens, and lines of young eucalyptus trees appear at the edges to shade us from that impossible sun. I wonder if Simon planted them. The white house beckons at the end, teethed with simple Doric columns, and as I peer eagerly through the glass, holding Evelyn on my lap, a figure emerges through the front door, under the shadow of the portico, dressed in pale clothes. My chest seizes up.

"Who's that?" I say.

"What's that?"

"Who is that, out front?"

Clara strains her neck, and in that instant of pause, I realize the person standing on the stately front portico of the Maitland plantation house is wearing a dress.

"Her? I expect she's the housekeeper. Unless she's one of Simon's mistresses, in which case we shall shortly have an awkward scene indeed!" Clara says gaily.

"Of course she wasn't his mistress."

"Oh, don't be frosty. I was only joking. Anyway, you shouldn't care." The lane is drier here, protected from the rain by the trees, and the gravel spurts from our tires. "I spoke to her on the telephone yesterday, to tell her we were coming. She's quite kind, actually. I think you'll like her."

"I'm sure I will."

The lawn draws close and the Doric columns loom large, and the Packard begins its swing into the circular drive. I try not to stare at the woman waiting for us on the steps, but there's something about her carriage, something about the pale blue drape of her dress—really quite up-to-date, for a housekeeper—that draws my attention. And something else.

"Why, she's a Negro!" Clara exclaims.

GOING TO MAITLAND WAS CLARA'S idea, to begin with. My own head was too muddled. When I awoke, the morning after the attack on the beach, I thought I was back in France. I thought, in fact, I had never left, that the year was 1918, and the war hadn't yet ended, and I was still unmarried. I thought I lay in a bed at the American Hospital in Neuilly, and these anxious faces surrounding me—Clara and Samuel and the local Cocoa doctor—had no meaning.

Where's Simon? I mumbled, and everyone exchanged a look, Clara to Samuel to the doctor and back, and it was Clara who came close and took my hand and reminded me that Simon was gone, darling, Simon was dead, and I was in Florida, and I had gone walking on the beach and stumbled into a nest of bootleggers, landing rum out of Bimini, and it was a lucky thing that someone heard the commotion and sounded the alarm, because that gang had left me for dead.

At her words, the pieces of memory began falling into place, conscious and unconscious: the sense of myself as Virginia Fitzwilliam, widow and mother, and the sequence of events that had ended in a blow to my head. Which ached and rang in a terrible racket, once I thought about it. I asked desperately after Evelyn, and they brought her to me, and though my limbs were weak and the contents of my skull all shaken up like an especially potent cocktail, I managed to convey to her that Mama was awake and feeling better, there was nothing to worry about. I just needed a little rest.

And that was when Clara snapped her fingers and said she had the most wonderful idea. We should go away from the bustle of town, we should go to Maitland for my convalescence. A thousand acres of peace and orange blossoms would be just the thing for me! And Evelyn, of course. Evelyn could have the run of the place. Every child should have a little freedom to run around, especially during the hot Florida summer. Samuel could stay with us, when business allowed. What jolly times we would have! But most of all, peace and quiet. Peace and quiet for my head to heal, for my bruises to fade. What did I think of that?

Well, I didn't care about Maitland one way or another. At the time, lying there in that white, fresh bed, battered, having just escaped death, I only wanted to leave Cocoa. I wanted to leave Cocoa, and the beach, and the vision I had encountered there. I wanted to gather up my daughter and get the hell out of Florida itself. But I couldn't go all the way home to New York, not when I could scarcely sit up. Not on the brink of July, when New York was at its worst. Clara was right, I needed to convalesce. And Maitland Plantation was fifty miles from Cocoa—I knew that much from Mr. Burnside—and remote from the coast, where the bootlegging gangs did their work.

But I couldn't tell Clara the real reason I wanted to escape. How could I possibly explain what I had seen on the beach last night? How could I explain that I had, in receiving those blows, been struck with a terror far more crucifying than physical injury? So I would go to Maitland, and when my eyes stopped swimming I would write to Sophie, and together my sister and I would think of something. Together we would take Evelyn and go to live with Sophie and her new husband, somewhere no one could find us, somewhere no one would hurt me again, somewhere we would be safe.

And in the meantime, I had Clara and Samuel to protect me. Clara and Samuel, who had been right all along. Whose vision remained clear, when mine was distorted by a longing I had never learned to conquer.

THE HOUSEKEEPER GREETS US AT the entrance of Maitland as if she owns the place—which, if the world were more just, I suppose she would—and introduces herself as Miss Portia Bertram.

"How was the drive?" she asks, while a neatly dressed man appears from around the corner of the house to unstrap our trunks from the rumble seat. The introductions have already been made, and still Clara stares with a kind of rapt fascination at Miss Bertram's cheek.

"Not too bad," I say, just as Clara reports cheerfully: *Hot as blazes!*

Miss Bertram smiles. "Cook's just made up a fresh pitcher of iced lemonade. And *you*"—she bends down to Evelyn, who hides behind my skirt, clutching one hand, and this time her smile is genuine—"you must be Miss Evelyn. My, aren't you just the picture of your daddy."

Evelyn's nose slides against the side of my leg, and I look down to see that she's actually peering out from her sanctuary. Meeting the friendly inquiry of Miss Bertram's face.

"What a big girl you are," Miss Bertram says. "You must be six years old!"

Evelyn giggles.

"Seven?"

Another giggle.

"*Eight?* You can't be eight. No, ma'am. You're not big enough for eight."

"Two!"

"*Two? Two* years old?"

"She'll be three in December," I say, stroking Evelyn's hair. "She's tall for her age."

Miss Bertram straightens and winks at me. "She gets that from her mama, I think."

"Rather," Clara says. "We're a funny threesome, aren't we? Samuel is enormous, and I'm tiny, and Simon was just in between. I don't think he was quite six feet, was he?"

"Just six feet, I think. An inch or two taller than me."

"Was he as tall as that? I suppose I always think of him next to Samuel. I say, though, this *is* grand. How on earth did Simon fix it up so well? I understand it was practically in ruins."

Miss Bertram's smile disappears. "Not *quite* ruins. We did the best we could."

"Have you been here so long?"

"All my life, Miss Fitzwilliam."

I intercept Clara's arm before she can ask any more questions. "Let's go inside, shall we? I could do with a glass of lemonade."

The house was designed for the Florida climate, all deep porches and shuttered windows and high ceilings and a vast column of a staircase wending upward in the center, and Clara exclaims at the coolness inside. I think it has something to do with the furnishings, too—what there are of them, anyway—spare and sparse, light in color and texture, creating a dreamlike atmosphere. There are hardly any doors. Miss Bertram leads us from room to room, separated by a minimum of walls, and I remark on the paucity of furniture and decoration.

"Mr. Fitzwilliam wanted it that way," says Miss Bertram. "He thought you should be the one to decorate the house, once it was finished."

"Isn't it finished already?" Clara asks, depositing me on a lonely sofa. She wanders to a tall French window and fingers the diaphanous drapery.

"Not quite. The library annex was just begun when—"

"When he died."

Miss Bertram stares at the back of Clara's head. "Yes."

Clara turns and lifts one of her delicate eyebrows. "You must have been awfully upset when you heard the news."

"Of course. We have endured a lot of trouble together, Mr. Fitzwilliam and I."

"Fixing up this old ruin."

"Yes. And turning the plantation back into a working farm, Miss Fitzwilliam. That was a whole lot of work, believe me. We were just coaxing those poor old trees back to life, you know, and now this."

The sofa is plain and white and comfortable. I sink against the cushions and watch Evelyn as she scampers from window to window. "What a terrible inconvenience."

Miss Bertram folds her hands behind her back. Her face, turned toward mine, is really quite lovely. I know she must be thirty-five or forty—about the same age as Clara, in fact—but she hasn't got a single line. Just that patient expression in her eyes, which are not brown but a kind of opaque, unexpected gray. She says softly, "I'd hate to see all our hard work go to nothing."

"Mrs. Fitzwilliam could sell the place, of course," Clara says briskly.

"That's true. It's my property, isn't it? Some rich bootlegger, maybe, with money to burn."

Miss Bertram stiffens. "Sell! Sell Maitland?"

"Why not?"

"Why, because the family's owned it for generations!"

"Not *my* family," I say. "My husband's family."

"Aren't they the same thing, Mrs. Fitzwilliam? You married Mr. Fitzwilliam, I believe. You took his *name*. Bore him a beautiful child. He left this place to *you*, ma'am, not to anybody else. He trusted you to carry on for him."

"Then he ought to have considered my wishes, instead of his own."

Clara smiles at Miss Bertram. "She's had an accident, you know. As I said over the telephone. She's here to convalesce."

Miss Bertram accepts Clara's smile with a faint, sage curve of her own, and for a moment the two women seem locked in a kind of ethereal communication, back and forth between their stiff mouths and their bright eyes, and I'm struck by how pale Clara looks, when only a day or two ago I was admiring the apricot glow of her suntan. I glance down at my bare arms, and then back to Clara's cheeks, and then Miss Bertram's warm brown skin.

At last, Miss Bertram tilts back to me, and her expression grows kind. A pair of tiny lines pops out from the outer corner of each eye. "I understand. You'll want to rest now, won't you, Mrs. Fitzwilliam? I've had the beds upstairs all aired and changed, but I'm sure Mr. Fitzwilliam would have wanted you to take his bedroom. The master's bedroom. I remember how he chose everything the way he thought you'd like it."

I'VE NEVER BELIEVED IN GHOSTS. For one thing, if spirits could return to visit those left behind on earth, wouldn't my mother have returned to me by now? *I* certainly would, if some terrible sickness or accident parted me from Evelyn. I would shatter Valhalla itself to reach my daughter, if I had departed from her too early. If I had left her alone, without my protection. If I had some warning to communicate to her.

But my mother, in death, never gave me the slightest hint that her spirit lived on beside me, or protected me from the man who had murdered her, so as time went on I gave up any hope—or dread—of supernatural beings. I came to understand that we living people exist alone in this physical realm, and the departed spirits belong solely to the eternal one.

This I firmly believe, and yet, as I stand in the center of the master's bedroom at Maitland, while Evelyn tugs and tugs on the tall French door to the balcony, I can't shake the uncanny sensation that someone stands by my side, watching her with me. I think I can feel the shimmer of warmth, just to my right, prickling the hairs of my arm. For an instant I don't dare to turn my head, because I'm afraid of what I'll see. A pair of spots appears, floating in the air before Evelyn's head, and I realize I have forgotten to breathe. The room sways. Something brushes my arm.

"Virginia? My goodness!"

"Clara."

"Are you quite all right? You're all gray!"

"Just a little dizzy."

"Oh, you're exhausted, aren't you? My poor darling. Do sit down. There's a nice cushy armchair right here. Evelyn, sweetheart, you must wait just a moment."

She leads me to the chair, and I sink back and close my eyes and listen to her footsteps, light as a fairy, as she flutters about the room. A blanket comes down across my lap; Evelyn is urged from the room. A gentle draft caresses my face, from a window newly opened, and then the door closes with a soft click.

When I awaken, the room is dim and the air has gone quite still. The white curtains no longer flutter at the windows. I lift my head to find only a single lamp burning on the table by the side of the bed. A small domed silver tray sits underneath the lamp, and the reflection of the electric bulb creates a steady round pool around the finial, like the Arctic Circle.

A deep lassitude fills me, not unpleasant. The ache in my shoulder has receded, and my brain no longer hurts. I lay aside the blanket and rise from the chair, and only the slightest sensation of dizziness drifts into my head. I grip the bedpost and concentrate on the curtains across the room, long and generous, shielding the balcony from view, while the world steadies around me, scented with orange blossom. A vase of them rests atop the chest of drawers along the wall to my right.

Underneath the dome, someone has arranged a small supper of cold chicken and corn bread. I eat slowly, for I'm not especially hungry; I swallow the food only because I know I ought to swallow food, not because swallowing satisfies any particular desire within me. In fact, I have no desire at all. Every human want seems to have muted inside me, like a knife that has blunted from use.

Except, perhaps, for the scent of the orange blossoms on the chest of drawers. I can't seem to resist them. I wander across the room, curling my bare toes pleasurably around the soft nap of the rug, and when I reach the blooms I close my eyes and sink my nose among them, and all at once I stand on the worn stone steps of a London church, and it's springtime, and a man is kissing my lips to the music of a thousand eager birds. As if I've fallen into a dream.

I open my eyes, and there is a note nestled between the petals. A note, I would swear, that didn't exist before.

For some time I gaze at this piece of ivory paper, folded once across the middle, and the line of thin, black letters just visible underneath the shelter of the uppermost half. The edges gain and lose focus, though the fault is not in my mind or in my eyes. I feel, in fact, quite alert—almost acutely aware of the rub of each detail against my senses. The delicate rich scent of the orange blossoms. The white velvet texture of the petals. The silken wood beneath my fingertips, and the slow respiration of the house around me. A plump rag doll rests against the mirror, wearing a pink dress trimmed in tiny lace, and her button eyes address me solemnly. I lift one hand and pluck the note from among the flowers. The two halves part, revealing the message inside.

A single line only, just five words:

Everything you seek is here.

CHAPTER 14

Versailles, France, August 1917

I WOKE ON my stomach, for the first time in my life. A disorienting rearrangement of the universe. In panic, I lifted my head, and a hand fell on my hair.

"Shh. Go back to sleep."

"Simon?"

There was a low, chesty laugh. "Were you expecting someone else?"

My head dropped back to the mattress—the pillows were long discarded—and the tip of my nose resumed its communion with Simon's ribs. The air was dark and drowsy and thick with beloved details, like the rustle of Simon's breath and the texture of the old linen sheet across my back. His hand remained in my hair, stroking gently, and I recognized the smell of cigarettes. The brief, velvet depth of sleep from which I had just awakened. The strange serenity of my mood.

The absence of dread.

"How long have you been awake?" I whispered.

"About dawn. Go to sleep, I said."

"Can't."

"Rubbish. You've scarcely slept at all tonight."

"Neither have you."

"Yes, but I'm an old sinner, and *you* . . ."

I lifted my head again, and this time I propped my elbows underneath me. Simon took shape before me, colored in black and gray: lean, naked, smoking a cigarette. Not the pungent French kind, but a good, sensible

British cigarette, mild and good-humored. Parliaments or something. His hair was too short to be really tousled, but I thought I could see the multitude of tracks my fingers had left there, flattened here and parted there. Or maybe it was only my imagination.

I asked him what was the matter.

His hand still wove inside my hair. Nothing, he said. Nothing's the matter.

"Yes, it is. You're unhappy."

He touched my cheek with his thumb, the one holding the cigarette, and stroked along the bone to my ear.

"My God, how beautiful you are. More now than yesterday."

"Lies."

"No, it's true. It hurts to look at you. Like looking at the sun."

"Just look away, then."

"As if I could. That's been my trouble from the first moment, hasn't it? I can't look away from you. I want to lie here looking at you forever."

"I thought you said you were tired of beautiful women."

"Do you really remember everything I've said to you?"

"Every word." I turned my lips into his palm. This strange delight, so early in the morning, in the face of Simon's melancholy, was a thing of wonder to me. "Tell me what's wrong. You're not unhappy about *this*, are you?"

"I believe I'm meant to be asking *you* that question, my pet. How are you feeling?"

"Very well. I think."

"You're sure? No aches and pains? I *am* a doctor, after all."

"Not at all."

"Ah, you're only fibbing to save my pride. But then, you've never lacked for fortitude, have you? *Virginia.*"

I loved the emphasis he placed on my name, each time he said the word *Virginia,* as if it meant something more than ordinary identification. As if some code were hidden in its syllables. How I worshipped that sound, the sound of my name in Simon's throat. I never wanted it to stop. Last night he had said it over and over: as he kissed me, as he pushed inside me for the first time, as our flesh stretched and slid together, as he reached the limit of his patience and cried out *Virginia!* in a voice of almost agony. And I thought, at the time, this was the sweetest sound I had ever heard.

Afterward he had reproached first himself and then me. He had taken advantage of my innocence; he had indulged his own passion at my expense; he should have restrained himself. I should have said something to stop him; one word, he said, one word from me, one raised finger would have stopped him in his tracks. And I told him that I hadn't stopped him, I hadn't wanted to stop him. I wanted the opposite. I wanted this culmination as much as he had. The promise of love wasn't enough anymore. Before we parted, before we left each other and returned to misery and the relentless threat of death, I wanted to belong to him. I wanted the fact of love, the proof of it. I wanted to serve him, I wanted to give him joy.

"But you're wrong," he said, eyelids dropping, voice slurring, "it's I who belong to you, it's I who am your servant now," and I thought he was going to sleep, because the feat was accomplished and there was nothing else to do but rest until morning. In my ignorance, I never dreamed there might be a second act. I settled myself against him and tried to quiet my teeming mind, the strange restlessness of my thoughts. But a short while later he began to stir—hands sliding, lips murmuring—and showed me what he meant. What it meant to have your nerves overcome altogether and your body turned into a perfect physical instrument, plucked into music not by your own inefficient fingers but by those of a lover. A lover's mouth. A lover's flesh, invading yours, heavy and urgent, stretching you into infinity until you simply snapped from the tension. You couldn't help it.

That's what I meant, he said, a little smugly, and his head dropped and he fell asleep, sliding into a natural position alongside me, his joints fitting into the cavities of my joints, his heart settling into the rhythm of my heart, hair and sweat and skin mingled together.

Now here he sat, propped against the horizontal brass rail at the head of the narrow bed, solid and carnal amid the haze of his cigarette, smelling of tobacco and a scent I now recognize as that of human musk, speaking my name once more like a holy word, while his face—what I could see of it, in the half-darkness of a curtained room just after dawn—contained nothing but sorrow.

INEVITABLY, WE MADE LOVE ONCE more. *Inevitably* because there's something so sensual about waking in the dawn with your lover, something primeval and hopeful. All your modesty is laid waste. The nakedness of his chest, and the nakedness of yours. I was like another Virginia, a new and lustful Virginia born from the old, rigid, fearful one. I had forgotten who she was. I pulled the cigarette from his fingers and kissed him violently until he surrendered and rolled me to my back on the narrow mattress and stretched my arms high above my head, holding my wrists in a tender grip against the brass rail, while his mouth nipped at my neck and breasts.

It hurt terribly at first, but I didn't let him know. I didn't want him to stop. I angled my hips and endured the way he worked himself inside me, until my raw flesh softened and filled with heat; until I drove as ardently against him as he drove against me. In the end, I struck home before he did, crying out with great force, and at the sound of my shout, the arch of my neck, he opened his eyes and went still. Gazed down at me. Said something vulgar in an awestruck tone. Followed me, frenzied, a few minutes later. Roaring as if in anguish. Collapsing on my breast as if he had lost every bone.

An absolute silence overcame the room. Only the valves of our hearts continued to move, in slow, giant, synchronized thuds that unnerved me. I thought he had fallen unconscious. I said his name softly. He roused himself and rolled away and gasped, hand on chest, "That's it. Done for. You're going to kill me, aren't you? You're going to wring me dry."

I was so innocent. I lifted my head and said anxiously, "You're all right? You haven't hurt yourself, have you?"

"Irreparably, I think. But God knows, there are worse ways to go."

By the time we could move again, the room was much brighter. The furnishings took on color. Simon lifted himself upward and reached for his wristwatch, which he had wound the night before and left ticking on the bedside table, next to the ashtray. His cigarette had burnt out. He sat on the edge of the bed and lit another. I came up behind him and wrapped my arms around his chest.

"What now?" I said.

He covered my fingers with his left hand and smoked silently for a minute or two, staring at the nearby wallpaper. His thumb stroked my knuckles, counting out the seconds in precise little beats. From outside the window came the shout of a man, the honk of an angry horn. The shoulder beneath my chin moved in a massive sigh.

"Right now, my dear, I expect we'd better bathe."

HE DIDN'T ENLARGE ON THIS humble suggestion as we bathed and dressed, taking turns in the well-scrubbed *salle de bain* down the hallway, nor as we breakfasted in the small parlor downstairs. My modesty returned with my clothes. I could hardly look at him across the table, instead stealing glances over the rim of my coffee cup. (The hotel resolutely did not provide tea.) Simon busied himself with his breakfast and remarked on the weather. His cheeks were pink and fresh from his morning shave—he had contrived, somehow, to borrow a razor from the hotel—and he looked remarkably unlined, for a man of thirty-six years who had spent most of the night in vigorous sexual congress. Who had taken a virgin to his bed and drained himself three times by dawn. His hair bristled upward, still damp from his bath, the gray strands glinting like tinsel among the tawny brown, and I looked away, because I couldn't examine the texture of his hair without remembering how it felt on my skin.

As he ate, his cheerfulness grew. Madame returned and asked if he wanted more coffee, and he smiled broadly and told her, in French, that he would take another cup with pleasure, that he could not get enough of this fine, strong brew. Her cheeks turned pink. She went obediently to the kitchen.

"Right, then," he said, coffee finished, rising at last, tugging at my chair, "we had better catch that damned train, hadn't we?"

WE FOUND AN EMPTY COMPARTMENT on the 9:03 express to Paris and sat next to the window, across from each other. I couldn't think of a word to say. My head was too full; my chest ached. Between my legs, I was now throbbing with soreness and above all a strange oversensitive awareness, as if I could identify by name each individual nerve beneath my skin. Simon absorbed my silence for several minutes, while the train gathered speed and the buildings flew by, lapsing into green, and then he turned from the window, leaned forward, and took my hands.

"Why, you're cold!"

"Only my fingers."

"You're all right, aren't you?"

He looked anxious. I smiled forcefully and said, "Very much all right."

"Good. I am a dreadful cad, you know. I shouldn't have let that happen."

"I don't regret a minute."

"*Now* you don't. But this afternoon, when I'm gone, all whisked off to my wretched surgical hut—"

"I'll be grateful, tremendously grateful, for every moment we spent." The words were flowing better now, greased along by Simon's expression of easy remorse.

"So will I." He lifted my hands to his lips and kissed them both. "In fact, I believe I desire nothing else in my life than to create a few more such moments, if you can spare them."

"Yes."

"And I'll keep on writing, of course, and I do hope you'll read my letters this time."

"Of course I will."

"And the next time we meet, it will be a proper weekend, at a proper hotel. Here in Paris, or perhaps someplace on the seaside if we can manage a few more days. Although they're a bit more strict in the provinces. We may have to think up some suitable little falsehoods, in that case." He winked.

"Falsehoods?"

"Oh, Mr. and Mrs., you know. Don't worry. I'll sort it out. I can be very clever and deceitful, when properly motivated."

"I guess you've had heaps of practice at this."

"Don't say it like that. This is nothing like that sort of affair."

"Isn't it?"

"How can you suggest such a thing? You know how I feel."

"Do I? You haven't said."

"Haven't I? My God, what about yesterday? I poured my heart out."

In the face of his astonishment, my voice fell to a mumble. "But this morning. You seemed—you weren't very happy."

"Oh, that. Haven't you ever heard of the old Latin phrase? *Post coitum omne animalium triste est*. Common affliction, except among women and roosters, apparently. One perks up after a bit and sees the bright side. Namely, the fact that you've just made love to the most marvelous woman in the world, and might, if you happen to dodge the German artillery for a few more months, have the great luck to repeat the privilege."

"Oh!"

"Virginia. Dear one. Don't be afraid. Last night—you can't imagine what it meant to me. What *you* have meant to me. I was only melancholy because—well, you know it's going to take some time, all this wretched legal business. It may be a year or two before I am properly divorced, however willingly Lydia undertakes the matter. And then there's my parents."

"Parents?"

"I mean my family, and hers. They'll be rather shocked, I suspect, at the whole mess. The scandal of divorce, when they thought everything settled exactly to their liking."

I drew my hands away. "Haven't you told them anything?"

"Not yet. I wanted to see you first. And of course they know nothing about Samuel's part in all this. Nor will they, if I can help it."

"I see. I'm just an interloper, then. The woman who destroyed your happy marriage."

"No! Good Lord, of course not. I'd never put you in that position. As far as they'll know, Lydia caught me in bed with a whore and demanded a divorce, and you came along later and reformed me. Back to a sober, faithful chap, a credit to his family."

"But until then—"

"Yes. I'm afraid you must remain a bit of a secret, for now. At least from my own friends and relations. My parents and my sister."

"The one in the white dress? The photograph on your desk?"

"You've got a splendid memory. Yes, that's her. Two years younger. She's an angel; I shall have to be careful how I explain things to her. I don't think I can bring myself to besmirch her memories of Samuel." He added, after a pause, "Her name is Clara."

The train clattered through a junction. I turned my head to the window and watched the buildings slip by, hot and bright in the August morning. Through an opening I glimpsed a street, and a fleeting image of a woman dressed in black, carrying a straw basket. "Yes, of course. I don't want to create any trouble for you."

"Sweetheart, you're not *trouble*. You're the opposite. The trouble is *mine*, my own doing, though God knows I meant to do right. I promise you, as soon as the divorce comes through, we can be married. It's just that it will take some time, that's all. I need you to trust—"

"*Married?*"

"Yes. Married. Isn't that what you want?"

My heart seemed to seize in my chest at that unexpected word. I stared at his quizzical face and thought, as the panic ran up my throat and down my limbs, making me dizzy: Of course. Marriage was always the point, wasn't it? Every girl wanted to be married. Home and hearth and a husband who loves you. Children and a large, well-appointed house and a servant or two to help manage the whole works. All that marvelous domestic machinery, stamping out families without a fault. Until it didn't. Until an awful, irreversible fault occurred, and the machine trembled and groaned and fell to pieces.

"No." I locked my fingers together in my lap. "No, it isn't. I don't want to be married."

Simon tilted his head. Squinted his eyes. "I beg your pardon?"

"There's no need."

"But I thought—"

"I'm used to independence. I've never wanted to marry."

"A modern woman?"

"Yes."

He observed me in disbelief. "You're quite sure?"

"Quite sure."

"Then why—I don't mean to argue—but why, when you learned about Lydia why did you care? Why did you send that telegram?"

"Because I'd never wreck another woman's marriage. I couldn't bear that. Even now, knowing she doesn't care, it hurts to think what we've done."

"Virginia, darling, *don't*. I promise you I'll make it right, perfectly right. *With* Lydia's blessing. You haven't hurt anyone. There is nothing whatever sacred about this . . . this convenient legal fiction that constitutes my union with her. In God's eyes, it isn't even a marriage. What *is* sacred is my union with you. Which I mean, at the earliest possible moment, to make formal before God *and* man."

"That's not necessary."

"It is to *me*."

"I just—I can't be married. I've known that since I was a girl. I don't want that kind of dependence."

"I see. And what if *I* do? Want that kind of dependence? Want to marry you?"

"Then I'll have to refuse you."

Simon turned his head and looked out the window. The gray light coated his skin. "What a surprise you are, Virginia. What a series of surprises you've given me, in the past thirty-six hours."

"I hope you haven't—that you didn't make this decision thinking—"

"Thinking what? That we should be married? Of course I did. I wouldn't have done it otherwise. I'm afraid—naïve chap that I am—I assumed you had a more official connection in mind, when you decided to go to bed with me."

"Well, I didn't."

He turned back to face me. "Then what *do* you have in mind, Virginia? How *do* you wish me to serve you? What sort of future do you imagine for us?"

"Let's not think about the future at all. Why should we? We'll go on writing and meeting when we can—"

"A tawdry affair, then. I thought you didn't want that."

"It isn't tawdry. It's beautiful. Last night, it was so beautiful and right. And that's why—oh, I don't want to ruin it, I don't want to *darken* everything—"

"Marrying me would *darken* everything?"

"No! Not marrying *you*. Marrying anyone. I can give you anything else, anything at all, but not that. I wish you would just *understand*—"

"I'm afraid I don't. I thought you were the kind of girl who wanted a husband. A family to hold her dear. I thought, after last night—"

I felt my head grow dizzy, my fingers grow cold. My voice soared upward into a high, thin shriek, like a frantic animal, like some kind of cheap hysteric. "Well, I'm not that kind of girl. I never was. If that's what you expect from me, then I can't—we can't see each other again, we can't *meet* like this—"

Simon reached out and grasped my face between his cool, dry hands. "No! Don't say that. Don't be upset. Calm down; it's all right. No, I don't understand, but I'll do whatever you want, I'll do anything that makes you happy."

"Don't just say that—"

"I'm not. Virginia! Listen to me. We don't need to speak of marriage. Just don't—for God's sake, don't disappear. Don't go away again."

"You must understand."

"I'll try. Of course. I'll do whatever you want. Just—just allow me to see you again. On whatever terms. For God's sake. Can you promise me that?"

There was no looking away. He was so close, I could count his black eyelashes and the flecks of brown in his irises, if I wanted to; I could smell the trace of coffee in his breath. And yet his proximity, instead of increasing my panic, steadied my nerves. His fingers, instead of entrapping me, secured me in place. The pressure of his thumbs returned strength to my bones.

I nodded.

"I will do whatever you want, Virginia. There's no other choice. I can't be without you. The idea of never seeing you again is impossible. You know that. Don't look away."

Well, I lifted my gaze, which had swept downward in relief at his words, and I remember thinking I had never seen an expression so earnest as his. Brows knit carefully together, irises bright.

"I've got to run up to London next month. I've got to see this through, because I can't go on pretending to the world, I can't keep us—keep Lydia and myself—frozen in this damned morganatic tableau for the rest of our lives. And then I'm yours. Every possible chance, I'll find you. With or without the prospect of marriage. Is that perfectly clear? Whatever you're seeking, Virginia, I promise you, you've found it."

I nodded.

He sat back against the seat and said, "Thank God." His smile was huge; I can still picture its breadth. The sun caught his face. He reached inside the breast pocket of his tunic and brought out his cigarette case, made of gold, from which he selected a long, white cigarette that seemed to glow by itself in the glare of the sun. He placed it in the corner of his mouth and struck a match. The flame wobbled as he held it up, though I couldn't tell if this was because of a draft or a tremble in his fingers. I stared at his lips and felt the pulsing of my own blood against my skin. He shook out the match and blew a gentle breath of smoke to the side of the carriage, away from the window glass, and the pressure of his gaze forced me to look up into his eyes.

"This is only the beginning of us, darling," he said. "I swear it."

CHAPTER 15

Maitland Plantation, Florida, June 1922

I SUPPOSE I'M not surprised to see that Simon's plantation is thriving. By his own testimony, he was an accomplished horticulturalist, a man with an inborn gift for making things grow or die, according to his own whim.

Still, the sight of all those rows of trees, thick-leaved and green, undulating along the gentle slopes toward the horizon, traps my breath in my chest. A fine haze drifts from the treetops toward the rising orange sun. The air is heavy with perfume. I think how much work it must have been, how much sweat and travail, to create an orchard so lush.

"How many acres again, Miss Bertram?"

"One thousand four hundred and thirty-three, Mrs. Fitzwilliam. Not all of it's planted in trees, though. He's got gardens and a whole plot set aside for the workers. Fields for the horses, too."

"Horses?"

"Oh, yes, ma'am. Didn't you know? He's got a whole string of them."

"Of course. Horses. I remember."

"My brother looks after them. He's a good man with horses, my brother."

"Does your whole family live here, then?"

She hesitates. "Yes, ma'am. There aren't many of us. Just me, my brother, and mother."

"How nice."

"Yes, ma'am." She chirps to the pony, and Evelyn, somewhat lulled by the motion of the cart as we drove out, lurches forward in my lap. "Hungry for breakfast, yet, Mrs. Fitzwilliam?"

"Certainly," I say, but it's a lie. I took a little coffee and a sweet roll from the tray in my room before coming downstairs, and an hour or two later it's still enough for me. Something about the heat, I guess, stifling my ordinary appetite. It's eighty-two degrees already, settling on our skin like a warm, moist Turkish towel, and who could face breakfast in that? Well, except Evelyn. When I found her this morning, playing about the kitchen while Miss Bertram instructed the cook, she had already eaten a whole poached egg on toast and drunk a tumbler of fresh orange juice. (Oranges, you understand, are in plentiful supply around here.) Now she squirms against my leg until I free her, and grasps the side of the cart with her long, plump fingers and calls out to the pony.

"She's an angel," says Miss Bertram.

"Most of the time," I reply. "I wonder if Clara's awake yet. She'd like to see all this, I think."

"Clara? You mean Miss Fitzwilliam?"

"Yes, of course. She must be exhausted; she's usually such an early riser."

Miss Bertram chirps again to the pony, who's slowed to a lazy walk, parting the haze with effort. "Didn't she tell you? Western Union boy arrived last night. I don't know what the telegram said, but she packed up and left first thing."

"Left! Clara's gone?"

"Yes, ma'am." Miss Bertram stares straight ahead, between the ears of the pony. "Took her trunk to the Packard all by herself. Didn't even say where she was going."

BUT SHE LEFT A NOTE, which I discover when we return to the main house a quarter of an hour later. It's tucked beneath the vase on my chest of drawers, so she must have entered before I awoke.

Dearest Virginia,
   I've had a bit of terrible news from Miami Beach, a dear friend in straits, so

I'm off for a few days to sort things out. Hope you don't mind I've taken the motor.
Give sweet Evs a kiss for me.

> *Much love,*

> *C.*

I gaze at the letters for some time, in much the same way as I read the note last night, until some whim strikes me and I open the top drawer, where I put the earlier message. I hold the two in the air, side by side, framed by orange blossoms, but the notepaper of one is smaller, a shade or two creamier, and while both are written in opaque black ink, the really expensive kind, Clara's handwriting is quicker, spikier. They are really nothing alike.

But I already knew that, didn't I? I already know whose hand wrote that note last night. I know the cast of those words like I know my own.

I glance up to my reflection in the mirror, and I'm surprised to see that I look rather well—at least, next to the white cloth face of the doll leaning against the glass. Still too thin, maybe, but my color is warmer, my eyes less anxious. I've taken an aspirin, according to the doctor's instructions, and the headache that was threatening the sides of my skull has died away. Down the hall, I hear Evelyn squealing happily with Miss Bertram.

A low voice echoes in my ear.

Everything you seek is here.

I FOLLOW THE SQUEALING ALONG a wide, high corridor until I arrive at Evelyn's bedroom. "I was wondering where they put you last night, darling," I say, and my daughter puts down a bright-colored alphabet block and runs to wrap her arms around my legs. I want to lift her up and blow raspberries into the warm skin of her tummy, as I usually greet her in the morning, but the act seems too raucous for my present tranquil mood, and besides, we've already reunited. Instead, I lower myself to the floor and return her embrace. Her hair smells of oranges.

"What a picture you are," says Miss Bertram. "It's a shame Mr. Fitzwilliam can't see the two of you like this. He did want all these rooms for his children."

I look past Evelyn's head to the bedroom wall, which is painted a bright yellow, the color of sunshine. A pair of perfect windows, curtained in pink polka dots, gaze out on the second-floor balcony and the grounds beyond. On the white-painted bed, a pink-and-yellow quilt has been covered with sleeping dolls of all shapes and dresses.

"When was this room decorated?" I whisper.

"Oh, now, I don't remember exactly. When the rest of the house was finished, I guess. Mr. Fitzwilliam always wanted a girl, you know. Boys, too, but there always had to be a girl. I think he has a soft spot. And now look! Here she is."

I stroke Evelyn's cheek with the backs of my fingers and swivel my gaze around the bookcases and dollhouses, the miniature table set for afternoon tea, the enormous stuffed bear in a rocking chair near the leftmost window, dressed in overalls, as if he had just returned from picking fruit in the orchard.

"Here she is," I repeat.

THERE ARE FOUR OTHER ROOMS in the children's wing: another decorated for a girl, two more in blues and greens, stocked with fire engines and soldiers. Each has a bookcase lined with all the childhood essentials: *Peter Rabbit* and *Squirrel Nutkin,* illustrated Bible stories and fairy tales. The fourth room contains a single bed and spare furniture of adult size. Miss Bertram explains that it's meant for a nurse or nanny. "Though you don't seem like the kind who hands her children off to the help all day, Mrs. Fitzwilliam," she observes as she closes the door.

"No. I kept Evelyn in my own room during her first year."

"That's what I thought. Still, it's a good thing to have another pair of hands around, especially if you've got more than one."

"More than one?"

"More children, ma'am. Children do come, one after another." She says it baldly, without tact, as we wander down the airy corridor toward the staircase, swinging Evelyn between us.

"Not in my case, however."

"Why, you never know what the future brings. You're such a young thing. And then you don't have a mama of your own to help out."

"How do you know about my mother?"

"Mr. Fitzwilliam told me. I hope you don't mind. I'm awfully sorry. I can't think of much worse, for a child to grow up without her mama. Or her papa."

"Well, I can't help that."

Miss Bertram doesn't answer, and we reach the top of the staircase, long and sinuous, curving down to the front hall like the neck of a swan. I know I must question her more closely; I know I must urgently learn more about Miss Bertram's role in my husband's life. How she came by her knowledge. How much more she knows. How closely her intentions aligned with his.

And yet I find I haven't a thing to say. Not a single query. A wholly unjustified contentment wells up inside me, as I regard the beauty of Simon's house, the symmetry of its architecture, the marvelous sight of our daughter clambering down the steps of the elegant main staircase, gripping the rails as she goes, because she's too small to reach the bannister. The light from the fan window floats in tiny motes before me. The raw edges of my nerves have all smoothed and rounded away. A smile forms on my lips.

After all, Miss Bertram lived here long before Simon, didn't she? She belongs to the house, not to him.

"She's a beautiful child," says Miss Bertram. "How I wish Mr. Fitzwilliam could see her like this."

"Yes," I say, and I follow Miss Bertram down the stairs, while she takes up Evelyn's small hand protectively in her own.

THE STRANGE THING IS, I missed my mother most not when she first died but years later. When Evelyn was born.

The pregnancy and delivery, I suppose, went as easily as these things can go. My tall frame seemed to absorb the changes in my body without much fuss; until I was six or seven months along, you might hardly know I was expecting a baby at all. Even then, I maintained all my usual habits of exercise and activity, right up until the onset of labor itself, which occurred in the evening, as we were sitting together in the parlor, reading in quiet unity while Father's gramophone played "Oh, Dry the Glist'ning Tear." (I can still hear the melody in my head.) At first I thought the stiffening of my abdomen represented only the familiar pangs of false labor, but as the contractions grew and grew, each one coming sooner and harder than I expected, I realized what was happening. And for a few terrible minutes I didn't know what to tell them. How do you explain to your father and your virgin sister that you're about to give birth? What words, pray, do you utter to illustrate the delicate nature of your predicament?

Eventually Sophie noticed my distressed face and sprang to her feet, calling for the cook and the housemaid, both of whom had already gone home for the day. I think Father caught the drift and went for the telephone. Evelyn slid into the doctor's hands only a few hours later, just under eight pounds, and a nurse came by arrangement to see us through the first two weeks.

But an unknown, disapproving, tight-lipped nurse from a Manhattan service is not a mother, is she? How can you tell her about your absolute unfamiliarity with babies and their ways, your paralytic terror at every sneeze and hiccup and change of color? How can you describe your fear and your ineptitude and your adoration? When it's two o'clock in the morning and your baby fusses and fusses at your breast, and you're weeping silently into her hair, shuddering chest, aching eyes, no idea what's wrong, not the faintest clue why she won't nurse and won't sleep, who is there to embrace you and assure you that everything will be just fine? Who is there to take the baby into her warm, grandmotherly arms and ease your burden for a minute or two, so you're not alone on this earth? Two o'clock in the morning with a newborn is the loneliest hour in world.

And then again, who is there to share your inexpressible joy when she sleeps at last, when her velvet cheeks go still and her tiny petal lips twitch, as if she's dreaming of milk? Who is there to share this love that is more than love, this love that allows you—at last—to glimpse the nature of God's love for the universe?

No one.

AND I AM REFLECTING ON all this, remembering those feverish early weeks, as I recline on a picnic cloth and watch Miss Bertram play with Evelyn in Simon's garden at Maitland. Some sort of counting game, I think; I'm too drowsy and content to investigate. Evelyn's laughing and so is Miss Bertram, and now they rise and chase each other between the trees. No urgency requires me to follow them. For once, I don't feel the familiar stir of uneasiness as Evelyn leaves me, in the company of another woman. The sweet floral scent of the orchard hangs in the hot air. Beneath the picnic cloth, the grass tickles my skin. I suppose I'm falling asleep, and I tell myself it's a good thing, because my head is healing, my brain is healing from a serious blow.

WHEN I WAKEN, THE SUN'S hardly budged from its fierce quadrant in the sky. Maybe it was only a few minutes. It seems like hours, though. It seems like I'm a different person from the woman who went to sleep. I sit up and draw my knees to my chin, gazing at the neat row of boxwoods before me, and it occurs to me that boxwoods aren't the sort of shrubbery you expect to find in the middle of tropical Florida. Although I'm no expert, am I?

So I rise and shake out my dress, and I wander toward the boxwoods, which reach nearly to my waist, clipped to a square, straight edge. A gap in the middle pleads to be stepped through, and though my head and my limbs weigh heavy with lassitude, drenched in the drowsiness that follows an afternoon nap, I make my way to the opening to discover what lies beyond. I find myself wandering past spicy eucalyptus, past verbena, past rows of densely blooming roses and flowers I can't name, all arranged in a kind of tantalizing succession, so that you step past one charming planting and another one beckons around a gap, or the corner of a stone wall, until you arrive at a sunken oval edged in boxwood, planted in that natural, overgrown English style with a thousand blooming perennials engaged in intricate cohabitation. A low curved bench occupies the turf on the other end. I descend a few stone steps and tread into the center of the oval, thinking that I must be Alice and this is Wonderland, or else I'm still asleep on the picnic cloth. But do dreams smell like this? A succession of perfumes, one after another. The heady mixture of citrus and eucalyptus and warm, damp earth; the green scent of plants growing rampant. And I think, this is Simon's garden; Simon planned and planted this.

I've entered the oval on its long side, and I've almost reached the center before I see the long, tranquil pool stretching from top to bottom. Almost like a canal, and at both ends—I can see them now—a pair of small stone fountains play softly. If you sit at that bench on the other side, I believe you can watch them.

"It's lovely, isn't it?"

How I jump! But it's only Miss Bertram, speaking gently from the entrance behind me, wearing her long, low-waisted dress of blue cotton that I admired earlier. I smile in relief and agree that it's a lovely garden indeed.

"He started plotting it out right away." She folds her arms and follows the curving line of boxwoods with her eyes. "Mr. Fitzwilliam. He has a real love for gardening."

"Yes, he does. Since he was a boy."

She nods. "So he told me. It looks almost wild, doesn't it? The flower beds, I mean. As if they just grew up there naturally. But I can tell you, he planned every detail. Dug each hole with his own hands. Wouldn't let another man touch this part of the garden."

"I can't imagine where he found the time."

"I guess he just wanted what he wanted. You know how it is, when you want something bad enough."

"Who looks after it now?"

"I beg your pardon?"

"Now that Simon's gone. Who takes care of this garden?"

Miss Bertram hesitates. Her eyes flicker to one of the fountains and back again. I can hear them now, those fountains, rattling softly into the miniature canal, like the patter of a never-ending rain.

"My mama does," she says, in a way that makes me think she didn't want to have to say it.

"Your mother's a gardener, too?"

"She always loved her flowers. And her house is close by." Miss Bertram nods at some point over the boxwood hedge. "I know Mr. Fitzwilliam wouldn't want any old gardener to look after his secret garden."

The words *secret garden* strike a strange little chord inside me. "If it's a secret, it's not very well hidden," I say. "I found it pretty easily, in fact."

"Well, he would have wanted you to, wouldn't he?"

Instead of answering her, I cross the canal in an awkward leap and walk to the bench. It's longer and deeper than I thought; the kind of furniture on which you could lie down and take a nap, if you didn't mind the stone mattress. Behind me, I hear the rustle of vegetation that betrays Miss Bertram's approach.

"Where's Evelyn?" I ask.

"My mama took her into the house for cookies."

"Your mama?"

"Yes. Mama wanted to meet her. She's Mr. Fitzwilliam's daughter, after all. We've been just dying to see her."

"Yes, she is." I'm not really paying attention to her words, in fact, because in staring down at the surface of the bench I've noticed a set of small initials carved into marble at one end: my own.

And, at the other end, Simon's.

"Do you like it?" asks Miss Bertram.

"He went to a lot of expense, that's for certain."

"I guess he did. He used to tell me that was why he worked so hard, to provide for you. So you wouldn't be giving anything up, moving from your father's house to his."

"That wasn't necessary. It wasn't about the money, at least on my side."

Miss Bertram barks. "Oh, honey, everything's about the money."

"Not to me. I hate it. It distorts everything; it obscures what really matters. People will lie and cheat and do all kinds of things for money, and when they have it, they aren't any happier than they were before."

"Is that true? I guess I wouldn't know. Sure is nice to have enough money, I've always thought."

I turn away from the bench to face her. "Of course no one wants to be poor. But wealth . . ."

"Then I guess it's a shame you've got so much, isn't it?"

"*I* haven't got it. I've made sure of that. It's all gone—or going—to Evelyn. In trust."

Miss Bertram's expression goes all bemused. She's stopped halfway across the garden, just on the other side of the miniature canal, and under the shade of the garden her complexion loses its honeyed undertone, so that she appears almost as a shadow herself. Except for her eyes, which are bright and curious, riveted to my face, and more specifically to my lips, from which those rather bold and revealing words have just escaped.

"To Evelyn?"

I hesitate. But the secret's already out, isn't it? "Yes."

"Well," she says. "Well."

"I just don't want it. I don't want to wonder whether someone's making love to me because of my money. And the attention. The way the newspapers—the newspapers—" I seem to run out of breath. Or words, or something. The will to speak.

"I see."

"Do you?"

She shrugs her shoulders. "You can do as you like, I guess. But it seems to me, you've just made your money poor Evelyn's problem instead. You've made *her* the object of all this unseemly desire. And poor child, she's not yet three."

My lips move, shaping words that don't come out. A bird starts singing in the trees nearby, and such is my ignorance of birds and their distinct voices, my city dweller's inattention to the details of nature, that I don't have the slightest clue which bird it is. A faint panic stirs at the base of my brain, from which I'm told such instincts rise.

And maybe Miss Bertram recognizes my panic, or maybe she thinks she's overstepped her bounds. The sharp, bemused position of her face softens, and she holds out her hand. "Come. Come on back to the house, Mrs. Fitzwilliam. Evelyn's having her cookies. And you look as if you could use a glass of lemonade."

"Do I?"

"Yes. Come on, now."

I start forward obediently. She takes my hand to help me over the canal, before she tucks it into her elbow, and we leave the garden so quickly, I don't have a chance to say good-bye. Just a quick glance over my shoulder before the bench disappears from view, and then we strike off through the rows and the beds, toward the main house and the promised lemonade.

December 24, 1919

Dearest V,

I imagine I really shouldn't write to you just now, as I'm feeling immensely sorry for myself and have, in consequence, drunk far too much wine at dinner. You see, this is not quite how I imagined my first Christmas Eve as a married man. I had dreamt of a roaring fire, and a tree trimmed with all sort of ridiculous objects, and a dog at my feet, and Sammy in his pajamas, and best of all my wife at my side, curled up perhaps on an old and venerable sofa. Possibly she should be in the family way by now, and I should be rubbing her poor feet, as properly belongs to a husband who has got his wife in an interesting condition. We should be speaking of the happy year just past, and the delights to come in the year ahead. When the hour is ripe, we should retire upstairs to our bedroom, where I should make my wife comfortable in whatever way she likes best, or at the very least provide a warm shelter in which to give her rest during the holy Christmas night.

Alas, my dream remains inside my head. There is no fire, roaring or otherwise, as the temperature hovered around seventy-three degrees for much of the afternoon; no dog, no comfortable sofa. Sammy and the other children are all abed. The tree is a meager one, hung with tinsel made hastily from old wrapping paper by my heroic housekeeper, who realized my melancholy around four o'clock this afternoon, I believe, and did her best to lift my holiday spirits.

But worst of all, there is no wife. Dogs and trees and sofas may be dispensed with, but Virginia is essential to my Christmas contentment, and so I have retired to bed in hopes of conjuring her here somehow, at least in spirit: so far I have succeeded in picturing your hair and your face and that glorious, supple tall figure of yours, but for some reason I cannot find your eyes, even though I know their color and shape. I cannot picture them somehow, and it grieves me so much, I can hardly hold this pen to paper. Forgive me. I hope I haven't upset you. Or perhaps I hope that very thing: isn't that why I'm writing these letters to begin with? To move you, to soften you toward me, so that this dream of mine may become reality by next Christmas.

Next Christmas! There we are. I'll think of that instead. The house will be finished by then. This room will be new-painted and furnished. I have tried to *imagine how you would want our bedroom to look, and I'm afraid it's rather hard going, as the decoration of houses was the very last thing we were ever inclined to discuss. But I have the feeling you would like something in the classical style, with plenty of light from a series of tall French windows, one of which should open onto a balcony—what they call sleeping porches here, because it grows so hot and close during the summer, you would rather sleep outside, on a balcony screened against the mosquitoes. I think you would like something open and airy and light in color, and simple furniture, and plenty of shelves for books. I hope you won't be disappointed when you see what I've done, though of course you can redecorate in any style you like.*

A knock has just sounded on the door, and Miss Portia has brought in some warm milk to help me sleep. She is our housekeeper, as you may recall from my earlier letters, but more than that: she is really a kind of manager for the plantation itself, and we have worked together closely on all aspects of the repair of the house and the orchards. I should tell you that I have recently discovered something rather shocking about her. Prepare yourself. Having observed her appearance and education and her fierce loyalty to Maitland, I often wondered whether she has some deeper connection to the place, and it seems I was right. She is in fact Lydia's natural half-sister, a few years younger, conceived—I am afraid— during the course of the Gibbonses' marriage, when Mr. Gibbons came to visit my father here at Maitland. Her mother was the schoolteacher for the children of the workers, back when the place was in some sort of order and harvests were regular. I suppose that explains her passionate love for this place, to say nothing of her tenderness to me, which I don't flatter myself I did anything particular to deserve.

In any case, I do hope you won't hold her birth against her, though I believe you never would; you are too kind and fair-minded for that. I suppose, in God's eyes, she has just as much right to this business as I do. I mean to ask her, one day when we know each other a little better, how well she knew her father, and whether he took much interest in her upbringing. Whether Mrs. Gibbons knew of her existence, and whether she cared.

Are you the jealous sort, love? If you are, you never gave me the slightest hint. Somehow I think you would hold out the branch of forgiveness, in Mrs. Gibbons's place, and would love the child itself regardless of the shame of its conception. But maybe I have only begun to idealize you in my mind, to hang virtues upon you as Portia and Sammy and I hung our makeshift tinsel upon the tree this evening.

I believe I had better finish my milk and go to sleep now, dearest wife. I hope you have spent your Christmas Eve in joy, surrounded by the love of your sister and father. You have certainly been well loved here, inside the heart of your faithful husband,

S.F.

CHAPTER 16

D o you know how long it takes to grow an orange? Why, all year, almost! The blooms first come out in the spring, just as they do on the fruit trees back home, but the harvest doesn't begin until winter. And in the meantime, those trees just keep blooming and blooming, for no reason I can see. Miss Bertram says they tend to put out new blossoms after a good fall of rain—hedging their bets, I suppose—but as we get regular cloudbursts in the afternoons, I don't see why those trees should take it personally like that.

Anyway, I don't mind. It's such a heady fragrance, mingled with the ripening citrus flavor of the oranges themselves, so that when the wind is just right, passing through the orchard to your open window, it fills your head like a drug of some kind. A most marvelous medicine. Miss Bertram always makes sure a vaseful ends up in my room, and I sink my face into the blooms at morning and at night, every chance I get. Every time I gather enough strength to rise from my bed and drag my unwilling body across the room.

Everything you seek is here.

Five simple words, so familiar a young child could read them, and yet I still can't quite grasp their meaning. Maybe it's the fog in my head. But what did the author mean? Everything I seek is here in the room? Inside the house itself? Or all of Maitland Plantation? Well, it doesn't matter. I'm not going anywhere, am I?

I haven't left this room since the second morning after my arrival.

THE DOCTORS, I THINK, ARE stumped, although they pretend not to be. Doctors can't show that kind of weakness, can they? Not in front of the patient herself. They examine me knowingly, making all the right noises of assurance and professional competence, and then they retire with Miss Bertram to confer. I have been given various pills and ointments and elixirs, all of which I refused to take, hiding them instead under my mattress or down the drain of the bathroom sink—an act of rebellion that required a supreme physical effort. It's not that I don't trust them. Why, Miss Bertram couldn't be more concerned about me. You ought to see her face, all compressed with worry, her eyebrows nearly meeting in the middle. She brings Evelyn to see me twice a day, and Evelyn sits on the bed and plays card games with me until my brain can't keep up, until the effort of keeping track of the cards overwhelms me. That's when Miss Bertram purses her lips and plucks Evelyn from the bed and whisks her away, because Mama needs her rest so she can get all better, isn't that right?

But Mama's not getting any better.

I figure it must be my head. The feeling, you know, is not dissimilar to the way I felt after an accident at the end of the war. My head took a bad knock then, too, and I lay in a hospital bed for months. My memory of that time remains hazy to this day. So this mental strain, this sort of febrile disorientation (though I haven't got a fever, haven't got measurable symptoms of any kind) isn't entirely unknown to me.

But I'm not foolish, even if I can hardly make it to the bathroom under my own power, and require Miss Bertram's help to bathe properly. I won't take their medicine, which isn't going to help anyway. I won't take palliatives of any kind. Except aspirin for my headaches, one at night and one in the morning.

That's all.

WHEN EVELYN'S TAKING HER NAP and Miss Bertram's other duties aren't claiming her, she comes to sit with me in my bedroom. That's when she brings the fresh flowers and lemonade and we talk. For as long as my mind can hold a conversation, that is.

She's worried about me, of course. She smooths my pillow and straightens my blankets, and I can tell she's keeping busy because she doesn't want me to see the expression on her face. She asks me how I'm feeling. I always say I'm feeling better. I don't want to disappoint her. This particular morning, which I believe to be the second week of July, though I can't be absolutely sure, I add something more, for effect. Something about how Maitland Plantation is better than any hospital for the recovery of one's head after a blow like that.

"I've always thought so," she agrees, pouring the lemonade, "though I guess I've never taken a blow to the head, myself."

"They heal so slowly, you know. Brain injuries, I mean. I saw so many of them among the soldiers. You start to think you're feeling better, but you're really not yourself. Not for some time. So you want to be somewhere safe. Like an animal in its den."

"I see. And Maitland's your den?"

"Yes, it is. I am so glad Clara brought me here."

"So am I, Mrs. Fitzwilliam. You can stay just as long as you like, you know. No need to go dashing off back to New York."

"New York? Of course not. Not yet, anyway. I find I'm liking Florida far more than I thought I would, when I first arrived."

"The state does grow on a person, I'm told. I guess I was just lucky to be born here, so I never had to experience much else."

"Never? You've never been outside of Florida?"

She lifts a shortbread from the tray. There are always shortbreads, too, though I never eat any. Only Miss Bertram does. "Except for college, I guess."

"College!"

"I went away to Radcliffe for a couple of years."

"Radcliffe! In Massachusetts? You went to *Radcliffe*?"

"Yes, indeed. The very one. I think I told you my mama was a schoolteacher? She had such hopes for me. Such big old dreams. And my daddy, why, he would do anything my mama asked of him. He doted on us both."

"Your father? Does he live here, too?"

She laughs. "Oh, no, ma'am. My daddy's passed on, a few years back. And he never did live with us. I was born on what we call the wrong side of the blanket, you know. My daddy's a white man, a businessman who used to come out here from time to time. He was friends with old Mr. Fitzwilliam, though Mr. Fitzwilliam visited the place but once or twice. But my daddy met my mama here, one of those times, and they fell in love, and— well, here I am. Not of one world nor the other. Betwixt and between."

"I'm sorry."

"Nothing to be sorry about. You can't change folks, and you make yourself unhappy trying. Why, I was lucky, by any measure. I had everything I needed. My daddy did love my mama, loved her dearly, even if he had a wife elsewhere. A family elsewhere. He was one of those fellows who possessed what you might call an excess of love for the female sex. And he did want the best for me. He surely did. Paid for me to go up north and study at the finest college money could buy. But we didn't suit, Radcliffe and me."

"Oh, dear."

"Now, Mrs. Fitzwilliam, don't you go giving me that look."

"What look?"

"That pity look. *Poor little Negro, she woulda had such a bad time among all the white folks.* It wasn't like that. No, ma'am. I was their pet darkie. You just about had to invite me to lunch or to teatime, if you wanted to pass muster your first semester. All those clever, rich Brahmin girls, they simply couldn't wait to be my bosom friend." She plucks at the cookie, examining each piece against the light before popping it into her mouth, so that I can't help wondering what she's looking for.

"So what happened?"

"I got homesick. Who wouldn't?" She makes a long gesture of her arm, toward the tall French windows. "For one thing, Florida's got all these characters. It's like the Wild West sometimes. Billy the Kid got nothing on some of these moonshiners and gladesmen."

"I wish I could meet one of them."

Miss Bertram snorts. "No, you don't, Mrs. Fitzwilliam. Not especially in the state you're in."

"Why, what state am I in?"

She sets down the remains of the shortbread, dusts the crumbs from her fingers, and strokes my hand. "I'm going to tell you a little story, Mrs. Fitzwilliam. I think it's about time you had to know it."

"Know what?"

"It's about Mr. Fitzwilliam. It was just after Christmas, you see. He'd had a big old dustup with his brother, over there in Cocoa. Had to do with all those ships and what they were carrying."

"Moonshine."

"Oh, so you figured that out, did you?"

"It wasn't hard."

"Well, but you're just a New Yorker, Mrs. Fitzwilliam. You don't know from moonshine. Anyway, it wasn't just what was going out, you see. It was what was coming in. Rum, mostly. Rum from Cuba, rum from the Bahamas. A nice little business. Anyway, you know how it is with business. Once you start to make a little money, other folks want a piece of your action. And the folks who wanted a piece of Mr. Fitzwilliam's action, well, they weren't nice folks. So Mr. Fitzwilliam, like a good gambler, he decided he was going to quit while he was ahead. He was going to use that profit to pay off the outlaws once and for all and go back to the ways things were. Honest cargo."

Her voice, low and sort of rhythmic, affects me like a lullaby. I have to fasten on each word, to concentrate, to part the veils of fog in my head. To remind myself that this is important, Virginia, *important*. Pay attention. Simon and Samuel, they had a fight.

I say, "And I suppose Samuel didn't agree. He liked the dishonest cargo just fine."

"That he did. You see, Master Samuel, he still wanted to make some money. I guess he didn't feel the orchards and the ships were making enough. And he and Mr. Fitzwilliam, they had a big old fight, and Mr. Fitzwilliam came home and told me about it. He said Mr. Samuel had offered to buy out the shipping business from him, and he said no. And he told me he thought Mr. Samuel was in deeper than he was letting on. And he said he was going to do something about it."

"Like what?"

"That, I don't know. He wouldn't say. But he did tell me this, Mrs. Fitzwilliam." She squeezes my hand and leans closer, almost over my face itself, so I can smell the sweet shortbread on her breath. The tang of lemonade. "He said I was to watch out for you. If you was to come down here to Florida, looking for him, I was to keep you safe. He said to me, Portia, if anything happens to my wife, why, I'd never forgive myself. She is the most important thing in the world to me. Everything I do, I do for her sake."

"Is that true? Did he really say that?"

She leans back in her chair. "He did."

My head is beginning to ache. My stomach is sick. Across the room the curtains are drawn over the windows, because my eyes are so sensitive to the light, but I think the sun must be setting. The glow that surges past the edges of all that white fabric is thick and molten, like you could hold it in your hand. You could hold it in your hand, but if only you could get out of your bed to try. If only you could lift your arm and stretch out your fingers toward the sun.

You might think, at this point, that all sorts of questions should be rattling around inside my skull, and they are. Rattling and screaming and carrying on. But I can't quite seem to grasp them. I can't quite seem to make them hold still and talk sense. As if I'm staring at a jigsaw puzzle, not a terribly complicated one, not all that many pieces, and I can't remember what I'm supposed to do. What to do with those pieces, lying there on the table before me.

I just lie there, gazing at the thick yellow line between the two nearest curtains, and I think, *She knows so much*. How does she know so much?

And: *She wants me to stay here*. Safe and sound.

Which sounds lovely—staying here at Maitland, in this tranquil room, in this tranquil state of being—but it's not. There exists something deep inside my tranquil, tranquilized brain that doesn't *want* to stay here. A small worry, a particle of fear. An atom of anxiety. I am not where I am supposed to be. I am not doing what I am supposed to do.

I want an aspirin. How long until I can take another aspirin?

My lips move. I hear myself asking Miss Bertram if I can see my daughter.

EVELYN CHEERS ME UP. EVELYN always makes me feel better.

It's an effort, but I manage to climb out of bed and into a chair. I don't want Evelyn to see me like that, all motionless, lying prone on a four-poster with the blankets up to my chin. A little girl shouldn't have to see her mother like that.

Instead, I sit in the large wing chair in the corner, wrapped in a dressing gown, my toes balanced on the edge of the matching footstool. Evelyn's just finished her dinner, and I'm grateful to see that she displays none of my symptoms. That her cheeks are pink and healthy, her eyes bright, her movements unfettered. She rides an imaginary pony around the room and tells me about her day, in the random, unconstructed sentences of a small child. The grapes she ate for lunch. The giraffe in the book Miss Portia read to her. The toy soldier Sammy let her play with.

"Sammy, darling? Who's Sammy?"

Sammy is the boy she plays with.

"Whose boy?"

She shrugs. Just the boy.

(I am concentrating very hard. Thinking *Sammy, my God, Sammy. What does this mean?*) "Where? Where does the boy live?"

Miss Portia's house.

"Is he Miss Portia's boy?"

Yes. Miss Portia boy. He THIS many years old.

(She drops the pony's reins, tucks her doll underneath her elbow, the rag doll that used to sit against the mirror atop my chest of drawers, and holds up seven fingers.)

I ALWAYS TAKE MY ASPIRIN late in the evening, when the house is quiet, because I don't want anyone to catch me. Also, I'm starting to run low, and I think that if I take this pill just before I go to sleep, the effects will somehow last longer. The aspirin will see me through the night, the beautiful black velvet night, so thick and so heavy that I can just about live there, free of all pain, until morning comes.

Until the aspirin runs out.

What will I do when the aspirin runs out?

I wait until the atmosphere is absolutely still. Until every last floorboard has gone silent. And then I lie there a little longer, gathering my strength, because it requires such a *vast* amount of strength to push back the covers and rise from the bed. Such a colossal *will* to stagger across the width of the bedroom (sometimes I actually crawl, you know, because the effort's so immense) and open the bathroom door and then, on top of all that, to open the door of the medicine cabinet and grasp the bottle of aspirin that the doctor gave me in Cocoa. A hundred little white pills, only there aren't a hundred there anymore. Not even close. I try to count what's left, to figure out how many days of relief I have remaining, but I lose myself in the middle. Well, never mind. I can always send out for more aspirin, can't I?

But what if I can't? What if I don't remember? What if I entrust this task to Miss Bertram and she brings back the wrong kind of aspirin? What if— even worse—she decides I don't need the aspirin anymore?

The bottle is shaking before me, rattling the little pills within, making me think of a snowstorm. One of those glass globes you brought back from your holiday in the mountains, filled with liquid, depicting some miniature landscape, and you shake and shake until the delicate white flakes within blur into a miniature blizzard, obscuring the miniature landscape within. Sophie bought one of those for Evelyn when we visited Switzerland last year. Geneva. Or was it Zurich? How Evelyn laughed. How she shrieked with delight.

And I realize that the bottle of pills isn't shaking by itself—of course not. That my hand holding the bottle is shaking. That I am so desperate for my evening dose of aspirin, I am actually *shivering* with the force of my anticipation. One arm braced on the washstand. Mouth dry. Eyes hazy. Brain aching.

And I think—the first really *clear* thought I've had all day, maybe all week—

This isn't really aspirin, is it?

CHAPTER 17

France, August 1918

I FIRST MET Samuel Fitzwilliam in the small, badly lit café near Château Thierry where the evacuation hospital staff used to go for a little food and company on our few hours off, that last August of the war. I was eating dinner with a couple of nurses, whose names I forget; he sat alone with a bottle of sherry and watched us silently.

I knew he was there, of course. I noticed him right away, not just because he was that kind of man—tall, marble-faced, shoulders wedged like anvils into a corner too small for them—but because his gaze was so familiar. His eyes, I soon discovered, were the exact shade and shape of his brother's.

One of the nurses leaned confidentially over the table. "Don't look now, but there's a fellow in the corner over there, watching our every move."

Everyone looked, except me.

"Ooh, very nice," said one of the other girls. I think her name was Mary. "I do like those British officers. They're such gentlemen."

"Not all of them," I said.

"Well, he's too big for me," said the first one. "Too big and too dark. And I don't like the look in his eye. Like he wants to eat us up."

"I wouldn't mind *that,*" said Mary. She was sitting opposite me, and the officer sat diagonally to her right. She sent him a look that I supposed was flirtatious, and he must have acknowledged her in some way, because she laughed, and her skin turned a little pink.

The waiter came then, and we ordered our dinner. It was only five o'clock in the afternoon, but we were due back on duty by eight, and the hospital lay an hour's walk away. Outside, the sun was still high, and the air was hot and salty, like a seaside holiday. I didn't have much appetite, and the food at the café was terrible: usually cassoulet, made mostly with beans and only a little canned meat, or else a gritty stew made of shellfish. Hazel, who was on duty at the moment, called it *mal de pesce*.

But free afternoons were rare, and the food at the hospital canteen was usually much worse, so those of us lucky enough to be off-duty at four o'clock in the afternoon always met in the hospital courtyard, rain or shine or hail, for the walk down to the village and the Papillon, with its red-checked tablecloths and its decent vin de table, served in small, old glasses that the waiter wiped with his apron.

He was wiping them now, examining them critically against the light from the window, while I vigorously ignored the familiar, tactile sensation of being watched. The buzz along each hair on my scalp and arms; the awareness, as we ordered four plates of cassoulet and a bottle of wine, of each small shift in his position, each twitch of his fingers, though he sat behind me and to the left, just outside the limits of my vision.

The waiter nodded and left to fetch the wine. In his absence, I felt exposed, like an animal that has stepped outside its cover.

"He's getting up!" whispered Mary, but I didn't need the warning. I already knew that he was rising, sidling away from his corner, straightening his tunic. Beneath the edge of the wooden table, my hands gripped each other. A shadow cast itself over the red-checked cloth.

"Good evening, mademoiselles," the man said, in a voice that I remember finding rather sinister at the time: velvet-soft and drawling, and yet so resonant it seemed to rattle the wineglasses. Mary's eyes goggled. The other nurses shrank in their seats.

He went on without a pause. I had the impression that he was used to that kind of reaction, and that he didn't give a damn. "Have I the honor of addressing Miss Fortescue?" (He laid a touch of ironic weight on the word *honor*.)

Someone gasped; I wasn't sure who. I was taking in the giant size of this man's hands, which gripped the tiny sherry glass as if it belonged to a dollhouse set.

"I am Miss Fortescue."

"I'd like a word with you, if I may. Briefly."

I looked up finally at his face, and the sight of his eyes sent a shock through my nerves. And yet I didn't recognize him. I knew those eyes, but I didn't know *how* I knew them. My brain couldn't quite connect this giant man, whose hands looked like shovels, with the trim, professional figure of Simon Fitzwilliam.

"Excuse me. Have we been introduced?"

His eyebrows lifted. "Do we still need that kind of thing?"

"*I* do. I'm in the middle of a private dinner. I'm not about to run off into a corner with any stranger who asks."

"Oh, I see. In that case." He set down the glass and placed his fingers along the edge of the table. The action tilted his torso forward, so that he loomed over the salt cellar and the meager jar of yellow chrysanthemums like a large and meaty thundercloud. "My name is Samuel Fitzwilliam. I understand you're acquainted with my brother, Simon."

WE SAT AT THE CORNER table, under the furtive surveillance of Mary and the other nurses. The bottle of sherry stood between us. He had pushed aside the chrysanthemums to make room. My nerves were still splintering from shock, and my chest was cold and fearful. I had brought a glass of wine with me—the bottle had arrived just after Major Fitzwilliam—but I didn't drink. I wasn't sure I could hold the glass without spilling it.

"Simon said you were killed."

"Did he? Not quite. I was taken prisoner."

"Prisoner! For how long?"

"Over three years. I was in the regulars when the war started, you see. The Coldstream Guards, to be precise. Second son joins the army; it's a kind of tradition with those of us in the landowning classes, when there's only so much land to go around. It meant I was among the first men to set foot in France with the BEF. Captured by a damned patrol at the end of October and sent to Breslau."

"How awful."

"Better than getting killed, I suppose, which is how I'd have ended if the Boche hadn't got their mitts on me. Every last officer in my regiment—below the rank of major, of course—is now feeding the French soil."

"But how did you get out? Were you released?"

"Released? You mean for good behavior? No. I escaped." He poured again, slow and exact, and pointed out that I wasn't drinking my wine. Was there something wrong?

"No," I said. "I've never been a great drinker."

"That's a shame. It's the only human pleasure worth its price." He saluted me with his glass. "Cheers. To you and to my splendid brother. I understand you're well acquainted."

I hesitated. "Yes."

"You've been carrying on with him for a year or so, if I heard the story right. I've been told I don't always pay close attention to people's stories. Especially about my brother."

"Who told you this? Simon?"

"Ha-ha. No, not Simon. A little birdie. Is it true, though? You and Simon?"

"I . . . we . . ." There was no point in lying, was there? Not to Simon's brother. And—the thought now burst into bloom, the wondrous implications of Major Fitzwilliam's return from the dead—wouldn't he greet this news with delight? "We're in love. We—we've had to keep it secret, of course."

"Oh, of course. But in the meantime . . . ?"

In the meantime. Well, what was I supposed to say? *In the meantime, while Simon's getting his divorce from the woman you love, the mother of your child, we've been carrying on a love affair.* A love affair, true, in which our meetings had been short and furtive, and our surroundings bleak, and our partings desperate. Letters crammed with passionate longing and plans for the next time, always the next time, a few days in Paris or a night in Amiens, the German offensive throwing everything into chaos last spring, the Allied counterattack reversing our direction yet again. And now, at last, the prospect of hope. The end of the war. The possibility, at last, of something longer and more permanent, a week together, a month together. A cottage by the sea instead of a room in a sordid hotel. The lifting, at last, degree by degree, of the shroud of dread from my shoulders. The new and brilliant dawn at my window.

"In the meantime, we are in love," I said.

"How marvelous. I expect you've been meeting up for dirty weekends and that sort of thing. Knowing my brother."

"I don't think—"

"Of course you have. Because the thing about Simon, he always gets what he wants. Since childhood, really. Did you know that we're twins?"

"I think he mentioned it."

"Well, it's true. Shared the same womb and all that, and it seems we made a little trade, while we were swimming around in the primordial bath. I got all the size, and he got all the charm. And if Simon decided he wanted you in his bed, well, he certainly wasn't going to let a little thing like matrimony get in the way, was he?"

"What a terrible thing to say!"

"Well, now. I suppose it is. But then, we've never been close."

"But why not? You're brothers, you're twins!"

He closed one eye and examined the sherry in its glass. "I'm afraid that's rather a long and knotty tale, Miss Fortescue, strewn with all the usual incidents of brotherly affection and family accord, and—as you've kindly made clear to me, in your forthright American way—you haven't got much time to waste on idle chatter with strange men. So, in the interests of brevity, soul of wit and all that, I'll just skip right over the trivial details of the family history and—what's that wonderful phrase I used to hear, when I was in New York once? *Cut to the chase,* that's what they told me. Cut to the chase, sonny. I haven't got all day."

He finished the sherry and reached for the bottle. It didn't seem to be having the slightest effect. I guessed that was fair. A puny bottle of sherry wouldn't stand much chance against that enormous frame. And yet he wasn't fat. Every ounce of him was carefully rationed, without a dimple of prodigal flesh. He was just bone, and the necessary muscle to cover it, and the bulk of an officer's uniform over that. I thought he could probably swallow his brother whole and nobody would know the difference. I tried to imagine him confined in a German prison, and failed. But I could imagine what it might have been like. How he would have suffered. The bitterness it must have worked on his mind and spirit.

And then to break free at last, and realize what you had missed.

"At least you're alive. Your family must be so happy," I said.

"What's that?"

"Your family. Simon. I suppose you've been to see them already?"

He transferred his attention, which had wandered briefly to Mary and the nurses, back to me, and for an instant I was truly frightened. His eyes, which so uncannily resembled Simon's, such that the sight of them made me lose my breath, contained a strange intensity of emotion—as if he were one of those spoon benders in the curiosity show, and I were a spoon. No one had ever looked at me like that. Not my father. Not even Simon. No one had ever wanted to *bend* me before.

"Well?" I said. "Haven't you seen them? Don't they know you're alive? You have no *idea* what—"

"But I did write, Miss Fortescue. That's the thing. I did write. They do, in fact, know I'm alive. They *have* known, from the beginning."

"From the beginning? You mean since you were captured?"

"Yes. The Red Cross gets the letters out. Didn't you know?"

"But that's impossible. They must not have received them."

"They did receive them."

"No, they didn't. Simon said—"

He laughed. "*Simon* said."

"What does that mean?"

The glass was empty again. He poured another—the bottle was running low—and asked me if he could light a cigarette, though he didn't wait for a reply. Just pulled out a packet and a book of matches from his tunic and lit himself up.

I leaned forward. "Well? Are you certain they *know* you're alive? Have you been to Cornwall and *spoken* to them?"

"A better question, I think, is whether *you* have been to Cornwall. Have *you* ever seen my family? Spoken to them?"

"Of course not. I've had no business with your family. No opportunity to travel, even if I did."

"Only with Simon?"

"Just Simon."

"Ah, Simon. My dear brother. And Simon told you that I was dead, didn't he? That I'd been killed at the beginning of the war."

"He said—I don't remember exactly what he said. That you went missing, I think, and were presumed killed."

"How convenient of me. Terrible blow."

"Well, it was! He said it was! He'll be delighted to know you're alive. In his last letter—"

"Oh, I'm sure he said all kinds of decent things in his last letter. Simon's superb at saying decent things. Though I expect you're already aware of that."

My head was spinning a little, trying to pin down facts that refused to stop shifting around. I placed my palms on the table and stared at my knuckles.

"I'm afraid I don't understand. You can't be saying that Simon *knew* you were a prisoner all this time."

"Of course he knew."

"But that's ridiculous! Why on earth would he say the opposite? Say you were killed? When he had every reason to want you alive! Didn't you know that? Didn't you know you have a—you have a *child?*"

Major Fitzwilliam dropped a long crumb of ash into the chrysanthemum jar. "Ah. Now we're getting to the truth of the matter. The reason I came to see you, of all people, in this godforsaken little French hole in the mud. The fact is, I *didn't* know there was a child, and if I *had* known, I would have been happy to tell anyone who cared to ask that it wasn't mine."

"*What?* How can you say that?"

"Because it's the truth." He tapped his temple. "There are things, Miss Fortescue, about which a man can be pretty certain, and the question of whether or not it's possible he's fathered a child on a particular lady is one of them."

"But then who is the father?"

"An excellent question. I'll give you a moment or two to ponder it."

"You're not saying Simon . . ." I couldn't finish the sentence. The blood in my cheeks seemed to interfere with the ordinary function of my jaw.

"Got my fiancée with child, as soon as I'd marched off to war? I can't say for certain, of course," he drawled. "Since I wasn't there at the moment of conception."

"He wouldn't have. He wasn't in love with her."

"You don't have to be in love, Miss Fortescue. Where do you get these ideas? You only have to want something. If you're my brother, it's usually something you shouldn't have. Your brother's fiancée, for instance."

For an instant the image blinked before me. A pretty girl in a white dress, trimmed in lace; wearing, perhaps, a wide-brimmed hat with a pink grosgrain ribbon and an air of moneyed desirability. The heiress, the one whose wealth was meant to save the family estate.

I whispered, "You were actually engaged, then? You and Miss . . ."

"Gibbons. Yes, we were engaged. I rather thought she was in love with me. We hadn't told my parents, of course, or hers. It wouldn't have done for her to marry the second son. A waste of perfectly good capital."

"But you never—"

He squinted at me. Squeezed the glass in his hand.

"Never . . . ?"

"Don't make me say it."

"Never went to bed with her? Let's just say that I know the baby isn't mine, hmm? The birth of young Samuel Fitzwilliam came as a cracker of a shock, when my family got a telegram through with the news. A rather brusque telegram, if you must know. There I was, rotting away in a German prison camp, kept alive only by my faith in the love of a precious girl—the only girl, I might add, who has ever liked me better than my charming, elegant brother . . ."

He paused grandly to pour himself another glass. I thought, *Surely he ought to be drunk by now, even a big man like him*. But he wasn't. He was exquisitely lucid, his movements elastic and precise. The sherry didn't wobble as it fell happily into the glass. His thick, dark hair remained in place. Only his mood showed any sign of poisoning: maudlin and reckless, like a man on the brink of some self-destructive act.

"It's not true," I said softly. "I know Simon. I know what he told me. Why would he lie?"

"To get you into bed, of course. It seems to have worked."

"He asked me to marry him. It's a sham, you know, his marriage to—his marriage. It was only because of the baby. They aren't intimate. He's divorcing her, with her full support."

"Is he? I haven't heard anything about that."

"Because you've been in prison."

"I hear news, believe me. Heard that he was enjoying himself with an American nurse, for one thing—"

I made a little noise of outrage, but he held up his hand and went on.

"I don't give a damn, Miss Fortescue. I really don't. Long since given up counting Simon's conquests, let alone blaming them for being conquered. My parents, of course, and then the nannies and the governesses. Even Lydia, it seems, though she used to see through him. When we were young, I mean."

"Or maybe she only sees him clearly *now*."

He shrugged. "As you like. Anyway, it's always come up trumps for good old Simon, which—as I said—doesn't bother me a bit. But I thought you should know what's really going on, that's all. That you're being led down the garden path, just as I was."

"I'm not being led down the path. Any kind of path. I'm sure there's a perfectly good explanation for all this."

"Really? I can't think of one. Either Simon's been lying to you all this time, or I have. Naturally you'll say it's me. But the question is, Miss Fortescue, the question you have to ask yourself is *why*. Why would I lie?"

"Because you've conceived a terrible and ungrateful bitterness for your brother, just because he's a good man, just because he happened to be born before you. And you think he's betrayed you, when in fact he's only done the right thing, a *noble* thing, giving your poor child a name—"

"Ah! Is *that* how he won you over? God, what a rotter, my brother. A true rotter. If I were you, I'd consider this a lucky escape, provided you're clever enough to take the opportunity. Before he gets you into real trouble. Or has he already done that? Gotten you into trouble."

I rose. "If you'll excuse me."

"Oh, now, don't cut up like that. I beg your pardon. I have a habit of saying the wrong thing to a lady—again, the exact opposite of Simon. I like to speak plainly, and it's no more than the truth, you know."

"That's quite enough."

He held up his hand. "Forgive me."

"Why should I? You're not really sorry. You like to say things that disturb people. You relish it. You *enjoy* being the exact opposite of Simon, don't you?"

He tapped his enormous thumb against the base of the sherry glass. He had remained seated while I stood— not a very courteous stance, on the face of it, but I didn't mind. I felt a little power return to me, as I stood there next to the table, glowering down at the shiny, monochrome waves of his hair—again, so unlike Simon, all mottled in gold and silver—and

I later wondered if he understood this, if he kept his seat out of generosity instead of rudeness, defying a custom that must have lain very close to instinct.

But that was only later, when I had the time—weeks and years—to examine every detail of this conversation in my mind, over and over. In that August of 1918 I thought Samuel Fitzwilliam was simply a boor, in addition to being a vengeful, bitter liar. I didn't understand him at all. *I* was the one who couldn't see him by any other angle, except in opposition to his brother.

"Well," he said at last, "I can see you're not his usual sort, anyway."

"Thank God for that."

"I suppose that explains why he went to such lengths to seduce you. I don't blame him for that, at least."

"That's generous of you."

Samuel parted his thick lips—he had a strangely sensual mouth, for so blunt a man—as if he were about to say something. I felt the nearby stares of the nurses, who had given up pretending to make conversation, and the weight of so much silence became unbearable.

"Well? Do you have something else to say, or are you finished? I'd really like to return to my friends, Major."

"Nothing at all, really. I'm just finding myself in a damned odd position. Wanting actually to *defend* the poor bloke, for once in my life."

"You don't need to bother."

"The truth is, Miss Fortescue, as I said before, you're better off without him. Better off without the whole family, really. We're a bad old lot, deserving of extinction, I expect. Only the animal instinct for self-preservation keeps us going, like one of those wind-up toys that refuses to stop ticking along, crashing his silly little cymbals. I suppose I can't even blame him for Lydia. He has to find the money somewhere, doesn't he?"

"Of course not. There are others ways to make money."

"Spoken with the ridiculous optimism of an American. Yes, I suppose there *are* many ways to make a stinking great pile of money, the kind of money you need to keep up moldering estates and pay the taxes on them, too. But not for a humble surgeon in the medical corps. That's another thing he wanted and got. Well, now he's got to live with the consequences, hasn't he?"

"I don't understand."

"I mean he insisted on his medical course, instead of doing the sensible thing and reading, say, law or history. Something that might lead to riches in Temple Bar, or the City. I don't know how he got our parents to agree. Why the devil it meant so much to him. I suppose he just likes to have the power of life and death over someone, like some kind of god, which is rather a chilling thought. But there it is. And now he can't see why he's got to make a choice between love and money. Because he does, you know. Lydia's fortune is all tied up. If you're hoping he'll divorce her, I'm afraid you'll be waiting for eternity." He finished his glass and set it down on the table, next to the bottle and the pot of yellow chrysanthemums that matched the one on the table occupied by my friends. "But I've taken enough of your time. I'm not in the habit of doing Simon's women any favors, and I only really came here out of curiosity."

"You've wasted your time."

"Have I?"

"Yes. I'm happy you're alive, Major, and I do hope you come to your senses. But you've wasted your time. I have nothing but faith in Simon, and if you could have seen him, if you could see him for what he *really* is, what he's suffered, I think perhaps you might change your mind."

Samuel Fitzwilliam folded his arms across the vast khaki field of his chest.

"What a damned shame, really. At least on our side."

"A shame?"

"A shame that you haven't got any money."

"It doesn't matter if I haven't got money. You'll see. Simon and Lydia will divorce, and the two of you will at last have your chance to be happy together, if you can set aside your pride and seize what lies before you."

He turns back his head and starts to laugh. "Oh, my dear girl. What a beautiful innocence you have. But you do know that's illegal, don't you?"

"What's illegal?"

"Why, marrying your brother's wife. It's against canon law. There's some talk of allowing a chap to marry his brother's *widow*—the Deceased Wife's Sister's Marriage Act passed Parliament some while back, at least, and now that the war's taking all their husbands, the women are clamoring for the same opportunity—but to divorce one chap and marry his brother is quite beyond the pale. I'm afraid we're done for, Lydia and I, unless we escape to some heathen isle. My brother's fortune is safe from temptation."

As I said before, I never liked wine. I never liked the smell and the taste and the instant recollection of dread. In most cases, I could force down a sip or two, just to make myself social, but at the moment I stood before Samuel Fitzwilliam in that small, sweaty café in Château Thierry, I had never once taken so much wine as to make myself drunk. Never once experienced even the slightest sensation of inebriation. Nor had I ever known the desire to feel anything other than perfect, reassuring sobriety.

And yet I thought—as I listened to Samuel Fitzwilliam speak, as I heard him say *We're a bad old lot, deserving of extinction,* as I examined the familiar, exciting outline of his eyes and the faint yellow reflection of the chrysanthemums against his jaw—I thought, *Maybe I would like to try a little sherry.*

I lifted the bottle, which was about two-thirds full, and poured a reckless splash into Samuel's empty glass. The vessel looked much larger, now that it stood on its own, outside of his giant hand, and the old-fashioned facets splintered the glow from the guttering candle in the center of the table. I sniffed the rim once: no black dread, no throttling panic. Just a vague, sweet excitement that made me feel capable of anything. Any possible folly.

I swallowed quickly, before I lost my nerve, and as I returned the glass to the tablecloth, I said, "Just how much money does she have? Simon's wife."

"Lydia? Quite a lot. I expect her father's worth a hundred thousand or so, at least."

"A hundred thousand? Is that all?"

"I call it a decent fortune. But perhaps you feel cheapened?"

"Cheapened? Not at all. Just struck, I suppose, by the irony."

"The irony? Of a hundred thousand pounds?"

To my left, four steaming plates of cassoulet had been brought to the table where Mary and the nurses were sitting, including one set before my own empty seat. I smelt the earthy flavor, the beans and herbs and the meager, mealy sausages, past the sweet haze of the sherry that still fumed about the passages of my throat. I was hungry now, hungry as a lioness, and wanted to eat. But not yet.

Not before I leaned forward and said something utterly out of character, straight into those disturbing hazel eyes.

"Yes, irony. You see, Major Fitzwilliam, *my* father's a millionaire."

CHAPTER 18

Maitland Plantation, Florida, July 1922

I'M TRYING TO write a letter to my sister, Sophie, but I can't seem to make any sense. I'll etch out a sentence, or a few restless words, and I'll read them over again and there's no meaning there. Or maybe it's too much to explain. Too strange and far-fetched, too hysterical. Or maybe it—all of it, the whole story, the tale of my existence here at Maitland—maybe it's just crazy. I'm crazy. That knock on my head alongside the midnight ocean, it scrambled my brains.

I only have three aspirin left in the bottle. I'm hoarding them carefully, so they don't run out too soon, leaving me with nothing to soften my state of misery. I can be terribly disciplined, when I must. Have been taking only one each day for the past week. At night, always. I can get through the day without an aspirin if I must, but I can't face the black night in this state. Agitated and nauseous, sick and confused and sleepless. Sweating through my nightgown. No, at least this way I can look forward to my nightly dose of relief. I can count down the hours and the minutes until the peace descends, brief and precious, and my brain unravels like a spool of tight-wound thread released from its spring. *That,* of course, is the moment when I should pick up a pen and write a note to my sister, but I can't. I don't have the will. I just want to lie in my white-clad bed and watch the drift of the curtains in the moonlight. The slow, silver silence of the room around me.

And then I awaken. Agitated and sick. And I think, *Something's wrong.* Something is certainly wrong. I need to do something. I need to let Sophie know. I need to tell Miss Bertram that I'm running out of aspirin.

That's what I tell myself, anyway, even though I do understand that more aspirin won't help. Because the aspirin isn't really aspirin, don't you know.

BUT I HAVE TO DO something. The moon is waning again, and soon it will disappear altogether for a few pregnant black nights. And this is terribly important, this moonlessness, though I can't quite remember why. Life and death.

I finish the letter to Sophie. I address the envelope in a handwriting not my own, to the house on East Thirty-Second Street that I scarcely now remember. But whom shall I trust to post it? Miss Bertram, of course. Miss Bertram will mail this letter for me. In the morning I will place this envelope on my breakfast tray and Miss Bertram will carry it downstairs to be stamped and mailed.

The letter has taken all day. My hand is tired, you understand, and I'm interrupted constantly. Miss Bertram and the maid who comes to clean the room at ten thirty every morning, Evelyn and the doctors. I had to hide the drafts under the mattress whenever a knock sounded on the door. Pages and pages. I'm burning them all now, in the flame of the kerosene lamp on the chest of drawers, while my legs tremble under the strain of my weight. The black scratches disappear into the maw of the fire, and the paper curls and fries and crumbles into ash. The reek scorches the lining of my nose. I turn to the vase instead, the nearby vase of fresh orange blossom, and my God, for an instant it's like I'm all better, it's like the nightmare has dissolved, it's like I'm twenty-one years old and newly married, and a damp London spring blooms around me.

And then a brilliant agony sweeps up the nerves of my arm, and I realize my fingers are burning.

I stumble back and drop the burning papers onto the floor, atop the fine pale rug, and the rug smokes and the air turns acrid. I seize the vase and toss the water and the flowers onto the pile of fire. Well, that's what I mean to do. But my arms are weak, you see, and my muscles don't obey my commands as precisely as they used to, and as I sweep the vase sideways and jerk the water free, the delicate crystal bowl strikes the corner of the chest of drawers.

All of which occurs in the space of an instant or two, and yet as I experience this series of small disasters, the pulse of time slows to an almost unsurvivable tempo, like the thud of your heartbeat in the moments after sexual intercourse. I watch my own actions as if I've flown straight out of my body: the spasm of my fingers, the fall of the paper, the burst of flame, the fatal trajectory of my arm. The extraordinary shattering of the vase, like the burst of an explosive artillery shell upon contact with the earth. The clutch of my hand, trying to retrieve the fragments from the air—to reverse this terrible destruction—and the way one inevitable shard slices straight across my right palm.

I watch the blood bubble up from my skin, first in drops and then in a passionate dribble, tumbling over the ridge of my thumb and onto the rug. The stains are bright and red, next to the burning paper, nearly extinguished, and the strewn flowers. A few dark spots pop out into the air before me, like the reverse of stars, and I drop to my knees, cradling my hand, unable to speak, transfixed by the flow of blood and by the strange pattern it makes among the orange blossoms.

I think not of my own wound, or of the pain in my burned fingers and my scored palm, but of the bottle of aspirin waiting for me in the medicine cabinet, and how I will now miss my evening dose, because I cannot possibly rise from this floor again. I am too sick. I have lost too much blood. I am just plain drained.

CHAPTER 19

France, August 1918

ONE TIME, WHEN I was about twelve, I got lost. Only for an hour or two, but it was January and quite dark by the time I found my way home, and my father was frantic, though not for the reasons you'd think.

The whole incident should never have occurred, as he reminded me often in the days following. My father had strict rules about our travels: I was never to go beyond the limits of our single square block without him, and Sophie was never to leave the house alone at all, and if I had stayed within those limits, I would never have lost myself.

But I was twelve, you see, and I was beginning to experience stirrings of rebellion. I thought my father was absurdly overcautious; I thought he didn't understand how capable I'd grown. I was angry at him, too, for reasons I didn't want to examine. So one day, when he was busy in his workshop down the street, and Sophie played downstairs with the nice Irish lady who rented our basement apartment, I slipped outside and took the sharp January air into my lungs and set off for a little walk. Just to show that I could.

I headed west, toward the bustle of Fifth Avenue, and when I reached Fifth I hesitated and turned south. I thought I'd go as far as Madison Square, maybe, and see the famous Madison Square Garden tower, where Thaw murdered Stanford White. And when I reached Madison Square and admired the tower, I thought I might just go down Broadway and see a few of the great dry goods emporia—Lord & Taylor or Wanamaker, which Father would never dream of entering—and I became so enthralled by the shop windows and the lighted displays and the sheer illuminated thrill of Manhattan that I kept on going and going, imagining I could just walk right back up Broadway again, or head east and take the Second Avenue El uptown, and then I realized I wasn't on Broadway at all, and that the streets were no longer numbered, and instead of lying flat in an orderly, easily understood grid, they sprawled in every possible direction, intersecting at odd angles, creating triangular patches of contested pavement, overrun by horses and delivery trucks and streetcars and people in strange, worn clothes chattering in every possible language under heaven. I was lost.

Now, any sensible New York City parent would teach his child, if she somehow lost her way amid the hustle-bustle of downtown Manhattan, to find the nearest policeman and ask for help. In our house, things were different. I was never, under any condition, to approach a policeman. A drunk on the corner was preferable to a policeman. I was to avoid speaking to policemen as if they carried an especially virulent strain of typhoid, transmitted by words. If a policeman happened to catch my gaze as I walked along the street, I was to smile absently and turn my face in fascination to the nearest shop window, even if that shop was a morgue.

And a number of blue-suited members of the Metropolitan Police swiveled their heads and narrowed their eyes at the sight of me, neat and clean and young in my blue wool coat and hat and muffler, my sturdy leather shoes, all worn and plain but well made. I hurried along as if I knew exactly where I was going—you must always assume an air of confidence as you navigate your path through New York City, whatever the neighborhood and whatever your age—and thought, I'll just keep going until I spot something familiar, a landmark, City Hall or the Brooklyn Bridge, and then I'll know exactly where to go.

And then I plowed directly into the chest of a cop.

He was terribly nice, pepper-haired and blue-eyed. He told me, as he escorted me personally back to my home on Thirty-Second Street, boarding the Second Avenue El at the Canal Street station (*How had I missed it?* I thought in agony) and getting off at Thirty-Fourth Street, that he had five girls of his own, and he didn't want to think what might have happened if I'd rounded the wrong corner and ended up on, say, Delancey Street. Next time, as soon as I lost my way, I should head directly to the nearest policeman and ask for help. Would I promise him that? (We were now walking west on Thirty-Second Street, my house only a half-block away.)

I promised him.

You can imagine my father's expression when he opened the door and saw the two of us, Virginia and the policeman. The look of unfiltered terror, which Officer Shea innocently interpreted as a parent's natural fright.

Father disguised it quickly, of course, and the policeman went away amid a torrent of thanks. Only when the door was closed at last did Father's horror find its true node. How much had I told the policeman? What name had I given him? Where had he found me, and did I mention how long we had lived in the city? Did I even realize what I'd done? The danger to which I'd exposed us all?

I think I managed to answer all his questions without breaking down, but the shame hung over my head for a week. The lesson sank through the pores of my skin and into my bones. Say as little as possible about yourself. Don't attract attention. Follow the rules. Be self-sufficient. Never, ever ask for help.

But I think Father learned something, too, about the possible effects of keeping your daughters under lock and key, without the chance to stretch their legs. Because the morning after my little adventure, next to my plate at the breakfast table appeared a folded paper, which—unfurled—turned out to be a detailed map of Manhattan Island.

ALL OF WHICH, MAYBE, IS apropos of nothing, but I found myself thinking about that awful January afternoon as I drove Hunka Tin—a new Hunka Tin, belonging to the American Army Ambulance Service, but almost exactly the same as the old one, so that I nearly forgot they were two different vehicles—along the road toward the field hospital at Epieds, where the advancing Fourth Division had been sending back a stream of casualties since the end of July.

The night before, Major Fitzwilliam hadn't asked me anything more about my father and his extraordinary new fortune. I guessed he was too astonished, or maybe that kind of financial interrogation just wasn't the done thing between ladies and gentlemen. (Not that social custom likely carried much weight with Samuel Fitzwilliam.) Or maybe it didn't matter. Money was money, and the means of acquiring it—like children—should be rarely seen and never heard.

Still. Those silly, awful words kept on repeating in my head, in time with the whining rotation of Hunka Tin's engine. *My father's a millionaire.*

The news had come from Sophie. Of course. A letter arrived soon after I reported for duty at the new American base hospital in Rouen. I remember how the sun lay high and hot in the pale August sky, and the few men— training accidents, mostly—were drunk and cheerful. They hadn't seen battle yet. I dropped into my chair in the mess and caressed the envelope. Sophie wrote several times a week, but the letters tended to come in bursts because of the shipping, or not to come at all. Sometimes I had to piece the information together and guess at what was missing. I'd asked her to number the letters, so at least I knew what I didn't know, but she rarely re- membered, or else muddled the numbers because she had forgotten where she was. You would think, with her mechanical aptitude, she would be more methodical. But she wasn't methodical, not unless she had a machine to focus her mind.

I didn't mind. The rush of pleasurable relief engulfed me so entirely, I was only happy to know she was alive. That a letter existed, and so did Sophie. There was only one envelope this time, so I took my time opening it. The windows stood open, allowing a warm draft to shiver the paper, which I held to my nose—as always—in hope of catching some scent of home. Sometimes I thought I found it: the faint smoke of the parlor fire, the honeysuckle of Sophie's soap. And then it was gone, and I figured the sensation was just my imagination: the smell of hope.

Darlingest Virgo . . .

She always started off that way. We were everything to each other, after all.

> *It's been a few days since I last wrote, and I'm sorry for that, but Brigid left* *us on Wednesday without any notice at all* [naturally, Sophie didn't specify which Wednesday, and she'd neglected to put either the date or the number at the top of the page] *so I've had to do all the cooking and cleaning besides my* *schoolwork. I made a horrible mess of a chicken pie last night—lost track of time,* *as usual, and the crust nearly broke poor Father's teeth—but I guess today's* *soup isn't so bad. The agency is sending over a new one tomorrow. A cookmaid,* *I mean, not a soup!*

So it went. It was morning, and I was about to eat my breakfast, one hand gripping my fork and one hand gripping my letter. There was no more well-stocked sideboard here, no fresh cheese and fresh bread and tender new carrots from the garden Mrs. DeForest had decreed at the château last April. Just canned meat and a sticky, unsweetened porridge. The other nurses had already eaten, and there wasn't much left.

I set the fork on my plate and turned the page over.

> *But that's not the most exciting news, oh no! I've saved that for last. Brace* *yourself, my dearest one! Would you believe that we got a letter yesterday, and* *the Prudent Manufacturing Company wants to license Father's patent for the* *pneumatic oxifying drill for its new factory? They're offering him a dizzying* *amount of money so he won't go to a competitor first. He won't say how much,* *but I can tell it's heaps and heaps, because he's going about the house whistling.*

Whistling, Virgo! I know you'd disapprove if you were here, but I can't help smiling. Who knew Father could whistle?

Now, you must understand something. Since our arrival in New York, after Mama died, we had been poor. Well, maybe *poor* wasn't quite the right word. We'd been getting by, mostly on the money and the jewelry that Father managed to bring with him, and the income from renting out the basement apartment. But prosperity? I could hardly, in that summer of 1917, remember what prosperity was like—what it meant to live in a spacious house, smelling of lumber and fresh air and flowers, and watch the lugubrious sea twitch beyond your window. To have lots of pretty dresses to wear, and luxurious lunches you couldn't possibly finish. Horses to ride, and tennis racquets, and hazy afternoons at the club. Sailing on your own boat. Opulent picnics on a lawn of green velvet.

But there's so much difference between prosperity and getting by. We had a cheap cookmaid, it's true, and Father always managed to scrape together the tuition for the Kingston Girls Academy each year. So we weren't dead broke. And yet, when I thought of money, there came this idea of finitude. There was only so much money, in a small imaginary pot you couldn't refill. At the bottom of that pot lay poverty. Lay starvation and misery and humiliation.

So at first I couldn't quite fathom the notion of such a great quantity of money—so great, it encouraged Father to whistle—and I set the letter aside. I thought Sophie had been mistaken, or had taken a few facts and daydreamed them into a fortune. But as the weeks and months passed, it became clear that, if anything, Sophie had underestimated the scale of Father's success. That small imaginary pot of money had grown to a colossal dimension, an infinite dimension. The strangest twist of fate. *My father's a millionaire.*

Only four words. Nothing at all, really, compared with the terrifying scope of what I had revealed to Simon, by the side of the Grand Canal in the gardens of Versailles. Since then, I had taken such care. I hadn't said any more about the murder or the circumstances of our life in New York—not because I didn't trust Simon to keep my secrets but because I couldn't bear the sight of his face when he learned them. The possibility of his doubt, the idea that he might not share my faith in my father. And who would want a woman whose father might be a murderer?

So I had answered his gentle questions in the way I had been trained— revealing things without really revealing anything. A few small, unimportant details to make him think he understood. Anyway, we didn't leave much time for talking, did we? On the four occasions we had managed to meet since last August, we wanted only to make love and to sleep—that peculiar, enchanted depth of sleep that comes only after intense physical release—and that was all. We were so exhausted, you see. The war was extracting everything out of us. We had nothing left to give each other, except a peculiar carnal comfort, and silence, and slumber. Precious gifts we could obtain nowhere else.

We wrote, of course. We wrote as often as we could, but the wonderful thing about letters was that you could choose the subject. You could conveniently forget to answer any questions from his letter, or choose your answer carefully, or write in such haste—*We are moving again; I can hear the German shells beating closer*—that you couldn't write everything.

Until yesterday, then, I thought I was cured, that I had cured myself of this stupid tendency to lay myself bare. To confess such secrets as I could never, ever reveal. I thought I had regained control of my lips.

My father's a millionaire. Why?

My God, it was a sultry day. August in France. The heat was immense, the air full of dust and exhaust and misery, the hot blue sky meeting the ruined, busy earth. I couldn't hear the distant war boom above the noise of the road, but as I drove, I felt the familiar shock of artillery striking the earth, vibrating the tires and the metal frame, traveling through the steering column and into my fingers. The sensation of battle. The armies were moving now, moving at last out of their trenches and into the shattered woods and the open ground, first the Germans pushing us back through the spring and early summer, and now us returning the favor at last. Fresh American boys in their millions feeding the tide. I squinted at the road ahead, dust-white and rimmed by the splintered remains of the linden trees that had once shaded travelers. It doesn't matter, I told myself; nothing else matters compared with this.

But it did.

Don't tell anyone, Sophie had begged, in her most recent letter, almost as if Sophie knew that her sister had someone to tell. *Father says it's supposed to be kept secret.* But the pneumatic oxifying drill—whatever it was—had proven a smashing success, a complete revolution in a certain specialized section of mechanical design, and some cunning lawyer had made certain that he didn't sell the patent outright but instead negotiated a series of licensing contracts to several manufacturers: licenses that had already banked a million and a half dollars, with more to come, on and on into the future. (Sophie had only learned this by inadvertently opening a gleeful letter from the lawyer in question, which she thought was a bill from the butcher, since they shared the same last name.) *Don't tell anyone*, Sophie had begged, and I had gone and done just that, in a fit of—what? Jealous pique? Wanting to stick it in Samuel's eye. Wanting to prove myself better, somehow, than Lydia Fitzwilliam, than Simon's wife, as if money actually made you better than your fellow man. As if the fact of my father's strange new riches made any difference at all. As if Simon would care how much money I had.

Because of course Samuel had lied to me. For one thing, I knew Simon had begun the divorce proceedings—he had told me all about the sordid arrangements for the woman in the hotel, and the private detective—and the meeting with his lawyer. The outrage of all four parents at Simon's apparent perfidy: *I found myself almost overcome with a desire to laugh, when I was called on the carpet to explain my appalling behavior. Didn't I know such things were to be kept discreet?*

For another thing, I knew Simon. His tender concern for my welfare, his anxiety that I might be engaging in something I really didn't want. *You don't have to meet me like this, Virginia. We can make everything proper. We can wait until the divorce comes through, and get married.*

And of course I had told him that he was ridiculous, that I had no need or desire for marriage, that I was perfectly satisfied with our relations as they stood. That was what I said out loud. What I thought was this: *I can't go on without the hope of seeing you again in a few weeks, a few months: this reassuring contact, this wordless expression of devotion, this intimate physical connection between two human beings that keeps the dread from my window. I cannot stop and say, let us be married before we come together again. Don't make me stop. Don't make me give everything up.*

And in between those few precious rendezvous, when I woke alone in my cot in the nurses' hut, I had poured my soul into the war. I had taken on extra shifts, I had volunteered for every special duty, I had filled every possible moment with work. My zeal had won special commendations from the head of the service, who was astonished by what he called my inhuman devotion.

But that was the easy part. Devotion was easy. Self-control I had in spades. So I couldn't understand what had possessed me in that café, when the bitter lies of Samuel Fitzwilliam made no difference to my future. I had actually *bragged*—that was human, perhaps. But what was worse, what was unforgivable, was that I'd exposed such a vital secret about myself. About my father, about my family. Worst of all: to a stranger, a venal man who couldn't possibly be trusted. *Why?* What was *wrong* with me?

Either Simon's lying to you, or I am.

And then: *Why would I lie?* Why, indeed.

Was that it, then? Had Major Fitzwilliam actually wedged some kind of chisel into my outrage, producing a crack of doubt?

I remembered my father's stricken face as he opened his front door to discover his missing daughter on the stoop, in the company of a grim-browed officer of the New York Metropolitan Police. Before me the road curved ahead, hot and shimmering in the August sun, choked with dust from a train of supply trucks up ahead. I eased back the throttle to give myself a little more room, because the German bombers were getting desperate now, trying anything, dropping ordnance in full daylight on the Allied supply lines.

Why? Why had I done it? Exposed myself like that. Pulled apart my ribs and shown this man, this stranger in his uniform, the heart that beat inside. Given him a piece of precious, vital information, a club that he could wield, if he really wanted revenge against Simon.

You're better off without us. Was that the nature of Samuel's revenge? A love for a love? Steal my lover, and I will drive away yours.

My chest shook as I gripped the wheel. The dust cleared, but my eyes remained clouded and wobbly, and I realized that they were wet. I reached up to brush the corner of my eye, and at that instant a light exploded before me, like the flashbulb of a newsman's camera, and I'm afraid I really don't remember anything more.

June 28, 1920

Darling V,

Here's something that may shock you: my brother Samuel has arrived from England, dead broke and desperate, and I've given him a _job_. I hope you don't mind, although I suppose there's no reason you should, other than the fact that you never had a high opinion of him exactly. But there wasn't much left after my parents died, you see; nearly everything was sold off to pay the debts and the death taxes—including, as you know, the poor old house itself—and he and my sister have run out of what little remained. He has resigned his commission, and there are no honest jobs to be had at the moment, with so many soldiers out of work. So he's come here—buried his pride, you might say, as a last resort—and I suppose I haven't the heart to refuse my own brother.

Not that I have much to give him, at present. I have taken out a massive mortgage on the property in order to fund the building of the new steamships—nearly complete—and the repair of the orchards and the house. But the fact is, I could use the help of someone whom I—well, if not trust utterly, at least understand. Left to myself, you know, I should much rather spend my time mucking about on the plantation, while Samuel is, by nature, better suited to the civilized warfare of the business interests in Cocoa. And since I can't be in two places at once, I imagine this arrangement will make the best of both of us: he managing the day-to-day affairs of the hotel and the shipping company, I turning my orchards into a thriving vale once more, and neither of us having to do more than is absolutely necessary with the other.

Well, I shan't bore you with any more business details. I daresay that's the last thing you're interested in. In any case, there's a luminous, golden-pink dawn dreaming outside my bedroom window, and the haze is rising slowly above the blossoming trees, and I would really rather slumber on and think of _you_ than do anything else at all.

But that would accomplish nothing, would it? So instead I shall finish this letter, rise from the armchair, and don my trousers and work boots. I shall head out into that fragrant dawn and see to my trees and garden, and when I return I shall bunker down in my study and attend to business over a pot of fresh coffee.

Try to make these sums in my account books stretch out a little longer. Just a bit longer, and then in another year, God willing, I can approach my wife, hat in hand, heart in throat, and explain everything. Ask her to join me in this new home I am building around me.

Until then, I remain your <u>own</u>

S.F.

CHAPTER 20

Maitland Plantation, Florida, July 1922

SOMETIME IN THE night, I open my eyes to the strange perspective of the bedroom floor, illuminated rather luridly by the glow of the kerosene lamp above my head. I suppose I've fallen asleep, though I can't imagine how. My cheek sticks to the fibers of the rug. My hand throbs. Damned scorching thirst fills my throat. And my head! My God, how it hurts. Not a headache as you ordinarily experience them, but a kind of unbearable, itching, spider-crawling pressure, as if my brain is going to burst from my skull.

I must have aspirin.

There's no question of standing, let alone walking. As I detach my face from the rug and place my left palm against the floor to hoist my torso a few inches upward, into a world that swings violently back and forth, I think I've never tried so hard to accomplish anything else in my life. Even giving birth to Evelyn, for which at least God and nature granted me a certain reservoir of strength. Here, I have nothing. I have only will. Just *need*.

Because of the injury to my hand, I crawl across the floor on my knees and my elbows. I cross the edge of the rug, and now the bare wooden floorboards grind against my bones. Why is the bedroom so large? It's like scaling a continent. I pass the open French window, and a draft of damp air engulfs me, cooler than you might expect on a July night in Florida. I think—trying to distract myself—maybe it's another thunderstorm, about to pull across the night sky, and just as this thought takes its fuzzy shape in my mind, a distant groan troubles the atmosphere. I would say ominous, but the thunderstorms come so regularly here, drenching us daily, rattling the roof tiles and coursing down the drainpipes, bathing the orchards and the turf until the sun bursts out again and all that water turns to steam—as I say, the thunderstorms are such frequent visitors, they're like old friends. Not ominous at all. I imagine, as I reach the threshold of the bathroom, how lovely it would feel to dance in the rain at midnight.

The mere act of dragging myself across the bedroom floor seems—paradoxically, maybe—to have restored a little life to my limbs. I gaze up at the elegant basin, and the medicine cabinet above it, and I might just manage it. If I brace my good left hand on the marble and gather my feet underneath me. If I use my legs to lever myself upward, and my arm for balance, and I set my teeth against the myriad agonies blooming inside me. Outside the bathroom window, the thunder rumbles again, imminent now.

I have always considered myself a woman of tidy habits. Everything in its place, you know, and even though I never flinched at the prospect of those muddy battlefields, I always cleaned myself afterward, to a meticulous standard, before I allowed myself to collapse in bed. I don't know why. I wasn't an especially tidy child. I had such a multitude of toys when I was young, so many dresses and hair ribbons and God knows what else, I could strew them around me and not care what became of any particular item. And then we moved to New York, and my earthly possessions could—and did—fit into a single satchel, and suddenly the disposition of those possessions actually mattered. The orderly arrangement of my hair mattered. The clean symmetry of my face and hands mattered. A speck of dirt on the hem of my dress became a subject of immediate anxiety. A scuff on my shoe sent me into a panic.

And now. Just look at me in the mirror.

My face, smeared with blood. My nightgown, stained. My right hand crusted and clotted and swollen. My hair matted and limp. Wan, hollow-eyed, dull, blurry. I turn on the tap. Hot and cold running water, terribly luxurious. I must clean myself, of course. Clean up this terrible mess I've made of myself.

But first. Aspirin.

Tap off.

The fingers of my right hand have lost all strength. Shaking and vulnerable. A kind of panic fills me as I fumble and fumble with the bottle, and then I turn it into my left hand and use my teeth to screw open the lid and it pops off, satisfying sound, and I pour one tablet—just one!—onto the marble edge of the basin, and my fingers are shaking so hard, my muscles are trembling so violently, that when I try to grasp that darling, delicious tablet it careens down the side of the basin and disappears into the drain.

(A brief double flash outside the window. A quiet crash of thunder deepens into a rumble.)

Calm down now. (The breath saws along my throat.) Calm down. Close your eyes. You can do this.

I can do this.

All I need is an aspirin. Just one little aspirin and I can clean my face and hands and change my nightgown, I can find that perfect tranquillity of mind and become myself again. Virginia. Whoever that is. Clear everything away.

Open your eyes. Take the bottle in your left hand—the left, now!—and tilt it carefully, carefully, to the marble. There are two tablets left. Wait until the first one slides to the edge of the rim. Now tap. Once. There it comes. Atta girl.

Now, try this instead. Wet your forefinger and just press it into the tablet. Gently, now. Just until it sticks. That's the way. Now lift your finger, nice and slow, holding your wrist so the poor thing doesn't shake quite so much. Except your right hand is making it shake even more! So drop the right hand. Bring your mouth to your forefinger. Open your lips.

It's not there.

Eyes open. Look down. Tablet sticking to the curve of the basin. Scramble, scramble. The tablet tips off the edge of the finger, rolls like an unattended tire right down under the edge of the drain.

Angry now. Angry! Goddamn fingers, goddamn aspirin! Take the bottle and shake it and it's EMPTY! EMPTY! But there were two tablets left, you were sure of that! TWO! Where's the other one? WHERE? You shake again and tilt the bottle to your lips, because maybe it's stuck, but there's nothing there, nothing, and you throw the bottle on the floor— SHATTER!—and dig your fingers around the drain, DIG DIG DIG, gore melting from your skin and staining the porcelain, DIG! fingers scraping on the pipe, and you lift out a dirty, hairy white tablet—TWO dirty, hairy white tablets, stuck together!—and SHOVE them both into your mouth just as the thunder goes CRASH outside your window, and the bedroom door goes CRASH against the wall, and you crumple gratefully to the bathroom tiles and dimly, dimly, hear a familiar, anguished voice calling your name.

HE WANTS TO KNOW WHERE Clara is. I say I don't know. I thought she was in Miami Beach. That's what she said, that she was going to Miami Beach. She took the Packard and just *left*. He runs the washcloth over my face and arms, and I let him. Feels so good and warm, scented with soap. He swears and asks me how I cut my hand. I tell him it was the flowers, and I point through the doorway into the bedroom, and he follows the direction of my finger, I guess, because then he swears again and says that cut is going to have to be stitched up.

Okeydokey, I say.

He tells me to open my eyes. I open my eyes.

He swears a third time and asks me what I've been taking, what they're giving me here.

Aspirin, I say. I point to the bottle on the floor.

He takes me by the shoulders. "Where the hell is Clara? Tell me!"

"Miami Beach. She said she was going to Miami Beach."

"When?"

I close my eyes again. "Maybe a month ago. The day after we arrived here. She got a telegram."

"What telegram?"

"I don't know. She left a note."

"Where? Where is the note?"

I point again. "Top drawer."

He drags me along the floor and props me up against the bathtub and runs to the chest of drawers, and do you know something? I don't mind a bit. Really.

Tranquillity.

HE'S CARRYING ME OUT OF the house in his big, strong arms, and I still don't mind. Not. A bit. Someone is arguing with him. Miss Bertram, I think. Oh, she's furious! My, my. I raise my head and tell her it's all right, he's not going to hurt me.

Miss Bertram shouts. "What have you done to her?"

"What have *I* done to her? I found her like this! On the bathroom floor!"

"Take her back to the bedroom! I'm going to call the doctor."

"The hell with your doctors. She's coming with me."

I raise my head again. "Evelyn!"

He shouts to Miss Bertram. "Bring the girl!"

"Oh, no, you don't! That little girl is staying right here."

(Menacing.) "I said, *bring the girl*. Or I'll fetch her myself."

"You will not!"

He doesn't answer. He just swings me around and marches out the door and into the warm, wet night, and he deposits me into a car of some kind, smelling of leather and oil and rain. Don't move, he tells me.

As if I could.

He leaves, and I hear them shouting, Miss Bertram demanding and remonstrating, and I just close my eyes and let them shout. This seat is so comfortable. I'm fresh and clean, all washed up, dressed in a crisp new nightgown and a dressing gown, my hair pulled back, my right hand wrapped in a thick white bandage. The leather is soft and beaten smooth beneath my cheek. I allow my hand to fall *kerplop* to the floorboards.

Tranquillity.

I WAKE UP RETCHING. THE car skids to a stop. Footsteps crunch. Door opens. He pulls me out of the seat and holds back my hair while I vomit into the grass by the side of the road. Vomit and vomit. Sweating. Spots popping. Slump into his arms.

I whisper. "Evelyn?"

"She's all right. Everything's all right. I'm going to make everything all right, okay?"

Okay, Samuel.

CHAPTER 21

Neuilly, France, September 1918

L ATER—I DON'T REMEMBER when—they told me that I hadn't been hit by a German bomb, as I thought. Hunka Tin's right front tire had exploded, sending me into the hood of an oncoming truck, packed with soldiers coming off the front line.

I asked them, *How does that explain the flash of light?* And they couldn't give me a satisfactory answer. I don't suppose I'll ever really know. They never gave me the name of the other driver, either, who must have seen what happened. It's a terrible thing, believe me, not remembering something so important.

In fact, the gap of memory lasted over a month. I'm told I wavered in and out of a conscious state, but when I search my mind for details—the crash itself, the rescue, the fight to save my life—I can't find anything at all.

One thing only: the profile of a trim, gray-haired man in a British Army uniform, standing by my bed while he spoke, in great animation, with an American doctor whose name I forget.

ON THE LAST DAY OF September, when I could sit up at last without feeling dizzy, Simon Fitzwilliam walked down the long ward and stopped at the end of my bed. It was about four o'clock in the afternoon, and golden light flooded the windows behind him, but I knew it was him.

"Thank God," he said. "You're awake."

"What are you doing here? How did they let you in?"

"I came last month, on a forty-eight-hour pass, when you were first brought in. I don't suppose you remember. You were half-dead. I was never so afraid in my life. You're looking much better."

I didn't answer. I hadn't yet dared to look in a mirror, but I had touched my bandaged face and shorn hair just that morning. I knew that my skin was still bruised, my eyes swollen. "Thank you," I said drily.

"Do you mind?" he said, after a moment. "Do you want me to leave?"

"No, of course not. I'm just—I'm not very good company for you."

"For God's sake. You don't need to say a word. Just be alive, that's all. Be *Virginia*. That's all that matters."

"I think I can manage that."

"Good. Because I had the devil of a time getting more leave. There's a war on, in case you didn't know."

The old charm. It stole over me, like the sunlight behind him, warm and familiar, driving away all the shadows. The doubts that had shrouded me, the words that had drummed and drummed inside my skull as I lay on this bed. And I was too tired to fight. My limbs hurt. I tried to smile. "Is there? I hadn't noticed."

He walked around the corner of the bed toward me, and his face jumped out from shadow, along with his hand, which contained a pair of books. He held them out to me. "For you."

"Thank you."

There was no nightstand, at least for my use. He laid the books on the blanket beside me. "Aren't you curious to see what they are?"

"I haven't been able to read yet. The words keep swimming."

"God, yes. Of course." He sat down respectfully near my left knee. "*A Tale of Two Cities* and *The Story of an African Farm*."

"I haven't read the second one."

"I think you'll like it. It's not very long, however." He took my hand and laid his first two fingers on the inside of my wrist, feeling my pulse. "Hmm."

"Better?"

"Yes, much." He moved his fingers but didn't release the hand. His palm was warm and dry. "It's good to see you, Virginia."

"Is it? I'm not exactly an object of seduction anymore."

"You never were. Why would you say such a thing?"

"I don't know. I don't know anything about you."

He leaned forward. His thumb pressed into my palm. "My God. You know everything about me! What's the matter? What have I done?"

His face, I now saw, was lined with fatigue. His hair had taken on more gray, and his cheeks were thinner, and his tunic hung roomily on his frame. His eyes were unnaturally bright, as if he were existing on nerves alone, and he fixed upon me with desperation.

"Your brother," I whispered. "Your brother came to see me."

His shoulders fell. "Yes. So I thought."

"He told me terrible things. But I didn't believe him. I couldn't believe him—"

"Of course not. Of course you didn't believe him. Because you have faith in me, dearest. You trust me. You *must* trust me."

"I trust you."

"It was a terrible shock when he turned up. A wonderful shock and a terrible one." His hand gripped mine like a manacle. "I won't say more. I don't want to tire you. I'll be off in a moment. But I swear, Virginia—"

"You don't need to swear anything. I could see how bitter he was, how he resented you. How he's resented you all his life. I understood right away."

"But you doubted, just a little."

"Not really. I just—I needed to see you, that's all. To hear the truth from you."

"That I love you. That I cannot imagine my life without you. Don't believe anything else, not for an instant. Do you hear me? Do you *understand* me?"

He spoke, as I did, in a low, husky voice—conscious of the dozen occupied beds on either side of us, the bored ears straining to catch our conversation. A nurse strode by, carrying a tray, and her gaze slid away as I glanced at her.

"Yes," I said.

Simon went on, focusing his words to a tone of such deep privacy that they reminded me, for an instant, of his brother's voice in the café. His other hand touched my cheek.

"You are the only *true* thing in my life, Virginia. The only thing left intact. The only thing that matters anymore. Since the day you drove your damned ambulance through the mud of that courtyard, I have thought of nothing but you. Have *dreamt* of nothing but you. Your skin and your lips, your beautiful eyes. The scent of you. The weight of you, lying in my arms, sleeping in my bed. I have been obsessed with you. Scheming for the next meeting, and the next, scarcely existing in the meantime. When I got word about the accident, I nearly went mad. You can't imagine—but that's enough. Look at you, you're exhausted."

"No! Don't stop. Don't go." I closed my eyes. "I am much better. Much better now."

"Good. You must get better as quickly as possible, do you hear me? I have laid such plans for us, but they all depend on a Virginia who's herself again, all put back together and full of her usual ardor and determination, behind her wonderfully prim façade."

"Plans?" My eyes cracked open again. "What kind of plans?"

"Never worry. I have it all worked out. I've made arrangements for you at a private hospital near London, as soon as you can be safely moved—"

"What?"

"I'm not going to be taking any more chances with you, phantom girl. I know one of the doctors there. You'll be in excellent hands, safe and sound. The war will be over in a matter of months. Did you know that? The Germans are back on their heels. They can't last much longer, not while you Americans flood in endlessly. And then there will be nothing left to stand in our way. This entire nightmare will be over at last. We shall be man and wife by springtime."

"Man and wife!"

"Yes. I won't take your objections any longer. I have discovered, in the past month, an absolutely invincible need to marry you. What do you say?"

My lips moved, but nothing came out. I must have looked astonished, or frightened, because Simon leaned forward and spoke in his doctor's voice, terribly soothing.

"We *must* be married, dearest. This scare you've put into me, it's brought me to my senses. For practical reasons, if nothing else. Just think if anything should happen to one of us. If you should have a child."

I tried to remember all my earlier objections. I tried to conjure the sensation of dread, the picture of my mother, but the image was too blurred, a relic of a distant childhood, and anyway Simon's face was too near. His words were too comforting. I sat there on my bed, seeking the well of my resistance, and I couldn't find it. As his hand massaged the bones of my fingers, I lost the will even to search.

"Virginia, please. Whatever your fears, I promise you I'll extinguish them. I shall never intrude on that marvelous independence of yours. I shall guard you and serve you and strive for your happiness every moment of my life. But I want you as my wife. I need you to marry me. Before God and the law."

"But what about Lydia? Your brother?"

"Everything will be settled soon, I promise. The way will be clear. I'll sort it all out; you're not to worry about a thing. Just promise me you'll be mine. No. No, that's not it. It's the other way around. You must promise *me*, my dear phantom girl, you'll do me the very great honor of allowing *me* to become *yours*. To show you what marriage can be, with the right person." He smiled. "With *me*."

SOMETIMES, IN QUIET MOMENTS, AS I lie in my bed and count the strokes until midnight, I wonder how different a course my life would have taken if I had withdrawn my hand in that moment and said *no*. If I had refused him then, if I had remained firm in my refusal ever to marry. My refusal to take on the trappings of ordinary domestic life, like the other girls. Like my mother did, until she was murdered.

But I know this exercise is pointless. Because how could I have refused him? Lying there as I did, on my hospital bed, bandaged and helpless, while he pressed my hand reverently and begged me to marry him. This man who had restored the promise of dawn to my life. This man who, in my blackest hour, injured nearly beyond repair, had not abandoned me but had instead brought me back to life. How could I not trust him?

Though my memory of those weeks inside the American Hospital in Neuilly remains dim and indistinct, even to this day, I do remember how this most seductive thought began to unfurl inside my brain at that moment, as Simon spoke. How a heady sensation overtook me, as if I'd been looking at a painting upside down all this time, and now, as if by enchantment, it turned right side up. And the revelation was more beautiful than I could have dreamed, if I had ever known how to dream such things.

I thought—yes, my God, I actually thought this—*I will be safe now.*

"Yes," I said.

His eyes widened. "I beg your pardon?"

"Yes. Yes, I'll marry you."

"My God." He kissed my hand. Wrapped it up between his two palms. "Splendid. My God. Say it again."

"Yes!" I tried to laugh, but my ribs hurt and it ended in a wince.

"Careful!"

"Yes. I will marry you, Simon Fitzwilliam, you dear and foolish man. I can't imagine why you're asking. But if you're so stupid as to want to marry me—"

"Only if *you* want to, Virginia. Only if you're as stupid as I am, as splendidly and marvelously stupid—"

"I am! I—oh."

He shook his finger. "No more of that laughing, Miss Fortescue. I won't have you setting yourself back."

"Yes, sir. No more laughing."

"You have only to think about getting better, about healing this precious body of yours. Your head and your ribs. This left arm I saved personally from amputation at the hands of that damned pompous surgeon. That's all you need to concern yourself with, at present, until it's time to find your wedding dress and choose a bridesmaid. You're to leave everything to me and take care of *yourself,* for once. Your own dear self."

He kissed my hand—the right one, not the left, which was still stiff in its massive plaster cast—once on each knuckle, and then he turned my fingers over and kissed my palm. His short hair bristled from his scalp. When he was finished, he lifted his head, laid my hand against his cheek, and said, "You are to have *faith* in me, is that clear? *Mrs. Fitzwilliam.*"

I remember how I smiled at his earnest expression. The warm echo of his words. The sunshine of his voice, burning away the last of my doubt.

I remember how I touched his upper lip with my thumb and replied, "Perfectly clear."

November 28, 1921

Darling V,

I do wonder sometimes if you shall ever read these letters. Whether I've been foolish to keep them back from their envelopes: foolish and rather vainly hopeful that you might, one day, find the courage or the forgiveness or the simple curiosity to seek them out. But I well remember how you treated my letters once, when you thought me guilty of another crime, and if there's any chance at all that I might, by this method, preserve a record of my true thoughts for you . . . well, I suppose I have always known my chances were long, where you were concerned. That I was risking my all for a reward too bright even to contemplate.

Or maybe it doesn't matter. Maybe the act of writing is enough. I don't know. I do know that it helps me, somehow. When the day is long & weary, and everything seems to be falling apart—as if you're replacing a book on a bookshelf, & another one tumbles to the ground just as soon as you've fixed the first one, and then you put that one back and another one crashes down—when, as I say, life seems impossible & insupportable, I find comfort in scribbling these lines to you. Whether or not you see them. Whether or not you read them. Almost—but not quite—whether or not you care.

But you must care, mustn't you? If you didn't care, I should have been served divorce papers by now. Each day, you see, I tremble when the post arrives, just in case there should be some dreadful legal-looking envelope from some sort of New York firm, informing me that my wife no longer wishes to be my wife.

And each day, I am reprieved, & believe me, my darling, I am fully grateful for this reprieve. You can't imagine. Today, for example, I have been up to my ears in the accounts, instead of tramping about my orchards as I prefer. The reason? I am contemplating a change in business strategy. The trees returned a decent harvest last winter; the ships are running out full and returning—well, let us say they are returning with some valuable cargo indeed, cargo that I believed would set us up beautifully for the coming year, enough to get ahead at last. But while revenues are tumbling like—well, like ripe fruit, if you don't mind the phrase, ripe fruit into our waiting coffers, they are going out again in the same abundant manner. This valuable cargo of ours has attracted so many strings, so many distasteful connections, so many unsavory characters, I am determined to wash my hands of it and return to what I do best. The long, slow journey, instead of the quicker one. As I said, I don't mean to be tedious, and I expect the less you know about all this, the better.

I wonder if I can live up to him. Your father, I mean. Whether, in all my striving, I can ever give you anything like the comfort & luxury he has provided. I admit I am jealous of him. Jealous of his riches & the genius that made him rich. It seems that however I try, however abundantly I call my orchards to give forth their fruit, it's never enough. The growing of fruit, I suppose, is a far more commonplace genius than the invention of industrial gadgets.

On that note, I am off to do what my meager talents allow. Coax my trees unto fruitfulness.

Ever your own,

S.F.

CHAPTER 22

London, March 1919

B Y THE TIME I married Simon Fitzwilliam, on the last day of the following March, at ten o'clock in the morning, my bones had knit and my eyes no longer swam when I read. I wore a new suit of pale gray and a matching hat of gray felt, though my shoes were old. For good luck, I told myself.

I wrote my name confidently in the parish register of Saint Mary Abbots, at the bottom of Kensington Church Street, and gave my bouquet of pink hothouse roses to Hazel, who was my bridesmaid. We stepped outside into the watery sunshine. The robins sang from the blossoming trees, and the daffodils thrust up from the earth. Simon stopped me on the church steps and turned me about for a long and somewhat indecent kiss. Everyone applauded. "Mrs. Fitzwilliam at last," he said, when he lifted his face from mine, and he smiled and tucked my arm into his elbow. Hazel, delighted, brought out a Brownie from her pocketbook and took a photograph, which she gave to me later.

We held our wedding breakfast—such as it was—at the Savoy. Corporal Pritchard was there, and Hazel, and a few of Simon's medical corps friends, boisterous and respectful. Of Simon's family there was no sign. Not even an arrangement of congratulatory flowers. Never mind. We went through four bottles of champagne, toast after toast, and when the last man staggered away at half past four, Simon bore me upstairs to a hotel suite bursting with new spring flowers. The sky was still light and blue, but we made love anyway, swift and voracious, for the first time since June, when Europe was still at war.

AFTERWARD, SIMON ROSE TO OPEN another bottle of champagne and light himself a cigarette, while I lay on the bed, too happy to move, and watched him tread naked about the room in an utterly unselfconscious way, attending first to the cigarette and then to the bottle of Pol Roger in its silver bucket. This is marriage, I thought, when you have the right to each other's bare skin and humble errands. I admired the squint of one eye and the patient play of muscle in his forearms as he worked the cork from the stem, while the cigarette dangled from the corner of his mouth. A soft pop, a gentle fizzle of air. He set the fat cork next to the ashtray.

"What an expert," I said.

"Every gentleman should know how to open a champagne bottle properly." He poured a glass for me and then for himself and carried them both to the bed. "To my beautiful new bride."

"To my gallant husband."

"What? Not handsome?"

"Handsome, of course. And charming. Invincibly charming."

"Faithful. Devoted." He kissed my lips. "A trifle zozzled at the moment, I admit, but that's to be expected. I say, is it too soon to make love to you again? I don't believe I'm much use for anything else at the moment."

"I didn't know there were any rules like that about making love. If there are, we've already broken most of them."

Simon glanced at the window. "Twice before sunset might be tempting fate, but then we're married now. Surely the gods will forgive us."

"Yes. After all, we've already done our penance, haven't we? Both of us. We've suffered enough."

He smiled, stubbed out the cigarette, slugged down the champagne, and reached for my hips.

"My thoughts exactly."

I THINK WE BOTH MUST have fallen asleep after that. When I woke up, the sky was dark and a gentle spring rain caressed the window glass. Simon lay on his stomach, one arm flung across my breasts, one leg straddling mine. His sweet, drunken breath dampened the air. The bedside lamp was still on, and I could see the vivid, irregular scars on my left forearm, where both radius and ulna, snapped in two, had torn through my skin seven months earlier. I wriggled my fingers. A miracle, really, that they still existed, that my hand still existed and sprang whole from my wrist. A miracle wrought by the man now sleeping beside me.

My head throbbed a little from all the wedding champagne. My mouth was dry and sticky. Seized by restlessness, I slipped myself out from under my bridegroom and rose from the bed to pour a glass of water.

I drank and poured again and drank. The hotel creaked lazily around me. The clock on the mantel, slender-armed and gilded, claimed five minutes to eleven o'clock. Not so late, then. I emptied the ashtray and turned out the light. Simon didn't stir. For a minute or two—I really can't say how long, only that it seemed like ages—I hung there, like the phantom he called me, until my legs failed and I sat on the edge of the bed and gazed opulently at him, my new husband, murky and shadowed among the tangled bedclothes, only just visible in the midnight glow of the city outside our window. Without quite touching him, I traced the outline of his long, trim limbs, the angle of his shoulder. The line of his jaw, glittering with peppery stubble.

I thought, *I will know him always, he will father my children, we will grow old side by side.* We will make love ten thousand times and plant fifty gardens in the springtime, and when winter comes we will lie together and keep each other warm, until the sunshine returns.

WE SLEPT THROUGH THE NIGHT, and at dawn I woke to Simon's kisses.

I remember how I wrapped my arms around his neck and inhaled the warm, sleepy scent of my husband's skin. I remember thinking *How luxu-*

rious. How luxurious that we could take our time, now that the first urgency was satisfied and a lifetime stretched out before us. We moved from the bed to the armchair to the floor to the wall, enthralled and perspiring, mating in a kind of exotic, primal waltz, and at one point, near the end, while the rain drummed against the window and we drove desperately toward resolution, Simon wrapped his long fingers around my jaw and the back of my head and said, "I am so sick of death. I am so sick of watching men die. I want to make you pregnant this second. I want to deliver our child with my own hands."

So I dug my passionate young heels into the backs of his legs and prayed, too, prayed for a baby with Simon, prayed with all my strength that he would start a baby inside me on this tender April dawn: not because I had ever craved children, or imagined myself as a mother, but because I trusted my husband so profoundly. I believed his words. I believed that Simon, after four years of battling death, needed desperately to create life.

I don't know if God was listening, or whether He still heeded the prayers of mortal men, or whether He gave and withheld His gifts for His own capricious reasons. From what I had seen of the hospitals and battlefields of France, He had probably abandoned humanity altogether.

But you will observe that the following December I gave birth to Evelyn, so I suppose it is quite possible—though by no means certain—that our wish that morning was granted.

LATER THAT DAY, AFTER WE had bathed and had breakfast, we drove down to Cornwall to meet Simon's family.

We hadn't discussed them at all. Every time I'd raised the subject, during Simon's visits to the small hospital in Hampstead, he had laid his finger on my lips and said I wasn't to worry, he would take care of everything, they would accept me and love me once we were married. Once the whole affair was an accomplished fact. Once they knew me.

A week earlier, I had asked about the wedding, and whether any of the Fitzwilliams would attend.

No, he replied, looking away. I'm afraid they're not ready for this. Everything has happened so quickly, and they are terribly old-fashioned.

I took him at his word. Why shouldn't I? At the time I had no reason at all to doubt Simon Fitzwilliam, other than the preposterous accusations of his envious brother. The opposite. I had a hundred reasons to trust him. Hadn't he rushed straight to the private hospital in Hampstead where I had lived since Christmas, immediately after his demobilization in January? And he'd hardly left my bedside since, except to make the necessary arrangements for our future together, the mysterious errands about which he refused to reveal any details. He had been devoted and attentive. He had seen to my every comfort. He took me on long walks to build my strength, he devised exercises for my eyes and my brain and worked me patiently through them, until I could read long chapters and solve puzzles without breaking down in fatigue and frustration. Until the sap began to rise inside me at last, and run in my veins.

"You're back," Simon said a few weeks earlier, as we collapsed laughing against a tree after some shared joke, I forget the subject.

I wasn't altogether back, not quite. I felt sometimes as if I had changed, in some small yet fundamental way. My memory, from time to time, played tricks on me—not forgetting things, exactly, just scenes going in and out of focus, so that I couldn't rely on my own recollection, like I used to, which unsettled me. I thought I had lost some tiny spark of defiance, some fraction of my independent will, when my head shattered Hunka Tin's windshield last August.

But Simon's will had filled the void. He had poured his strength into my broken body and molded me back together, and he had sealed my recomposition yesterday, when he slid a slim gold band over the knuckle of the fourth finger of my left hand and said, in a voice packed tight with sincerity, not missing a single word: *With this ring I thee wed, with my body I thee worship, and with all my worldly goods I thee endow: In the name of the Father, and of the Son, and of the Holy Ghost. Amen.*

How could I possibly question him, after a speech like that?

We drove out of London along the Richmond Road, while the sky drizzled delicately upon the roof of Simon's battered two-seater Wolseley. He had bought it last month from an old Harrow friend of his, an infantry officer who had lost both legs at Passchendaele and no longer needed a motorcar—or at least the kind of motorcar you drove yourself—and the gears ground noisily from disuse. The terraces passed by, gray and wilting, separating eventually into semidetached houses and then to boxy suburban villas. We kept a comfortable silence, shoulder to shoulder, listening to the roar of the motor, and I believe I dozed off once or twice, exhausted by the wedding and everything that followed, by too much champagne and too little sleep. In my haze, I felt the car slow down and turn, and I raised my head to the hoary English sight of a half-timbered public house, dripping rain from the eaves.

"Lunch," said Simon.

THAT NIGHT HE TALKED ABOUT his parents.

"It was a love match, actually. They were most spectacularly in love, or so I'm told. Isn't that strange? One never imagines one's parents in that condition."

"No," I said. "I suppose not."

"Of course, the trouble was, they never really loved anything else half so well as each other. I often thought that there wasn't room for another person between them."

"Not even you and your brother and sister?"

"No. That's the trouble with devotion, you see. They were always off on romantic escapades. They left us with nannies, Samuel and me, when we were three months old. Took off to Borneo for a year, to dive for pearls."

"Dive for *pearls*?"

"Oh, it was good fun, no doubt. Some friend of my father's—it was Lydia's father, in fact—he lured them out with the promise of adventure and riches. You have to learn how to hold your breath properly and that sort of thing, and I doubt there would have been a surfeit of clothing. Terribly improper for my mother, of course, back in those days, though that was part of the allure for her. She was always a bit daring and headstrong. Anyway, it was all marvelously exotic—I've seen the odd photograph— but of course you don't want babies along on that kind of expedition, and once we were out of sight and reach, you see, they more or less forgot our existence. Like a pair of pets left behind. I'm not at all certain they would have come back altogether, if Mummy hadn't gotten pregnant with Clara. I think she was cross about that, actually. Babies were such a nuisance to her. Father was certainly cross. I remember how black-faced he was, when they returned."

Simon lay on his back, smoking, his head propped by a pillow. We had stopped for the night at some sort of seaside village outside of Exeter, dreary with rain, and after a tasteless supper under the surveillance of a lean, red-faced landlady dressed in faded black bombazine from another century, we had raced each other up the stairs to our room in the rafters, dominated by an ancient, creaking bed frame that could have left the poor woman in no doubt of our entertainment. Afterward, Simon had rummaged through the luggage and produced a bottle of brandy—liberated last autumn from an abandoned German staff billet in the Argonne, he told me—which he now drank in small, disciplined sips from a tumbler on the bedside table.

"Did you mind?" I asked.

"I don't remember. I was only a baby. I should add that my grandparents looked after us as well—my father's parents—so it wasn't as if we were surrounded only by professionals. I was awfully cut up when Granny died. She was great fun. Gave us far too many sweets. Then Mummy came home and had Clara, and I don't think they ventured any farther than the Continent after that, at least until I went away to school. But the unavoidable fact is that they were bored by home and hearth, that's all. The inconvenience of children. And Mummy never really liked Cornwall anyway. Too cold and rainy, even in August, and anyway she had loads of blunt in the beginning, she could do what she wanted. A Home Counties heiress. Granddad and

Grandmama thought she was throwing herself away on Father, because we're a third-rate family, really, no title or anything like that. Just a damp pile of stones near the sea. A few neglected acres of citrus in America. Until the money ran out, why, you couldn't keep them there longer than a week."

I turned on my side to face his profile. "It won't be like that for us."

"Won't it? We *are* terribly in love, after all. Just as they were."

"But you're not like that. You're going to be a wonderful father. You were born to give life to others."

He reached for the ashtray. "I hope so."

"You're melancholy again."

"Oh, it will pass, never fear. Where the devil did I leave my cigarettes?" He heaved himself from the bed and found the battered case on the floor next to his discarded shirt.

I sat up and held out my arms. "Come back."

"I told you, it will pass. It's nothing to do with you."

"*Everything* about you has to do with me. Don't you remember? For better or worse. Richer or poorer. So you *have* to tell me what's troubling you."

"There's nothing troubling me." He lit the cigarette and stepped to the window. The London drizzle had turned to a steady rain in Hampshire, and now a gale was picking up, lashing the water against the glass. "By God, it's rotten out there. It had better blow itself out before morning. I don't fancy driving along the cliffs through all that, not in Jock's old Wolseley."

"Simon, you can *tell* me."

"Tell you what?"

I lifted my arms again, spreading them out, palms raised, and for an instant, in my lamblike faith, I might have been Christ on the cross. "Look at me. I'm healed. I'm all better. You don't need to protect me anymore. It's time you tell me what's troubling *you*. To let me share *your* burden. That's what I'm *supposed* to do. I'm your wife now. Richer and poor. Better and worse. Isn't that right?"

He turned: first his head, and then the rest of him, pale and naked in the dim light of the old oil lamp on the bedside table. He was still too thin. Too thin, his hair overtaken by gray, his face strained. How had I not noticed the new lines in his face? His sturdy, perfect bones poked against his skin. His belly was concave, and I could count the muscles of his abdomen, the movement of his ribs as he breathed. As he watched me, as his gaze dropped from my eyes to my breasts to my waist, as the cigarette dangled unloved from his fingers, I thought how I wanted to feed him. To nourish him with my own body, if I had to. The body I offered him now.

"My wife," he said softly.

"Yes. Yours. We're bound together by God. That *means* something, at least to me."

His body roused, but he didn't step forward to claim me. He looked away, at the ceiling and then the window, and then he made for the bottom corner of the bed and sat down, cradling the cigarette between his hands. "I suppose I should tell you. I *have* to tell you, before we reach the house."

"Tell me what?"

"I've been putting it off, like a coward. I knew it would upset you, and I thought—I don't know what I thought. I didn't want to ruin everything. Didn't want anything to cloud yesterday. Our wedding day. I wanted it to be perfect for you. But I suppose it's now or never."

I went on my knees and crawled toward him, laying my cheek on his back. My mouth dried. My blood ran light and cool, anticipating some shock. Some terrible thing. "What's now or never?"

He leaned forward, bracing his forearms on his thighs, nearly dislodging me. I curled my hands on either side of his waist.

"Tell me. I'm strong enough. You've made me strong again. We're married, nothing can change that."

"It's Lydia."

Lydia.

I licked my lips, which were dry and swollen.

"What do you mean? About the divorce? Was there any difficulty? Is she upset?"

He lifted the cigarette to his mouth.

"The child? Little Sammy? Is he all right?" I raised my head. "Your brother! Has he been to see her? Was there trouble?"

Simon detached me gently and rose to his feet and walked around the side of the bed to the table, where he stubbed out the cigarette in the ashtray and finished the brandy. His throat moved endlessly as he swallowed, and when he set the tumbler down his face had hardened into glass.

"I'm afraid Lydia's dead."

CHAPTER 23

Cocoa, Florida, July 1922

I'M AFRAID THE doctor's not pleased with me. He stitches up my palm and examines my eyes and ears and all that, as duty requires. He asks me to describe my symptoms, and when I've finished—before the last word has left my lips, in fact—he demands to know what on God's green earth I think I'm doing, taking opium. A young mother like me.

I tell him I haven't been taking opium. Just aspirin.

Oh, the *look* on his face. He doesn't think much of the moral constitution of Mrs. Virginia Fitzwilliam, that's for certain. He checks his watch (he's been taking my pulse, for maybe the dozenth time) and releases my wrist. On his way out the door, he glances back over his shoulder and shakes his professional head. Presumably on his way to lecture Samuel.

Well, I don't give a damn what he thinks. At the moment, I don't care about anything except Evelyn, and she's sleeping off the mad night in her own little bedroom in Simon's apartment. *My* apartment—I must remember that. I close my eyes and recall the weight of my daughter, packed tight into the hollow of my shoulder as we drove down the lurid midnight highway, past the wet earth and the close-packed vegetation drizzled with moonshine. Her warm bones tucked along mine. The lumpen shape of her doll digging into my ribs. And I wonder what it is I'm really craving, the pills or the love, the chemical tranquillity or the real kind: the kind that can only be transmitted through human skin. I'm sweating again, sweating and aching and exhausted, and just as sleep begins to settle over my forehead, a name emerges from the darkness.

Sammy.

"WHATEVER HAPPENED TO SAMMY?" I ask Samuel when he jolts me awake sometime later, by the act of opening my bedroom door.

"Sammy?"

"Your son."

He crosses his arms. "That boy is not my son."

"He's still a person. A little boy. What happened to him, after Lydia died?"

He stands there at the foot of the bed, scowling at me. He brought a tray with him, and it's resting on the round table by the side of the bed. The smell makes me sick. I don't want food. I want something else. Aspirin. Evelyn. Something.

"It was Clara," he says. "Clara looked after him."

"And afterward? When Simon left for Florida?"

"Sammy went, too."

"And who's taking care of him now?"

"That woman from Maitland, I assume. The housekeeper. That's where Simon always left him, at the plantation, with the housekeeper and her mother. Didn't you see him?"

"No. But I think Evelyn played with him, when I was sick. Why would Miss Bertram keep him a secret, though?"

He frowns a little more. Looks at the tray and back at my face. "God knows. You're still sick. You look terrible."

"Thank you."

"Who gave you those pills?"

"The doctor in Cocoa."

"Some doctor." He uncrosses his arms and walks to the window. "Have you remembered anything more about Clara?"

"I don't understand. You say she's gone missing?"

"I haven't heard from her since June."

"June!"

"Yes, June! You stupid girl." He grabs the edge of the curtain. "I'm sorry. I didn't mean that. It's just—well, she's got this unfortunate tendency to get into trouble from time to time, she's a bit headstrong, you know, *impulsive,* that's the word, and—this note. The one in your drawer. She didn't say anything else? Whom she was meeting?"

"Not that I remember. I wasn't feeling well, that first night—"

"I'm not surprised."

"For God's sake, Samuel, I was attacked! The doctor gave me pills for my headache!"

He turns his face toward me. "Attacked?"

"Didn't you hear about it?"

"No."

A funny little silence nestles in between us, right in the middle of all that soft, drunken morning air. Samuel stares at me, and his eyes turn a little wild, and his face turns a little tender. A little something else. I can't tell what. He doesn't move, though. Not a flinch. Until his lips move.

"What happened?"

"I was with Clara. We went to this—this place in Cocoa Beach, this restaurant a few miles south, after dinner."

"A gin joint, you mean."

"I don't know. I don't know anything about places like that. Anyway, she was—well, she was flirting, I guess, or something like that, and I went for a walk on the beach."

"By yourself?"

"Yes. I wanted to see if it was true."

"If what was true? If *what* was true, Virginia?"

"That the rumrunners landed on moonless nights. And there was no moon out, so I thought, well, I'll just take a look . . ."

"My God." He steps forward, looms by the edge of the bed. Reaches out and touches my cheek. "That was *you?*"

"Me?"

"Are you all right? You weren't badly hurt?"

"No. I don't remember it, actually. I think I'd had too much to drink, and someone hit me on the head . . ."

"Oh, Christ. Oh, Virginia." His hand travels along my jaw. Inspects my chin. The shape of his eyes softens and rounds, suggesting remorse. But then, it's Samuel. You can't read Samuel. Maybe it's remorse, maybe it's pity. Maybe it's something else. He reminds me of a bear, all huge and brown and bristling, looming over me. Nudging me with his paw, to decide if I'm still alive. "And you don't remember? You don't know who did this?"

"No."

"I'll find him."

"No!" I push his hand away. "Please, don't. Please don't have anything more to do with this, do you hear me? It's done enough damage, this business."

"What business?"

"You know what I mean."

Well, his face goes hard again, just like that. His eyes squint. He steps back and sucks his lips into his mouth. He says, or rather growls, "And this happened just before Clara disappeared, was it?"

"Two nights before. We left for Maitland the next day . . ." And my voice trails away, because you see, I don't think I really understood him until now. Understood what he meant, that is, by *missing*. Clara missing. Busy, energetic Clara. My head's still fuzzy and restless, my thoughts swinging and swaying like those round-bottomed dolls you push with your finger. Revolving around my own needs, my own physical maladies. Now the dolls are going still, the light of reason is spreading and spreading, and I think to myself, for the first time, *Nobody's seen Clara in weeks*. Not since she motored right back out of Maitland in Simon's blue Packard, the morning after we arrived.

"And she left in the morning," he finishes.

I say, in my mumbling, scratchy voice: "You haven't heard a word from her?"

"Not a damned word. Not a note. Not a message."

"Do you think something's happened to her?"

There is a lamp balanced atop the sleek modern table, a few feet away from Samuel's enormous body. He picks it up—a lovely, curving, elegant object, made of reflective mercury glass spun into symmetry by some expert hand, priceless—and hurls it against the wall.

"Of course something's happened to her! What the bloody hell else could it be? Do you think this is all just an extraordinary coincidence?"

I'm shaking all over, shaking and sweating. Nerves shrieking. "Who, then?"

"You tell *me*! Simon's dead, it can't be him."

I roll over. Turn my face into the mattress. Seize the pillow and squeeze it across the back of my head, around the cartilage of my ears. Samuel shouts something else, but I can't hear it. Just beautiful, muffled silence.

But you can't block out the world forever, can you? Especially when you need to breathe. You don't *want* to breathe, maybe, but you need to. So you turn your head sideways to allow a little air into your starved lungs, and there's your brother-in-law, standing by the edge of the bed, staring fiercely. Dark hair tousled like a ruffian's. Jaw set. Hazel eyes burning straight through your skull.

"At least Evelyn's safe," I whisper.

"Well, that's a damned clue in itself, isn't it? The little heiress remains intact." He runs a hand through his hair. "Miami Beach. Who'd you see there?"

"Lots of people. I don't remember them all."

"There must have been someone."

"There wasn't."

"You hesitated."

"I was trying to remember, all right? There wasn't anyone in particular. Where's Evelyn?"

"Still sleeping."

"Where are you going?"

"Miami Beach. Call me at the Flamingo if you hear anything. There's your breakfast tray. I suggest you start by eating something, if you still want to call yourself a mother."

He slams the door behind him, and I stare for some time at the white-painted wood that replaces him. At the shattered lamp next to the wall. At the silver dome on the tray on the bedside table, keeping my breakfast warm.

MAYBE IT'S THE SCORN IN Samuel's eyes. The doctor's eyes. Nobody's ever looked at me that way before. Pity's bad enough—I've had plenty of that, especially during Father's trial. Oh, the pity in everyone's eyes, as they gazed upon Sophie and me, the motherless girls, practically orphans, sitting quietly in that courtroom! But scorn. That's another perspective altogether. And the tone of his voice! *If you still want to call yourself a mother.*

Nothing quite so vicious as that, is there? *If you still want to call yourself a mother.* You can bear anything but that. Anything but the accusation that you, Virginia Fitzwilliam, have failed your own daughter.

When you have lived the past three years in devotion to her. When your daughter is the temple at which you have worshipped, the single clean object left in your universe, the magnet, the gravitational force, the molecular glue that holds you together. Keeps your component pieces from cracking apart and falling in noisy shards to the floor, the way your own mother fell to pieces.

Like any really effective blow, the denunciation takes a moment or two to work its intended effect. First, there's the instinctive *No, but—!* The angry *Stupid bastard!* The resistant *He doesn't understand.* And then the truth, you know, the *truth* of it works its inevitable way into my gut. Fills my eyes. Sticks and chokes in my throat.

My Evelyn, my daughter. I've failed her.

Aspirin, indeed. I knew all along, and still I went on fooling myself, taking any little excuse to grant myself relief. Now look at me. Look at me! I deserve Samuel's scorn. I have fallen apart. I have deconstituted my mind and my body into a thousand broken pieces. I am not Virginia anymore. I'm not even a human being anymore, not even a mother, and it's all my own doing. My undoing is my own doing. I am not strong enough. The same method by which I fell in love with Simon: I thought I was stronger than I really was.

And it turns out, I was only untried.

Like you, Mama? Were you only untried? And then the rains came, the darkness came, and you succumbed to them. You gave in. You fell apart and reassembled your brokenness into somebody else. And I judged you for it, I found you wanting, and it turns out we're the same. I'm no better than you were.

ALL OF WHICH REFLECTION, YOU might say, represents nothing more than a giant salt bath of self-pity in which to wallow without purpose. Oh, I know about all this modern psychology. How helpless we are in the aftermath of our parents' crimes, how imprisoned by the iron facts of our childhoods.

But as I lie there, wallowing, face immersed in a white down pillow of my husband's choosing, I start to get a little angry, too. At what, exactly, I'm not sure. I'll leave that to all those fashionable new head doctors to decide. Just a sort of inchoate fury, or frustration, or some damned thing. I don't want to be this person, lying on this bed. I don't want to be my mother, just because of some universal law of human transmutation, some inevitable psychological destiny.

I want to be Virginia. Whoever she is.

And I'm sick, you know, I'm feeling pretty damned lousy, as a purely physical diagnosis, and I think, well, I've been sick before, haven't I, and I've pushed myself out of bed. Because I had to. Because there was no other choice. One leg after another. One limb at a time. One foot sliding down the mattress to the rug, like that, and then you brace your good left palm against the pillow and lift yourself upright, and the other foot slides down to the nice soft rug, right next to the first foot. And there you are. Standing. Miserable, but standing. On your own two feet.

A SOMNOLENT LATE-MORNING ATMOSPHERE SITS on the walls and the furniture, the few objects in Simon's parlor. The clock on the wall says half past ten. In the wake of the thunderstorms last night, the sky has cleared to a pungent, unclouded blue, and the Indian River glitters restlessly outside the windows. I grip the back of a nearby sofa and consider the emptiness of the apartment, the lazy lonesomeness. No one to bother us up here. Door bolted, our whereabouts unknown. Except to Samuel, and he's miles out of town by now, on his way to Miami Beach, to save his sister. Wouldn't that be lovely, to have a brother desperate to save me? A man I could trust.

But I don't pause to savor the beauty and the pity of it all. I make my way straight to Evelyn's room, as quickly as my unsteady legs and uncertain balance will carry me. That's why I'm upright to begin with, isn't it? What got me out of bed: that sensation of danger streaming through my innards, like the unstoppable river that passes outside, carrying goods to market.

Goods. *Goods,* indeed.

Evelyn's bedroom lies down a hallway on the other side of the parlor. One of three chambers, in fact, all of which are decorated in warm pastels, in soft furniture, as if waiting for children to populate them. A month ago, the sight of those expectant rooms touched me with an uncertain tenderness, almost like hope. Now I regard Evelyn's white-painted door—left a few inches ajar—in panic. The nausea strikes again, overturning my guts, so that I lurch against the wall, holding myself up with one palm, and I make a drunken, disgraceful path down those remaining yards, until my hand pushes forth from the wall to land on Evelyn's doorknob. The hinges give way silently, sending me staggering inside.

The room is cool, shielded from the sun by a set of thick curtains, and for an instant I can't see the bed, or my daughter inside, and my heart stops beating. I blink and blink, trying to penetrate the shadows, and as my pupils dilate, taking their time, I stretch out my impatient hands and step forward.

The bed. There it is, framed in white iron, clean and hygienic. The mattress, the soft quilt.

A small, oblong lump: Evelyn's foot.

The breath rushes from my chest. I slump forward, supporting myself on my hands, one bare and the other clubbed in bandages, and inch my way upward to the pillows until I find her shoulder, the smooth fiber of her hair. Her ribs, moving steadily in the rhythm of a deep and untroubled sleep. Her cool, healthy cheek.

I don't know if you've ever felt that kind of relief. I suppose everyone has—everyone who's ever loved another person, I mean. Because sooner or later we all experience that extraordinary, irrational terror, all the more paralyzing because you don't quite know why you're so afraid. Someone's late coming home on a stormy night, or a child goes to bed with a fever, or a siren wails delicately in the distance, and you're certain, you're certain, you're *certain* something must be terribly wrong, this is it, your number's come up. The bell tolls for thee.

And then comes the deliverance. The door opens, the child wakes up smiling, the siren passes. And the relief, my God, the relief almost kills you, it's so mighty. You double over, you're faint. You press your hand to your stomach and thank God, thank God. You're safe. For this moment, your world remains intact. Your daughter's alive and well, sleeping under your fingers, inside the sanctum of her bed. You tuck a lock of hair behind her darling ear and listen to the whisper of her breath. You smell the nectar of her skin. You say, maybe out loud or maybe just in your head, I'll never let this happen again. I'll never let anything harm you again.

AND I MEAN IT, YOU know. I tuck the blanket an inch or two higher on Evelyn's chest, and I kiss her forehead and her white, exposed cheek, and I drag my bag of bones into the hallway and the telephone in its cubby in the wall.

I instruct the hotel operator to connect me to the front desk, and I ask the front desk if I have received any letters.

Yes, madam. Shall we send them up?

Yes, please.

You might think, after a month's absence, I'd have any number of letters waiting for me in my pigeonhole in the hotel's front desk. In fact, I've taken the strictest care to make sure this isn't the case. I didn't want any curious being to know where to find me. Not even Sophie. To my lawyers in New York I gave the address of the Phantom Shipping Company, care of. So when the red-suited Phantom Hotel bellboy arrives at the apartment door, trying not to widen his eyes at the derelict sight of me, he's carrying only two white envelopes. One bears no identification, other than my name and that of the Phantom Hotel. The other one is from the National City Bank of New York.

I sit down at the desk in the corner of the drawing room and open the anonymous note first. I'm not surprised to learn that Agent Marshall—in his brief, efficient manner—inquires after my health and well-being, and any information I may have discovered in the weeks since my injury in Cocoa Beach. How kind. I fold the note back into its original creases and then rip it into small, fastidious pieces, an action that requires just about all the strength I've got left in my fingers.

The second letter, on the other hand. That's the one I really want, and yet I find, as I gather the scraps of Agent Marshall into a neat pile, which I then brush over the side of the table into the small metal wastebasket I've fetched from the corner for that purpose, that I'm delaying the moment of discovery. That I really don't want to know the details. That I'm afraid. Of course. I'm always afraid, aren't I? Fear and dread, my old companions. I set down the wastebasket and pick up the remaining letter. My name is typed on the outside of the envelope, rather than written, and it's a solid new type, black and unscarred, punched in by ten expert fingers that make no mistakes. The kind of professionalism you expect from your New York City bank.

Except it isn't my bank, exactly. I've never had an account at the National City Bank. That was, more or less, the substance of the inquiry I wrote and mailed to their offices a month ago, in between my visit to the First National Bank of Miami and my excursion to the Miami Beach casino, along with a cheerful postcard sent to my sister. This, I presume, is the bank's answer. A vital piece of the puzzle, you might say, and yet I think I already know what it says. The gist of what's happening here. And I find, as I slide a slim silver letter opener along the edge of the envelope and pull the contents free—two pieces of ecru paper, folded together into precise crosswise thirds—that I'm right. Of course I'm right. Didn't I expect all this from the beginning?

Dear Mrs. Fitzwilliam,

In response to your inquiry of the 21st of June, I regret to inform you that, since the account holder is now deceased, the Bank cannot divulge any such information without proof of your identity as his legal agent. We can, however, confirm the details to which you referred in your inquiry: namely, that the account holder instructed payment in the amount of $100,000.00 to be made on the account of Mr. Fitzwilliam at the First National Bank of Miami. Any further details must be applied for in person . . .

The usual compliments follow, but I don't read them. Instead I fold the letter and slide it back into its envelope, and I tread carefully across the enormous drawing room to the master bedroom, where my valise lies under the bed. My valise of important papers. I open the valise and find my father's cracked leather portfolio, the one marked FITZWILLIAM, and I slide the bank correspondence inside, next to the thirty-odd envelopes postmarked from Florida, with nothing inside them.

My hand pauses. I don't know why. Maybe it's the muddle in my head, the uncertainty that roils between the folds of my brain. Outside the window, a steamship lets out a distant, prolonged belch. A Phantom steamship, possibly? I pull the stack of empty envelopes from the portfolio and untie the string that holds them together.

Again, that handwriting. Strikes me in the stomach, where I need it least. I touch my finger to the word *Virginia* and think how I once used to welcome the sight of this word, in that particular pen stroke, how it used to send a current of joy into that selfsame stomach that troubles me now. As the tip of my finger glides across the ink, wondering what kind of letter ought to have been contained inside, and what information it should have contained, so does my eye wander across the paper, until it lands on the round, black, innocuous postmark in the corner. Just to be sure. Just to make certain I wasn't dreaming, or hallucinating, or merely mistaken.

And while I'm sitting there, reabsorbing the meaning of this information, a sound drifts through the open bedroom door and interrupts the rhythm of my thoughts, such as they are.

The distant, unmistakable voice of a metal doorknob, when it's rattled by a hand without a key.

THE FUNNY THING ABOUT COURAGE—at least in my observation—is that it tends to rise and fall in proportion to what's at stake. I now shudder to remember the way I drove that damned Hunka Tin through mud and shellfire, without regard for my own safety. But why wouldn't I? I had only my own paltry life to lose, and who gave a damn if I lost that? Certainly not me. Simon, maybe, but not for the reasons I then imagined.

Now it's different. Now I have Evelyn, and while I still don't particularly value my life for its own sake, I value it for hers. I know what it's like to grow up without a mother.

And, of course, there's Evelyn's life. My daughter's precious, irreplaceable life. I could die this moment, and Evelyn would grieve, but she would go on. Like Sophie, who was three when Father killed Mama, she wouldn't even really remember me. Though the loss of me would open a giant chasm in her life, she would survive it. But if my daughter died, and I lived? I couldn't survive that. I could not survive the loss of Evelyn.

As I stand in the doorway of the bedroom and listen to the rattling knob—carrying across the drawing room, from the direction of the entry hall—the sound changes entirely, replaced by jolts, as if someone's given up on the lock and has now resorted to brute force. I realize I have two choices, if I want to live, and I want Evelyn to live. I can hide us both, or I can fight. Which is really no choice at all, because where could we possibly hide where a determined intruder won't find us? We're on the eighth floor of a hotel in a strange, hostile town. There's nowhere to go.

So it's not really courage that propels me from the bedroom's threshold, closing the door behind me, but fear. I have no choice. There's nowhere else to go. Nothing else to be done.

Outside, in the drawing room, the air's gone quiet. Maybe he's given up; maybe he's left. Maybe it's just Samuel, returning for a forgotten object. My nightgown is damp, sticking to my skin, and my vision swims. I walk across the room and gaze about in search of a weapon of some kind, a thing that could be used as a weapon, anything. A painting? Too heavy, even if I could operate both hands.

The knob rattles again, more softly. As if there's a key this time, a key trying to loosen a stiff lock. Someone who lives here, or used to live here.

Knives. The kitchen. But the kitchen's all the way on the other side of the apartment. I cast about, frantic now, and with my uninjured left hand I snatch a ceramic vase from a sleek modern sideboard and secure it with my right thumb. I turn toward the entry foyer just as the door cracks open and a hand wraps around the edge.

There's nowhere to hide. I turn and flatten myself against the wall, just around the corner from the foyer, and listen to the creak of the door. The careful footsteps on the rug. The clink of something landing in the china bowl on the entry table.

Footsteps again.

I lift the vase above my head, thinking that at least I have surprise on my side, at least I'll go down fighting, by God, a vengeful pale Valkyrie in a sweat-soaked nightgown, hair matted, head swimming, limbs as weak as a kitten's.

A foot appears—not the foot I was expecting—but my reflexes are so primed that I whirl anyway, hurling the vase before I can stop myself.

Clara screams, ducks, and collapses onto the floor, while the vase shatters against the door. In her distant bedroom, Evelyn wakes up and starts to cry.

CHAPTER 24

Cornwall, England, April 1919

THE GALE DIED away during the night, and the sky was now a chilly, uncertain blue, pockmarked by dark-bottomed clouds. Simon put the top down on the Wolseley and glanced anxiously upward as we plowed down the muddy road along the coast, toward Plymouth.

She had disappeared a few weeks after Christmas, he had told me the night before. He had gotten the telephone call soon after arriving in London, in the days following his demobilization. No sign of her anywhere, her suitcase untouched, her wardrobe full. I had asked if there was a note, and he said there wasn't. Just the customary pile of clothes next to the sea. Her father had died of the 'flu during the autumn, and though she had escaped the illness herself, she went into a decline. Shut herself in her room, wouldn't talk to anyone. Everyone said it was her broken heart, of course. She had drowned herself out of heartbreak.

I stared out the side of the motorcar, bundled against the draft in my thick service overcoat and Simon's woolen muffler, which he had wound around my neck with his own hands as we stood in the courtyard of the inn. The distant sea appeared and disappeared in little glimpses between the cliffs. "They're going to hate me, aren't they?" I said wearily. "Your family and friends."

"They're going to hate us both. I'm the faithless husband, remember? The blackguard who slept with London whores on leave, while the sainted Lydia tended to our child in the country."

"And you won't tell them the truth."

"I can't. For one thing, they wouldn't believe me."

"No, of course."

"Anyway, there's my brother. Still refuses to own the child."

"But that's disgraceful!"

"It's a bloody mess, is what it is." He glanced at me, and back at the road ahead, which was in terrible condition: unpaved, slick with mud from yesterday's rain, rimmed by treacherous hedgerows. "In fact, I was rather thinking, as soon as we've done our duty here . . ."

"Thinking what?"

"I was thinking we might sail to New York sooner rather than later. To see your family. I'm sure you must miss them intolerably, after all, and I, for one, should very much like to meet them. What do you think of that?"

New York. The two words settled on my chest.

"Oh! I don't—I hadn't thought of that."

"What? Don't you want to see them again?"

"Yes! But I was thinking—I was really thinking we might just have them come to visit us, instead. Here in Cornwall."

"In *Cornwall?*"

"Aren't we going to live here? In Penderleath? Near your family?"

He lifted his right hand from the wheel and fumbled for the cigarettes in his jacket pocket. "That wasn't the plan, no. Anywhere but here, really. It's going to be bloody awkward around old Fitzwilliam Manor for the foreseeable future, for one thing. That's why I was thinking about New York. I daresay your family would be over the moon to see you again, after so long. Especially after the accident. And I should hope they'd like to meet me. The English gent who's swept you off your feet."

He was having trouble with the matches. I took the matchbook and the cigarette from his fingers and bent down under the dashboard to strike the flame. Several tries later, I handed Simon the cigarette, trailing a fragile line of smoke from one end.

"Thanks awfully, darling." He transferred the cigarette to his right hand, which was propped on the doorframe while his left hand operated the steering wheel. He inhaled quietly and glanced again at the side of my face. "To be perfectly honest, I seem to have developed the most powerful desire to make an entirely fresh start in life. Leave this damned war-weary continent behind. All these terrible memories, these ghosts upon ghosts."

"But what about your profession? What will you do?"

"I don't know. Something. Not medicine."

"Why not? You were born to be a doctor."

"Was I? Maybe the old Simon was." He rubbed the corner of his mouth with his thumb. "Now it turns my stomach. It does. The idea of opening some damned surgical practice in London. The smell of blood and antiseptic. I'm sick to death, Virginia."

I stared at his left hand, ridged and bony beneath its leather glove. The first two fingers, pointing upward, pinning the cigarette between them, tremble visibly. Or maybe that was just the vibration of the motor? *Sick to death,* he said, and I remember his lean, bare shoulders as he made love to me the night before, his silvering hair, the graceful hollows beneath his cheekbones.

"Well? What do you think?" he said.

"I think—well, of course we should visit New York, if you like."

"But not to live there?"

"It's just—oh, Simon. I do hope . . . you see, I don't think I *want* to live there anymore. I don't think I *can.* I thought—I thought instead that . . . but I didn't want to say anything, not until I'd spoken to her . . ."

"Spoken to whom?"

"Sophie. My sister. I thought we could invite her here, to live with us."

"Oh."

"Do you think that's a terrible idea?"

"No, of course not. She's welcome, if she wants to come." His thumb tapped the wheel. "What sort of girl is she? You don't speak of her very much."

"She's a darling. Lovely and absent-minded and mechanical."

"Mechanical?" He smiled.

"Yes, she takes after our father that way. But she's not like him otherwise. She's really very sweet. I think you'll adore her."

"I'm sure I shall. But will she *want* to move to England? Awfully long way, you know, and most everything's still rationed. Everything worth eating, anyway. Besides, I'm sure she has her friends in New York."

"Not really. We weren't encouraged to have friends, Sophie and me."

"What's that? Why not?"

"Because of our circumstances." I looked down at my hands in my lap, gloved like his, except in black leather instead of brown. "My father."

"Ah. Yes. I'm sorry. I'd forgotten about that. Not forgotten exactly, but—"

"But you understand? Why I'd rather live anywhere else than there?"

He made a noise that might have suggested anything. Sucked on the cigarette, briefly inspected the remaining stub. "About your father."

"What about him?"

"Well, what sort of fellow is he? Apt, for example, to greet sons-in-law with suspicion or generosity? What's his attitude toward this reckless foreign marriage of yours?"

"I don't know." I found the ring on my fourth finger, underneath the glove, and twisted it back and forth. Such a strange, alien thing, a piece of metal bound around a piece of your body. I had never worn a ring before. "I haven't told him about you."

There was a brief, stunned silence.

"You're joking, aren't you?"

"No. He's not—as you know, as I've said before, he's suspicious of outsiders. We weren't allowed to make friends, at least the kind of friends we could invite home. So I didn't know how to explain. How to make him understand that you could be trusted. I thought he might forbid me to marry you. Order me home at once."

"So you went ahead and married me anyway?"

I tried to laugh. "I did once hear that it's far better to ask forgiveness than permission."

"Yes, but that's . . ." He crushed the spent cigarette against the doorframe and tossed it into the draft. "Marriage *is* rather a larger matter, you know. Are you saying you haven't mentioned my existence at all? What about your sister? Surely you've told *her*."

"No. I was afraid she would blurt something out. She can be impulsive."

"My God." He grasped the brim of his hat and worked it up and down against his forehead. "I suppose he'll be furious at us both."

"I don't know. That's why—"

"What's that?"

I raised my voice, which had fallen into hoarseness. "Why I thought we might make our home here, at least for now. Live here and send for Sophie."

"I see."

"You don't approve."

"I just think it's a bit shortsighted, that's all. You're not afraid he might—well, cut you off?"

"Cut me off?"

"Leave you without a penny. Or whatever it is you have in America."

"Pennies. I wouldn't care about that. I couldn't take his money, anyway."

"*What?* Why the devil not?"

"We can make our own fortune."

"You make it sound so easy. Have you ever *tried* to get your hands on a decent sum of money? Enough to set yourself up in reasonable comfort? It's bloody difficult. It's going to be even more difficult now, with the war over, and everybody out of work."

"I'd rather be poor than take Father's money."

Simon lifted his hand back to his forehead and rubbed his thumb against his skin, just beneath the brim of his hat. "Would you, now," he said, so softly that I had to strain to hear him over the noise of the engine. "May I ask why?"

The road grew rough, winding about a set of small hills. The draft whistled past our ears. Simon slowed the car and put both hands back on the wheel, gripping it with such intensity that his knuckles seemed to burst beneath the brown leather of his gloves.

Tell him, I thought. Tell him why you're afraid.

Tell him the thing you haven't told anyone. The thing you haven't told Sophie.

The thing you haven't even told yourself.

I stared at those hands, at the tight bones of his knuckles, and said, "There's no reason. I suppose it's just because *I* want a new life, too. *I* want a fresh start. A fresh start with you and Sophie. That's all."

I DON'T SUPPOSE I'LL EVER forget the sight of Penderleath, glimpsed between a pair of overgrown elms as we crept around the final curve of the drive. *Fitzwilliam Manor,* Simon had called it, in his jaded voice, but I thought it was beautiful in its damp, crumbling humility.

"I see they've given up on the north wing," Simon said. A few drops of rain spat upon the windscreen, and he reached for the dashboard.

"What's in the north wing?"

"The nursery, for one thing. And the billiards."

"But I thought Lydia's money was supposed to save the house."

"Yes. Well. As it turned out, there wasn't so much money as my parents hoped. The fortune was all cleverly tied up by the lawyers. And her father lost a few ships to the damned U-boats, apparently, and required the capital himself. A thing he never troubled himself to mention, of course. We only discovered the extent of the mess after his death." He paused to switch gears. "And then came the divorce proceedings."

"Oh, God."

"Not your fault."

"But in the eyes of your parents . . ."

Simon slammed his foot on the brake pedal. The Wolseley skidded to a stop, rear wheels sliding along the mud. He turned and caught the back of my head. "You are not to care what my parents think," he said fiercely. "You are not to believe a word they say, do you hear me? Leave them to me. I know how to manage them."

"Are they really so awful?"

"They're not awful. They're only . . . they're bitter. And rather furious with me."

"Then why are we here? Why not wait?"

"God knows." His hand turned gentle and stroked my cheek. "Maybe just to show you what it *could* be, one day, when it's ours. The way I've dreamed it. Central heating and sound roofs and bricks all repointed. Fresh paint and new furniture and children running about. And *love*, Virginia. Just imagine it."

I looked over his shoulder at the ancient gray dimensions of Penderleath, the comfortable jumble of Palladian symmetry and Jacobean fretwork, all softened up by age and weather. "I think it's perfect the way it is."

He barked and put the car back in gear. "That's because you haven't been inside."

NOBODY CAME OUT TO GREET us as we pulled up in the exact center of the drive, before the pilloried entrance. The gravel was patchy and ragged with weeds. Simon switched off the engine and went around to open my door.

"What's the matter?" I said, touching his chin.

"Nothing. Come along, Mrs. Fitzwilliam. Into the lion's den."

He led me around the car and up the crumbling steps. "I suppose I ought to carry you over the threshold, but it's not really ours yet. Nor especially homelike, for that matter. Still . . ." He flung open the door, grasped my waist, and swooped me inside. His voice boomed about the entrance hall. "Mother! Father! The prodigal returns."

"Don't joke," I whispered.

"I'm not joking."

No answering voice reached us from inside. The atmosphere was cold and damp and uninhabited, smelling of mildew and something else, sweet and slightly rancid. Simon released my waist and gathered up my hand inside his. "I'd offer to take your coat, my dear, but I daresay you'll need it."

"But where is everyone?"

"Sitting resolutely in the conservatory, I imagine. Wrapped in old furs. Drinking tea and setting their teeth against us. I shall have to work every wile to thaw them out."

"Your brother said you were good at that. Getting your parents on your side."

"Well, they're very much like children themselves, you know. Utterly incapable of dealing with practicalities, like the size of the overdraft and the necessity for paying one's tradesmen. Buying coal over buying new evening frocks. Improving one's estate as an investment for the future."

We passed along a long, dark gallery, papered in striped Victorian burgundy and shrouded by portraits of murky ancestors. A thick film of dust coated the windowpanes, adding an unnecessary layer of gloom. "Do you see what I mean?" Simon said. "If all this were cleaned up and brightened. See that plasterwork, ruined by damp. It's a disgrace, really. And it was once the most magnificent house for miles. Look at this portrait, here."

He stopped before a painting, larger than the others, framed in gilt. The dusky air nearly swallowed the subject, so that I could make out only a crimson dress and a sumptuous abundance of creamy skin.

"Who is she?"

"Augusta Fitzwilliam. Married my great-whatever-it-is grandfather when she was just fifteen. She made the family's fortune, three or so centuries ago. Mostly on her back, so the legend goes. She was an ardent Royalist. Look how beautiful she is."

I peered forward and saw a pair of large eyes—color indeterminate—and a firm, well-crafted chin. Hair the color of honey, hidden behind a gold headpiece. For an instant, her face reminded me of Simon's.

"She was the mistress of Charles II, for a time. He quite adored her, or so I was told, and not just because she was such a beauty. She was a terribly brave woman. Kept the house as a refuge for the Royalists during the war, despite several attempts by Parliament to arrest her. Hid him for the night, so the story goes, on his way to exile in France, when he was only about sixteen. Naturally she fell into bed with him once he returned. Most women did, if he wanted them, especially the pretty ones. But I believe she fucked him on principle. Doing her bit for the monarchy."

"Didn't her husband object?"

"I imagine he had little to say about it. After all, they were both rewarded handsomely when the king was restored to the throne. The house was left crumbling to bits after the war—much as it is now, what irony—and Charles chucked a grateful pile of gold their way, so who was Mr. Fitzwilliam to complain? This was his king, after all. He did refuse a title for his wife's services, however. He had his pride."

"It all sounds so venal."

"Well, of course it was venal. Most human acts are venal, to some degree. But it did the trick, didn't it? Saved the house and the fortune for generations to come, when the Roundheads nearly destroyed them." He paused. "Besides, it wasn't as if she didn't care for him. They carried on for years. She had at least three children by him. In fact, the eldest of them ended up inheriting after his half-brother went to London and died of the plague, so we're really not Fitzwilliams at all. Properly speaking, I suppose, we're Fitzcharleses."

"*What?*"

"Yes. I'm a prince, of sorts. At your service." He made a little bow.

"I don't believe it. King Charles was your *grandfather?*"

"Well, most likely. Several greats ago, of course. You look so astonished."

"I *am* astonished! It's—it's amazing. You're—his *blood* runs in your veins! Why didn't you say something before? Doesn't it amaze you?"

"I don't know. It's just a fact to me. Something I've known all my life. I suppose it *is* rather extraordinary, to an outsider." Simon returned to the portrait. "Though I daresay there are thousands of us, scattered around the country. He was a damned promiscuous bloke, and a generous one. Let that be a lesson to everyone. It pays to tip well."

"You sound as if you approve."

"Not exactly. But it was a different age, you know. I don't see the harm in it, if everyone got what they wanted out of it. Husbands, wives, and king."

I blurted out: "But if it were *me?* Would you care then?"

He was still holding my hand. I thought I felt his fingers move around mine, in a slight spasm. "What a strange thing to ask."

"You know what I mean."

Simon's hand released mine, just long enough to tuck my arm inside the nook of his elbow. "You must know the answer to that," he said quietly, and he turned us both away from the portrait, down the remainder of the gallery. The shabby carpet muffled our steps, until we came to a large, rectangular drawing room, flanked at both ends by tall, mullioned window seats. The furniture was covered in yellowing sheets.

"Oh, how beautiful!" I said.

Simon released my arm and went to one of the windows. He shoved his hands into his pockets and stared at the drizzling garden outside. "It will be. It will be, by God."

I joined him and rested my head on his shoulder. I loved his old tweed jacket, the absence of his army tunic. The material smelled of wool and cigarettes and camphor—it had spent most of the war in a wardrobe, locked in battle against moths—and I remember thinking how comfortable a combination that was, how perfectly evocative of Simon. I remember thinking how that scent would always belong to him. Always belong to our life together.

"We'll make it beautiful again," I said. "We'll do whatever we must."

He put his arm around me. "Yes. Whatever we must."

I don't recall how long we stood there, gazing out the grubby windows at the gardens beyond, overgrown and weedy and coated in mist. The damp crept through the cracks in the windows and filled the air. I pressed my cheek against the dry warmth of Simon's tweed shoulder—I recall that detail clearly, because it was the last sensation of comfort I was to receive for a terribly long time.

Whatever the period of time we stood—a minute, ten minutes—the interruption inevitably came. Simon heard it first. I felt his arm stiffen, and an instant later I heard the signal, too: the clatter of footsteps down a flight of wooden stairs.

"Samuel! Is that you?" called the voice of a young woman.

We turned together, Simon and I, and I was about to ask him whose voice this was—who this young woman could possibly be—when its owner flew around a corner and into view before us, light and miniature as a fairy, wearing a gray dress and a stained white pinafore apron. She stopped at once and put one hand to her mouth, and I saw that a white surgical mask dangled from the side of her face, while her hair was bound in a white scarf.

"Clara," said Simon. His voice seemed a little cold. "How good to see you."

"Simon! What are you doing here? Is that—?"

"My wife. We were married the day before yesterday. Virginia, darling, this is my sister. Clara."

"Hello," I said.

Clara looked at me and at Simon. I remember thinking how plain she looked, how lank her hair and how large her mouth, but I now believe that was only because she was so pale and wan, because the skin beneath her eyes was bruised with fatigue.

"Oh, my!" she gasped.

Simon's hand gripped mine. "Yes. Where are Mummy and Father? I should like to present their new daughter-in-law."

"But you can't!"

"Why not? Have we been forbidden?"

Clara wrung her tiny hands, like a nurse in a play, and perhaps it was that—the image of Clara as nurse—that made everything fit together: the empty, yearning house and the cold and the damp and the familiar expectancy of disaster. Made understanding creep over me like twilight, even before she opened her pink mouth and told us the truth.

"No. Because they're ill. They're both terribly ill. I think it's the 'flu."

February 12, 1922

Dear Mrs. Fitzwilliam,

For so you remain, at least for the moment, and I don't want to waste what might prove my last opportunity to address you with the name you were so good as to accept from me, three years ago.

This morning I received a letter from your father. Something of a shock, I'll admit, as he has never troubled himself to address me before. Even more shocking that he wrote this singular epistle from inside the Fairfield County Jail in Stamford, Connecticut, and now, my dear wife, now I understand how I have been a fool. A fool to leave you alone like this, all these long months and years, and not to find you and speak with you and understand why you have shunned me like this. The terrible secret you have been harboring under your skin. The terrible courage with which you must have placed your hand in mine, in that long-ago churchyard in Kensington. And I did not understand. I thought—forgive me—I thought your trust and love in me must have been very weak indeed to fall away so easily under my brother's persuasion. Now I know.

And we have a daughter. Her name is Evelyn, and she has my eyes and my smile. How I stare at those words. <u>Daughter</u>. <u>Evelyn</u>. It cannot be true, and yet your father assures me it is. I want to weep. I want to rage. I don't know whether I adore you or hate you for granting me such a gift and then never telling me it existed. How could you? But then you could. You had to. You had this fear of me. You were afraid I was a monster, and that the terror of your own childhood would be revisited upon her. Excuse the poorness of this handwriting. I cannot seem to steady my distress.

I will return to your father's letter.

It was long and full of fear: for you, Virginia, and your sister. He turns to me now, for all my faults, in the event he can no longer watch over your interests himself. Without my knowledge, he has investigated my affairs—I suppose that is no more than any father would do—and has changed, or at least softened, the implacability of his resolve against me. In consequence, he has bequeathed me a sum of money with which he hopes to purchase my loyalty. He promises more if certain conditions are met.

It is a strange letter, and stranger still that it should arrive at such a moment, as I contemplate the balance sheet before me and realize that I have no choice but to take some kind of action, or lose everything for which I have labored these past few years.

I shall have my wife at last. And now I shall have a daughter, too.

My fingers are shaking so fiercely, I can hardly hold this pen. I am filled with a strange exhilaration, as if I have caught at last that tide in the affairs of man, to which Shakespeare urged us.

I am not making any sense, am I? Fear not, my beloved. I shall explain everything when the time comes.

And in the interim, my dear, you are not to worry if you haven't heard from me for some time. You are not to think that I have succumbed to any ill. I am only doing what must be done, as I have always done when faced with obstacles. I am <u>determined</u> to win back what I have lost, even if this gamble requires the most desperate stakes I have yet had the courage to summon.

But then, only the brave deserve the fair.

Still (and <u>ever</u>) your own

S.F.

CHAPTER 25

Cocoa, Florida, July 1922

THE SMALL BODY cowering on the floor of the foyer might belong to my sister-in-law, but she's not the Clara I remember. Not the Clara who drove confidently down the drive of Maitland Plantation a month ago.

I sink next to her and take her cheeks in my hands. "Clara! My God! Are you all right?"

"You're hurt!"

"It's nothing, nothing. But you!"

I stroke her dirty hair, her bruised little face. Her wan skin.

"It doesn't matter," she whispers. "As long as you're safe. Are you? You look like hell."

"So do you!"

"I've been living in a hole in the ground for the past four weeks, that's why. A damned hole!"

"Where?"

"Somewhere between here and Maitland."

"But what happened?"

"I escaped, of course. What do you think?"

I stare at her, amazed, and she returns my stare and laughs. "Oh, that hurts!" she says, and goes on laughing, holding her stomach, and I start to laugh, too. Laughing and crying together. "A hole in the ground?" I gasp.

"A basement. These terrible men—"

"Who? What men?"

"Oh, darling . . ."

Evelyn walks in, hair all tousled, and we turn to her in the same movement. "Dolly gone," she says, starting to cry. "Where my dolly?"

Clara holds out her arms.

"Evvie, darling!"

And Evelyn runs straight into her auntie's embrace.

I FIND THE KITCHEN AND boil water for tea, while Clara runs a bath. The room is the absolute latest, all hygienic sanitary tiles and fitted metal cabinets, like a laboratory. A new Western Electric range squats in the corner on its four curved legs. Evelyn tugs on my dressing gown and tell me she's hungry. I pour her a glass of milk from the icebox. Slice bread and butter it thickly. Everything's fresh, and yet I haven't seen a maid. A bowl of green apples rests on the marble-topped table in the center of the room. I cut one apple into pieces and Evelyn eats them all, one by one. The lost doll seems to have been forgotten.

"Now, that's better," Clara says, wandering through the doorway, sitting at the table. She's wearing an ice-white robe and her head is wrapped in a towel. "Your turn. I'll watch Evelyn."

I lift my right hand. "But my bandage!"

"Just hold it out of the tub." She puts the tea in the strainer and the strainer in the cup, and she pours the hot water over all, just as if she's not sitting there wearing a bruise along her jaw, wearing pale, fresh-scrubbed skin and wide, exhausted eyes. When I continue to stand there, smoothing my hands on the sides of my dressing gown, she looks up. "Go on! You'll feel much better. We can't think clearly until you're fresh and clean."

"Think clearly about what?"

"What's to be done, of course. We can't let them win. They'll kill us if we do."

I want to ask her who, but I suppose I already know the answer. There is only one *who* here, isn't there?

Only one man who wants my money badly enough to kill for it.

SHE'S RIGHT, YOU KNOW, EVEN if I don't quite understand what she means by *thinking clearly* until I emerge from the bedroom half an hour later, wearing a skirt and blouse and cardigan and black stockings, skin scrubbed and hair brushed, teeth cleaned and stomach actually hungry. Dizzy, weak, restless. Hand hurting, head hurting. But more recognizably Virginia than at any moment in the past month.

Clara's moved to the parlor with the tea. She sits on the sofa next to Evelyn and turns the pages of a book, while Evelyn points out everything in the pictures. When she sees me, she smiles and reaches for the teapot.

"So, my love. What's happened to you?"

"You first."

"Oh, darling. It's so much to explain."

"You don't seem surprised."

She sets down the cup and takes my hand. "Virginia. There's so much I haven't told you. I didn't want to burden you, you know, with everything you've been through."

"I'm not a child."

"No, you're not. But you've endured so much. That was why I took you to Maitland, you see. I thought you'd be safe there, away from everything, and look at you!" She brushes my cheek with her thumb. "Where's Samuel?"

"He went to look for you. To Miami Beach."

"The Flamingo?"

"Yes."

"Good. We'll ring them and leave a message and stay right here, safe and sound, until he gets back. And we'll plot, you and I, what's next to be done. What's the matter?"

"What's the *matter*? My God! Look at us! You act as if nothing's happened! And he's trying to hurt us. He wants control of my money. Of my daughter, don't you see? And you were in the way, you were protecting me, so he tried to get rid of you. And it's my fault. I should have known better. I shouldn't have softened like that. I shouldn't have come. I shouldn't have brought Evelyn into this, and now we're trapped. He won't let us go until I give him what he wants. What he's always wanted from me."

Clara glances at Evelyn, who's taken over the book. The subject is horses, I think. Evelyn's studying each plate carefully with her grave hazel eyes.

"*Who* won't let you go?" Clara asks quietly.

I lean forward and whisper: *Simon*.

OF COURSE, SHE THINKS I'M crazy. I don't blame her. In the first place, the idea's absurd. What kind of man goes to such lengths as to burn down his beautiful villa by the sea, in order to enact the fiction of his own death? For what possible purpose? Simon's own brother identified his body. Agent Marshall of the Bureau of Internal Revenue confirmed it personally, summoning a great deal of sympathy as he did so. Not one person has disputed the fact of Simon's demise, not even those who cared if he was alive.

And where is my proof? A postmark on an envelope. A letter from a bank. A distrust of revenue men. A pair of hazel eyes, staring at me in fury in the instant before I was struck down on a criminal beach at midnight.

"You must have imagined that," Clara says. "It's simply not possible. You said yourself, you didn't remember a thing from that night."

"Nothing except that."

"Well, isn't that suspect in itself? That you don't remember anything else. You only think you remember it. You've seen Simon's eyes a thousand times. It's just a memory of him, shoved awkwardly into the wrong spot. Round peg, square hole. Because you *want* it to be true."

"*Want* Simon to be alive?"

She takes my hand. "Darling, don't think for an *instant* I don't know. The human heart is such an unreasonable little organ. You loved him so. You still love him, even though you know how thoroughly bad he is."

"I don't love him anymore."

"Yes, you do. You're absolutely obsessed by him. Why else would you come all the way down to Florida in search of him? It's the truth, dearest, and I don't blame you for it. But you've got to be sensible. I *know* who kidnapped me. I saw his face, and it wasn't my brother Simon, I can tell you."

"That doesn't mean anything. He might have been acting on Simon's orders."

She waves her hand. "Surely you know what kind of trouble Simon was in, before he died. How he got on the wrong side of some rather unpleasant chaps—"

"Yes, I know."

"Well. There you are. However cold and calculating my dear brother was, he wasn't going to get the better of the Ashley gang."

"The Ashley gang. That's their name?"

Her tea is cold. She leans forward and takes the pot delicately by the handle, and as she performs this little ritual, milk and sugar and tea leaves and water, I'm struck again by the ease of her manner. Why, she's just escaped from a terrible ordeal! And she's beaten up, she's pale and bruised, but she's thoroughly, terrifyingly intact. Drinking tea on a sofa. As if she's got some kind of unending reservoir of British glue inside that small, playful body, holding all her parts together. How did she come by it? What awful things has Clara endured, over the course of the past few years? Her entire life, when you think about it. Hadn't Simon said that she was a terrible inconvenience to her parents? Like Eve—or like the apple, really—she had caused the love-drunk Fitzwilliams to be exiled from their Eden in Borneo. Pearl fishing with their old friend Mr. Gibbons. This tiny little outcast, nothing like her brothers.

I think how inadequate I am. How weak, how easily overturned by the slightest obstacle.

"Samuel told me all about them," she says. "They're a primitive sort of family from the swamps. They don't follow any laws, just one another. I suppose when you grow up in the wild like that, you don't care much for the lives of outsiders. Anyway, they saw what Samuel had done—you do know about *that*, don't you? You're too clever not to have noticed."

"Bringing in liquor."

"Nothing very big, you understand. Just a bit of honest smuggling. It's in our blood, you know. Cornwall. My great-grandfather made a bloody fortune shipping in brandy when the French were cutting up, did you know? Then that beast Wellington spoiled all our fun!" She makes a soft little laugh and sits back with her tea. "Maybe it was bad of Samuel—you Americans are so terribly strict about your little laws—but they needed the money, and he wasn't hurting anybody. Until the Ashley chaps decided they wanted a share of the business. So do you know what they did? It's rather fiendishly clever, actually. They would wait until the ships came onto shore, all filled with rum and whisky and that sort of thing, on those dark nights without any moon, and they'd intercept them! Take all the cargo for themselves!"

"My God!"

"Isn't it frightful? And naturally Simon was furious. He never did like to share what he considered rightfully his, even if it was illegal to begin with."

"No, I suppose not."

"Anyway, they had a great big row, Samuel and Simon. Samuel wanted to pay the buggers off—that was what they really wanted, after all—but Simon's not the accommodating type. He thought he could do better. Take them on and take them over. He had some sort of scheme, Samuel said, but they were too clever for him. That gang, I mean. And that's when they got him." She lifts her hand and makes a slicing movement along her neck.

"Got who?" asks Evelyn. She looks up benignly from the floor, where she's moved with her horse book, sitting small and cross-legged, the pages open on her lap. A thin layer of dried milk crusts the skin above her upper lip, and her sandy hair floats about her shoulders. Her father's eyes are so wide and innocent on her face, I want to rage. I want to swoop her up and cradle her against my ribs, but my arms are so weak.

"Oh, nobody, darling," Clara says.

I open my arms anyway, because I must. Because my daughter sits there before me, and we are all that's left. She flings the book out of her lap and rises to embrace me, and I'm not one to waste such riches. I turn my face into her curling hair and breathe in the peculiar fragrance of childhood. The same honeysuckle with which I used to wash Sophie's hair, when she was little.

"Sweetheart," I whisper.

"Angel," Clara says tenderly, laying her head on my other shoulder, and we sit there on the sofa, breathing in unison, while the sun climbs into noon. While the clock chimes.

But Evelyn's not yet three, and her nap is hours away. She wriggles back down and strikes across the floor, following God knows what trail, and Clara's lips move against the fabric of my shoulder.

"You can't risk her. What should we do without her? We've got to wait for Samuel. Samuel knows what to do. He's a soldier, you know. They are terribly competent."

I watch Evelyn's head bob next to the window. She has something in her hand, a small rubber horse, which she gallops along the sill. *Neigh, neigh,* she trills, and then she moves to the next window, a few yards away. Below her the Indian River flows past the docks. Past the Phantom Shipping Company warehouse, reconstructed into usefulness. The white light makes her cheek glow, like the side of the moon.

"Samuel will protect us," Clara says dreamily. "After all, he's in love with you."

"That's not true."

"Yes, it is. You'll see. Everything will be just fine, darling. What a happy family we'll be. I've always wanted a happy family, where everybody loves each other."

"Oh, Clara."

She slides down and settles her head in my lap. Evelyn gallops her horse across the room. The tea cools before us: Clara's thick and milky, mine clear and amber, beneath a paper-thin wedge of Maitland lemon.

"Simon's gone, darling," she murmurs. "He can't hurt you anymore."

I stroke her soft brown hair and observe the movement of my daughter's tanned, rhythmic legs. Back and forth. My face feels stiff and hot. Inside, my brain is teeming. Charged and spinning, like an electric dynamo, throwing off sparks to the wind.

"Yes," I say. "Of course."

WHEN CLARA IS THOROUGHLY ASLEEP, I slide out from beneath her and lead Evelyn to her bedroom, where we play with her rubber animals for a few minutes, until she's immersed in her barnyard and doesn't notice my departure.

The telephone is down the hall, in a small nook built into the wall for the purpose of discreet conversation. I take the card from my pocket and read off the exchange and number to the operator. Collect, I tell her. From Mrs. Fitzwilliam.

To my surprise, the call connects in less than a minute. But then, maybe he's waiting for me to find him.

"Mrs. Fitzwilliam," he says, in his urgent American voice, like the passing of velvet over stone. "What can I do for you?"

CHAPTER 26

M<small>Y LAST CLEAR</small> memory of my mother came a week before she died. She was a little more herself that day, for whatever reason, and in the absence of either gloom or mania we baked a cake together in the large kitchen on Field Point Road. She wore a yellow dress the color of primroses and a white pinafore apron. Like me, she was tall and long-boned, but she had Sophie's face, or rather Sophie has hers: large, soulful eyes and honey hair, which she had pinned in a loose and graceful knot on the top of her head. She was also several months gone with child, and her figure exuded that luscious, rounded quality of an expectant mother. I thought she looked beautiful. I remember I couldn't wait for the baby to be born. Another sister. I could almost picture her, like an infant doll.

My mother wasn't all that experienced in the kitchen, and the cake was a simple one: white layers alternating with lemon curd. She didn't want to use the lemon curd that our kitchen maid had already cooked and put in jars for the winter, so we created our own out of fresh Florida lemons and sugar. When it was finished, I stuck my finger in the bowl and tasted it, and it was awful, not nearly as good as Charlotte's, grainy and sour, and I puckered my lips in disgust. *What's wrong, darling?* Mama asked, and I said, without thinking, *It's not as nice as Charlotte's lemon curd.*

In that instant, the rare, hopeful radiance of her expression turned dark, and I realized the awfulness of my mistake. I stammered something out, some kind of mitigation, but she was already reaching for the bowl, already lifting it high above her head and hurling it to the polished wooden floor.

I remember how the sticky yellow curd splattered everywhere, studded with tiny shards of porcelain. I remember how Charlotte came running into the room, her face a picture of shock, and how Mama picked up a rag from the sink and threw it into Charlotte's chest. *Clean up this mess!* she shouted. I can hear those words now, and the exact tone in which she said them. I can still feel the misery that bore down on my ribs, because it was my fault. My fault for saying such a thing, when I knew better. Knew better than to suggest that Charlotte, of all people, held any sort of advantage over my mother.

Charlotte picked up the rag, of course, and silently cleaned the floor of the lemon curd my mother and I had made together. What else could she do? She was only a servant. A week later, my mother was dead, and it turned out that the baby she had been expecting was not my sister after all, but a brother.

And to this day, I'm really not sure which loss hurt me the most, in that terrible time after Sophie found her body on the kitchen floor, covered with blood: my mother or the sister I had imagined, who never really existed.

MY MOTHER. I THOUGHT ABOUT her constantly during the week after I arrived at Penderleath. For one thing, there wasn't much else to do. Simon, shortly after rushing upstairs to assess his parents' condition for himself, had driven me to this small, strange little cottage so I would be out of the way of germs, he said, and while the shelves contained books (old ones, bound in cloth) and a sort of village washerwoman brought me my meals, I found I couldn't take much interest in either. My brain was too charged, my stomach too clenched. I would take down a book from the shelf and try to read, and find myself in the middle of a chapter without any idea who the characters were, or what had happened. I would be thinking instead about that last summer in the house in Connecticut, which was also by the sea: a friendlier sea, a wholesome, soft-lipped shore on Long Island Sound, where anybody ought to have been happy. But she wasn't. That whole summer, I felt as if some thundercloud were driving in from the west, about to blacken the sky, to blacken the whole earth. And now that premonition had taken hold of me again. I could not get the image of thunderclouds out of my mind.

I took walks instead. The cottage snuggled next to the sea, in a crevice along a series of cliffs, not far from a path that I imagined might have been used by smugglers, some day long ago. Or perhaps it was still used by smugglers; who knew? This was Cornwall, after all: a strange, remote claw dragging into the confluence of three seas. The skies remained gray, the drizzle intermittent. The air softened by springtime but not yet warm. I liked to stand at the point where the cliffs made their highest ascent and stare west across the gray-green wash, brooding and tempestuous, where America eventually lay. If I looked northward, along the coast, I could just see the headland where the shore bent inward to Port Isaac.

But I didn't venture into Port Isaac. Simon had warned me not to, in case there was more influenza. The disease was terrible; it was ravaging everybody, especially the young. So I remained isolated in the cottage, obedient to my husband's orders, fed only by the washerwoman and the terse, anxious notes that arrived daily from Simon and my own imagination, until one afternoon when the rain dried out and the sun appeared, and Samuel Fitzwilliam walked up the pebbled path and found me sitting on a boulder.

For so large a man, he moved with utmost quiet, and I must have jumped a foot when he stopped behind me and said my name.

"What are you doing here?" I asked.

"Pack your things."

"What? My God, has something happened?"

He was smoking a cigarette, nearly finished. He threw it down on the path and crushed the stub under the heel of his shoe. "You could say that, yes. Are you all right? You look pale."

"Just tell me what's happened! Is Simon sick?"

"No. No, Simon is not sick. Not with the damned Spanish flu, anyway." He reached out to me with his large shovel hand and dragged me down the path. "Your husband is just fine, Mrs. Fitzwilliam, as he always is."

"Then what are we doing? Your parents—?"

"My parents are dead, or will be shortly."

"My God!"

"They're dead, and you've got to leave, Mrs. Fitzwilliam, leave the lot of us here in Cornwall and go back to New York where you belong."

I dug my heels into the path and skidded along until he stopped and turned to me. His face was thunderous and bewildered. "What are you doing?"

"What am *I* doing? What are *you* doing? What's going on? Has Simon sent you?"

"No. Simon has *not* sent me, by God. I've sent myself. He's ruined enough, hasn't he? I'll be damned if he ruins you, too."

"He hasn't ruined anything! He's been risking his life, trying to save your parents, which is more than—"

"Save them? *Save* them?" Samuel's cheeks were red. He dropped my hand abruptly, so that I nearly fell to the ground, and ran his hand through his dark hair. "No, Mrs. Fitzwilliam. You've got it all wrong. He wasn't trying to save them. The opposite."

I reached out for a nearby boulder and sat down. My ears felt as if something had started whirling inside them. "What are you saying? Simon's not—what are you saying?"

"I'm saying he wanted to get rid of them. Get rid of them and claim his inheritance, before it's gone entirely. He already has, almost. I was just in the village, and the word is they're both unconscious, death expected any moment. Mind you, I don't half blame him, but—"

"But that's ridiculous." I stood. My legs wobbled and held. "We arrived a week ago, and they were already sick."

"Yes, of course they were. Because my brother came down here a few days before your wedding and *made* them sick. Poisoned them. The same way he did his father-in-law."

"That's the most preposterous thing I've ever heard! Poisoned his father-in-law?"

"Well, it wasn't 'flu, was it? The magistrate himself told me that—in strict confidence, of course—straight from the coroner's mouth. A magistrate and a coroner, mind you, who just happen to be on excellent terms with one Simon Fitzwilliam. They are all terribly snug with one another, the local gentry."

"But Simon—it's impossible. It had to be 'flu. What kind of poison could make you sick like that?"

"God knows. I suppose a chap like my brother might be up-to-date on all the most modern methods of poisoning."

"Stop it! Stop saying such things! It's ridiculous. Simon would *never*— you've got no proof—he would *never*—"

"You can believe what you like, of course. You're in love with him."

"And you're the opposite. You despise him. You want to think the worst of him, whatever the evidence."

Samuel shrugged. "I know what I know."

"Besides, Simon didn't go to Cornwall last week. He couldn't have. He was busy making arrangements for the wedding."

"Is that what he said? Well, I daresay it wasn't an absolute lie. He drove down here to ask them to go to the wedding after all, to give the whole affair the appearance of their approval. Naturally they refused. Told him exactly what they thought. A frightful old row, or so I've heard. Not having darkened the old doorstep myself, in recent years."

I opened my mouth to say that this was a lie, too, but the truth was, I hadn't actually seen Simon in the days before the wedding. For a week or so before, he had been away—running errands, as he told me—interviewing with some hospital about a position, squaring away the license and that sort of thing. I hadn't asked him to account for himself, and he hadn't given me any details. But I remembered, now that I thought about it, how haggard he looked when he visited me in my private room at the hospital in Hampstead, upon his return. It was the night before the wedding, and I had just finished packing my trunk, which he loaded onto the back of the Wolseley. I told him he looked tired, and he said he'd done an awful lot of driving, and I kissed him and said he should go to bed early and rest. Because to-morrow was a big day.

Yes, he had said, kissing me back. Tomorrow is a very big day, indeed.

I said, Aren't you happy? You don't look happy.

He had pushed back my hair from my forehead and told me he was the happiest and luckiest man in England at that moment.

But I thought, at the time, he was putting up a bit of a front. That the strain of everything had taken too much hold, and maybe it was the divorce. Divorce was always a tremendous strain, I'd been told, even if both parties approached the dissolution amicably, and he'd always been reluctant to share his troubles with me. He had always wanted to protect me from upset.

And I thought, as I searched his face that evening, how this had to stop. How I would do everything in my power to make it up to him. I would do everything I could to be a good wife, a wife who brought joy and comfort to her husband.

I said to Samuel Fitzwilliam, "I suppose it's possible he visited them. Obviously, he wouldn't have told me about it, if your parents were awful about the whole thing. He hates to upset me."

Samuel stared at me without replying. The breeze lifted the hair on his monumental forehead, but that was all that moved. The muscles of his face lay still; the knuckles of his right hand pressed into his waist, while his left fingers braced against his thigh.

"You don't know anything, do you?" he said. "Of course you don't, or you wouldn't have married him."

"I know everything I need to know about Simon. I know how good he is—"

"Did he tell you about Lydia?"

"Of course he did. He was awfully upset. Drowning like that—"

"Drowning! Is that what he told you?"

"Yes. He thinks it was suicide."

"Suicide. Oh, that's rich. That's priceless. Suicide. Tell me something.

You never thought it was a little bit convenient, that poor old Lydia—what was it?—that she vanished into the sea, after proving so unexpectedly difficult to divorce?"

The strangest thing. The sun still shone, in its feeble April way, but I felt as if a cloud had swallowed it. I felt as if the small warmth lighting my cheek had winked out.

"Of course I didn't think it was convenient. What a horrible thing to say. I didn't even know she was gone, until after the . . . after the . . ."

My voice faded.

"Ah. Didn't he bother to tell you until after you were good and married, then? How odd."

"But the divorce wasn't contested," I said. "Not at all. She agreed to everything. She wanted Simon to be happy."

"Really? Did you ask her?"

"Of course not. I've never met her. Did *you* ask her?"

He glanced at the sea. "No. I hadn't seen her since the end of summer. But I do know that her father kicked up an almighty fuss and said that if they divorced, he'd take back her inheritance."

"Simon didn't care about that."

"Didn't he?"

"He said that her father"—I tried to concentrate my memory—"he said that her father needed the capital anyway, to replace the shipping he'd lost to the U-boats. So it wasn't even worth the trouble."

"Hardly that. There might not have been much cash left, but the ships remain, the ones still afloat and the ones being built, and I daresay they're worth a great deal to somebody. And in order to inherit it, Simon and Lydia had to remain married, because that was the point, of course, the whole point of the marriage, combining the ships and the orchards. The dream of some future empire to rescue the family fortunes. Lydia's father was obsessed with it, God knows why. So you can see why his death was a marvelously timely development indeed for my dear brother, coming before the divorce papers were signed, so that Simon and Lydia get the whole lot, without any irksome clauses. And then Lydia drowns herself soon afterward."

I thought I might be sick. The seconds passed, the wind stiffened. This time a cloud did scud by, sending a shadow across Samuel's face.

I thought, *Just like Mother.*

"It's not true," I said. "It can't be true. I'm sure Simon will explain everything."

Samuel laughed. "Oh, I'm sure he will. He was always terribly clever at explaining himself afterward. Let me guess. You find out some inconvenient fact from another party. You start to have doubts, to renounce him in your head. And then he turns up at just the right moment, brimful of some wonderfully reasonable account of the crime, allowing just a touch of human fault but largely exculpating himself of anything but the very noblest of intentions. Does that sound at all familiar?"

"Excuse me." I pushed past him, down the hill toward the cottage. In my mind I tried to fight back the creeping blackness. To think of Simon's face, heavy with emotion as he placed the ring on my finger. *With this ring, I thee wed. With my body I thee worship.*

"She didn't just drown!" Samuel called behind me. "He went to visit her because she'd lost her nerve, she was thinking about rescinding the divorce petition because of her father. She wanted to try to make the marriage work instead, because that's what her father wanted. And the next day she was gone."

"Stop! Just stop!"

He took me by the arm. "Can you honestly say it wasn't Simon? Can you honestly say he didn't want it badly enough?"

"Want *what* badly enough? Her money?"

"No," he said. "Not hers. *Yours.*"

"I don't have any money."

"Stupid girl. I mean your father's money. His millions."

"But he doesn't know about that. Not how much, anyway."

"Yes, he does."

"I never told him!"

"You told *me*."

He looked even larger now, looming over me, a step or two higher on the steep, pebbled path. At that moment he looked astonishingly like Simon, though his expression had changed to one of anger: eyes fierce, mouth clenched. The sea crashed below us. *One good push*, I thought, and in my madness I didn't know whether I meant I should push him or he should push me.

Simon's voice: *Of course it was venal. But it did the trick, didn't it?*

"And naturally you had to tell him," I whispered. "You had to taunt him with it. You had to test him. Because you didn't think he meant to marry me."

"Dear girl, *nobody* thought he meant to marry you. Nobody at home knew a thing about you. He hadn't said a single bloody word to anyone, least of all his wife."

"Then how did *you* find out?"

"The usual gossip. You can't easily hide a love affair from your fellow officers, it seems, however discreet you imagine yourself. Any number of well-meaning chaps stood ready to tell me the fascinating news."

I stood there, panting. Unable to speak.

Samuel went on. "But of course, he *wouldn't* say anything to us. A gentleman never speaks to his family about his mistress."

I slapped him then. I didn't think about it; I just lifted my open hand and struck Samuel across the face. He flinched and touched his cheek with one finger. "Well done," he said calmly. "But I'm afraid you've got the wrong man."

THE STRANGE THING WAS, WHEN the door of the classroom opened and the headmistress motioned to my teacher, I knew what was wrong. I knew it was something to do with my mother, something terrible. I knew in my heart long before I accepted the fact of her murder in my head. It *fit*, that was all. All the wrongnesses in the house, one on top of the other. They were all leading to this.

My father was waiting in the headmistress's little office. He had forgotten to take off his hat. I remember how his hands shook, how he smelled strangely metallic: a scent I now recognize as that of blood. Blood, and the strong lye soap that had washed it away. He took me by the hand and led me outside. We had an electric Columbia runabout in those days, the kind that used a tiller instead of a steering wheel. He helped me inside, into the seat next to his, and on the way home he told me what had happened. That Charlotte had found Sophie in the kitchen with my mother, and my mother was dead. He didn't give me any details; I discovered those later. How she had been stabbed violently, and Sophie was soaked with her blood. Father just told me to be careful with Sophie, to hold her close and to protect her, because of what she had seen.

She probably won't remember anything, Father said, because she's so young. At least, I hope she won't.

I think he wiped away a tear, though at the time I thought he was only adjusting his spectacles to see the road.

When we arrived home, there were policemen everywhere, wandering about my house as if it were a shop or a hotel, as if it belonged to them. Father took me upstairs—through the front of the house, so I wouldn't see the kitchen—and told me to pack my things. We were going away. We couldn't stay here, not after what had happened.

I did as he asked. I packed my things, one by one, all by myself. I packed everything, because I knew, even then, that I wouldn't be returning to this bedroom, to this house, for the rest of my life. I knew, without being told, without thinking through any of the details, or resorting to any kind of human logic, that our happy days were past. That the night had come.

That I had only myself to rely on, in this unknown world that now lay before me.

BACK IN THE COTTAGE, I packed my few things with military precision. I poured all my concentration into the knife-edge sharpness of my folds, the squareness of the piles in my small valise. Hairbrush, cold cream, soap. Enamel writing case, containing pens and notepaper. I put on my coat and hat and gloves and opened the cottage door.

Samuel sat on the bench outside. He stood and removed his woolen cap. "I'll drive you to the railway station in Truro, if you like. It's a damned long walk to Port Isaac, and the 'bus doesn't run but once a day."

"All right."

"You're welcome." He took the valise from my fingers and set off ahead of me, down the crooked little path to the road, where a battered Daimler saloon stood on the verge. He swung the valise into the rear seat and opened the passenger door in the front.

The drive to Truro took more than an hour, and I don't think we exchanged a single word throughout. I stared straight ahead, clutching my pocketbook on my lap between my cold fingers, while Samuel drove with one hand and smoked with the other. The same way Simon had, I thought, driving from London. How strange, the small ways in which they were alike. The large ways in which they were different.

When we arrived at the railway station, Samuel switched off the ignition and looked at my lap. "You're still wearing your ring."

I glanced down and saw that he was right. I wriggled off the slim gold band and handed it to him. "For driving me here," I said.

He pushed my hand away. "Keep it. You may need the money sometime."

"You'll need it before I do. Anyway, I don't want it."

He considered this for a second or two and took the ring back.

"I can go with you to Liverpool or Southampton. Help you book passage."

"That's all right. I can manage myself." I reached for the handle of the door, and when I rose and shook out my skirt and closed the door again, Samuel stood next to me, holding out the valise.

"What should I tell him?" he asked.

"Are you going to tell him anything?"

"Only if you want me to."

You must understand that I wasn't really thinking at this point. If you had asked me to sit down and write, in logical order, the list of reasons why I should have believed the accusations of Samuel Fitzwilliam over my faith in Simon, I couldn't have done it. I didn't want to try. I was afraid that I could convince myself that he was innocent, that by wishing to make him innocent I would make him so, in my head, and I would then be a prisoner to unconscious doubt, looming outside my window, for the rest of my life. I would be a prisoner to this terror that boiled at the back of my mouth, along the edges of my skull.

And I had already been a prisoner for so long.

"Can I ask, at least, where you're going?" Samuel said when I didn't speak. "Home to your family, I assume?"

I nearly laughed. The hysteria rose in my throat, the true madness of my situation. Out of the frying pan, I thought. Now the fire?

"I'm going to find my sister," I said, "and then I guess we'll see what happens next."

BY THE TIME I LANDED in New York Harbor, three weeks later, I knew I was carrying Simon's child. My menstrual courses were late, and they were never late, not even when I was sick or lying near death in a hospital bed. Only Simon's child could interrupt the precise biological rhythms that governed me.

I hadn't wired ahead, so I was surprised to see two familiar figures standing among the milling people on the quayside as I disembarked. Father and Sophie.

My sister darted forward and threw her arms around me. "You're back!" she screeched, kissing each cheek over and over. The smell of honeysuckle made my eyes sting with tears.

My father's hand closed over my own. My left hand, which now bore a slim gold ring I had purchased on the ship.

"Welcome home," he said.

CHAPTER 27

Cocoa, Florida, July 24, 1922

I N ALL THE months that followed my return to New York, as the summer wore on and my waist disappeared, my father never once asked me what had happened when I was overseas. I spoke to Sophie, of course. (Sisters will confide, you know.) I spun her the loveliest tale—based in truth, as all good stories are—about how I had fallen in love inside the cab of a Model T ambulance, about how we had written to each other as war raged around us, about how my beloved had cared for me tenderly after the accident that nearly killed me. How—my goodness—he had brought me back to life! Like a saint performing a miracle.

How his parents' deaths had left him penniless because of the taxes, how he had left for Florida to make a fortune for us. Because of course he wouldn't take money from Father, oh no! He was too honorable for that.

And Sophie believed this story, all of it. Bless her dear, innocent heart. She held my hand and told me how she just *knew* my husband would send for us, any day now. She never once asked why a devoted husband couldn't make time to visit his bride in the last weary weeks of pregnancy, or why the birth of his only child drew from him no more than the usual monthly letter, or why the passing of holidays and birthdays never tempted him to visit us. I don't know. Maybe Sophie *did* suspect the truth and was only pretending for my sake. Complicit in our little household fraud. The innocent ones always understand more than you think.

Anyway. While I tried to stick to the truth, the part about not taking money from Father was a bald lie. I knew this because I'd seen the letter that arrived on the hall table in June, directed to Father from an address in London I didn't recognize. I opened it, of course. You can't just leave such a thing untouched, in the state I was in that summer of 1919. Without the slightest hesitation, I opened the London envelope and learned that the sum of ten thousand pounds sterling had, according to Mr. Fortescue's instructions, been herewith deposited in the account of Mr. Simon Fitzwilliam of Penderleath, Cornwall. That the bank would be happy to oblige Mr. Fortescue, should he have any further business to transact in the kingdom of Great Britain, and, in the meantime, remained his obedient servant, et cetera.

And I suppose that's why Father never asked me about Simon. He already knew everything he needed to know.

I TELL YOU ALL THIS not out of spite, or for pity, but because you may think I was unreasonable, judging Simon so harshly, without any proof except for the word of his brother.

Or you may think Clara's right. You may think there's a simpler explanation, that she was kidnapped by the Ashley gang, as part of this brutal war with Simon and now Samuel over control of the lucrative bootlegging trade on the Florida coast, and that the doctor gave me those pills only in order to help me heal from that blow to my head. You may think that regardless of whether or not Simon was a villain, he's dead, and that I ought to move forward. To begin my life anew. Fall in love with someone else, someone I can depend on.

The man, for example, who's standing at the end of the pier before me, dark and enormous in the moonless night, while the river rushes softly at his feet. Or maybe it's not Samuel. After all, I can't see much in this blackness; only the feeblest hint of the Cocoa streetlights reaches us here, on the Phantom Shipping Company pier, and as I said, there's no moon. Only the starlight, dimmed by that summer haze that coats the Florida sky. The world is so still and black, you can hear the groans of the alligators in the water below, the whispers of the night birds. The low mutter of the frogs, the squeaks of the crickets.

"Samuel!"

The man whips around. A light springs from his right hand and strikes my eyes.

"Christ! What are you doing here?"

An English voice. Samuel's voice. (I'm right, you see. I've been right all along.)

"Looking for you."

The light shuts off, and the darkness coats us once more. "Why?" he asks, and then, hastily: "You shouldn't be here."

"If you're waiting for the ship, it won't come."

"What do you know about *that?*"

"I just know, that's all."

Samuel swears.

He hasn't moved, not since that initial start, when I called out to him from my position halfway down the pier. I can't really see him; I can only perceive his shape by the way it blocks out the pinpricks of light from the opposite shore. I believe the scientists call this indirect observation. It's how they discover certain celestial bodies, or the constituent parts of an atom. You posit the existence of something by its effect on other objects.

"I know what you're doing here tonight. I know that you're expecting a shipment from Cuba—rum—and you've paid off the gang so they won't steal the goods as they come in, but you're wrong. They're double-crossing you, Samuel. They're taking your money and they're stealing the rum anyway, because Simon's with them."

"Simon?"

"Yes."

There is a shattering little silence.

"Simon's dead, Virginia. He's gone."

"He's not gone. I don't know whose body you found inside that house on Cocoa Beach, but it wasn't Simon's. It was all for show. He wanted everyone to think he was dead, because the business was losing money, he had all these debts and he couldn't pay them anymore, he couldn't keep it all spinning, so he thought he would start fresh, and he created this elaborate lie, this—this forgery of his own death, in order to escape his debts, and my father paid him to do it, to go away from our lives for good—"

"Your *father?*"

"Yes. My father paid him off, directly after the fire. I saw the letter from the bank. And then when Father was found guilty, Simon must have realized I was an even better prize than before, an heiress—"

"Oh, Virginia—"

"Except that he's got to get rid of you and Clara, so there will be no one left who knows the truth about him. And perhaps to get rid of me, too, so he can simply collect all my money, without the nuisance of marriage. I believe he's already tried—I think Miss Bertram—"

He cuts me off by the simple act of moving forward and snatching my hand. "Come along," he snarls, dragging me back down the pier toward the warehouse, which he opens with a key from his trouser pocket. Inside, he lights a kerosene lantern, and the sight of his face—square, blazing— sends me stumbling backward a step or two. He takes me by the elbows and tells me to be careful.

"You don't believe me, do you? You think I'm hysterical. Delusional. Because of everything that's happened to me, all these terrible things—"

"It's true, then? You're not still in love with him?"

"My God! How could I be?"

The room is hot and packed with atmosphere. Samuel tugs on my elbows, and I step forward, closing the gap between us. He bends down and kisses me on the mouth in a blunt, straightforward attack, opening my surprised lips and then turning tender, cupping the back of my head with his hands, so that it's no effort at all to stand there and kiss him. He's been drinking; his tongue tastes of liquor, his breath is pungent with it, intoxicating me in a small, reckless way. My arms, now free, slip around his thick waist, and it seems that my hands can't begin to encompass him, that

I'm reduced to a miniature of myself. Small and dainty and safe, for once in my life, in the middle of a bootlegger's warehouse on a moonless night. Imagine that. He lifts his head and his breath, reeking of brandy or more probably rum, touches my face. His thumbs run across my cheekbones. I keep my eyes closed, because he's still so close, and I don't want to look at him. Not yet. I don't want to know if I love him. If I care for him at all. If I'm still capable of that kind of thing.

"Should I apologize?" he asks.

"No."

He kisses me again, brief and firm, not so much ending the kiss as interrupting it. He circles his giant arms around me and draws me into his chest and stomach, whispering words into my hair that I can't hear, because the muscles of his shoulder lie against one ear and his hand rests against the other. His cotton shirt is damp with sweat. Stifling. The ridge of a button presses against my cheekbone, and I think, *How strange; my cheek used to reach all the way to Simon's shoulder.*

Samuel says aloud: "I'm taking you back to the hotel, Virginia. This is no place for you."

"I won't go."

"You don't have a choice. I'll carry you if I have to. These men—"

"They aren't coming *here*, Samuel. That's what I came to tell you. They'll be on the water, right now, on the ocean just off the coast, and Simon's with them. He's going to show them exactly where your ship plans to land, and then they'll take the cargo for themselves."

"How do you know all this?"

"Because I know the revenue agent who recruited him. The revenue agent who's going to be waiting on the shore to arrest the gang, and then to arrest you, too. It's a double cross, Samuel. Isn't that the word? He's getting rid of you and coming out all clean and lily white himself, a real hero, all his problems solved, except for me."

He lets me go. "Christ. A revenue agent?"

"Yes."

"My God."

"He's the man who helped Simon with his forgery. An agent for the Department of Internal Revenue, who's trying to—I don't know—clean up the Florida coast, stop all the liquor smuggling. He admitted the whole plan to me. I told him a pack of lies, how I loved Simon and couldn't bear it any longer, and I was going to go out on the beach and find those Ashley men myself if he didn't tell me the truth, so he told me. It's astonishing, really, what a man like that will admit when confronted with a woman's weakness."

He makes an agitated movement with his arm, the kind of gesture I've never seen in Samuel before, whose every physical act smacks of slow deliberation and purpose.

"This is the truth?" he says finally.

"Of course it's the truth!"

"Simon's still alive."

"He's alive, Samuel, he's alive and he's just off the coast, right now, waiting to . . . to strike, to . . . attack his own ship, or to *pretend* that he's attacking. To lead the gang into the trap. To finish the job."

"To this agent of yours. Waiting on the beach."

"Yes. This very minute."

"And this agent. He doesn't know you're here with me?"

"Of course not. He thinks I'm at the hotel, waiting faithfully for Simon to return."

"Evelyn?"

"Asleep. Clara's watching her."

He swears again and turns to walk to the other side of the room.

"Why are you telling me this?" he says.

"To warn you, of course."

"It's too late. What the devil am I going to do about it? Go up against the Department of Internal bloody Revenue? Go up against the Ashley gang?"

"No. You—we—we're going to tell them—tell the Ashleys—tell them this *second* that Simon's about to betray them. That it's all a frame-up."

He swivels around to face me, and the action is so swift and vicious, it disturbs the cloying, liquor-laden air, causes the lantern to swing gently on its hook. Causes the kerosene flame to lick luridly on his cheek. "*Tell* them?"

"Yes. I know where the men are waiting on shore. We'll go to them right now and warn them."

"My God. Do you have any idea what they'll *do* to him? To Simon?"

"Yes."

"And you don't care? They'll kill him, Virginia. They'll shoot him like a dog, without the slightest hesitation."

I'm wearing a loose, light jacket over my shirt and skirt, the same one I wore in the Japanese tea garden at the Flamingo Hotel, not because the night is cool—my God, it's like the devil himself is heating his brimstone under our feet—but because it's got large patch pockets on either side. I stick my right hand inside the corresponding pocket and draw out my Colt Model 1911 pistol.

"If they don't," I say, "I will."

THE PISTOL. MY FATHER GAVE me that pistol. It was a day or two before I left for France, I think, or maybe a little longer—that last week went by in such a hurry. Such a strange, flourishing panic that terrified and delighted me. Anyway, Sophie went to bed early for some reason, I forget why, and Father rose and turned off the gramophone and left the room, and I thought how strange that was, because Father usually outlived us all in the evening. He was always the last to bed, climbing the stairs in a heavy, pendulous tread that made me think of the Grim Reaper, or else Blackbeard. Sometimes he would pause on the landing—his bedroom was on the second floor, while Sophie and I slept on the third—and I would wonder if he was contemplating the next flight, whether he would knock on my door and want to speak to me, or just push the barrier open and not say a word.

But instead of saying good night and climbing the stairs, he returned a moment later with a box in his hand. I put down my book and knotted my hands in my lap.

"This is for you," he said gruffly, holding out the box.

"What is it?"

"A gun. A pistol."

He opened the lid and showed me. I looked back and forth between the pistol, nestled in old green velvet, and my father's face, red-tinted and serious, and asked what it was for.

He looked amazed. Amazed and maybe pitying.

"To protect yourself, Virginia. Every woman who sets out on her own should have a means of protecting herself. The male sex is endowed with the greater share of physical strength. A pistol is a means of redressing that imbalance."

I said that I didn't know how to use a pistol, and he said he would show me. He took the instrument from its hollow in the old green velvet and made me hold it, explained to me what type of pistol it was and how it worked, all its constituent parts. He showed me how to take it apart and clean it—the imperative of cleaning a pistol properly, of making sure that an object so precise and lethal as a gun remained in absolute pristine condition, not a speck or a smudge to affect its reliable performance—until, I suppose, I managed to satisfy him.

The next day he woke me at dawn and drove me across the East River to a field on the remote outer fringes of Queens County, where he showed me how to fire the thing, and while I was no sharpshooting prodigy, it turned out I had a steady hand and a good eye, and by the time the sun crept high enough to touch the telephone wires that stretched across one corner of the field, he again wore that expression of satisfaction, or maybe relief, and made me unload the pistol by myself and pack it back correctly into its case.

He didn't say much on the way home. It was November, and the wind was cold on our faces, so that you couldn't operate your mouth without great muscular effort. But in Brooklyn we stopped at a coffee shop and had breakfast, and Father said something, into the smoky silence, that shocked me. He said, in reluctant, gruff words: "Your mother would be proud of you."

And that was the only time we ever spoke of her.

AS A RESULT, WHENEVER I hold that pistol, or think about that pistol, I think of my mother, or rather the memory of my mother accompanies the pistol. Also the taste of coffee, the damp, greasy smell of that Brooklyn shop, frying bacon. And my father, looming over all.

Speaking of looming. There's Samuel, planted a few yards away, made monstrous by the swinging lantern, staring in shock at the pistol in my hand. He says, *You can't be serious,* as if he really means it, as if he doesn't think a woman with a pistol knows her business.

"Of course I'm serious," I say.

And I think my mother would be proud of me.

THEY SAY THERE ARE NUMEROUS sharks off the Florida coast, man-eaters. Maybe it's true. Florida still seems like such an exotic place to me, like the Antipodes, dangerous, sharp-fanged creatures lurking in its swamps and waterways, brimful of poison and malice. And I've always thought how ignoble they were, those poisonous lurkers, hiding inside the tranquillity of the water where nobody expects them, and then—*snap!* Not what you'd call honorable.

On the other hand, as I now perceive, the sharks and the alligators and the snakes have to eat, don't they? And we each destroy our necessary prey in the manner offered to us by Nature. We do what we must to survive in this harsh and bitter universe.

Still, the universe, or at least that infinitesimal fraction of it laid out before us now, seems anything but harsh and bitter. The air is dark and warm, the automobile's engine drones in our blood. The headlights slide across the twists and snarls of the mangrove on either side, while ahead of us the gray road blackens into shadow.

We pass a small signpost, indicating that the beach lies half a mile ahead, and Samuel brings the car to an easy stop. Sets the brake, switches off the headlights, cuts the engine, and for a moment there is nothing to see, nothing to hear except the faint roar of the surf, moving in rhythm with my breath. The whir of insects. Samuel finds my lap and wraps his hand over mine. His palm is dry and strong. I feel as if we're in a womb, waiting to be born.

"It's awfully dark," I whisper. "How are you going to make your way?"

"I'll manage."

"That's where he made his fortune, you know. Carl Fisher. He invented the first really practical headlight for cars. The Prest-O-Lite."

"Fisher? That chap in Miami Beach?"

"Yes. Clara's great friends with them. The Fishers."

Samuel makes a noise of assent that suggests he isn't nearly so fond of the Fishers as his sister is. How strange, to be whispering about headlights and tycoons at a moment like this. He leans down to the floorboards and finds the electric torch, which he lights for an instant or two, under the protection of the dashboard, just long enough to check his watch.

"I should start," he says.

"I should come with you."

"No!" His voice rises. Then, back to a whisper: "No. For God's sake. Stay here with the motor. Be ready for when I return. We're going to have to bolt out of here like lightning, do you understand? Can you still drive?"

"Of course."

"As soon as I leave, get behind the wheel. If you hear anything, start the engine. Not the headlights, just the engine. I'll move as fast as I can. If you see anyone other than me, just leave. Drive straight on back to the hotel and pretend you've never left. Clear?"

"But how will I know what's happened? How will I know . . . ?"

I can't say it.

"Because I will find you and tell you," Samuel says. "I'll see to it myself. I promise you, Virginia, I'll finish this for you."

You might think he whispers this sentence with passion, but he doesn't. He speaks with as much passion as a man promising to bring home meat for dinner, and I remember that he's a soldier, that he's gone into battle, that he once spent years inside a German prison and then escaped. And I remember the nature of what he's promising—to kill his own brother, partly for his own sake but mostly for mine—and of course you must steel yourself for a thing like that. As dangerous and wicked as Simon is, he shared a cradle with Samuel, they're twins. And maybe Samuel isn't going to strike down his twin by the force of his own hand, but the result's the same. Simon's going to die tonight, and Samuel is going to make sure he dies.

Though the air is thick and warm, not the slightest breeze off the water, I start to shiver a little. To tremble. I haven't been myself in so long; I haven't been strong and healthy in so long. I can't separate the sickness of the past month from whatever it is I'm experiencing now. Samuel hears the chatter of my teeth and asks if I'm all right, and I tell him yes. Just anxious.

His palm appears on the side of my face. "Don't be anxious. I'll see this through."

"Yes."

"When it's finished, when I'm back—"

"Don't say it."

"But you know."

"Yes."

His face is close to mine; I can feel its warmth. "I'm no good at this. Not like Simon."

"I don't want you to be like Simon."

"If I could, I'd show you. I'd make you mine this moment."

The shock of those words sends me into a kind of daze. I remember what Clara said, that Samuel is somehow in love with me, and the idea—

making love to Samuel, the act of intercourse with Samuel, the act of intercourse with anyone at all—is so strange and perverse and alluring that my stomach heaves. His mouth hovers next to mine, but he doesn't kiss me. I have the feeling he's waiting for me to say something, to give him permission, and that if he kisses me he might actually do the thing he's just suggested. Here in the dark, in the quiet, hastily and without any wooing: just copulation, brutal and primitive, the way soldiers do before they go into battle. Or afterward. And there is a corresponding urge in my belly to play my own part in this age-old transaction, to open my lips and my legs and allow him a warrior's rights, the way his own beautiful Fitzwilliam ancestress opened her lips and her legs to her king. (How strange that I should recall that story, at such a moment.) But this is my husband's brother, about to stain himself with my husband's blood, and I find that this urge in my belly, this daze in my brain is more like nausea, more like shame absorbed into physical symptoms.

"Not yet," I whisper. "Not like this."

He lifts his head away and opens the door of the car. "Remember what I said."

"Yes."

He slips quietly out of the car and shuts the door in such a manner that the sound stays put, like a cough suppressed in your throat. I clamber over the gear box into the driver's seat and look up to whisper good-bye, but he's already gone, gulped up by the teeming Florida night, and I have nothing to do but wait.

I THOUGHT I HAD MEMORIZED the territory around Simon's house on Cocoa Beach when I came here yesterday afternoon, squinting in pain at the sun. I sketched out the dirt road and the edge of the mangrove, the placement of the dunes and the other solitary houses, the exact number of steps between the road and the stone fountain in the center of what had once been Simon's courtyard (where the Ashley gang are to lie in wait), and the possible positions where Mr. Marshall and his men might station themselves: the watchmen stalking the predators.

But the darkness disorients me. I become aware of the stars, and the skin of black ocean at the horizon, boiling with phosphorescence. As the minutes pass and nothing else emerges, no shapes resolve from the shadows, charcoal on midnight, not the mangrove nor the beach nor the nocturnal beasts that surely prowl and scurry over the earth around me, I begin to lose myself. I've forgotten the effects of a blackness this intense, so thick you feel as if you're pushing it aside at every breath. How are you supposed to know your distance and your direction in a soup like that? Only the ocean saves me, the crests of the waves, the foam that returns just enough light to the universe, just enough sound and fury that I can at least find east, and if I can find east, I can find west, north, and south.

Can't I?

My hand hurts. The thick bandage applied by the doctor is now just a slender wrapping of gauze atop the neat sutures—eight of them—holding my flesh together. I cradle the right hand with the left and close my eyes, and it's too peaceful, too sacred, as if a human tragedy isn't about to play out—isn't right this moment playing out—a quarter mile away. On the beach. Simon's beach. Simon's house, and at this mere echo of his name in my head, a tremor strikes my chest, a blow of anguish. I bend over, sobbing, thinking of Evelyn, of how we made Evelyn, Simon and I, and now I have destroyed the father of my daughter. Evelyn, who never even knew him, and the Château de Créouville, the courtyard there, and the smell of Simon's cigarettes. The fountains dancing on the canals of Versailles. The tulips that thrust from the earth on my wedding day. The taste of Simon's skin. And I cannot push them away, cannot cleanse myself of these impressions, which are part of my flesh, the molecules of Simon invading the molecules of Virginia, and I have killed him. I have destroyed him. And he is my husband, he is the father of my daughter.

I spill, somehow, from Samuel's Ford and stagger down the road, toward the beach. It's too late, I have made the most awful mistake, he is wicked and only wants to deceive me, only wants my money, but I can't let him *die*. Cannot return to a world in which Simon does not exist. His molecules are my molecules; his wickedness is mine. Let him have my money. Let him have what he wants, but let him *live*. For God's sake. He is Evelyn's own father. And my throat revolts, my hand throbs in fear, but I cannot bear him to die. To *die*. His skin torn. His blood in the sand. By *my* hand.

Except I'm too late.

I know this, as I plunge through that darkness, that terrifying absence of light, except for the glimpse of ocean ahead. I know I have already set this train in motion, that I can't stop the inevitable crash ahead, and *still* I push forward, desperate now, wanting to reverse the flow of time, to send the earth spinning in the other direction so I can take it all back, return to the beginning, and that's when the gun cracks the air, a single shot and then a whole volley, *rat-a-tat-a-tat-a-tat-a-tat-a-tat*, the familiar deadly cadence of a Thompson submachine gun, and out of the blackness before me emerges a bouncing yellow light, a shadow behind it, a figure, a person, a man, and I can't see his face but as I stop, feet planted in the dirt, I know who it is.

The beam of his flashlight catches my chest an instant later. He skids, checks. The beam jolts to my face, and I cry out at the sudden blindness, and Simon says, "Virginia!"

Only a yard away. Alive. Slight glint where his hair should be—maybe the starlight. The lurid yellow glow of the flashlight illuminating his features like a monster's.

"Simon!"

He starts forward and snatches my arm. "Come with me!"

"No!"

"Now!"

I struggle free and reach for my pocket, and Simon swears foully and takes me around the waist, hoisting me over his shoulder, making me scream in agony as my injured hand strikes his back.

But my other hand. My left hand. Contains the gun.

The Ford's only a short distance up the dirt road, maybe fifty yards. Simon carries me along, almost at a run but not quite, and my torso slams against his shoulder and the muscles of his back, while I wriggle my left arm helplessly, trying to maneuver the gun into some sort of position, some angle by which I can strike him. But his bones are too hard, his arm too heavily braced around me, and instead I just pound the gun against his kidneys, over and over, thinking if I could just get him to drop me, drop me, and then Simon makes a noise of joy, sees the Ford probably, and the next thing I'm swinging through the air to land over the passenger door, crosswise into the seat, my head bouncing against the cloth.

"Sorry," he grunts, and jumps in after me.

I don't know how I scramble upward, brain sloshing in its case, dizzy and sick, but I do. I scramble upward. My left hand grips the gun and brings it shaking up to the level of Simon's ear and I say, STOP! I'LL SHOOT!

He turns his head and says, *What the devil.*

"Get out of the car."

"Virginia! My God. It's *me*, for God's sake! It's Simon!"

"Get out. Now."

"Don't be stupid. They're right behind me."

"I'll shoot."

"No, you won't. You won't shoot me. You can't."

My thumb lifts the safety catch. *"Out!"*

"Virginia, it's me. It's Simon."

"I know who you are."

"Christ," he says. "Virginia, no. It's *me*. It's Simon."

And for a second or two I believe him. The flashlight is off. He hasn't switched on the ignition, hasn't turned on the headlights. His head is just a smudge, the glossy curves of his eyeballs catch only the tiniest glint from the hazy stars above us. I can't see his face; I can only hear his voice, quiet and deep and doctorly, the way it used to reach me in bed, during our rendezvous in France, when we shared words in the middle of the night, and the absence of light and vision seemed to bring us into an even deeper communion than the acts of love we had just committed, in such fervor, during the hours before. He smells of cigarettes and the pungency of the ocean and his own peculiar perspiration, and such is the power of scent on the animal mind, the power of primal recognition, I want to plunge my hands around his waist and kiss his stomach, his chest, his neck, his mouth, his everything.

I suppose he senses this instant of weakness. He always did. He touches my shoulder and then wraps his hand around the side of my face, his thumb lying along the bend of my cheekbone and his fingers finding the tenderness under the curve of my skull. "Virginia, it's me. It's Simon. For God's sake, you've got to trust me, you've got to give me that gun right now."

And then: "Please, Virginia. Darling. My *wife*. Have mercy."

I lift the gun to the back of his head and slide my shaking finger to the trigger.

The air shatters around us, a bang of unearthly noise, and Simon slumps onto my chest. For an instant I think I've done it, I've shot him, and a hysterical scream rises in my throat.

But a pair of arms looms over my head and grips Simon by the shoulders, tossing him into the air and onto the dirt at the side of the road.

"Thank God," says Samuel, landing in the seat beside me, and without the slightest pause he starts the engine and grinds the gears, tearing the dirt, spinning the wheels, while I grip the side of the door and hold on for dear life, back up the road to the wooden bridge across the Indian River, while the sound of gunfire fades into the mangrove behind us.

SAMUEL TAKES ME NOT TO the hotel but to the Phantom Shipping Company offices. I ask him why we're here, in a stunned, quiet voice I don't even recognize, and he says we'll be safer here. What about Evelyn? I ask, and he says he's going straight over to the hotel, right now, and he's going to bring her and Clara to the offices, too, and then we will drive out through the night to Maitland. We'll be safe there.

Safe, I say. Safe from what? Simon's dead.

Just safe, he says. Away from all this.

I must look a little pale, because he pours me a glass of brandy from his office and makes me drink it all down, a waterfall of fire, pooling in my stomach. I set down the glass. He asks if I want a blanket, and I say I'm all right, I just need to lie down for a moment. He takes me to the sofa in his office and says I can rest there. He'll be back as soon as he can. He'll lock the door, just in case.

All right, I say, and I close my eyes.

The sofa is soft, the brandy is warm. I have the strangest feeling that I'm floating, drifting quietly to the ceiling, watching my sleeping body from above. Somewhere, just out of reach, hovers the horror of the evening, the reality of what has just occurred, but I can't quite grasp it. My head is too blurred. My bones too wispy. I can't seem to feel a thing. Just the cushion under my cheek, the brandy fire simmering in my stomach, the weight of my eyelids like a kind of paralysis, creeping over me, minutes ticking away in a grotesque rhythm until one of them—the minutes, the snitch of seconds on the clock—strikes an electric charge in the center of my chest.

Evelyn.

I leap upward. Heart pounding in my ears. Evelyn. I need Evelyn.

It's all right. Samuel has gone to fetch her. To fetch her and Clara, and we will drive to Maitland together, where we will be safe.

But there is something missing in this idea, some giant hole I cannot name, and into this void pours such a panic as I have never before experienced. I brace my hand on the arm of the sofa and haul myself to my feet, wavering, trembling from every pore, thinking, *Don't be silly, Simon's dead, we're safe now,* and that's when I realize I'm clutching something in the crook of my elbow, something soft.

I look down. A doll. Evelyn's missing doll, the rag doll that sat on my chest of drawers at Maitland.

I think, *Of course, she left it in the car.* In Samuel's car, as we drove through the night back to Cocoa. I had forgotten. And now I'm clutching it like a talisman; I have carried it without thought from the car to the office, close to my ribs, seeking any kind of comfort I can find.

Everything you seek is here.

The words echo in my head. I stare at the doll's brown button eyes, her pursed thread mouth. She's a large creature, comfortable and homemade, constructed of some kind of sturdy cambric. The delicate pink dress, tied at the back of the neck, covers a lumpy abdomen that sounds crisply when I turn it over in my hands.

Not the orange blossoms, I think. The doll.

In the gap between the two sides of her dress, a seam runs all the way down her back, sewn together clumsily in large black stitches. I insert my finger beneath the thread and rip it off, and the doll's cotton stuffing sags away, revealing the sharp white corner of a folded paper tucked inside.

I seem to have stopped breathing. I sit down, dizzy. Grasp the paper at the corner and work it free from the stuffing.

A letter, written close in small, black, familiar script, folded into a square.

I stick my trembling fingers back inside the doll. One by one, I pull them out, thirty-four of them in total. Thirty-four letters without envelopes, hidden inside the body of a rag doll.

I READ SWIFTLY, BECAUSE SAMUEL will return any moment. Because when you're gorging yourself, you cannot slow, you cannot stop to ponder the nature of what you're gorging on. I try to read them in order, though I seem to be having trouble with the months and the days, and where they belong in sequence. My mind is too overstruck, I think. By the time I finish the last one, the longest one, written on the last day of February, passionate and devastating, I have gone numb, the way you might go numb if struck by an electric charge too intense to bear. If you have just been told, on perfect authority, that the earth is no longer a sphere but has turned into a cube. If you have just learned that your mistaken testimony has sent an innocent man to the gallows.

I think, *Evelyn.* I must get back to Evelyn. I must find Evelyn at once.

I stand and grasp the edge of a chair for balance, swaying a little, and that's when I notice the small, delicate figure standing in the doorway. Wearing a thin cotton dress and a worn cardigan jacket. Staring at me from a face at once unknown and familiar, mouth altered and hair lengthened, like a statue of soft clay that has been reshaped by its creator.

"Virginia?" she whispers.

"Yes."

Her voice is clipped and English, somewhat timid. "I'm sorry to disturb you. I arrived on the train this evening, and I didn't know where else to go."

I stand there, blinking at her. Holding the knob of a chair for support. Pulse knocking in my neck like a woodpecker. An expression of concern takes over the woman's face, which is dainty and worn, empty of any cosmetics, a sad, dear, old-fashioned, elegant little face. One I feel I should recognize.

"I say. Are you quite all right?" She glances at my right shoulder. "Has something happened? Was that Samuel a moment ago? I'm afraid I'd fallen asleep in a chair. Such a long voyage, and then the train."

"I—I beg your pardon. Should I know you?"

"Know me? Why, don't you remember? Although I suppose we only met once, and not under the kindest of circumstances." She holds out her hand. "I'm Clara. Simon's sister. Just arrived from England."

February 28, 1922

Dearest V,

   The time has come to confess my sins, I think. You may think I should have done this sooner, and perhaps you're right, but in admitting my own culpability I must necessarily deal in the culpability of others, and I suppose I still retain too much of my childhood sense of fair play. Only a bounder tells tales on his comrades.

   But I have undertaken a rather uncertain project, you see, and above all I should hate to die without any hope of your one day knowing the truth, and perhaps excusing me in some small measure for the faults of my own hand. Your father has asked me to watch over you and Evelyn, in the event of calamity, and I will stand ready to obey him. Rather than returning his generous gift, which he sent to my bank without first seeking my approval, I have applied this sum to the mortgage I raised on Maitland three years ago, in order to fund the rejuvenation of my Florida enterprises. This fortune, therefore, redounds to you and Evelyn, who will inherit the plantation in the event of my misadventure. But the choice to rejoin me—to rejoin this marriage—remains yours. I can only hope that the events that follow will lure you in my direction, so that I may one day have the chance, if not the certainty, of winning you back, and allowing me the privilege of sharing in your future and that of our daughter.

   Of course, I may not survive the trial of the next few months, in which case your choice will be a simple one.

   Now to the confession. My first sin is fornication, which I suppose, since it occurred before we first met and resulted in no living issue, ought to be an affair that lies only between me and God. But as the effects of this act may illuminate what follows, and because I want no secrets left between us, I feel you should know of it. You see, in my great weakness, and to my even greater shame, I allowed myself to be seduced by Lydia in that fateful autumn of 1914, though I knew, even as I yielded, that I was violating what ought to have been a sacred trust—that of brotherhood—as well as God's own law.

   I won't say any more about the act itself, because I don't wish to wound you with details, except to assure you that it occurred only once, in extreme grief and confusion of mind—we had just received the War Office telegram, reporting my brother missing in action and presumed killed—and, I'm sorry to say, though of course this is no excuse, under the influence of a great deal of drink. So great, indeed, that I remember almost nothing of the moment itself, or its aftermath, and was therefore stunned when Lydia came to me a short while later to announce that she was expecting a baby.

As a physician, I naturally doubted that a pregnancy discovered so early could be any fault of mine, but I accepted my own responsibility to her—the fiancée of a brother I thought dead—and forbore to question her honor in the matter. We married at Christmas, as I told you, remaining chaste by mutual consent, and when she gave birth to Sammy six months later, I knew with certainty that a newborn of such size could not possibly belong to me; moreover, since my brother had departed for France fully ten months earlier, I had my doubts on that score, as well. Still I guarded her secret and loved the babe for his own sake—what else could I do, after all? The poor boy could not help the circumstances of his conception—and so I told you what I did about Sammy's origins. I acknowledge that this account was not wholly true, but at the time I had no wish to betray Lydia, who had suffered so much, and moreover I was afraid, deathly afraid, that to admit any intimacy with <u>her</u> might mean losing <u>you</u> entirely.

I will add, however, that I had no idea I had been so cleverly manipulated until much later, which brings me to a second (and less worthy) deception, made for much the same reason as before: because I was afraid of losing <u>you</u>, who had, by then, become so necessary to my existence.

When I went to Lydia in September of 1917—my next leave after our time together in Paris, which sealed me to you forever—and asked her for a divorce, she surprised me by refusing. By the terms of the settlement, she reminded me, her father's fortune would go to the two of us only if we remained married. If our union dissolved, the shipping company and all his other assets would revert back to him, to be divided upon his death between his two natural daughters. One of them, as I already told you, is Portia Bertram.

The other is my sister, Clara, whom he sired in Borneo.

(I tell you this in strictest confidence, for Clara herself is unaware of the con-

nection, nor would I have realized it myself had not Lydia revealed it to me, after our marriage. I know I can trust your discretion, dearest one.)

Until that moment, I had no idea that Lydia's motives were so thoroughly venal. I pleaded with her, I even insinuated that I knew she had lied to me in the matter of Sammy's paternity, but she held firm, throughout the winter and spring. You will remember my state of mind, during that time. I believe you thought I had doubts, that I lacked conviction. In fact, the opposite. I was frantic that I would lose you. I thought, if you learned of Lydia's objection to the divorce, you would cut me off altogether. And I was increasingly desperate to be free of a marriage that—as I soon perceived—was not just poisonous but fraudulent. You see, Samuel arrived back in England the following summer, alive (as you know) and having just escaped from a German prison: a fact I learned not from Samuel himself, but from a mutual friend. I was subsequently astonished to discover that the War Office had known of his imprisonment since November of 1914, and that the Red Cross had duly facilitated an exchange of letters. Naturally I confronted Lydia—who had been living at Penderleath since the early weeks of the war, ostensibly to comfort and assist my parents, insinuating herself into their confidence and taking charge of all household matters—and though she denied it, I could only conclude that she must have hidden the fact of his imprisonment from us all this time. That she had intercepted the telegram that should have told us the news, intercepted his subsequent letters and answered them in our name: chosen, in fact, to allow her lover to believe his family had <u>abandoned</u> him rather than reveal how she had maneuvered me into marriage. After he escaped, she naturally got to him first; I can only imagine what lies she told to convince him of her innocence. Samuel, under her spell as ever, accepted her story. He never once visited Penderleath, never once saw my parents. When at last I contrived to meet him and attempt an explanation, he almost murdered me. There was nothing I could do to shake his faith in her.

I don't know how any of this might have ended. I expect, desperate, I might have come to you and revealed everything, throwing myself on your mercy, begging you to take me anyway, to live with me as husband and wife in some other country, where no one could call it a lie. But then Samuel, out of spite, went to *meet you in France, and from that meeting Lydia learned that you possessed a fortune of your own. She immediately conceived a plan: she would allow the divorce in return for ten thousand pounds.*

I was desperate. I agreed. I thought I would find the money somehow, even if I had to beg your father to advance me that sum, which I was determined to repay.

And now we come to the third sin.

Lydia, it seems, had no intention of giving up her birthright to her illegitimate sisters. It was, I think, a point of pride with her, almost to obsession, that she alone should inherit her father's wealth, or what remained of it by the end of the war. She moved back into her father's house once the divorce petition was submitted, and there she poisoned him, little by little, in order to disguise her actions in what seemed like a natural decline. Suspicious, I went to visit, and upon a physical examination I knew at once what she had done. She wanted him to die before the decree absolute came through, so that Clara and Portia would never come into possession of her father's business. I threatened to expose her; she threatened to withdraw the divorce petition. We argued for some time. In my fury, at one point, I said I would kill her if I had to. I am sure the servants heard me. They all thought she was a saint, you see; she was a terribly convincing actress. When I left, I tried to take her father with me, but he was too sick to move, and in any case the servants prevented me. By then it was late in the evening. I went the next day to find a lawyer, to obtain some sort of court order for his removal, but before I could begin, I received the news that Mr. Gibbons had died in the night, and I knew what had happened. I knew she had killed him.

I suppose a more noble man would have gone straight to the police. And I should have done, as it turns out. But murder trials are messy things, you know, and everything would be laid bare, Clara would be ruined; my dearest, upright Virginia might recoil in horror at what she learned and leave me. And I thought I was so frightfully clever. I thought I could bargain with her. I went to Lydia and said that, as a doctor, I could initiate an inquiry into the death, insist on an autopsy of the body, and have her prosecuted for murder. In exchange for my silence, she was to hand over to me both the Florida shipping business and the sole guardianship of little Samuel, whom I was frantic to protect, and she was to disappear from our lives forever. She agreed. I thought the whole affair was set-tled. You and I and Sammy would move to America, build our lives and fortunes there, and have nothing more to do with her. Then, once my parents were gone, so I thought, I would tell Clara the truth of her parentage and give her a rightful share in the business, and perhaps have earned the means to restore our ancient family home to its old splendor.

But Lydia, you see, she doesn't like to lose, and she lost a great deal in this bargain. I should have been suspicious that she agreed so quickly. And I had neglected one important detail: at the time of her father's death, while the decree nisi had been issued, the decree absolute had not. We were not divorced. So that when she disappeared—not in the sense that I meant, that she would simply leave us alone, go off with Samuel perhaps, but actually <u>disappeared</u>, in such a way that everyone thought she was dead—we were still married.

Of course, I chose to believe, as did the rest of the world, that Lydia really was dead. I told myself that she had committed suicide, had drowned herself, not out of sorrow but guilt. But I knew there was a possibility she was still alive. And I married you anyway. The precious dream in sight, almost within touch, I could not face the agony, the protracted wait, perhaps years, before I could call you my wife. When, a few weeks later, the half-ruined body of a woman washed ashore some twenty miles up the coast, resembling Lydia in all respects, claimed by no one, I saw my chance. I convinced the local magistrate—an old friend of the family—to produce a death certificate on the face of the evidence: her mental state, the clothes piled by the sea, the body I swore was that of Lydia, though I could not absolutely be sure, given the advanced state of decomposition. And before God, before witnesses, before the registrar of the Borough of Kensington, I stated, in good but not perfect faith, that I was free to marry.

My final crime: I am a bigamist.

I never saw Lydia again. But she exists: I know this because she contrived to win her ten thousand pounds after all, using my name to extort this money from your father, under some promise of leaving you in peace. I presume she told him the same story she told Samuel: that I had somehow caused my parents' deaths, instead of having fought day and night to save them. As a result, he refused any attempt on my part to address him directly, and I dared send you nothing more than those empty envelopes, for fear that he might forbid even that slender communication.

I have recently heard rumors that she lives in London, under another name, spending extravagantly, but I have not been able to discover where. Samuel insists he knows nothing about her, and I can only speculate whether he is still her creature, or whether he still believes me guilty of her crimes. I suppose this suspense is her revenge on me. Or perhaps she clings to this last card—the legal fact of our marriage—in case she finds herself in need again. That is all we are, to a woman like that: cards to be played and discarded, according to her desire and our usefulness. Even to my dear Sammy, who lives and thrives with me here at Maitland, she has made no overture of maternal love, and I admit, I am deeply grateful for her neglect. He is far better off without her.

So there you have it: my sins laid out before you. My full confession, each fault committed out of either carnal weakness, or else the desire to protect you from evil, or else base fear—fear of losing you, who always seemed to me like a bird: impossible to cage, only slightly tamed, liable to fly off at the slightest alarm, never to return. I can only hope that you will <u>understand,</u> at least, why I have committed these crimes, even if you cannot forgive me. Certainly I have not forgiven myself.

I have entrusted these letters to Portia Bertram, and asked her to convey them to you at such time as she believes you are ready to receive them: so that if I should fail in this enterprise I shall shortly undertake, I can hope at least this little testament will reach you, as a final remembrance of a man who will remain yours, now and in whatever life is to come,

S.F.

Postscript. I have, from what few ready assets I possess, set aside the sum of five thousand dollars in trust for little Samuel, in case I should not survive the adventure I now undertake. I only ask that you have the goodness to ensure there is no difficulty in its administration, and that, in a full generosity of spirit, you will grant him whatever further share of my estate you judge fair, and allow him to know the sister to whom I have not yet had the privilege of introducing him.

CHAPTER 28

Cocoa, Florida, July 25, 1922

DURING THE COURSE of our affair, Simon hardly ever spoke to me of his wife, and I wasn't inclined to ask, for all the obvious reasons. For one thing, I was jealous. Though I believed him when he told me that he and Lydia shared no more than a name and a child he hadn't really sired, she was still his wife. She might, if she wanted, decide to claim his love, and she had that right. If she said *No, I've decided I want this to be a real marriage after all, a genuine union of man and wife*, Simon might feel honor-bound to obey her, mightn't he? So I was jealous of that right that belonged to her—only to her—and any allurements she might possess that would sweeten its employment.

For another thing, I was afraid to ask. Didn't the whole affair seem just the slightest bit far-fetched? What man is really so noble as that? How was it possible that Simon had never slept with his own wife, not once, not on their wedding night, not just to make things official? Not in loneliness, not in despair, not in affection, not in human lust? Had he said that only to comfort me? To forestall such jealousy as I describe above?

One time—just that one time—I asked whether it was difficult to love a child who wasn't his own, and he said it wasn't. Samuel was his brother, after all, and so Sammy was his nephew. His blood ran in Sammy's veins. And the boy was such a delight, such an upright, clever, inquisitive chap. Just such a son as any father would be proud of. And his face took on animation, and his eyes crinkled in pleasure at the recollection of Sammy's charms, and I found myself thinking that Sammy's mother must be a fool, not to be in love with this man, to want a real marriage with this man.

A fool, or else a woman with no heart to give.

BUT THIS IDEA LASTED ONLY a moment and never returned. And now? As I stand, gazing at this woman before me, whose wide-mouthed smile belongs exactly to Simon, I cannot quite comprehend what this means. The full dimensions of the charade that has been practiced upon me.

The woman is still speaking. Clara, she calls herself. Clara Fitzwilliam. I interrupt her to ask, if she's actually Clara Fitzwilliam, who the devil is the woman at the Phantom Hotel who claims to be her?

"I don't understand," Clara says.

"Clara Fitzwilliam's been in Cocoa since February. Staying with her brother. Staying with Samuel."

Clara grips her hands together at the intersection of her ribs. "My God. Then it's true. She's here. My God, she's actually done it."

"*Who's* here? Done what?" I take her by the shoulders. "Tell me the truth! Who the devil are you? Who the devil's she?"

"I'm Clara Fitzwilliam! I've already told you! Don't you remember? We met in the conservatory at Penderleath. When you and Simon were just married, and my parents were sick. It was frightful. I ran downstairs wearing that surgical mask—"

"No! That's impossible! Samuel's with her. Samuel ought to know his own sister!"

"Of course he knows his own sister. He knows *me*. He's just going along with her charade. Don't you see?"

"No, I don't see! Why on earth would he pretend someone is his sister when she's not?"

"Because he'd do anything for her. He always would. Poor Samuel. He's been under her spell since he was a boy. Doing whatever she asked him. But this! My God, the nerve of her!"

You know, the human memory is an extraordinary thing, malleable and indestructible all at once, capable of reason and deceit, capable of anything. As I gaze at this woman, thinking, *It's impossible, I cannot possibly have mistaken one Clara for another, I can't possibly have been such a dupe*, her grave, pale face seems to change before me, transforming into the face buried deep in my recollection, half hidden by a hygienic surgical mask, hollow-eyed and desperate, during a brief, frantic moment in a crumbling Cornish manor. Or maybe it's the memory that changes. Maybe I have been remembering her all wrong, ever since Clara Fitzwilliam danced into my bedroom six weeks ago, calling me sister. Pouring herself into the vast depression inside my heart.

I dig my fingers into her thin shoulders. My stomach is cold with fright.

"The nerve of whom?" I ask huskily. Even though I think I already know the answer. I think I already know what she's going to say.

She whispers back: *Lydia*.

SHE DIDN'T BELIEVE HIM AT first, she says. Before he left for Florida, Simon warned her that Lydia might not be dead after all, and that if she reappeared, Clara was to let him know, and to avoid her at all costs, because she had murdered her own father. Because she would do anything to get what she wanted. You can't believe the deceit of which she is capable, Simon said.

"And then I got the terrible news about Simon." Clara's eyes fill with water. "There was this letter, an awful letter from his lawyer, because Simon left me a bequest from his estate, and the very next day *she* turned up on my doorstep."

"Lydia?"

"Yes. She demanded the money, she said it was her birthright. She made the most terrible threats, and then she left. I thought she'd return—I went to stay with a friend—but she never did. So I decided to come to Florida and find Samuel and warn him—"

"You're too late for that. She arrived here in February."

"Oh, God. And Sammy?"

"Sam," I say slowly, "is at Maitland. In good hands."

"Is he? I suppose as long as he's safe from Lydia . . ."

"Safe from Lydia?"

"Well, he's Simon's son, isn't he, poor chap? My brother must have set something aside for him. And that's what she wants. Simon's money. However she can get it."

However she can get it.

Until this instant—those words—I don't think I've really understood. What this woman is trying to say. That Clara is really *Lydia*, Lydia Fitzwilliam, the first Mrs. Fitzwilliam, a Lydia Fitzwilliam who is a fiend. A fiend who wants my money. The fortune Simon left to me.

That is all we are, to a woman like that: cards to be played and discarded, according to her desire and our usefulness.

How is this possible? She was so kind. She was so sympathetic. She wanted me to be happy; she wanted me to enjoy myself and to fall in love again. How could she want me to fall in love with Samuel, her own lover?

You cannot conceive the deceit of which she is capable.

"Poor Samuel," Clara says. "Poor fellow. You see, he wasn't like Simon. Everybody loved Simon. Lydia was the first girl who took an interest in him. I say, what's the matter? Where are you bolting off to like that?"

"The hotel!"

She follows me out of Samuel's office. "But you're hurt! Look at you! What hotel?"

I fling open the office door, I don't know from what reservoir of strength, and run down the corridor to the stairs.

"Who's Evelyn?" Clara calls after me.

"My daughter. *Our* daughter!"

"My God! And you left her with Lydia?"

I can't answer her; my terror paralyzes my throat. And I have no breath to waste on words. No time to think through what Clara has told me—the *real* Clara, she claims, the one I met briefly in Cornwall, with her gray dress and her gray face, and yet so eerily echoing the other Clara, the Lydia-Clara, like two saplings grafted from the same tree, one watered with tears and the other with champagne.

Outside, the street is deserted, except for Samuel's Ford and the Packard parked on the opposite curb, not far from the entrance to the hotel, just between the umbrellas of light shed by a pair of streetlamps. Relief drenches me. They haven't left yet; they haven't taken her away. And then: Of course not. Stupid woman. They need me, don't they? If this new Clara is telling me the truth. If Simon wrote me the truth.

Or perhaps she clings to this last card—the legal fact of our marriage—in case she finds herself in need again.

They need my fortune, don't they? The fortune Simon left to me. Or far better, the fortune my father left to me. My God, what a windfall. They need me married to Samuel, perhaps, and then dead by some convenient accident, so common in this unruly state, rife with disease and predators.

Or maybe they haven't left because *this* woman is the liar. This woman is the false Clara.

My head hurts. My guts ache. My right hand throbs beneath the bandage.

Clara catches up and joins me on the pavement, breathless, clutching her hat. I turn to her and grip her arm. "Tell me something, quickly. How did your parents die?"

"My parents? What do you mean? They died of the 'flu."

"Are you certain? Absolutely certain? You were there, you nursed them."

She looks bewildered. "Of course I'm certain. I came down with it myself, the day after you arrived. It was weeks before I recovered. Poor Simon, he was beside himself."

Her expression is utterly without guile. I release her arm and say, "Do you know how to drive?"

"Yes." She hesitates. "Well, a bit."

"Wait in the Packard. Don't go inside, or they'll know I've caught on."

"But what about you?"

I turn away without answering and push my two hands on the revolving door of the Phantom Hotel, until it gives way into the lobby.

The desk clerk looks up with surprise. "Mrs. Fitzwilliam!"

"Good evening, Clay." (The clock above the lobby mantel reads half past two o'clock.)

"Good—good evening. Mrs. Fitzwilliam. Are you—shall I call a doctor?"

"No, thank you, Clay. I'm not hurt."

I walk across the lobby carpet without another word, conscious of the blood on my clothes, the state of my hair. I avoid the clerk's gaze, though I can tell he's shocked, he's thinking of reaching for the telephone and calling the police, raising the alarm, and I suppose that Samuel probably had the wit to use the back entrance, where no hotel staff might be encountered at this hour.

I reach the elevator and step inside, and I speak very gently. "Ninth floor, please, Potter."

Potter starts from his daze and says, "Yes, Mrs. Fitzwilliam." Operates the grille and the door, turns the lever, and only then does he catch a glimpse of me on the shiny brass interior. He makes another start, fully awake now, and turns his head. "Mrs. Fitzwilliam!"

"Yes, Potter?"

"Have you had an accident, ma'am? Do you need a doctor?"

"No, thank you." I stare very hard at the elevator dial, the creeping hand. "I don't suppose Mr. Fitzwilliam and his sister have been out tonight, have they?"

"No, ma'am. Not in *my* elevator."

"Thank you, Potter."

A light appears on the board of numbers next to Potter's shoulder. The call signal for the ninth floor.

"Why, now. That might be Mr. Fitzwilliam right this second," Potter says, voice of wonder, waiting for me to reply, to shed some illumination on these mysterious doings, but I don't reply. I wait for the hands, the damned hands to reach the raised brass 9 at the end of the dial, and the car jolts and stops, and Potter rises from his velvet stool and opens the door, making visible a slight female figure behind the grille, holding a sleeping Evelyn in her slender arms.

"My goodness! Virginia!" she says. "Have you had an accident?"

CHAPTER 29

Outside Winter Park, Florida, July 22, 1922

W E ARE FLYING through the warm night in Samuel's Model T Ford. I lie in the backseat with Evelyn, pretending to sleep, while Lydia—I can't quite seem to comprehend this—*Lydia* and Samuel sit quietly up front. Samuel is driving, and he does it well, changing gears smoothly and taking every turn at just the right angle, not too fast or too slow, clean and rapid.

Because my eyes are closed—feigning sleep, remember?—I can't see the two of them, occupying the front seat, side by side. Every so often one of them speaks, but neither voice is loud enough to overcome the roar of the engine, and if I weren't so terrified and determined, so invincibly and uncontrollably alert, I might fall asleep. I am so tired. The night is so warm. The vibration of the motor so soothing. In my arms, Evelyn lies beautifully unconscious, her eyelids twitching from time to time in the grip of some dream I cannot fathom. I stroke my thumb against her forehead, like a promise.

We drive west, toward Maitland. Fifty miles away. I didn't have a choice, really. No chance except to conceal my suspicions, to do nothing that might rouse them to some kind of rash, violent action. I have no one else. No one left to help me. No one left to trust. In all the world, there's only me and Evelyn. And my eyes release a pair of tears, one at each corner, which melt into the cloth beneath my head and stick my eyelashes together, because of what I have done this night. This awful night.

At some point we stop at a service station, or maybe just one of those farm stands with a gasoline pump, and Samuel honks and raises his voice to rouse the proprietor. I yawn and raise my head, as if the commotion's woken me from my rest, and Lydia turns her head and smiles at me.

"Go back to sleep, darling. We'll be there soon."

The owner emerges, swearing a little, and he and Samuel engage in some kind of negotiation about how much a fellow should charge for a few gallons of gasoline in the middle of the night. Lydia gets out of the car and walks a few yards away, into the grass, where she lights a cigarette and stares at the dark road ahead, propping her elbow in the palm of the other hand. Evelyn stirs in my arms and opens her eyes, and I tell her the same thing Lydia's just told me.

Go back to sleep, darling. We'll be there soon.

ON THE ROAD AGAIN, ABOUT a half an hour later, Samuel and Lydia begin to argue. Their voices rise. Evelyn twitches in her sleep, and I crack open my eyes, just a little, as if that will somehow make the words more clear.

Of course, I can't see much, just the outline of Samuel's ear and the profile of Lydia's nose against the dim sodium glow of the headlights. She's turned her head toward him, and she's doing most of the talking. I have to concentrate to hear her words, down here on the rear seat, holding Evelyn in my arms.

Listen, Virginia. For God's sake, *listen*. You have got to pay the strictest attention to these words. You have got to figure out what they're saying to each other. You have got to know what they're doing.

". . . not going to *invite* you, Samuel. For God's sake. She's a . . . [mumbling] . . . just go in there and take her."

Samuel barks something back. I can't seem to catch my breath; the tiny, feigned rhythm of my chest isn't enough to keep up with a desperate new desire for more air. More oxygen.

". . . be rape, you damned fool, my God . . . wants you . . . half in love with you already, or haven't you . . ."

More from Samuel, of which I can distinguish nothing, since his face continues to meet the road instead of his companion.

"Yes, she will." Louder, now, and passionate, the way you speak when you don't realize how loud you are. "She's the kind of woman who falls in love with the men she sleeps with. And she's dying for it, look at her. Hasn't been properly fucked in years, poor thing. Just be *bold* for once. Unless you don't think you're capable."

Samuel turns at last, so I can hear him. "Unlike you, I haven't had practice."

"At what?"

"Sleeping with someone I don't love."

My throat catches in some kind of gasp. I dig my fingers into my opposite wrist, praying the little noise goes unnoticed, and maybe there is a God after all, maybe He's allowing me some little crumb of mercy from His table, because a yard or two away, in the seat before me, Lydia's shadowed profile doesn't flinch.

Yes. The real Lydia. I know that now.

"Don't be stupid. You don't need to *love* her. She's pretty enough. She was pretty enough for Simon, wasn't she?"

Samuel turns his head and replies briefly.

Laughter. "Well, you can come to me when you're done with her. That should thrill you, shouldn't it? You chaps are all promiscuous devils at heart."

He makes some kind of movement, touching her I think, angry, and she makes a little cry and tilts her head back almost joyously, reveling in whatever complicated manipulation is transpiring between them. Reveling, I think, in her power to anger him like this, because he can't bear that she's instructing him to seduce another woman. Because he loves her so much more than she loves him. She says, head still back: "It's just for a little while, just until she agrees. And then we're free."

"Free," he says bitterly.

"Free," she says, and she curls down, out of sight, and Samuel makes a noise, a soft howl, a groan, a strange call of anguish and capitulation, and his hands clench hard on the steering wheel. For some minutes there is the most teeming, active silence, a replacement of noise with emotion, an interminable rising tension, until Samuel releases a series of sharp, quiet breaths and Lydia lifts her head, wiping her lips with the back of her hand, straightening her dress against her shoulders, tucking her hair back into place.

As she does so, a glance happens to fall on the backseat.

"Pull over, darling," she says. "She's awake."

THEY DIDN'T WANT TO HAVE to do this, Lydia assures me in a kind voice. It's just that there was no other way.

"If you needed money, I would have given it to you," I say.

"Of course you would. You're such a darling." She asks Samuel for a cigarette, and he pats his jacket pocket until he finds a cigarette case. Hands her one. Lights it for her. She smiles as she takes it out of her mouth and releases the first cloud of smoke like a ghost into the air, luminous in the glow from the Ford's headlights. Behind her, the sky is still dark and heavy, the dawn unknown. "But you see, it's *my* money, really. My father's company. My orchards, too. That was part of the marriage settlement, you know. Papa's grand idea, to bring together the fruit and the ships into a single empire. He was obsessed with it."

"But you don't give a damn about empires, not really. You don't care about the business itself. You just want to keep anyone else from having it."

Lydia stares at me. Waves her hand to clear the smoke, which hangs about foggily in this thick night air. "Tell me something. How long have you known?"

I press my lips together.

"Oh, just tell me. My goodness. What does it matter?"

"Since this evening. When Clara arrived."

"Clara!"

"Yes. The real Clara, I mean."

Lydia smiles. "Oh, right-ho. Of course. I suppose I knew she would turn up eventually. But where is she now?"

I shrug my ignorance, and it's the truth. The sidewalk was empty when we left the hotel, the Packard untouched. No sign that Clara had been there at all, and it occurred to me, in that instant, that I hadn't told her about Simon. Or did she still believe he had died in February?

Lydia reflects on this. Glances at Samuel, who's standing next to a tree, arms crossed, wearing an expression of deep discomfort. "We're sisters, you know," she says idly.

I shrug again.

"My father sired her in Borneo. Nobody ever mentioned it, of course—terribly awkward—but you only have to look at us together. And then we were born in the same week. One can only imagine, eh?"

She means to shock me, naturally. Maybe I'm shocked; I don't know. I'm so accustomed to shocks, they've left me numb. Numb and rather cold, you see, so that I no longer feel any particular emotion at this singular detail of Clara's conception, except a raw and painful fear reserved for Evelyn, sleeping now along the length of the Ford's backseat—a fear I keep in check by force, because I must. And a sort of otherworldly curiosity. I've never seen Lydia's father, either in person or in a photograph, but I now imagine he was a slightly built man, handsome, and his eyes were almost certainly blue.

"Borneo seems to have been a bad idea all around," I say calmly.

"Doesn't it? Except I reckon Clara would rather have been born than not, even if she's a cuckoo in the nest." She says this without bitterness, but as she speaks I wonder if this piece of information, flung so carelessly into the open, isn't the key to everything. That's what the psychologists would say, isn't it? That the sins of the father redound on the head of the daughter, penetrating deep into the chambers of the unconscious where they shoot about like tennis balls in a drawing room, smashing all the china and disfiguring the paintwork.

"Look," I say, "if it's money you want, you can have it. I don't give a damn. I'll write you a check the instant we arrive at Maitland, if you'll promise to leave us alone. Leave Florida, leave the country. Go back to England."

Lydia sucks on her cigarette and turns to Samuel. "You see, darling? This is why I adore you. Everybody else only wants to get rid of me."

"How much?" asks Samuel. Addressing me.

"Fifty thousand dollars."

A burst of laughter from Lydia. "Not nearly enough, I'm afraid. That's— what? Ten thousand pounds or so. Do you know how long that lasted us in England? Three years."

"Three years?"

"Less, really. I'm rather extravagant." She looks modestly at her hands.

The headlights make a lurid, conical glow on our bodies. I gaze at Lydia and her small, self-satisfied smile, then at Samuel, whose stiff face reveals no emotion at all, no human pleasure, and my mind seems to expand, like the coming dawn, to take in all of this, the vast reach of their fraud. And I think, *Why, this is the real proof, isn't it?* A piece of hard, genuine evidence that Simon, in his last letter, was telling me the truth.

"You tricked my father. That check he sent to Simon, to keep him from bothering me. That was you. *You* were the one who took his money, not Simon."

"I hadn't much choice, had I? Simon left me with nothing. Not even my own child."

"As if you cared about Sammy. Either of you. I'd ask which brother he belongs to, but I don't suppose it matters."

"Oh, I'm happy to tell you. He belongs to Simon, of course. A little lie, I understand, on the part of my dear ex-husband, which amuses me terribly, even now. But that was always his weakness. Women, I mean, not lying. But the one usually follows the other, I've found."

Samuel turns away and puts his hand on the trunk of the tree.

"Yes," I say. "Look at Samuel. Everything he's done for your sake. All the lies he told me, and I believed him. Because of my father, you see. Because my father killed my mother, and I saw everything—everything—through a glass, all distorted, so that whatever Simon said or did—"

Lydia starts to laugh. "Oh, you poor dear child. You poor deluded thing. You really haven't heard?"

"Heard what?"

She turns to Samuel. "You didn't tell her? Show her the newspapers?"

"I don't read newspapers," I say.

"My God. The story was everywhere. I tried to keep it from you—that's why I took you to Maitland to begin with—but I thought you *must* have learned by now—"

"Learned what?"

"Dear child. Your father didn't kill your mother. It was the kitchen maid. Well, her lover, rather, but your lovestruck father decided to protect her. All those years." She shakes her head.

I stare at her and then at Samuel. The air reels around my ears. "Is this true? Father's innocent?"

He shrugs. "Yes."

"I'm afraid he's dead now, however," Lydia says. "There was a confrontation. The lover shot him dead, to keep him quiet. I don't remember the details."

"Lydia, stop! For God's sake. Look at her."

I'm sinking to my knees in the warm grass. Hands over mouth. I think, *It's too much.* And then, *She's lying, she must be lying.* I turn to Samuel, whose familiar eyes regard me with a rare expression of pity, though his arms remain crossed over his broad chest, and the yellow glare of the headlamps shadow his face like a demon's. He shakes his head and turns away, and I know it's true.

"Good news and bad news, you might say," Lydia chirps. Lifts her cigarette carelessly to her lips. "But at least it's relieved you of a tremendous psychological burden. I have a friend who's an analyst, a head doctor, and he says there's nothing more damaging for a girl than a father she can't trust. Why, anyone can see what it's done for you! But better late than never."

My hands fall to my sides. A curious numbness overtakes me, as if my nerves, vanquished, have simply switched themselves off. I think, *I must stay calm.* I must set aside all these things, all this grief clawing at the back of my head, because of Evelyn. To save Evelyn. I rise to my feet—my God, the effort—and I hear myself saying, in a cold voice, "No. It *is* too late. Simon's dead, too. Samuel killed him."

Lydia flicks a nub of ash into the dirt. "So I understand. Terrible shame. But it doesn't change anything, does it? You've still got all the money. His final revenge on me."

"It wasn't revenge at all, I think. It was only justice."

"Of course it was revenge. Or some sort of insurance, if you like. Either way, they mean the same thing. *Justice* is a beautiful word, a damned noble word, but it's just revenge, all dressed up for legal purposes. He had no right to rob me like that. My father's business. No right at all." She grows a little passionate now, tossing the cigarette into the dirt and smashing it with her heel. "Thank God he's dead now. What a favor you've done me."

"It was Samuel who pulled the trigger."

Samuel says nothing to this. He stands apart, hands braced in his pockets, staring east as if to haul the sun above the horizon by the power of his gaze. Or else to smash it back down. To go back. I can see the edge of his cheek, a piece of his nose. The dark hair curling around his neck.

"My hero," Lydia says, not following my gaze. She's looking instead at the Ford. Her eyes are still fierce—penetrating the metal skin to my daughter sleeping within—but the smile's disappeared into a round, speculative knot. What a sharp little figure she makes, what a contrast to the soft-edged fairy who danced into my bedroom last month. As if she's taken the blade of a razor and applied it to her boundaries, trimming away the excess. In the silent, deserted morning, she might be a figurine on somebody's desk. But no. Now her hand forms a fist. Her voice bites the air. "I hope he suffered. Do you think he suffered, Samuel?"

"I blew his *brains* out, Lydia."

"Don't sound so bitter, darling. Remember what he did to you. Remember what he did to *me*. Stuck in that fetid basement for weeks. Do you know what I had to do to escape? I had to seduce one of my own guards. Lousy, stinking, ugly little chap. His breath, my God, like the stink of hell."

"Good," I say. "You'll be used to it, then."

Samuel whips around. "Be quiet!"

"You know I'm right, Samuel. You know what she is. My God, listen to her! Don't be such a fool."

"Samuel understands the truth," Lydia snaps.

He's breathing hard. I can see the movement of his chest beneath his shirt, the flex of his fingers.

"Samuel, please," I say. "Don't let her do this. You know what she's capable of. You know she won't be satisfied with money. She'll have to kill me afterward, because she knows I can destroy her now. She knows I know the truth."

"Oh, nonsense. All I want is what's mine. What belonged to my father and now belongs to me. I'm a terribly reasonable person, aren't I, Samuel?"

I raise my voice to a bark. "Your father ran that company into the ground, and Simon built it up again by his own effort. A thing you couldn't have done in a thousand years. You just take, that's all you do. You take things and chew them up and spit them out again, when they've given up all their flavor. If I gave you every penny I own, you wouldn't try to buy more orchards or invest in more ships. Oh, no. You'd just spend it all on hotels and dresses and jewelry and leave everything to rot."

Lydia smiles faintly and turns to Samuel. Her small, elegant hands make a cradle in the air. "Well, darling? Aren't you going to defend me?"

"I have stood by you through everything," he says hoarsely.

"Of course you have. As I've stood by you, haven't I? I've never asked a single thing of you that wasn't just and right. And I've suffered so much for your sake."

It's the strangest thing. As she speaks to him, supplicating, her soft edges have returned, blurring the outline of her in the sunrise, and I realize that she's wearing the same dress she wore when I first met her. That blue dress with the innocent white polka dots. Samuel gazes at her, his feet buried in the dirt, his hands clenched beside his enormous thighs. Utterly absorbed in the sight of her and the cadence of her voice.

"Your own brother took me like an animal in the garden," she says, "and you weren't there to help me. You were gone. I had come round to comfort your poor mother, and he was drunk, as ever, and he lured me outside and he took me in the grass—"

"Quiet!" Samuel says in anguish.

"—and he must have liked it well enough, because he came to visit me at my house the next day, and you know my father, he always turned to jelly with Simon, he adored him, he practically *threw* me at him. What could I do? You were *gone*!" She's sobbing now, actually sobbing in her throat. "He used to take me in the conservatory, that was his favorite spot, on the chaise, he would make me take off my dress—"

"She's lying," I say.

"Am I? Did *Simon* tell you that? That *I* was to blame somehow for *his* taking my innocence? *I* seduced *him*? Did he say—oh, let me guess—did he say we only did it *once*? Because *just once* is enough, you know, to start a baby—"

Samuel seizes her by the shoulders. "My God! Enough!"

"You see? You see why I couldn't ever bear to go to bed with you? I wasn't being cruel, oh darling, I just *couldn't*, not after the way your brother defiled me—look out!"

I'm sprinting for the Ford, throwing open the driver's door, trying to scramble inside. But Samuel—large, lumbering Samuel—takes on the agility of a tennis player. A tennis player chasing the deciding ball. He lunges for me. Catches me by the ribs, by the neck, drags me from the car into the dirt. I hear Evelyn's wail in the air above me, sailing over Samuel's angry head.

"Let me go," I whisper. "You've had your revenge. You've killed him. Just let me go, for God's sake."

"He's got to pay."

"He *has* paid."

"Just give her the money."

"She can have the money. Whatever she wants. Just let us go, please, let us—"

Samuel starts up suddenly, drawing me with him.

"Do you hear that?" says Lydia in a low voice.

I can't hear anything, next to Samuel's thick arm and his beating heart, except for Evelyn's hysterical cries. I would hear her voice through anything, through a stone wall, through an artillery barrage. My name. *Mama, Mama, Mama.* Her small arms, reaching toward me. Her red, wet, crumpled face.

Right here. Mama's right here. I strain against Samuel's arm, kick him, pound him, *Mama, Mama,* she calls, streaming tears, and a shadow moves between us and swoops her out of the Ford's open seat.

"Darling," Lydia coos. Cuddling my daughter close. Nuzzling her neck. "Sweetest darling love. It's all right. Auntie's here."

Evelyn cries, *Mama, Mama.* But with less conviction.

Lydia settles Evelyn on her hip, cradling that delicate, writhing, damp little body, humming and smiling. Her eyes are half-lidded, as if in bliss. "Auntie's here, sweetheart. Mama's busy with Uncle Samuel."

"Give her to me," I say in a terribly low voice. "Samuel, for God's sake, let me go."

"Quiet!"

"She's my daughter!"

"She's not going to hurt her."

Lydia, carrying Evelyn, turns away from me, cooing and soothing, the picture of an affectionate aunt, Madonna and child, and in the diminishing of Evelyn's cries, above my own desperate whispers, I hear a faint, high drone emerge from the east.

"Someone's coming!"

"Yes."

My body goes limp. A wild, frantic hope moves my pulse. I think, *I must remain calm. This is a gift from God, my only chance.* God above, let them stop. Let them see us and stop the car.

Samuel's head lowers to my ear. "Don't try it."

"Try what?"

"*Do* something." Lydia's voice carries across the air, singsong, from the direction of the tree. "They're going to think we've broken down. They're going to stop."

Samuel hesitates an instant, and in that precious speck of time I try to think of something to say, anything to soften him, to change his mind, while the drone of the car deepens and strengthens, focusing into a point up the road we've just traveled.

"Samuel—"

He turns me around and locks me in his arms and starts to kiss me. I try to move my hands, to maneuver them between our bodies to push his shoulders, but he's far too big, his body smashed against mine like a brick wall, his hands simultaneously pulling at my dress and trapping me in place. I lift my knee and he pushes me backward, against the door of the car, his mouth so hard and brutal I can't move my jaw, I can't speak, I can't breathe, my tongue tastes blood. Spots. I'm dizzy, I'm going to faint. The sound of the engine roars near, the brakes shriek.

"Need help, buddy?"

Samuel lifts his head at last. "Does it look like I need help?" he snarls, in a perfect American accent.

I reach deep in my lungs for enough breath to scream, but Samuel grasps the back of my head and his mouth smashes down on mine in a grotesque pantomime of sexual passion. I flail my arms, trying to make some kind of signal, some show of distress, but the engine revs high and the tires squeal softly, and Evelyn's laughter rings in my ears from some distant point, where Lydia is amusing her. *Help,* says my throat, says my brain, turning dark at the edges, the engine fainter and fainter, and Samuel lifts his head and lets me go.

I slide down his chest and legs to my knees, coughing and gasping, spitting out saliva and blood, and he takes me by the shoulders. "Sorry. Sorry."

"Bastard."

"I'm sorry." He hauls me back up and digs for a handkerchief or a cigarette, I don't know which.

"Put her back in the car," calls Lydia.

"Where are we going?"

"Why, to Maitland," she says. "Where else?"

CHAPTER 30

Maitland Plantation, Florida, July 25, 1922

I REMEMBER THE night we fled Connecticut. Only a few days had passed since my mother died, and we were staying at a hotel of some kind, I don't remember the name. Just that it was somewhere on the outskirts of town, and there was a small, blue view of Long Island Sound from one window.

Father woke me sometime in the middle of the night, when the sky was nearly black and the moon was absent. He had already packed our things. He shook me gently, and I woke at once and did as he said. I took Sophie from the bed (she slept next to me, curling like a giant doll into the curve of my arm) and wrapped her in a blanket. I remember feeling terribly guilty that we took that blanket without asking. We went down the back stairs and into the automobile waiting outside. The electric motor whirred softly. Though the air was warm, my father kept the top up, and we drove without speaking along the narrow lanes, avoiding the Boston Post Road until we were several miles south into New York state.

What I remember most was the silence. The dense, awful stillness inside that car, like a hole underground, surrounded by earth. Sophie slept on my lap, golden curls catching the rare glow from a streetlamp, while the air pressed intolerably against my skin. Father's hands clenched the tiller. He didn't smoke, had never so much as touched a cigarette in his life, and his fingers had nothing else to do. Just held that steering tiller in a dead man's grip and expressed nothing. Not a word passed his teeth. I had to guess where we were headed, why we were headed there, and it was not until the horizon climbed before us, the unmistakable ragged-edge skyline of Manhattan, that I knew for certain. And even then, I wondered if we were only passing through on our way to somewhere else.

And maybe I still feel that way. Maybe I'm still driving along that midnight road, which spent only an hour or two on the clock and seemed to go on into infinity. No possible end. No place to rest.

THE ENGINE OF SAMUEL'S FLIVVER runs louder than our old electric Columbia, and instead of setting her teeth in silence, Lydia keeps up a never-ending patter of conversation. Every so often she stops to ask a question of a purely rhetorical nature—*Don't you think, darling?* or *Wasn't it smashing?*—to which Samuel replies yes or no, according to her desire. Her mania exhausts me. I wonder if she's taken a drug of some kind, one of those drawing room powders you hear about, such is the furious, fizzy tempo of her speech, and then I think, no, that's not it. She doesn't need fairy dust. It's the thrill of the chase that's got her stoned. She's flying high on her own cleverness, her own capacity for deceit. The sheer joy of whatever evil she's about to commit.

But Samuel. Samuel hunches over the steering column—his body's too big for the car, his head submits to the height of the canvas top—and grips the wheel as if it's going to fly away otherwise—the same way my father's fingers clenched around the tiller of that runabout. Perspiration glosses his temples. He speaks only to satisfy Lydia, and even then his voice is so brief and guttural, it might as well be a skip in the engine, a cough of the pistons. Not human at all.

Me, I just sit there in the corner of the rear seat, holding Evelyn on my lap. Stroking her soft hair. Gathering my strength. Watching the horizon for the first sign of dawn.

BUT THE EARTH IS STILL dark when we turn down the drive toward Maitland, I don't know how much later. Black and quiet, the way the world lies in that hour before dawn, the deepest hour of the night. Though I peer through the windshield, I can't see the house itself, just the glow of the headlights on the track before us. When Samuel brings the car to a stop and sets the brake, I take the existence of house and gardens and orchards on faith. Or else dread: the recognition that we've reached the end of the road, Evelyn and I, and there's no refuge left to us.

"Out of the motor, now!" Lydia sings. "Chop chop!"

"For the last time," I say. "You can have everything. All Simon left to me. I don't care about it. I never want to set foot in Florida again."

"I daresay you might. And then again, you might not. Everything's gone into trust for Evelyn, hasn't it? So it's going to take weeks to get it back out again. Weeks! When there's a much simpler way."

She says those words so cheerfully, you wouldn't believe their meaning. And I suppose until that moment I didn't quite believe what Simon wrote. I didn't quite believe that she could possibly be such a monster, that she could so thoroughly lack any human empathy. When you think of such monsters, you think of men. You think of mad criminals, shackled and menacing, the kind you read about in newspapers. You don't imagine they could dance among you like fairies, charming and exquisite, laughing secretly at your credulousness. How could a voice so sweet convey such evil? It isn't possible.

I turn to Samuel. "You can't let her do this."

He responds by heaving his large body out of the driver's seat and into the open air. The engine's still running, the headlights lit. He opens the back door—not ungently—and takes hold of my arm. "Come along."

"No. I won't."

Before I can do more than tighten my hold on Evelyn, Samuel bends inside and grasps my daughter by the waist and shoulder. I cry out and fight him, kicking out my legs and twisting away, but he's too big and bound in muscle, and I'm sick and exhausted, wedged inside the back of a Ford. No leverage at all. He'll tear her in two if I don't release her. My arms give way, and Evelyn, awake now, starts to cry. Samuel hands her swiftly to Lydia and yanks me out of the Ford and into a firm hold, the kind you put on prisoners. I flail for my daughter, without effect. Lydia smiles and cuddles Evelyn close.

"There, there," she says. "Auntie Clara's got you, darling."

"Mama!" cries Evelyn.

"Mama's just fine, darling. She's with Uncle Samuel. They're going into the house now, and we're going to sit outside and play."

Evelyn points to the sky. "Night night."

"That's right. Night night. Such a long night for you, little angel. It's almost done now." Lydia looks up at Samuel. "Go on. What are you waiting for? You can see it's upsetting her."

She must *know*, I think. She must know what anguish it is, to watch your child burrow into the arms of another woman, a dangerous woman, and you helpless. I can see this knowledge in the smile she gives me. The way she turns her shoulder and bends her face to Evelyn's face and murmurs in my daughter's ear. Aren't children supposed to recognize evil? But Evelyn doesn't. Like me, she submits without question to Lydia's charm.

"Off you go," Lydia says again, over that shoulder, carrying Evelyn away, and at last Samuel moves forward, dragging me in the opposite direction, and I can't beg and sob, I can't plea and struggle, because Evelyn will hear me and be afraid.

So I stumble behind him and choke on my terror.

Stay calm, I tell myself. Mounting the steps of the front portico, Samuel's hand a vise around mine.

You *must* stay calm. You *must* find a way out of this.

This cannot be the end of the road.

AS SOON AS EVELYN'S OUT of earshot, as soon as Samuel has forced open the door and dragged me across the front hall, I start to talk. Low, steady voice. A cool customer, Mr. Burns called Simon. Well, I can be cool, too. I can be as cool as you please.

"You can't do this, Samuel. You won't kill me, even for her."

He doesn't reply.

"Let go of me. You know you can't live with yourself. She's killing you, bit by bit. Every word she's told you is a lie, can't you see? Let go of me. Let's save Evelyn together, let's save what Simon left behind."

Samuel growls, *Damn Simon!*

"All right! Damn Simon, then. But don't damn *me*." We're staggering down the length of the parlor now, past the closed door to Simon's study, rooms I hardly remember. In back lies the kitchen, beneath the children's wing. Miss Bertram. Where does she sleep? In the house? In her mother's cottage, near the orchard? I call out. "Portia! Miss Bertram!"

Samuel wheels around and raises his fist. Stops just short. "Be quiet!" he hisses.

"Portia!" Louder. *"Portia!"*

The hand comes down to clamp across my mouth, and I keep calling her name through his fingers, while he scoops me up and carries me the rest of the way, limbs flailing, into the kitchen. Plants me down on the table. Says to me in a fierce voice, still pressing his hand over my mouth, "Just listen to me, for God's sake. Will you shut the devil up and *listen*!"

I still myself and nod. Samuel lifts his hand from my mouth and curls it around my shoulder. Firm, unshakable grip.

"There's going to be a fire—"

I gasp and start upward. He pushes me down again.

"Listen! You're going to wait, you're going to wait until the smoke's going and you're going to flee, out the back, flee and find somewhere to hide."

"But Evelyn!"

"You'll get her back, I swear it. As soon as you sign over the damned inheritance, I'll get her back for you. Do you hear me? I'll get her back."

He's bending over me, staring at me with those hazel eyes that are so exactly like Simon's, so perfectly recalling the eyes of my husband, I have the strangest feeling, for just an instant, that Simon is actually speaking to me.

"How much?" I whisper.

"Everything. The company. The plantation. The bank accounts. Then you disappear. Move somewhere else, the other side of the country."

"How do I know you'll do it? If she realizes, if she makes you go back and finish the job—do her bidding as you've always done—"

"I'm not doing her bidding *now*."

"Yes, you are. You're still giving her what she wants. You think that this way, you can still square it with your conscience, but you can't, Samuel, you're her stooge, it's going to tear you apart, the way she's always torn you apart—"

The hand clamps back down on my mouth. "Enough. You don't know anything. You can't possibly imagine—"

"Samuel?"

A sweet voice carries from the doorway. Samuel closes his eyes and sags forward, and I spring against his hold, trying to slip free in this instant of his inattention, but his reflexes are too sharp. He grabs me back and turns to face Lydia, who's standing by the kitchen door, smiling a little, holding my sleeping daughter against her shoulder.

"I was wondering what was going on in here. Haven't you finished yet? The sun's going to start rising any minute." She meets my gaze and leans her cheek into Evelyn's soft hair. "She's such a dear. Goes right to sleep. Poor little mite."

I launch myself forward. She turns away, and Samuel gathers me back against his chest, arms bound like iron across my ribs.

"Tie her to the range," Lydia says over her shoulder. "That should hold her."

Samuel hesitates.

"*Now*, darling. Or else someone will spot the car. The light rises so quickly out here."

I can feel the thud of Samuel's heart between my shoulders. The heave of his lungs.

"Samuel! For God's sake. Don't be a coward."

Samuel's hands move to my waist. He lifts me into the air and hauls me toward the Garland range that hulks along one wall of the kitchen, and that's when I begin to scream. This time I don't spare Evelyn. I yell for help in a frenzy, flinging my arms and my legs against the barrier of Samuel's body, draining God only knows what reserve of energy.

With one hand, Lydia whips a handkerchief from her pocket and strides to Samuel. "Here. Put this around her mouth. I can't stand that awful racket."

Samuel drives me to my hands and knees on the linoleum floor and straddles me, pinning me in place with his great weight. My strength is failing now. He whips the handkerchief around my jaw and forces it between my teeth, the way you force a metal bit into the mouth of a reluctant horse. Calls to Lydia for some butcher's twine, on the double, and the drawers and the cabinets rattle softly, at some distance beyond the ringing of my ears, as Lydia obeys him. I can't seem to get enough air. The kitchen starts to darken around the edges. Fill with spots. My elbows buckle, my chest and head crash to the floor, and while I remain just conscious, I can't seem to move anything. Can't seem to summon anything more. Like a doll, a rag doll stuffed with folded paper, unable to tell anybody what's inside her.

AS I SIT ON THAT linoleum floor, limbs splayed, tied to the sturdy iron leg of the range by several loops of butcher's twine, I watch the scene before me as you might watch a scene in a play. As you might watch a film flickering on the screen of a cinema some Saturday night. It is not real. I am not really myself, I am not this person inside this room. There is no kitchen, no range; there is no massive man before me, straightening, taking the kerosene lamp in his hand.

Turning to the woman who stands in the doorway, holding a sleeping child in her arms.

The woman says, down the length of a long, narrow tunnel: "Hurry, for God's sake. She's getting awfully heavy."

"Get back, then. It's going to catch quickly."

"I want to watch you do it."

"Don't be stupid."

"Come on!" Her voice turns shrill. "What the devil are you waiting for? The sun's coming up!"

"All right. Just get out of the doorway."

She steps back a few paces. Her gaze remains pinned to the man in the center of the kitchen.

"Now," she says.

The man lifts his arm and hurls the lamp against the baseboard of the opposite wall.

The glass explodes in a shattering crash. A flame erupts from the floor, licking along the pool of spilled kerosene, making a strange whooshing sound as if all the oxygen in the world has been sucked instantly away.

The woman holds out her hand to the man. "Let's go."

"Just want to make sure it's catching."

"It's caught! Come with me!"

He stands there, staring at the gathering flame, the gray smoke as the plaster wall catches fire. The heat lands like a burning palm against my cheek, and I try to cry out, but the sound disappears into the damp handkerchief straining the corners of my mouth. I yank against the leg of the range. Eyes watering. Throat stinging.

"Samuel! *Now!*"

The man turns at last and strides toward her. Takes her hand and starts to bolt through the doorway to the hall beyond, the parlor and the front entrance and freedom, carrying the child, the beautiful child, into the night.

But as he does, he reaches into his pocket and pulls something out, some compact object he tosses behind him, so that it skitters across the floor to the leather soles of my shoes.

And in my confusion, in the smoke and heat and terror, I find myself staring at this object for several seconds before I realize it's a pocketknife.

STRETCHING. SWEATING. SHOE REACHES THE tip of the knife. Try to push it up, try to knock it toward my knee, closer, please God, help me.

Flames now spreading along the wall. Smoke filling the kitchen, curling around the furniture. Shoes too clumsy. Left foot to edge of right shoe. Push, push. Shoe flies off. Stretch again. Grasp knife between toes. Coughing now. Careful. Guide the knife upward, upward. Now a little push. Sweat trickling into eyes. Knife hits hip. Stretch hip, nudge, up, up, up to fingertips.

Can't get it.

Can't get it.

Please, God. A miracle, a miracle. Not for me. For Evelyn. My daughter. My *daughter*.

And then my fingers find the tip of the knife. Scrabble to gain hold.

Got it. Flick it open. Saw, saw, saw. Fire crackling now, lungs bursting with the effort of breathing so small.

The twine is tough. Of course it is. Made to hold flesh in place. Saw and saw and saw, blood trickling fingers, bandage ripping and tearing, stitches bursting, FREE

FREE

I TRY TO SPRING UPWARD, but all I can do is stagger, crippled, along the hot linoleum to the kitchen door, the door that leads outside, the service door. The metal knob burns when I touch it. I snatch a handful of skirt and try again, and this time the door opens, and the fire pauses and then roars in ecstasy at all this fresh, new oxygen flooding in from the pink-rimmed dawn.

And I think the heat actually propels me out, like a hand to my back, and I fall into the grass outside the door and breathe in massive, painful gusts of air that cut my throat with their cleanness.

Can't stay here. Have to get up. Have to get up and—

Help!

A human cry. A female cry. Streaking past the roar of the fire from somewhere behind me.

Somewhere inside the house.

And I do not know what instinct commands me to rise and turn, wet with blood, choked with smoke, and stare back into that hell. I mean I can hardly stand, I can hardly see at all. My limbs are made of liquid, of the thinnest possible jelly, sapped of all sap, bruised and torn and dirty. My daughter waits for me somewhere outside, in the arms of a monster.

But you can no more ignore a cry like that than you can ignore the urge to breathe. You can no more withstand that kind of raw human fear than you can withstand tomorrow. There is something inside the note of that voice that makes you cover your face with your skirt and plunge back through the doorway into the rising inferno, and maybe it's a kind of something you didn't realize you heard at first, because the sound reaches you again, as you tear across the floor, and this time you really do hear it, in yours ears and chest and blood: the wail of a hysterical young child.

I scream Evelyn's name and run down the hallway to the parlor, now filling with smoke, but nobody's there, the cry's now behind me, and I beat back to the kitchen, or what should be the kitchen, now crackling with fire along one side, spreading across the floor and walls, and that's when I see the other doorway, the one between the cupboards and the icebox, covered in smoke, and the pair of figures huddled just outside.

I think, *The back stairs.* The back stairs leading from the kitchen to the floor above. The children's wing.

This way! I scream. *Through the door!*

But even as I speak, I hear a groan above us, the sound of something failing, wood giving way, and they are starting forward toward me, the pair of them, and I scream *No!* and stagger across the burning floor, scorching my feet, passing across the center just as a beam crashes downward in an explosion of sparks, hitting the ground behind me.

I don't stop. I gallop on like some kind of greyhound, grab Portia by the arm, grab the small boy by the arm, urge them upstairs to where the fire is already burning through the floor. I can feel its heat on my skin, licking through the wall of the hallway, trying to find a way through from the room above the kitchen. The girl's room, I realize, Evelyn's room. Smoke fumes through the cracks in the molding, and it's going to ignite, it's like a bomb, I have no choice, I lead them down the hallway to the great staircase sloping back to earth, where the air is full of smoke but not yet fire, feet pounding and lungs coughing, the sharp crack of gunfire splitting the air, until we spill out onto the portico where the fragrant pink dawn illuminates a pair of automobiles.

A Packard and a Model T Ford.

EPILOGUE

Cocoa Beach, Florida, April 1924

S OMETHING WAKES HIM, in the hour before dawn.

Happens all the time. The house makes noises, or else his dreams take a wrong turn. A man's nerves, honed by war and by crisis, don't settle back into a peacetime lull simply because peace has arrived.

So he knows what to do. He remains still on his bed, eyes open, listening first for the steady music of his wife's breathing and then the larger rhythm of the surrounding atmosphere. The sleeping house, the velvet night. The scent of orange blossoms from the vase on Virginia's dresser, the smoky warmth of the sheets covering their bodies, nested one into the other: her bottom curving into his groin, his arm draped over the large, firm ball of her pregnancy. He counts the beat of her pulse. Lays his lips on her skin to test her temperature. Waits for the reassuring stir of the baby beneath his hand. A month to go, and he cannot stop checking these signs; his anxiety for wife and child cannot be satisfied. His world, from the moment almost of conception, has shrunk inside the boundaries of Virginia's skin.

And Sam and Evelyn. When his wife's heartbeat remains ordinary, and a tiny foot twitches against his palm, he eases himself from his haven and pads across the floorboards to the door. Lifts his dressing gown from its hook. Slips through the door and down the hallway to check on the children.

THERE WAS A MOMENT, AS he lay in the dirt of the road to Cocoa Beach, when he thought he might never see his own daughter.

He remembers how his mouth tasted of dirt and blood and salt. How he lay there without moving, aware only that something terrible had happened; something more terrible than the injuries to his body, of which he was aware without knowing, exactly, which parts of him were injured, and how. More terrible than the night that surrounded him, and the dirt and blood in his mouth, and the appalling confusion in his head.

Something had happened to Virginia. Samuel. Samuel had taken her away. Driven off. Beaten him.

He remembers how he spat out the grit and the blood, the awful taste of copper that made him sick. How his stomach heaved. How he lifted himself on his elbow and vomited into the earth, and by this action was made aware that his injury, at least the primary one, had something to do with his shoulder. That his head was sticky with blood, and he had lost the top part of his ear to Samuel's bullet.

He remembers how his heart beat wildly, but not because of this new awareness, the shock of discovering one's blood, realizing one's wounds. His heart beat wildly because Virginia was gone, Virginia had driven away with Samuel—he remembers the Ford, the smell and strength of Samuel heaving him over the side of the car and into the road—and Samuel would take her to Lydia, who had escaped from her prison—that much Simon learned from Marshall, in that brief telegram two days earlier, just before leaving Cuba, sending him into a frenzy of worry—and Lydia would do what Lydia had always done. Lydia would punish him, through Virginia.

Through his daughter.

He remembers how he made a fist and cried out again, a keening lament, and because the thought of Evelyn was nearly unbearable, he did the thing that hurt less: rose up on one hand, and then, with great effort, to his knees. And then, greater effort still, broken ribs straining under the necessary expansion of his chest, climbed to his feet, popped his dislocated shoulder into place—terrible agony—and listened carefully for the sound of the ocean.

How, when he found it, he set off in the opposite direction. Toward Cocoa. Toward Virginia and Evelyn.

Because he could not possibly die without seeing his daughter, just once. He could not die without finding some way to save her.

SHE'S SAFE NOW. LYING ON her bed, tucked under blankets, clutching a doll to her cheek. The window's open a few inches, screened against the damned mosquitoes, because Simon believes firmly in the virtues of fresh air. How she's grown in that year—now nearly two—since he first saw her! Bouncing against Lydia's hip, framed by the terrible billowing smoke that poured from the windows of Maitland. So small and flushed and confused. Crying out *Mama!* over and over, as he jumped free from the Packard, Clara shouting out something he couldn't hear—Clara, who had encountered him on the street outside the hotel, who had driven him to Maitland while he drank from a flask of rum and bandaged his own wounds—and then Evelyn's little head snapping sideways as Lydia slapped her.

That cheek now rests on a clean, white pillow, and the beautiful dark hair is brushed and shiny, the skin washed pink, the mouth full and twitching slightly under the influence of some dream. He doesn't quite remember how he saved her in that terrible dawn—he knows he attacked Lydia, he knows he snatched Evelyn away, he knows Lydia pulled a gun out of nowhere and threatened to shoot his daughter, he knows Samuel then took the gun and shot his lover—but these are details that were told to him later. In his memory the entire brief exchange is nothing but a grotesque blur, and maybe it's better that way. Maybe it's better that he only remembers the relief of collapsing in the dirt, clutching Evelyn to his breast, and looking up to find Virginia staggering across the portico with Portia and little Sam. Smoke pouring out behind her, bloodied and brave and alive, the kind of woman worth waiting for. Fighting for. Dying for. Living for.

HE VISITS HIS SON NEXT. Sam always sleeps on his stomach, crosswise, the sheets and blankets long kicked from the bed. Simon straightens him out and tucks the bedclothes back around him. Smooths his hair and says he loves him. The boy's been asking about England lately, out of the blue. Remembers the old house in Cornwall, the gardens where he used to play. Sometimes Simon wonders if they should go back and visit, whether Sam maybe deserves to choose whether he will be a Cornishman or an American. The other day, over breakfast, Clara mentioned that Penderleath has gone up for sale again—Clara and Portia now jointly own the hotel and the shipping business, he figures it's their right, while he and Virginia and the children spend much of their time at Maitland, tending to the orchards and the rebuilding of the house—and Virginia turned to him, eyebrow raised, meaning *What do you think?* Should we buy it, she meant. Should we do all those things you dreamed of, once, when you brought me to your home all those years ago.

He shrugged and went back to his newspaper, but his pulse beat hard, his mind teemed with possibility. Last night, as they settled into bed, she asked him again, this time outright, and he said, You decide, it's your money, and she kissed him and said no, it's *our* money, we'll decide together. And it seemed to him, in that instant, that his heart might actually burst, that there was no containing so much love in so small and human an organ.

ON THE OTHER HAND, FLORIDA suits him. He loves the unending warmth and the rampant way things grow under its sunshine and its abundant rain. Loves the way he can make love to his wife in the secret garden he planted for her, the way the sea beats against the sand outside his door in Cocoa Beach. How he rebuilt his marriage here, brick by brick; how he taught Virginia how to swim in the surf, and do you know, that was when she returned to him at last: swimming together at midnight under a full, bright moon. She came out of the sea, long-limbed and silvery, covered in nothing but salt water and moonshine, laughing for the first time in ages, collapsing in his outstretched arms. She looked up at him, and he looked at her, and it was time. Time to be man and wife again. Time to lie down together and remember what it meant to be happy.

A few months later she was carrying a child.

HE REALIZES HE HAS FALLEN into a reverie, standing there in Sam's bedroom staring at the glittering ocean outside the window, and he shakes his head and turns for the door. As he does so, he catches sight of something, a bit of movement through the glass, and he recalls the instant of waking, a quarter of an hour ago. What made him wake.

He steps to the window and looks out. Nothing. The moon—an old, waning crescent—has disappeared from view, but the sun is just starting to illuminate the horizon. To give shape to the waves and the stretch of unmarred beach.

No. Not unmarred. As he stands there, eyes adjusting to the darkness, he can just pick out a line of footprints, a double line, along the plateau washed smooth by the tide during the night. He can't tell which way they're pointing—Sammy's room is along the side of the house—or where they came from. How long they've been there.

But he does know that his brother, Samuel, disappeared that night at Maitland, after shooting Lydia through the heart, and nobody's seen him since.

He leaves the room and hurries down the hall to the staircase. In the cupboard near the door, on the highest shelf, he keeps his old service pistol in a locked box. He unlocks it now, a matter of seconds, and looks out the window. He has no patience for danger, no tolerance whatsoever for any kind of menace to this peace, this fragile joy, this precious family he has finally found after so many years of loneliness. If he has to kill someone, he will bloody well kill someone.

Movement. The corner of the porch.

He leaves the window and creeps to the door. Lifts the latch on the pistol. Heart thuds in his ear. Skin prickles.

A soft knock sounds on the door. A soft shout.

His name?

"Who's there?" he calls. Back against the wall.

Through the night, through the sturdy walls of his rebuilt villa on the Atlantic shore, comes a single word.

Marshall.

SO HE SIGHS AND LOWERS the pistol and opens the door a crack, though he doesn't replace the safety latch on his pistol until he sees the large, brown head of Agent Marshall bristling in the dawn.

"What the devil," he says.

"Sorry to turn up so early in the day, old boy," Marshall says.

"Think nothing of it."

Marshall ignores his dry tone. Sticks his boot in the doorway. "I need your help. Can we come in?"

"Simon! What's the matter?"

Simon turns swiftly to find his wife standing in the middle of the stairs, awkward with child beneath an enormous dressing gown. Her right hand grips a long, slim object that appears to be Sam's favorite baseball bat.

He turns back to Marshall and says, *"We?"*

Marshall pushes the door open, and now Simon can see that he's holding not a pistol of his own but someone's hand: a person who now comes into view from the shadows of the porch. A pale, sharp-faced woman in shapeless clothes, her weary blue eyes tipped up at the corners. Her bobbed red hair shining in the dawn. Bruise along one side of her face. Small, young girl-child blinking sleepily from the folds of her skirt.

Simon stares, open-mouthed. Nearly drops the pistol. Behind him, Virginia gasps, and not even this sound of shock from his pregnant wife can detach his gaze from Marshall's remarkable companions.

Marshall frowns, looks back at the woman, and clears his throat.

"I don't suppose you've got somewhere to hide them?" he asks.

AUTHOR'S NOTE

SOMEWHERE IN THE middle of writing this book—in fact, just as I was about to send Virginia off to her husband's plantation to recuperate from a blow to the head—I discovered that Maitland Plantation actually existed. My in-laws had recently sold their house and were sorting through all the vast accumulation of books, photographs, and family heirlooms, and I waltzed into the kitchen just as my mother-in-law was organizing her parents' letters. I picked one up at random. It was postmarked from Winter Park, Florida, in 1932. Carola Dommerich (faithful readers of my books will recognize that last name) had just arrived at someplace called Maitland and wrote to tell her then-fiancé about the journey.

"What's Maitland?" I asked my mother-in-law.

"A citrus plantation in Florida, owned by my grandfather. Sold off when he died."

It isn't often that writers receive such signs from above, so I obediently set out to transform Maitland Plantation into the beating heart of this book, and its owner a devoted horticulturalist. It was as if I'd found the key to his soul: until then, I wasn't completely sure if Simon would turn out to be (in my editor's words) the "goodie" or the "baddie." Several months later, when I visited Winter Park for a bookstore signing, I noticed the name "Maitland" on the map nearby, nestled comfortably among the suburban streets.

Nearly all of the characters in this book are purely fictional, though the

Ashley Gang did in fact exist, terrorizing law-abiding Floridians during the early Prohibition era, until they were massacred in an ambush at Sebastian's Inlet in 1924.

A final historical note: I based Portia Bertram's experience at Radcliffe on that of Zora Neale Hurston, who was also raised in Florida, at Barnard College, although Hurston persevered and earned a BA in Anthropology in 1928. In fact, a number of extraordinary African-American women came of age in the Everglades State during the early part of the century, founding colleges and newspapers and fighting for racial equality. I like to think that Miss Bertram may have a fascinating life ahead of her, as this particular chapter of it comes to an end.

ACKNOWLEDGMENTS

I GAVE MY formidable editor, Rachel Kahan, early warning that *Cocoa Beach* was proving a Very Troublesome Manuscript. The plot kept growing and transforming, throwing off shoots, like the gothic Florida vegetation itself. The central feint of the narrative had so many facets. The main characters—all of them survivors of deep trauma—were deeply reluctant to make their true selves known to me. Parts of the book were written and rewritten so many times, I couldn't even remember where I'd started. This had never *happened* to me! I wailed. It's all supposed to fall in *place* at the end!

So Rachel took the draft home and did what all the best editors do: she found what was good (much more than I thought, thank goodness) and told me what wasn't working, and how she thought I might fix it. I took the file back, followed her advice, found a few flashes of precious insight, delved deeper into my characters' human souls, and rewrote the ending entirely. If you enjoyed *Cocoa Beach* at all, you have Rachel to thank. Send flowers. Or chocolate. (She loves chocolate.)

My deep appreciation goes as well to the entire William Morrow team—Tavia Kowalchuk, Lauren Truskowski, Kate Schafer, and Liate Stehlik, among many others—who turn pixels into books and send them into the world. My copyeditor was tasked with watching out for "dead rabbits"—my personal term for the bits accidentally left behind when you (ahem) keep changing the plot—in addition to the usual proofreading and fact-checking, and I thank her gratefully, while accepting full responsibility for anything overlooked.

My agent, Alexandra Machinist of ICM, already knows how much I love and appreciate her, but it never hurts to remind her. Her ridiculously capable assistant, Hillary Jacobson, has saved my skin on multiple occasions.

Throughout this challenging process, the love and support of my husband and children kept me writing on, in music school waiting rooms and soccer sidelines, and I am forever grateful to them.

And to you, my readers, whose kind comments shore up my confidence over the trickiest of narrative hurdles, and remind me why I write these stories in the first place.

ABOUT THE AUTHOR

A graduate of Stanford University with an MBA from Columbia, Beatriz Williams spent several years in New York and London hiding her early attempts at fiction, first on company laptops as a communications strategy consultant, and then as an at-home producer of small persons, before her career as a writer took off. She lives with her husband and four children near the Connecticut shore.